RELIGION IN SOUTH ASIAN ANGLOPHONE LITERATURE

This volume studies the representation of religion in South Asian Anglophone literature of the twentieth and twenty-first centuries. It traces the contours of South Asian writing through the consequences of the complex contesting forces of blasphemy and secularization. Employing a cross-disciplinary approach, it discusses various key issues such as religious fundamentalism, Islamophobia, religious majoritarianism, nationalism, and secularism. It also provides an account of the reception of this writing within the changing conceptions of racial "Others" and cultural difference, particularly with respect to minority writers, in terms of ethnic background and lack of access to social mobility. The volume features chapters on key texts, including *The Hungry Tide*, *The Enchantress of Florence*, *In Times of Siege*, *One Part Woman*, *Anil's Ghost*, *The Book of Gold Leaves*, *Red Earth and Pouring Rain*, *The Black Coat*, and *Swarnalata*, among others.

An important contribution to the study of South Asian literature, the book will be indispensable for students and researchers of literary studies, religious studies, cultural studies, literary criticism, and South Asian studies.

Sk Sagir Ali is Assistant Professor at the Department of English, Midnapore College (Autonomous), West Bengal, India.

Goutam Karmakar is Assistant Professor, Department of English, BBTM College under Sidho-Kanho-Birsha University, West Bengal, India.

Nasima Islam is Assistant Professor in the Department of English at Acharya Girish Chandra Bose College, under University of Calcutta, Kolkata, India.

RELIGION IN SOUTH ASIAN ANGLOPHONE LITERATURE

Traversing Resistance, Margins and Extremism

*Edited by Sk Sagir Ali,
Goutam Karmakar and
Nasima Islam*

Routledge
Taylor & Francis Group

LONDON AND NEW YORK

First published 2022
by Routledge
2 Park Square, Milton Park, Abingdon, Oxon OX14 4RN

and by Routledge
605 Third Avenue, New York, NY 10158

Routledge is an imprint of the Taylor & Francis Group, an informa business

British Library Cataloguing-in-Publication Data
A catalogue record for this book is available from the British Library

Library of Congress Cataloging-in-Publication Data
Names: Ali, Sk. Sagir, editor. | Karmakar, Goutam, editor. | Islam,
    Nasima, editor.
Title: Religion in South Asian Anglophone literature : traversing
    resistance, margins and extremism / edited by Sk. Sagir Ali,
    Goutam Karmakar, and Nasima Islam.
Description: Abingdon, Oxon ; New York, NY : Taylor & Francis
    Group, 2022. | Includes bibliographical references and index.
Identifiers: LCCN 2021016075 (print) | LCCN 2021016076 (ebook) |
    ISBN 9780367744502 (hardback) | ISBN 9780367745462 (paperback) |
    ISBN 9781003158424 (ebook)
Subjects: LCSH: South Asian literature (English)—20th century—History
    and criticism. | South Asian literature (English)—21st century—
    History and criticism. | Religion in literature. | Secularism in literature
Classification: LCC PR9570.S64 R45 2022 (print) | LCC PR9570.S64 (ebook) |
    DDC 820.9/954—dc23
LC record available at https://lccn.loc.gov/2021016075
LC ebook record available at https://lccn.loc.gov/2021016076

ISBN: 978-0-367-74450-2 (hbk)
ISBN: 978-0-367-74546-2 (pbk)
ISBN: 978-1-003-15842-4 (ebk)

DOI: 10.4324/9781003158424

Typeset in Sabon
by Apex CoVantage, LLC

CONTENTS

CONTRIBUTORS

Sk Sagir Ali is Assistant Professor at the Department of English, Midnapore College (Autonomous), West Bengal, India. He can be reached at skali661@gmail.com

Avijit Basak is Assistant Professor at the Department of English, Maharaja Manindra Chandra College, Kolkata, India.

Swayamdipta Das is a SACT lecturer at Narasinha Dutt College under University of Calcutta, India.

Farddina Hussain is Associate Professor at the Department of English, Gauhati University, Assam, India.

Nasima Islam is Assistant Professor in the Department of English at Acharya Girish Chandra Bose College, under Calcutta University, Kolkata, India.

Sibsankar Majumdar teaches at the Department of English, Assam University, India.

Swati Moitra is Assistant Professor at the Department of English, at Gurudas College, University of Calcutta, India.

Kaushani Mondal is Assistant Professor at the Department of English, University of North Bengal, India.

Somjyoti Mridha teaches at the Department of English, North-Eastern Hill University (NEHU), Shillong, Meghalaya, India.

Rimi Nath teaches at the Department of English, North-Eastern Hill University (NEHU), Shillong, Meghalaya, India.

Haris Qadeer is Assistant Professor at the Department of English, University of Delhi, New Delhi, India.

Arunima Ray teaches at the Department of English, Lady Shri Ram College for Women, New Delhi, India.

Jai Singh teaches at the Department of Indian and World Literatures at The English and Foreign Languages University, Hyderabad, India.

INTRODUCTION

Religion in South Asian literature: fictions of the twentieth and twenty-first centuries

Sk Sagir Ali, Goutam Karmakar and Nasima Islam

I

South Asian cartography

Sheldon Pollock, the renowned historian and expert on the intellectual and literary history of India, while talking about the "sociolinguistic giant" (Pollock 2003: 4) that is South Asia, writes,

> The literatures of South Asia constitute one of the great achievements of human creativity. In their antiquity, continuity, and multicultural complexity combined, they are unmatched in world literary history and unrivaled in the resources they offer for understanding the development of expressive language and imagination over time and in relation to larger orders of culture, society, and polity.
>
> (Ibid.: 2)

However, Pollock is quick to point out, and aptly so, that such literatures from the non-West in general and from South Asia in particular have long been deprived of the scholarly attention they deserve, which is at odds with the kind of colossal relevance that these literatures have in the lives of people from the regions (Ibid.). Hence, this project undertakes the academic task of shedding some modest light on a hitherto neglected aspect of South Asian literary canon as well as South Asian lifeworlds – the thematics and problematics of the representation of religion in twentieth- and twenty-first–century South Asian Anglophone literature. Representation of religion in South Asian literature is one particular domain among many that needs sustained scholarly attention given the enormous impact the idea of religion has on the kaleidoscopic socio-cultural as well as political life of people from this vast subcontinent. The book not only situates the thematics of religion as an important interpretive kernel of the social, political and aesthetic lifeworld(s) of South Asia, but it also punctuates and disseminates the assumed canonical registers of the Anglophone literary oeuvre by understanding

DOI: 10.4324/9781003158424-1

how the transliteral network of exchanges and hybrid entanglements render obsolete the earlier definitive constatives regarding what should ideally constitute the South Asian Anglophone literary space per se.

To lay out the general cartography of South Asia, one may refer to Ayesha Jalal and Sugata Bose. They, in their book entitled *Modern South Asia: Culture and Political Economy*, suggest that "South Asia" is a recent geographically constructed category "which today encompass eight very diverse sovereign nation states of very different sizes – India, Pakistan, Bangladesh, Sri Lanka, Nepal, Afghanistan, Bhutan and the Maldives" (Bose and Jalal 2018: 25). According to the book, Myanmar's entry into the category of South Asia is both advocated for and contested. This vast geographical landscape houses around 25 percent of humanity (Ibid.: 26). Speaking of its diverse religious milieu, they argue,

> It is source of two of the world's great religions and the home to more devotees of a third than either the Middle East or Southeast Asia. Hinduism, with its ancient roots, modern transformations and multiple interpretations plays a vital part in the culture and politics of the subcontinent.
>
> (Ibid.)

Important to note here is that, along with Hinduism, they with equal care refer to the vast majority of Jains, Buddhists, Zoroastrians, Christians, Sikhs, and "more than half a billion of the world's 1.65 billion Muslims" who live in three South Asian countries – India, Bangladesh, and Pakistan (Ibid.). However, the cartographical reality of South Asia that this book would be dealing with is not that ambitious. Rather, honestly, it is much reduced in its scope, as a significant part of our contributions focus on the Indian literary landscape, since, apparently, India is the "geographical and cultural centre" of the region we today call South Asia (Mittal and Thursby 2006: 1). However, that should not be considered as an endeavor on our part to reduce South Asia to only one country, that is, India. For the record, we do recognize and acknowledge the "vastness" of the subcontinent called "South Asia" in every sense of the term, and it is precisely this enormity and diversity of the subcontinent that make it impossible for a single book like ours to do justice to the panorama of its literary-cultural landscape(s).

Religion as a category

There are innumerable ways of discussing "religion" as an analytical category. Using social scientific perspectives seems to be a potent one for more than one reason. As Gramsci shows, religion, having huge relevance in the overall lifeworlds of people, has both the affective and cognitive abilities that might both consolidate and disrupt any relationship of power (Williams

1996: 374). Therefore, we need to be attentive toward not only what religion is but what religion does. Or, to put it differently, we need to focus on not only what religion is but also why people *do* religion (Smith 2017: 3). Religion as a conceptual category can be defined as "a complex of culturally prescribed practices that are based on premises about the existence and nature of superhuman power" (Ibid.). But in the context of the real material world, interestingly, people use it for multiple empirical motivations, that is, as a means to achieve pragmatic ends. Smith calls it religion's "causal capacities," which is different from what religion is: "these include things like new forms of identity, community, meaning, self-expression, aesthetics, ecstasy, social control, and legitimacy" (4). It also might be used as a potent tool to "remythologise the present," which seems to have huge impacts on contemporary South Asian societies (Dimitrova 2010: 1). Scholars like David Ludden, while analyzing the phenomenon of the demolition of Ayodhya's "Babri Masjid" in India, uses the annihilation of the mosque as a metaphor for a window on the larger world where religion and politics are strategic bedfellows (Ludden 1996: 1). He writes, "We see Ayodhya as a window on a world of conflict that developed inside nationalism around the globe in the 1980s and as an instance of the global staging of national politics and cultures in the late twentieth century" (1–2).

He points out that since the 1980s, religion entered politics with renewed vigor in countries like the United States, India, Algeria, Poland, Iran, and Israel and elsewhere across the globe (3). Now, if we peep through this window and take even a quick sneak peak at the larger world outside, we would realize that almost in all the South Asian countries, religious nationalism has become a reality which has been controlling and regulating political systems and societies and escalating and having ever-widening impact especially in contemporary times. In the wake of statist initiatives like the National Register of Citizens (NRC) and Citizenship Amendment Act (CAA) in India, religion has once again become a head-turner in the South Asian public sphere(s) and been mobilizing public opinions. The strategic accession of the Bharatiya Janata Party (BJP) in India to power in the 1990s and again in 2014 and 2019 for two successive terms; Muttaheda Majlis-i-Amal's growing importance in the polity of Pakistan, along with many other Islamists' tremendous relevance as what scholars like Ali Riaz call "kingmakers"; Jamat-i-Islami's rise in the political horizon of Bangladesh as a coalition partner; and so on attest to religion's colossal political economy in South Asian societies (Riaz 2010: 1).

Weaponization of religion and fictional psyche

Now, if one turns one's attention towards studying the pragmatic weaponization of religion for specific politico-ideological gains, one has to study its many representations in popular literary-cultural expressions – fiction being one. To clarify, here, we use the category of "politics" not only in the partisan sense but also, as Ranciere suggests, as a set of perceptions and practices that shape a common world (2004: 10). Again,

> it is a partition of the sensible, of the visible and the sayable, which allows (or does not allow) some specific data to appear; which allows or does not allow some specific subjects to designate them and speak about them. It is a specific intertwining of ways of being, ways of doing and ways of speaking.

(Ibid.)

Therefore, it is interesting to explore what Ranciere calls the "politics of literature," where different regimes of representations and meanings of religion along with its myth-making power are employed. For example, interpretations of religious texts like that of *Manusmriti* or Islamic Hadith literature give birth to certain gendered division of roles in life for the sexes, which might better cater to a specific ideological interest, which in this case happens to be the patriarchal interests. Or, say, for example, in the Indian context, the fact that religiously motivated metaphors like that of the "Bharat Mata" that imagines the nation-state as a "Mother-goddess" with a quintessential Hindu connotation attached to it are invoked in the public imagination to demand absolute loyalty from its citizens is hard to miss.

Religion occupies a legitimate portion of the ideological-aesthetical imaginary of the South Asian fiction psyche. The fact that two of the most powerful South Asian countries – India and Pakistan – share a complicated history of partition, a traumatic phenomenon that has a lot to do with the religio-political antagonisms between the two countries from their very inception, is noteworthy here. Internationally acclaimed writers like Salman Rushdie have hugely cashed in on such politico-historical backdrops of nation-states and their mythical makings time and again to come up with fictional masterpieces. Also, over time, international and national phenomena like 9/11 (September 11, 2001, US attack) and 26/11 (26 November 2008, Mumbai attack) have proved watershed temporal markers that foregrounded religion as a hot topic for literary-cultural imaginations. Real-life phenomena such as these have proved potent grounds for fictional moorings as well. However, many times, such imaginations have been tempered with a deliberate and/or unconscious unidimensional ideological and politico-aesthetic representation of religions like Islam and communities like those of Muslims and dalits. Interestingly, on the one hand, such literary-cultural representations have contributed to the stereotyping and minoritization of these communities. On the other, the marginalization of such communities has pushed them to the receiving end of certain literary-cultural underrepresentation and, in a certain sense, mis-representation. The ethical is getting grounded when such literary-cultural representations do not go uncontested. Writers like

Arundhati Roy, Mohsin Hamid, Kamila Shamsie, Tabish Khair, Tahmima Anam, Zia Haider Rahman, Khaled Hosseini, and Nadeem Aslam – to name only a few – from the South Asian community of fiction writers have come up with diverse representations of such religions and religious communities. However, the mere existence of such literature may not guarantee much. It is because the politics behind the mainstreaming or canonization *vis-à-vis* marginalization or what we may call dalitization/subalternization of certain literatures is real: "the very criterion that distinguishes the 'literary' from the 'non-literary' is often a result of operations of power" (Abraham and Misrahi-Barak 52). Therefore, as Ranciere seems to suggest, the politics of literature is involved in partitioning the visible and the sayable that frames a political world; it is important to democratize different regimes of interpreting literature (10). Further, it is important to unearth their heteroglossic uni/pluriverse and amplify the polyphonies underneath the text. And one needs to do so in order to explore multiple representations of different religious, ethnic, and caste communities across literatures regardless of the celebrity status of the litterateurs involved. It is so, as different censorship mechanisms may produce villanized counter-celebrity status of litterateurs (figures like Salman Rushdie, Maqbool Fida Hussain, or Taslima Nasrin are cases in point) in their own homelands for allegedly "hurting" the religious/community sentiments of groups.

Religion, caste, and culture

Speaking of literary censorship, it is interesting to note that the more relevant religion becomes for politics, the stricter attitude the hegemonic power-brokers assume towards freedom of expressions that deal with religion. Even the fictional representation of religion or quasi-religious figures might draw the wrath of both state and non-state agents of censorship. In this context, the strategically engineered idea of "hurt" sentiment has proved a potent and convenient weapon in the hands of the censor. On the one hand, on the pretext of (religious) hurt sentiment, certain kinds of religio-cultural expressions are censored. On the other, some are encouraged that might help the existing regimes of power to ensure smooth prevailing of the dominant ideology. Such trends are not new and have actually been explored through many Marxist and post-Marxist analytical frameworks suited for analyzing the relationships among the categorical concepts like that of "base," "superstructure," "literature," "culture," "ideology," "hegemony", and so on. However, their re-appearance with the censoring juggernaut in the literary-cultural sphere of South Asia with renewed vigor is not good news for artistic freedom and democratic fervor of the subcontinent. Again, religion proves a fecund thematic for both fictional and non-fictional writings in the context of South Asian countries like India because of its unique relation to what we call "caste." In the context of the subcontinent, religion, along with caste, plays an important role in determining the constructed binaries between the "Other" and the "Self." In other words, religion and caste, as two identitarian categories, when they come closer and blend together, might offer a nuanced understanding of the notion of "otherness" in the context of Indian polity and provide insights into the history of communal violence in Indian societies (Abraham and Misrahi-Barak 2018: 120). The caste–religion combination has become a conspicuous identitarian marker that has given rise to both xenophilia and xenophobia shaping the politico-cultural milieu of the country. Caste atrocities and caste-based discriminations are continually being faced by those groups in the margins of history, whom Kancha Ilaiah in his seminal text *Why I Am Not a Hindu: A Sudra Critique of Hindutva, Philosophy, Culture, and Political Economy* calls "dalitbahujans" (2019: xii) on the daily basis of their existence gives rise to a fierce politico-aesthetic representation of their lived experiences in the contemporary fiction in general and sub-genres like graphic novels in particular. Representation of religious and caste perspectives in comic books like *Amar Chitra Katha* and graphic novels from Navayana as a "social agenda" are noteworthy here. We need to concern ourselves with many representations of religion in our cultural templates because that would equip us to study "secularism" (both as an experiential ideology and as state policy) as well. Given the fact that we are currently living in a world which is overwhelmed with different xenophobic hate politics, and religion along with ethnicity happens to be one of its many potent resources, we need to study the categories of "religion" *vis-à-vis* "secular" and their many representations more carefully. Also, we need to study many displays of religion to understand potential imaginaries of what renowned thinkers like Jurgen Habermas call "postsecular" in his article "Notes on a Post-Secular Society." According to Manav Ratti, Habermas uses the term "postsecular" to refer to the threats that increasing relevance and public influence of religion poses to the "secularised" societies of contemporary nation-states, especially when there seems to be absolutely no guarantee that in the wake of something called "modernisation" religion is going to take leave from the world over anytime soon (Ratti 2013: 6).

II

Religious possessions, myths, and importance of religion in South Asian history

Religious possessions in South Asia denote social changes and often preserve the long-lost past, reinvent the present, and project certain tactics for communities to "become visible in order to protect their place in the hierarchy or to compete for resources" (Jacobsen 2008: 10). Religious possessions symbolize various movements that address "the transformation of public sphere in South Asia" (Veer 2002: 173), homogenous and heterogeneous religious communities in the transnational space, and nationalization of religion in general. Multifarious social movements and transnational elements add value to the ethics, politics, and religious issues in the postcolonial nation-states of South Asian countries. So, the formation of the nation-state within the context of colonial and postcolonial space in a global context captures the impact of religion in this region, and "the interpretation of religion in South Asia thus requires an understanding of colonial modernity, of the postcolonial transformation of the public sphere, of religious forms of social mobilization, and of the dialectics between nationalism and transnationalism" (Veer 2002: 174). While religious practices and beliefs are communicated to socialize new generations through media and social movements, religion in this region plays a vital role in the politics of identity and belonging. Along with these, spatial mobility, conceptual acuity, and acute awareness of South Asian history are incorporated within the domain of religion in this region, and it is clearly discernible that "religion is utilized as a mobilizational ideology to establish justice sanctioned by the religion. The long and tumultuous history of South Asia reveals that religion has played both roles in the past" (Riaz 2010: 11).

This growing importance of religion in South Asia not only shapes and reshapes the political landscape and controls political mobilization but also becomes an extremely important political ideology. Here Ali Riaz's three arguments are worth mentioning, as they talk about the "long historical antecedents" of the interplay between religion and politics, the appearance of religion as "both an ideology of the ruling class and as a counter-hegemonic project," and the outcome of religious identity as "a result of ontological insecurity and existential uncertainty faced by individuals because of the pace and nature of globalization in recent decades" (Riaz 2010: 9). While maintaining a subtle distance from religion, the institutional role of faith is given major importance by South Asian countries in their respective constitutions. At the same time, "as states in the region have struggled to find a judicious balance between the absence of religion in politics and the use of religious symbols to bolster their power, political parties, particularly religio-political parties, have garnered support" (Riaz 2010: 1). Within a larger socio-economic environment of South Asia, the profound impact of globalization not only breaks the boundaries but also compels individuals to ponder "ontological security" and "existential anxiety," terms coined by Anthony Giddens. Being ontologically insecure, people in this region seek answers to their fundamental existential questions through their respective religion because "religion, like nationalism, supplies existential answers to the individual's quests for security by essentializing the product and providing a picture of totality, unity and wholeness" (Kinnvall 2004: 759). Within the context of ontological insecurity, globalization, and a neo-liberal economic agenda coupled with political cosmopolitanism, religion also acts as the prime medium of resistance, and religious identities often provide what Foucault terms "a plurality of resistances" ["des" resistances] (1978: 96). At the same time, it should be remembered that "religion and faith are central to the lives of ordinary people in South Asia is not something that is contested" (Robinson 2017: vii). The distinction of this region as an entity comes to the fore in the "tumultuous history of the societies that encompasses the South Asian region testifies to the fundamental role that religion and particularly the politics of 'majority' and 'minority' religions has played in shaping ideas of nation, state and citizenship" (viii). While in South Asia, the sharpening of the religious boundaries demands fluidity of faith and secular democracies, leaving behind the ethnicization in the political arena, faith is working as a mode of salvation and creates private space of spirituality to control ethnic violence and political instabilities. Even though people living in South Asia face certain difficulties due to religious mobilization in the political field, often religion here works as a divine social mirror that relies on beliefs which are further divided into *sacred* and *profane*, terms used by Durkheim, who opines:

> Beliefs, myths, dogmas, and legends are either representations or systems of representations that express the nature of sacred things, the virtues and power attributed to them, their history, and their relationship with one another as well as with profane things.
>
> (1995: 34)

Taking into consideration Durkheim's idea of "collective representations" and Catherine Bell's observations on "ritualisation," it can be asserted that certain rituals are followed, regimented, codified, and termed manifest beliefs in the domain of religion in South Asia.

III

Why religion?

After the Rushdie Affair in 1989 and in the wake of 9/11, we observe a shift in the change of consciousness among people across the globe as they are polarized along religious lines. British sociologist Tariq Modood experienced this, as he found a shift in his and his family's identity "from being considered Pakistani in the 1960s/70s, to Asian in the 1980s, and Muslim in the 1990s" (2005: 4). The Rushdie Affair, the terror attacks of 9/11 and 7/7, and the wars in Bosnia and Chechnya are integral in the change of perception of people's identities globally. And South Asia is not an exception to this pigeonholing of identity formation based on religion. What is important is that the disappearance or decline of religion in the wake of modernity is a myth, and it invites a psychological intervention. With the emergence of modernity, people across the globe believed religion was fast approaching an end, to be replaced by reason and science. In a conversation with Richard Kearney, Julia Kristeva contends that we are bound to think of religion "once again" but in a "recuperative, hermeneutic" way to current cultural issues. She does not define religion in the narrow, institutional sense, as she finds "a new religious revival" and that the old institutional religion died in France more than two centuries ago. Kristeva says that conventional religion "no longer speaks to us," and yet the spirit of religion wishes to be rediscovered. In general, "religion" remains saturated with institutional religions, and to her, "spirituality" is what signifies the shifting terms of the volatility of the present (Kristeva 2016: 97–99). Luce Irigaray, like Kristeva, also opines that we need to "think anew a religious dimension when many believe we have put an end to it" (2004: 147). She finds a mode of being which is in the process of becoming towards a continual transformation with a divine goal. She notes that recontemplating religion does not necessarily mean discarding religion but subjecting it to precise cultural critique (Ibid.). Slavoj Žižek has also declared that the present is defined by a "Messianic longing for the Otherness that is forever to come" (2002: 152). What emerges is that religion acts as an existential attitude, a mode of being rather than the institutional adherence of the masses across the globe. In a similar vein, Heidegger's phenomenology of religious life or man's being towards god cannot be understood within the normative dimensions of phenomenological hermeneutics, including that of Husserl, and must necessarily move beyond the ontotheological dimensions of *a priori* Western systems of metaphysics and theology. Religious life, thus, according to Heidegger, offers us radical and newer ways into the systems of phenomenological enquiry. After the eighteenth-century Enlightenment and the advent of modernity with the killing of the sacred, people have been articulating of the "death of God" and the demise of religion. But C.G Jung contends that religion, which was present in the mind of men across the globe from the very beginning, is similar to an instinct, and, "like every instinct, it has its specific energy, which it does not lose even if the conscious mind ignores it" (Jung 1936). Like the unconscious, it would reappear with considerable force as soon as conditions allowed. Jung finds psychic contents take on disruptive aspects when repressed. Like Freud's theory of the "great repressed" of sexuality, which returns in crooked shapes such as criminality, neurosis, and hysteria as it remains unconscious in individuals, Jung finds religion, too, will return with a vengeance in present times. This "return of the religious," according to Derrida, also has the semblance of the messianic meontological kernel of the "other," wherein it invokes everything that is dissimilar to the egological "self." He says this religion with its "explosive force" can "interrupt history" and "tear history apart" (Derrida 1998: 2–18). Religion, according to Derrida, would return with a violence, as it had been muzzled with violence. He finds religion swelling

9

like a tumor in society, as it had been rejected in our connection to reality. Like a pressure in the soul, it can explode at any time:

> Religious resurgence imposes itself upon us to suggest the redoubling of a wave that appropriates even that to which, enfolding itself, it seems to be opposed. It gets carried away, sometimes in terror and terrorism. Allying itself with the enemy, hospitable to the antigens, bearing away the other with itself, this resurgence grows and swells with the power of the adversary.
>
> (2002: 82)

Religion and violence

Recently, conflicts and violence in the name of religion seem to have been more widely recognized in South Asia. The connection between terrorism and sacrifice in South Asia is especially evident in Sri Lanka and Kashmir. Venomous organizations, which are apocalyptic and nihilist in nature, run terrorist activities constituting their own reward. During the last five decades, the structure of conflicts in South Asia can be chronicled as pathological in the sense that the image of the other is positioned on a perverted understanding of reality, coupled with fear and suspicion. The hostilities and tensions in the form of histories can be identified in space and time, such as the 1983 July massacre of Tamils in Colombo; the 1984 killing of Sikhs in Delhi; the riots in Karachi in December 1986; the 1992 demolition of Babri Masjid in Ayodhya; the 1993 Bombay blast; the assassinations of leaders like Mahatma Gandhi in India, Liaquat Ali Khan and Zia-ul-Haq in Pakistan, Sheikh Mujibur Rahman and Ziaur Rahman in Bangladesh, and Bandaranaike and Ranasinghe Premadasa in Sri Lanka; Taliban activities in Afghanistan and the consequent war on terror; the recent Delhi riots; CAA protests; and Tablighi Jamat vilification on religious lines. Since 9/11, religious violence in South Asia has had greater significance on the global scale, as certain cultures do not line up with the ethno-religious identity of a given culture but with "the desperation that has begun to crystallize outside the peripheries of our known world as a new bonding between terror and culture" (Nandy 2009: 173). This shapes the foundational basis for understanding the structure of present-day violence in the region. The contemporary structures of violence, according to Ashis Nandy, have shown unusual culturalist trends in the subcontinent, with its deep-seated pathologies of postcolonial skirmishes characterized by acute confrontations between different stakeholders on cultural, religious, economic, and linguistic grounds. He argues:

> In this respect, the killers who struck at New York on September 11, 2001, and the regimes that claim absolute moral superiority

over them share some common traits. Both believe that when it comes to Satanic others, all terror is justified as long as it is counter terror or retributive justice. Both believe that they are chosen and, hence, qualified to deliver life and death in the name of righteous causes.

(2009: 169)

Taking a cue from Nandy, the political theorist Banu Bargu finds the sources of the "cultures of violence" thesis in an unpalatable association between "[a] corollary of the religious fundamentalism argument" and "the constant presence of violence" (2014: 21) in topographies where self-sacrifice and the use of severe systems to obtain political gains are standardized. It would be interesting to ask how religion, in the post-ethical age, might embody very different and almost self-contradictory notions of ethics and self-sacrifice. While Levinas denotes the religious experience *vis-à-vis* the self-abnegatory gesture of Abraham as the true ethical encounter with the face of the other, the concomitant violence in the radical acts of self-sacrifice associated with religious fundamentalism gestures towards a subjective performative towards the monstrosity of the "other" (the political realm of the *le tiers*) which overwhelmingly refuses to be reduced to the primordial relationship with the singular "other" (the archetypal "neighbour" in biblical theology) (Lévinas and Lingis 1969).

Deeply connected with questions of religion in South Asian fictions, the chapters featured in this volume begin with a dissemination of religion with three main sections, each representing ideas and practices of the same in a conceptual manner. Organized into three thematic categories – Part 1, "Religion, Agency, and Cultural Memory"; Part 2, "Ethnicity, Myth, Caste, and Censorship"; and Part 3, "War, Trauma, and History" – the first section begins with a chapter titled "Fear of the Other: Narrator and Narratives in Tabish Khair's *Night of Happiness* and *Just Another Jihadi Jane*." In his travel narrative *Nine Lives* (2009), Dalrymple charts India's "elsewhere" – a traditional, religious, and cultural space of the periphery distanced from the technologically equipped modern urban centers of India – drawing an identity of the nation based on practices, rituals, and religious performances of the hegemonic belief system. What seems to strike out is his exploration of mystic and sacred India, although he wanted to avoid its many clichés. Similarly, he also repeats several stereotyped images of Islam and its culture in one of the stories. Considering this mapping of India, Farddina Hussain explores the othering of a community in fiction revealing the general thoughts about this religious community and a general discomfort by locating the other in a sphere of doubt and violence. By following Dimitrov's otherism and Khair's notion of new xenophobia, Hussain analyses two novels by Tabish Khair as Khair addresses the politics of viewing and representing the stranger, an "other" based on religion and culture. With the use of a narrator, Khair focuses on the dynamics of power, prejudices, and xenophobia in society. In his recent novel, *Night of Happiness* (2018), and his earlier novel, *Just Another Jihadi Jane* (2016), the ironic framework of the narratives exposes the problems of the individual against the collective in terms of identity formations and beliefs. In the second chapter of this section, "Kurukshetra and Karbala: *Mahabharata* in Intizar Hussain's Fiction" deals with Intizar Hussain's fictional world, a microcosm of the composite culture of the Indian subcontinent. By deploying narrative techniques which bring together the different modes of narration, Intizar Hussain delves deep into the pluralist culture of the past by populating his literary canvas with real and imagined characters from histories and mythologies. Haris Qadeer, in this chapter, explores how the traditions are cultural spaces of amalgamation and immense creativity by foregrounding the trans-Islamic framework of Hussain's fiction, especially the deployment of the *Mahabharata*, and mediates on the contours of syncretic culture, pluralistic traditions of the past, the idea of national citizenship, and the debunking of the myth of monolith Muslim cultural identity in South Asia. The chapter also gestures towards the ways in which the generic constatives of Anglophone literature might be critically punctuated and reworked through a transcultural poetics involving a comparative interpolation of literary texts originally written in South Asian regional languages with their translational counterparts produced and rendered readily consumable by the Anglophone readership. In the third chapter, Swati Moitra seeks to investigate how Ghosh negotiates the relegation of the goddess cults to the domain of the superstitious and the non-modern in his Sunderbans-centric novels. How do the marginal worshippers of the subaltern goddess cults make space for themselves on the pages of Ghosh's English-language novels, produced for the secularized marketplace for literary fiction? How do the goddess cults, themselves marginal forms of worship in increasingly homogenized visions of the secular and the religious, figure into Ghosh's urgent narratives about climate change and the future of humanity? Sk Sagir Ali looks at the overlapping parameters of religion, representation, recognition, and secularism that distinguish between Islam as a religion and Islam as a culture in Salman Rushdie's *The Enchantress of Florence* (2008). Ali deciphers the tensions between an individual subjectivity and a communitarian adherence to culture and faith that manifest themselves in the narrative, as they negotiate between the pull of a liberal individualist lifestyle and that of family, community, and religion, between speaking as an "I" and on behalf of a collective.

The second section, "Ethnicity, Myth, Caste, and Censorship," opens with Somjyoti Mridha's chapter, "The Poetics and the Politics of Kashmiriyat: A Study of Mirza Waheed's *The Collaborator* and *The Book of Gold Leaves*," which makes a timely intervention into the public debates on Kashmir. Mridha interrogates the political ideology of Kashmiriyat and its relevance or the lack of it in Mirza Waheed's novels, *The Collaborator* (2011) and

The Book of Gold Leaves (2014), proposing to theoretically engage with the concept of Kashmiriyat as it has evolved over the years. In most fictions emerging out of Kashmir in the aftermath of the armed resistance since 1990s, there is a conspicuous erasure of all other discourses apart from mainstream azadi seeking Kashmiri nationalism, primarily spearheaded by the majority Kashmiri Muslim community. Mridha compares and contrasts the idea of secularism in the non-Kashmiri Indian context and ideas of Kashmiriyat through its representation in the novels of Mirza Waheed, who represents various sections of Kashmiri society like the Kashmiri Pandits and the Gujjars in order to represent the complexity of the conflict situation and its many stakeholders. Arunima Ray, in the second chapter of this section, showcases the impact of the caste–gender relationship on women in both upper- and lower-caste communities. Keeping the specificity of the gender–caste relationship in mind, Ray has taken three texts – *Samskara* (1970) by Anantha Murthy, "The Remains of the Feast" (1993) by Githa Hariharan, and "Bayen" (2002) by Mahasweta Devi – to not only show the debilitating effect of the caste–gender nexus but also to point out how a scenario of identity formation takes place in the representations of the different authors concerned. She has used two stories as a minimized form of fiction, especially in the postmodern sense. In the next chapter, Nasima Islam focuses on one of the most crucial aspects – the idea of "religious hurt sentiment" that has time and again been used by the advocates of censorship as a potent rationale to demand banning of any text. By taking up what happened to Perumal Murugan's *One Part Woman* (2010) as a case study and analyzing its multiple ramifications, Islam unpacks the constructed notion of religious hurt sentiment in exploring the political economy of "hurt" only to enquire how hurt might be strategically engineered at the hands of mobilizers with vested interests to achieve certain ideological goals. Jai Singh, in his chapter, looks at the idea of religion in literature by using Deleuze and Guattari's theoretical framework. When we look at religion's representation in Indian literature, it is evident that religion and literature both turn out to be a kind of war machine, and in a very subtle manner, all other religions except one are either erased or misrepresented. *The Hungry Tide* (2004) by Amitav Ghosh on the surface level is about state atrocities on the lower-caste migrants who occupy the Sundarbans delta region; however, in a very subtle manner, it is about establishing the hegemony of one religion over other religions: the long discourse of Nirmal the schoolteacher on the Brahmanical idea of the Ganges and other rivers and the appropriation of Bon Bibi song within Brahminism. Singh's chapter will discuss how literature becomes part of the religious war machine in Indian ambience.

In the final section, Rimi Nath's chapter "The 'Long Shadow' of Bangladeshi Liberation War: Religion and Nationalism in Tahmima Anam's Bengal Trilogy," while interrogating the mutability of national identity, seeks to highlight how political events before, during, and after the 1971 War of

Independence altered/politicized individual relationships and the dynamics of conflict in Bangladesh. Tahmima Anam takes on protest and politics as she suggests that we can expand our notion of the political by extending it to the politics of family and relationships, and the chapter seeks to explore this facet of politics in relation to war, religion, and the national question. Sibsankar Majumdar's chapter in this section deals with the composite socio-cultural and historical traditions of the Assamese people, who have been gifted with a powerful multicultural tradition for centuries. Tilottama Misra's *Swarnalata* (1998) is woven around the reformist proselytizing initiatives of Brahmo Samaj and the central issues of Christian missionaries in transition at a critical juncture of history. In the next chapter, through a case study of Githa Hariharan's novel *In Times of Siege* (2003), the politics of "readism," historical carpentry, and ideological polarization have been shown through a conflict built around the teaching of history, historical knowledge, and institutional instrumentalization of hegemonized historical representation. Avijit Basak tries to show, by analyzing Neamat Imam's *The Black Coat* (2013), how the very process of binarization started with the invention of Mujibism while Mujib still was ruling Bangladesh. Taking cues from the post-structuralist/modernist theorists, Basak argues how the foundational trauma of the *Muktijuddha* led to the birth of a Bangladeshi Dream which was frustrated by the administrative failure of the Mujib regime, and in this context, the advent of a secondary Mujib figure in Nur Hussain is a disruptive event. Nur is not only a more daring and compassionate version of Mujib; he is also a true representation of what Mujib should have been as the ruler of the country. Against a backdrop of a raging famine, Mujib's force tried to appropriate not only the nationalistic narrative but also tried to appropriate Nur himself. This continuous agony of ideals versus real-life compromises exposes the failure of the appropriation, symbolizing the failure of a pro-nationalist, cult-driven state. Through the point of view of the narrator, Khaleque Biswas, we not only learn about the struggle of a nation but also the struggle of an intellectual who is torn between material achievements and intellectual bankruptcy. The downward spiral is symptomatic of the birth of crises leading to gradual radicalization and religious disharmony in a state which was founded as a secular nation. In the final chapter, Swayamdipta Das attempts to understand the etymological historiography of Buddhism and trace its origins through the corridors of power and thereby debunk the purist ideologue of seeing the iconography of the Buddha in terms of a trans-political realm in Michael Ondaatje's *Anil's Ghost* (2000). Das explores the relevance of a post-secular public sphere as enunciated by Jürgen Habermas in his writings and attempts to offer a critique of the neo-liberal currency of secularism (or the laicistic state) by understanding its complicity in triggering a rise in fundamentalist religious movements in South Asia, like the civil war in Sri Lanka in the 1980s.

14

The desire behind this collection is to contemplate the importance of religion in South Asian fictions while remaining careful of its limitations. In today's polarized world afflicted by the hegemony of western modernity and secularism, religion is seen as a primary cause of social division, conflict, and war, while it is also argued that this is a distortion of the true significance of religion, which when properly followed promotes peace, harmony, goodwill, transcultural cosmopolitanism and social cohesion. The multidisciplinary approach to the issues of religion, faith, and their affective registers in the South Asian modern nation-states in this volume of essays seeks to provide fresh insight into religion's increasing importance in the contemporary world-order, which is slowly transcending the hegemonic spectres of familiar interpretive structures like rational scientism and secularist modernity.

Works cited

Abraham, Joshil K., and Judith Misrahi-Barak. *Dalit Literatures in India*. New Delhi: Routledge, 2018.

Bargu, Banu. *Starve and Immolate: The Politics of Human Weapons*. New York: Columbia University Press, 2014.

Bose, Sugata, and Ayesha Jalal. *Modern South Asia: History, Culture, Political Economy*, 4th ed. London: Routledge, 2018.

Derrida, Jacques. "Faith and Knowledge: The Two Sources of 'Religion' at the Limits of Reason Alone." In *Religion*, edited by Jacques Derrida and Gianni Vattimo, Stanford: Stanford University Press, 1998, 2, 18.

———. *Acts of Religion*, edited by Gil Anidjar. London and New York: Routledge, 2002, 82.

Dimitrova, Diana. *Religion in Literature and Film in South Asia*. New York: Palgrave Macmillan, 2010.

Durkheim, Émile. *The Elementary Forms of Religious Life*. Translated by Karen Elise Fields. New York: The Free Press, 1995.

Foucault, Michel. *The History of Sexuality: An Introduction, Volume 1*. New York: Pantheon Books, 1978.

Irigaray, Luce. *Key Writings*. London: Continuum, 2004, 147.

Jacobsen, Knut A. *South Asian Religions on Display: Religious Processions in South Asia and in the Diaspora*. London: Routledge, 2008.

Jung, C. G. "Concerning the Archetypes, with Special Reference to the Anima Concept." (1936/1954), CW 9, part 1, par. 129.

Kinnvall, Catarina. "Globalization and Religious Nationalism: Self, Identity, and the Search for Ontological Security." *Political Psychology* 25:5 (2004): 741–767.

Kristeva, Julia. *Reimagining the Sacred*, edited by Richard Kearney and Jens Zimmermann. New York: Columbia University Press, 2016, 97–99.

Lévinas, Emmanuel, and Alphonso Lingis. *Totality and Infinity: An Essay on Exteriority*. Pittsburgh, PA: Duquesne University Press, 1969.

Ludden, David. *Contesting the Nation: Religion, Community, and the Politics of Democracy in India*. Philadelphia: University of Pennsylvania Press, 1996.

Mittal, Sushil, and Gene Thursby. *Religions of South Asia: An Introduction*. London: Routledge, 2006.

Modood, Tariq. *Multicultural Politics: Racism, Ethnicity and Muslims in Britain*. Edinburgh: Edinburgh University Press, 2005.

Nandy, Ashis. "Terror, Counter-Terror, and Self-Destruction: Living with Regimes of Narcissism and Despair." In *Civilizational Dialogue and World Order: The Other Politics of Cultures, Religions, and Civilizations in International Relations*, edited by Michális S. Michael and Fabio Petito. New York: Palgrave Macmillan, 2009, 167–180.

Pollock, Sheldon I. *Literary Cultures in History: Reconstructions from South Asia*. Berkeley: University of California Press, 2003.

Ranciere, Jacques. "The Politics of Literature." *SubStance* 33:1 (2004): 10.

Ratti, Manav. *The Postsecular Imagination: Postcolonialism, Religion, and Literature*. London: Routledge, 2013.

Riaz, Ali, ed. *Religion and Politics in South Asia*. Oxon: Routledge, 2010, 1–24.

Robinson, Rowena. "The Politics of Religion and Faith in South Asia." *Society and Culture in South Asia* 3:2 (2017): vii–xx.

Shepherd, Kancha I. *Why I Am Not a Hindu: A Sudra Critique of Hindutva Philosophy, Culture and Political Economy*. New Delhi: SAGE Publications India, 2019.

Smith, Christian. *Religion: What It Is, How It Works, and Why It Matters*. Princeton, NJ: Princeton University Press, 2017.

Veer, Peter van der. "Religion in South Asia." *Annual Review of Anthropology* 31 (2002): 173–187.

Williams, Rhys H. "Religion as Political Resource: Culture or Ideology?" *Journal for the Scientific Study of Religion* 35:4 (1996): 368.

Žižek, Slavoj. *Did Somebody Say Totalitarianism?* London and New York: Verso, 2002, 152.

Part 1

RELIGION, AGENCY, AND CULTURAL MEMORY

1

FEAR OF THE OTHER

Narrator and narratives in Tabish Khair's *Night of Happiness* and *Just Another Jihadi Jane*

Farddina Hussain

In his book *Nine Lives*, William Dalrymple charts the Indian periphery – a religious and cultural space – that he noted during his travel in India. He writes how these margins are distanced from technologically equipped modern urban centers like Delhi or Mumbai, projecting a sacred India of traditional practices, rituals, and performances like that of Theyyam dancers of Kannur in interior forest clearings or the singers of Indian epics in Rajasthan. For him, India is a mystic nation that breathes in multiple cultures and traditions belonging to diverse religious sects, and he attempts to "show rather than tell" that among the nine lives, each represents "a different form of devotion, or a different religious path" (Dalrymple 2013: xv). Although he wants to avoid the various clichés of mystic India, he nevertheless searches for a spiritual India to check if India can "still offer any sort of real spiritual alternative to materialism" (Dalrymple 2013: xiii). Western materialism and eastern (Indian) mysticism have always blighted writers in the west writing on Indian religions. This representation of India, which is not new, also reiterates writers' engagement with the hegemonic culture of India and its various religious sects. While writing of Devdasi in a Hindu temple, Jainism, Buddhist monks, Tantric traditions, and the Bauls of Bengal, mostly belonging to the majoritarian belief system, he writes of Sufism as Hindu-Muslim syncretism. National identity is often seen in terms of assimilation to the dominant paradigm. Sufism, which reached India in the twelfth century, recognizes the Almighty as a *Mashook* (lover), and its followers search for God within themselves. Their devotion is a kind of quest for *fana* – total immersion in the absolute. Bridging the gap between the Hindus and the Muslims, Sufism, as Dalrymple mentions, brought:

> many Hindus into the Islamic fold, [and] . . . also succeeded in bringing an awareness of Hinduism to India's Muslims. Many Sufis regarded the Hindu scriptures as divinely inspired, and took on the yogic practices of the Hindu sadhus: sitting meditating before a

DOI: 10.4324/9781003158424-3

blazing fire in the heat of summer or hanging themselves by the feet
to recite prayers – a practice that is still performed by South Asian
Sufis, who sometimes use the hat racks or luggage rails of trains
from which to hang.

(Dalrymple 2013: 114)

He writes the story of the Red Pari (fairy) to show how her life encapsulates
the complex relationship of Hinduism with the different forms of South
Asian Islam, "swerving between hatred and terrible violence on one hand,
and love and extraordinary syncreticism on the other" (Dalrymple 2013:
121). These Sufi devotees for him often follow Hindu 'sadhus' and 'tant-
rics' by completely rejecting conventions and becoming wanderers to seek
God on the road. Dalrymple's views not only epitomize the exotic India of
hanging 'sadhus' and 'tantras' but also expose his thoughts on Islam and
its practices in India. While delineating Sufism, he characterizes Islam with
conflict and orthodoxy. He mentions some of the general notions towards
Islam: "Behind the violence lies a theological conflict that divided the Islamic
world for centuries" (Ibid.: 135).

Considering this mapping of the 'other India' in non-fictions, this chapter proposes to explore the religious and cultural other in fictional narratives, particularly in Tabish Khair's novels like *Night of Happiness* and *Just
Another Jihadi Jane*. Certain events, occasions, and characters are highlighted to dwell upon the representations of Islamic community, with an
emphasis on prejudices, cultural symbols, Islamophobia, and self/other dialectics. To begin with one of the early Indian English novels, *Kanthapura*
by Raja Rao projects a complicated space occupied by a Muslim character
in the narrative. The village is presented with its caste-based geographical
landscape in opposition to the colonial establishment of the Skeffington
Coffee Estate, where laborers are brought in from other parts of the country. The narrator, an old Brahmin lady, introduces the villagers, the village
goddess, and the events of the Gandhian movement of Satyagraha, which
leads to an exodus at the end whereby a new village named Kashipur is born
out of the old village Kanthapura. Amidst the nationalist discourse, Raja
Rao draws the policeman Bade Khan, who seems to move between the two
locales as an outsider. He neither belongs to the village community, nor can
he dare to associate himself with the colonizers, although his *lathi* seems to
have limited power to scare off or threaten the villagers of Kanthapura. He
is scorned by the very narrator and presented out of place. Another Indian
English novel, *A Passage to India*, set against the backdrop of colonial rule,
was published in 1924, and E.M. Forster depicts the character of a doctor,
Aziz. He is looked at by the male colonizers with fear and doubt throughout
the novel, as the other is strange and different from self, that is, the British
male. It is this fear of difference, of not an unknown other but someone
who is visible and a part of the Indian society and culture, that becomes

significant. This novel echoes a general discomfort by locating the other in a space of doubt and violence. One of the major concerns of Amitav Ghosh's *In an Antique Land* is the divide and intolerance between communities and how, particularly in India, the "terror of symbols" separates people and leads to violence:

> tales that grow out of an explosive barrier of symbols – of cities going up in flames because of a cow found dead in a temple or a pig in a mosque; of people killed for wearing a lungi or a dhoti, depending on where they find themselves; of women disemboweled for wearing veils or vermilion, of men dismembered for the state of their foreskins.
>
> (Ghosh 1992: 210)

Cultural symbols and religion become the markers of social identities depending on which borders are drawn to separate one from the other, both in the East and the West. This creates a fear of the other, who is perceived as a stranger and, therefore, a threat. One of the fundamental concerns of Tabish Khair's *The New Xenophobia* is to explore the perception of the other and the act of making one a stranger in addition to elaborate on how new xenophobia extends the creation of a stranger through one's responses and thoughts. Xenophobia comes from the Greek words 'xenos' (stranger) and 'phobos' (fear). However, it is not simply a combination of a particular being, object, or stranger and the basic human emotion of fear. Whom we consider a stranger and what we fear can change over time and with the experience of power. Power, as Khair puts, following Foucault, exists only when it is exercised (put into action) and, therefore, requires a subject; this power in relations between self and other decides the production of the stranger in xenophobia:

> The construction and reception of the stranger of xenophobia, old or new, is always a matter of power, a relationship of power. It is, in this sense, that my study of xenophobia confines itself largely to the history of capitalism as the dominant structure of power, which arises identifiably in the eighteenth century (though with older roots) and transforms itself, again identifiably, in the late twentieth century. One can define power as the ability of the self to act upon the existence and consciousness of others.
>
> (Khair Xenophobia 2016a: 3)[1]

His notion of new xenophobia in contemporary times may not include physical violence because "power refers to any imposition, physical or not, of one consciousness upon another," although it operates with varieties of "'push-in' violence" (Khair 2016a: 4) which may mostly go unnoticed or unrecognized as violence. For him, a xenophobe does not avoid strangers but wants to reduce them, make them look inferior or demonic, like a vampire. It is also important to note that the making of the stranger is associated with the sense of self and its relation to other in social and psychoanalytical ways.

Any discussion on identities and self in Postmodernism must consider them as multiple and constantly in flux. Similarly, there can be no stability in the interdependence of self and other. They exist in a complex relationship with each other, and, like self, other is also a fluid entity, always evolving. An other is:

> a site or location upon which we project all the qualities that we – as individual subjects, social groups, or even nations – most fear, or dislike, about ourselves. In other words, the other is a construct. It is, moreover, a historically and culturally specific construction that is determined by the discursive practices that shape us into what we are. Thus rather than representing the real and diverse qualities of any given group or entity, such constructions reflect the values and norms of the individual or group that constructs it.
>
> (Childs et al. 2006: 164)

A self is understood in relation to the other, indicating that 'I' is actually dependent on a 'not-me' and self is predicated on the existence of 'other.' But it is not simply external; as psychoanalysts would believe, the other is inside us and their relation is never neutral, for "The strangeness of the stranger is always a definition of our own normality; without it the stranger ceases to come into being qua stranger" (Khair 2016a: 13). According to Khair, it is impossible to meet an unknown other or stranger in entirety: "it is almost impossible for a total stranger to appear . . . he has already been constituted within 'us'" (Khair 2016a: 12). This echoes the phenomenological position of other in relation to self that other is always a construct by self owing to power relations, whether rhetorical or ideological (or economic). Once the inferiority of the other is established, the self gains more power to imagine, represent, and re-imagine the 'other,' forming a loop from which there is no escape. Following India's partition into a Hindu-majority state and a Muslim-majority state, people who had shared a culture, past, or even a childhood found themselves pushed into the positions of strangers who had always been suspected. Even after so many years of that historical separation, termed by Zamindar the 'long Partition' (Zamindar 2010: 2) in her book *The Long Partition and the Making of Modern South Asia*, India sees Pakistan as an inverted, upside-down house,[2] as a not-me (us) part of self. With the turn of the clock or time, strangers are constructed and acted upon. These strangers are people whose differences are already known or perceived.

22

In *Night of Happiness*, self is a male, upper-class Hindu who is the narrator and protagonist, an insider to the story. As such, he occupies a privileged position in constructing a discourse of another person as 'not-me' through suggestive metaphors, body language, and tone. He delves into the psychological recesses of his own mind and presents an inversion of himself. It is the fear of this inversion/difference that makes him highly liable to distortions of both self-understanding and fantasizing about others; as Martha Nussbaum says, "Fear is a "dimming preoccupation': an intense focus on the self that casts others into darkness" (2012: 58). In doing so, a discourse is created offering the other as an object to be feared, and once the inferiority of the other is established, he engages in drawing his/her identity and culture in relation to his own; like a xenophobe, he puts his consciousness on the other and structures the narrative. Here, Mehrotra, the narrator, reveals more of the stereotypical gaze in looking at the other than letting him, Ahmed, speak for himself. The novel depicts the responses of a pragmatic Mehrotra towards his Muslim employee who has undergone a traumatic experience during the Gujarat riots of 2002.

On one level, the primary focus of the novel seems to be the self-other relationship between Mehrotra (self), an entrepreneur of a flourishing business, and Ahmed (other), his employee and aide. But, on another level, it is not simply a reductive binary that Khair explores in the narrative but a complex understanding of the self that constitutes the other within; his self is dependent on the other as a not-me part of self. Apparently, this other is not a stranger but office staff who leads a quiet life yet evokes a feeling of suspicion. Mehrotra has been dependent on Ahmed for his many business accomplishments and treats him as a trusted aide, which in due course begins to wane. This element of doubt emerges owing to the cultural and religious differences, although Ahmed helps him in his business. While introducing Ahmed's placid nature, he begins by saying that Ahmed is not religious and celebrates only one Islamic festival, *Shab-e-Baarat*, 'Night of Happiness': "a full moon day of devotion and celebration in the month of Shabaan in Islamic calendar" (Khair 2018: 15); this is presented ironically, as if celebrating one Islamic festival makes him less of a Muslim. On that particular occasion, Ahmed would ask for leave, a rare request for an otherwise undemanding person who never seems to need anything from others. The image of Ahmed is associated with his towel-wrapped tiffin carrier, odd aphorisms, and inconspicuous behavior. He is presented as a person who would stay away and not disturb anyone in the office. In the narrative, Ahmed's calm and composed behavior implies of a subtext which is certainly not peaceful but disturbing. It conceals more than what it attempts to reveal, forming a veil of mystery and doubt for the reader. Ahmed's composure suggests a secretive trait in him, which, Mehrotra feels, could be dangerous. In this case, fear is nourished by the idea of a disguised enemy and thrives on the idea of hidden-ness, of danger lurking beneath the façade of normalcy (Nussbaum 2012: 23). Mehrotra's seemingly liberal approach to the other apparently hides his prejudices, anxiety, and doubts about differences which he does not want to acknowledge. This makes the reader experience the narrator's social gaze at the other, who belongs to a minority community in Uttar Pradesh, India. It is fear of not just any stranger but a particular kind of stranger.

"A certain construction of difference is essential to xenophobia and the fear it sets out to evoke" (Khair 2016a: 20). This making of an other by the speaker-narrator begins with the Ahmed's résumé, which has a list of spoken languages apart from "the usual English, Hindi, and in his case of course Urdu, . . . Marathi Gujarati, Bhojpuri, Bangla, Arabic, French, German, Thai, Tibetan, Japanese and a 'smattering of Chinese'" (Khair 2018: 9). This extraordinary list makes the narrator Mehrotra skeptical at first until he has the details to support it. The other here needs to be rationalized in terms of his activities, culture, and knowledge to fit in. Ahmed's earlier profession as a tourist guide in his native place, Phansa, an imaginary town which is not very far from Bodh Gaya in Uttar Pradesh, gave him a chance to meet customers from all over the world visiting the Buddhist pilgrimage site. The list of languages seem incongruous due to Mehrotra's predetermined notions of Ahmed based on his religion and community: "in his case, of course, Urdu" (Ibid.). It is similar to the treatment of almost every Muslim character in Bollywood's numerous productions, irrespective of gender, with cultural symbols of kohl on their eyes and amulets on their chests. The most recent blockbuster showing these unchanging cultural signs is Zoya Akhtar's *Gully Boy*, released in 2019. In a review published in a leading newspaper of the country, the reviewer Keshava Guha calls it a "literary thriller [. . .] of varieties of Muslim faith in India" (Guha 2018: Reviews).

In the narrative, such cultural signs and prejudices are subtly and ironically used by Khair to reveal the (mis)representation of the minority community. His narrative techniques allow him the liberty of maintaining distance from the discourse and its implicit gaze. Both of his novels have narrators to lay out the plot and leave it for the silent prospective readers. They become the voice of the society and depict their preconceived opinions towards communities like Muslims. Although in *Just Another Jihadi Jane*, the writer/narrator of the novel, Jamilla, makes the narrative sound fictional: "There is death in the details, and there is guilt, crime and persecution. No, I won't give you too many details. I will give you names of places and people but seldom the exact ones" (Khair 2016b: 1), the story presents a relatable plot for Muslim immigrants in the West. Interestingly, the narrative is left to the discretion of the future reader to "make what you can of what I say" (Ibid.). This open-ended narrative which invites multiple readings has both a dominant and a muted story. Similar to the *Night of Happiness*, the narrative hides the writer's intent and purpose in the subtext as he writes of female agency in a racial and patriarchal society. Khair's treatment of the apparent theme of Jihadists becomes subversive as he projects death as symbolic and rhetorical.

Both novels begin at the end of the plot when everything has already happened and awaits a storyteller to narrate it through his/her memory. Mehrotra, the narrator of *Night of Happiness*, leaves the manuscript in a five-star hotel room to be read by specific readers:

> Maybe you are a businessman or a CEO, passing through this teeming North Indian city, and staying for a night in one of its five-star hotels. You could be a prosperous doctor attending an international conference, or an ordinary tourist from Denmark or the US. . . . But, no, you cannot be a mechanic, ordered to repair the air-conditioner, or the cleaning lady.
>
> (Khair 2018: 1)

This list of future readers noted by Khair belongs to an affluent section of society, and he categorically negates a class of readers like the maintenance man or the service lady. By drawing such clear distinctions, Khair ironically implies how the discourse of the other would be produced by the powerful for his affluent readers. The other remains as the not-me self for them, the discourse becomes a leisurely reading catering to the predetermined images of the strange other, and the other never gets liberated from such static spaces. The drawer containing the manuscript also has the *Bible* and the *Gita*. The *Quran* is conspicuous in its absence, stating a euphemism for religious tolerance/intolerance in India. The cancelled original title "The Spectral Infinitude of Small Distances" and the lines from the poem "The Rime of the Ancient Mariner" by Coleridge set the stage for the story of the other:

> They groan'd, they stirred, they all uprose,
> Nor spake, nor move their eyes;
> It had been strange, even in a dream,
> To have seen those dead man rise.
>
> (qt. Khair 2018: 3)

A dark world of eerie strangeness and mystery evoked in these lines begins the discourse of the 'other.' We, as readers, find in it a foreboding with the mention of death, disease, and the supernatural. The cancelled title introduces the subtext in the narrative of an inverted, alternative world replete with unease and fear of the ethereal.

On his first visit to Ahmed's house, in the beginning of the narrative, when Mehrotra decides to drop Ahmed home on the stormy evening of *Shab-e-baraat*, he describes the typical lower-middle-class apartment complex of the sort built by public corporations in the 1970s, with a dark parking lot that has looping insulated electric wires hanging in the pigeon-infested corners. He then mentions how "it was the kind of neighbourhood that often makes me sad and uneasy." He goes on to refer to an incident in the United States where, in an unknown neighborhood, a hugely built man demanded money from him. He reiterates how such areas exude a mixed feeling of sadness and fear. A detailed description of the building and the house convey the feelings of fear and strangeness, "stealiness about his right hand man" (Ghoshal 2018: Features), that grip Mehrotra as he walks through the corridor. He sits inside Ahmed's house at his invitation and is surprised to see a window open in such a bad storm. It challenges his notion of closed doors during a storm outside, whereas for Ahmed, "to seal a space is to shut out a soul" (Khair 2018: 25). Immediately, the readers share Mehrotra's unease and curiosity about the word 'soul.' This becomes a window of the unknown strange space: a space of mystery that Ahmed from now on would be associated with, an awe not too distanced from fear. Next the invisible *halwa* on the plate of *nimki* that is served to him further enhances the fear of another living in dark, middle-class apartments. The novel presents the economic divide between employer and employee along with the cultural gap of consuming Rooh Afza and *halwa* by Ahmed. He tells Mehrotra how his wife continues the tradition of preparing *halwa* in a certain way like his mother on the Night of Happiness; therefore, Mehrotra expected *halwa* to be served to him that evening when he was in Ahmed's house waiting for the storm to subside. To his surprise, it was missing on his plate:

> I felt only discomforted, confused; it was nothing compared to what I experienced the very next second, when Ahmed, with the gentle tinkle of spoon on china, scooped [the ghost of] *halwa* out of his plate and levered it, carefully, making sure nothing spilled, to his mouth. It was then that I broke out in a cold sweat.
>
> (Khair 2018: 35)

Little later, however, the narrator records that Ahmed's "calmness, so domestic, so normal, must have diffused my [his] sense of icy horror" (Ibid.: 35). He also senses steeliness about Ahmed that sends a shiver through him. This experience is immediately contrasted with a dinner party he went to with his wife in honor of a British writer of Indian origin who had won an award. In the party, his mind was full of his attempts to rationalize the act of Ahmed pretending to eat his phantom *halwa* from his plate. In the following days, Mehrotra, with his seemingly liberal mindset, could not confront Ahmed because of all his politeness and service. Subsequently, the element of doubt about his sanity loomed large followed by fear: "Would I detect signs of madness in him, a glitter in the eye, a fervor in the voice, a grasping of the hand, or would he still be as he had been for so many years: polite, considerate, orderly, reliable?" (Ibid.: 51).

26

This experience never leaves Mehrotra's mind; he keeps thinking of Ahmed all the time, with a growing feeling of mistrust and also guilt for being complacent in his liberalism. Many theories cross his mind about Ahmed's wife in the flat in devious ways. This almost becomes an existential issue, robbing him of peace and calm. He doubts Ahmed's sanity and even employs a detective to find out facts about his past years and personal life. The detective writes his account based on interviews and hearsay as he relates: "We do not go shadowing people most of the time. Maybe that is what private eyes do in the West, where no one seems to know his neighbour or second cousin, but this is India, where everyone knows everyone else" (Khair 2018: 62). The knowledge provided is more a social discourse than an analysis of factual evidence. This also exposes the rooted contemporary problem of surveillance, Islamophobia, and violence:

> While it references the past, the novel remains rooted in the present not just because of direct contemporary allusions within it, but in its most important narrative tool – that of surveillance. Data is the new capital and surveillance, the means of control in our times. The powers that be demand more and more access to our personal information while legislating opacity for their own machinations. Dubious detective agencies running out of dingy buildings employed chiefly by suspicious spouses are a thing of the past. They are now replaced with swanky businesses whose owners go golfing on the weekends. In the new environment, these firms have respectability as the backend industry of corporate law.
>
> (Maithreyi Karnor 2018: para. 6)

The issues of surveillance and control were explored in his earlier novel, *Just Another Jihadi Jane*, where Khair examines the use of the internet by terrorist groups. The internet facilitates Jihadists in contacting, planning, and recruiting young girls from the West. Khair writes of religious fanaticism and Islamist terrorism in a narrative that foregrounds binaries. The other is created on three different levels: national (White citizens/Muslim immigrants), cultural (West/Islam), and gender (Muslim man/Muslim woman). The primary focus in the narrative is women and the production of the other in patriarchal Islamic societies and also in Western societies. Women immigrants face greater marginalization and trauma than their male counterparts. All this is in an atmosphere of growing Islamophobia, "the West's insidious 'Other'" (Herrero 2018: 1), and the West's inability to recognize Islam as determining many historical experiences (as discussed in "Overhauling Islam: Representation, Construction, and Cooption of 'Moderate Islam' in Western Europe" by Haddad and Golson, 2007). Its multiculturalism is never a one-directional integration (if there's integration at all) but more complex in terms of identification and beliefs that affect the lives of Muslim immigrants.

In addition, the subtext in the narrative counters the binary structure to emphasize the complexity of the relationship between self and other, agent and victim, or life and death. Khair challenges the West's homogenizing view of non-western women, particularly Muslim women, as passive victims. The narrator, a simple Jane, tells the story of the experiences of her friend Ameena and herself in London and later in Syria as they join the Jihadists. In London, she and Ameena live in the same building working-class English inhabited earlier. They notice a cultural gap in the signs around them and how they change later as immigrant families move in:

> The lift would smell of vomit and beer then. And there were used condoms and syringes lying about. Then, of course, more of us moved in and more of them moved out. Some were glad to leave; some gave us the finger. But they left, slowly, one by one, the so-called white working class. Or the white drinking class. The so-called brown working class moved in. It was not the brown drinking class though; it was mostly the Muslim working class. The smell of vomit and beer disappeared. The syringes and condoms disappeared. The graffiti got multilingual. All the rest stayed as it was.
>
> (Khair 2016b: 3)

These girls live negotiating two different cultures and two different positions, one public and the other personal, represented in the novel through the use of London English outside home and Urdu at home. The personal and private and its strains are aggravated by the racial experiences of the girls. Both realize that no Muslim man, however orthodox he may be, would ever face even one third of the difficulties that Muslim women encounter in the West. They are viewed as objects, either as monsters or with curiosity about their bodies. Ameena tries hard to assimilate herself to the western lifestyle by smoking, hanging out with boys who give her slight attention, and also losing her virginity. Jamilla, on the other hand, rejects the established family practices of raising a daughter for marriage to a man selected by the family and a woman like her mother's outright acceptance of opinions and decisions made by the men in the family. She wants to pursue higher studies if she can manage a proper scholarship. She finds no respite in England, at home or outside, where she is shouted at or verbally abused for wearing a hijab by an elderly woman from the bus for letting down her sex and not fitting into the culture. So, for both girls, the Islamic nation, Syria, and Daesh promise belonging, where everyone would be brothers and sisters like the imagined community of seemingly like-minded friends on screen. For Ameena, Hijjiye replaces the mother who failed her. Their utopian expectations of homogenization and assimilation in Syria are soon shattered. In a way, the novel can be seen as a journey from London to Syria in search of truth: "Remember, I am a woman who started off with the conviction that nothing but the truth should exist. The One Truth, the Only Truth. I was suckled on that conviction, Ameena wasn't. I felt I had the truth; Ameena was seeking the truth" (Khair 2016b: 1).

The truth that they find out in Syria is no different; they are looked at as war trophies from the West, a victory of sorts, and use their presence to lure more young women via the internet. Women are used in these Jihadist groups as commodities. In the Syrian orphanage, there are three types of women – the older women, whose main function is to teach the younger ones; the beautiful younger women, who were meant to be brides of Jihadists; and mostly the uglier ones would be trained to be suicide bombers. All these women from different countries and cultures are clubbed together as Muslim women from a hypothetical Islamist community but, in fact, they have very little in common and speak different languages.

It is the internet that helps the girls learn about Daesh, an acronym for ISIS. Khair shows how young girls are lured and recruited via the internet as brides of Jihadists and then made suicide bombers. He depicts the effect of terrorism on simple ordinary Muslim women and reveals the marginalization and indoctrination of females within the community, leading to shattered, lonely lives for the young. For them, joining the Jihadists is an escape from patriarchy and the life of a racial and religious other.

It is emancipation and belonging that the girls look for, which seems to be a kind of fantasy for Ameena initially. In this, Khair denaturalizes the issue of female victimization or seeing female terrorists as an outcome of indoctrination. Through the narrator, Khair shows how woman is not a victim but someone with agency who decides to join a militant group:

> Mia Bloom's analysis of female militancy in which she, while insisting on an equal importance of choice and coercion, sums up the key motives of women to join a militant organization in four markedly personal Rs (revenge, redemption, relationship and respect).
> (qt. in Bazraktarevik 2019: 12)

Syria is seen as an alternative world to their frequent social deaths in London. Both girls learn their version of truth in Syria when they witness the violence, jealousies, and politics in the name of religion. She narrates one of the many experiences of prisoners in the orphanage, when the older Kurdish women spat in her direction. The incidents of violence and intolerance that she sees around her make her realize gradually the difference between her interpretation of Islam and the various orthodox views of the Jihadists:

> I had lost my belief in the exact ways I had been brought up to follow my faith in. It didn't make sense anymore – this intense

hatred and violence being practiced in the name of a religion that stood for peace, this endless nitpicking bureaucratic intolerance being practiced in the name of a God whose most common attributes, as I'd been told from the time I was an infant, was mercy and forgiveness!

(Khair 2016b: 152)

The narrative exposes the paradoxes of how, in the name of religion, extreme cruelty and impiety are carried on, leaving young girls alone and without a home to return to. This seems to be one of the primary concerns of Khair as a writer. He writes of heterogeneity to readers in the West who often think of Islam as a community of terrorists and suicide bombers. So, the tale of the two girls becomes relatable.

This raises queries on female participation and agency in Jihadist groups, as discussed by Faruk Bajraktarevic in his paper "Just Another Jihadi Jane: Transgressing to Transform and Transcend," to show how the narrative, to borrow Showalter's words, is "a double-voiced discourse, containing a 'dominant' and a 'muted' story" (qt. in Keyes 2008: 14). The silent text implies that more than religious reasons, it is the will to escape the prejudices and Islamophobia associated with immigrants in the West that these girls go to Syria as emissaries. Their experiences in the Islamic state reiterate the displeasure and dissatisfaction in a patriarchal world where they are mere objects to be used for the purposes of their possessors:

One of the reasons why I chose two women was exactly this . . . because my sympathies are more with female characters for a set of reasons. . . first of all it's a sexist movement. . . it is important because you have to recognize that these girls have agency – they are not just being brainwashed.

(qt. in Bajraktarevic 2019: 8)

The subtext furnishes a larger purpose of showing death both as physical and rhetorical. Regarding the life-death dichotomy, the narrative moves to an incident of suicide bombing and the symbolic death of the two girls (Ameena's death when she is reported killed in an explosion and Jamilla is thought to be dead along with her), although Jamilla chooses life. Instead of a social death by submitting to the motives and plans of persons in power positions, Ameena decides to end her life as an act of not only saving Jamilla but also showing her voluntary physical death as a victorious termination of the orders of Daesh leaders like Hassan and the larger process of militancy. It is seen as an act of "explod[ing] the social game" of oppression by "speak[ing] a word of truth to a tyrant" (Bajraktarevic 2019: 9). For Khair, it is an address to the larger world to see the anxiety and suffering of the gendered Islamic 'other.' He places Jamilla's narrative as an act of re-invention of herself with a new name far away from her family in London: "I wanted a place where I had no history, and where I could be with my beliefs without people who proscribed or prescribed" (Khair 2016b: 237). Religion as depicted in the novels is an individual response towards the Almighty, a rescue for the follower beyond otherism and religious fanaticism.

The narratives in both the novels by the narrators of the plot, the writers (Mehrotra and the future writer Jamilla) of the plot, and the novelist Khair himself are layered and profound. Meanings emerge from the interwoven discourse of the narrator, on one hand, and, on the other, out of the novelist's intent. It is the style adopted by Khair of using irony and metaphor that draws on his views in the subtext by maintaining a distance from the narrative. In *Just Another Jihadi Jane*, the narrative presents "a female militant neither as a full agent or victim," and this debunks the pre-given gendered standards defining agency and would seek to understand the actions themselves in a particular context so that it is "neither a philosophical absolute nor a tangible entity but a relational and contextual practice" (Brown 1995: 6). This is a new breakthrough in gynocriticism to explore female experiences outside the usual framework of female victimization. In *Night of Happiness*, Khair proposes that Ahmed is indeterminable or incomprehensible. The towel-wrapped tiffin box with the *halwa* is found at the end by Mehrotra on his office table. His confusion about how it found its way there despite Ahmed's long absence from the office makes him look for clues; the flavor of *halwa* haunts him, and he makes his way to Ahmed's neighbor, who informs him of Ahmed's death. Left with no clue, Mehrotra's representation of the other remains mysterious and uncanny. Jamilla and Ahmed subsequently become vampires because they are always dead in the eyes of the xenophobe:

> The stranger, like the vampire, has a body that is like 'our' body, but not really so. The stranger, like the vampire, might be innocuous in broad daylight, but is always a hidden dark, potential threat. The stranger, like the vampire, appears to be like 'us', but only by deception. The stranger, like the vampire, appears alive, but isn't really so. The stranger, like the vampire, can be killed without any commandment, sacred or secular.
>
> (Khair 2016a: 22)

Notes

1 Henceforth, *The New Xenophobia* will be cited as (Khair 2016a) and the other novel *Just Another Jihadi Jane* published in the same year as (Khair 2016b).
2 'Upside down house' is a term used by Amitav Ghosh in his novel *The Shadow Lines* to refer to the other side of the border that always looks inverted.

Works cited

Bajraktarevic, Faruk. "Tabish Khair's *Just Another Jihadi Jane*: Transgression to Transform and Transcend." *The Central and Eastern European Online Library*. Serbia, Mar., 2019. www.ceeol.com/search/article-detail?id=802701.

Brown, W. *States of Injury: Power and Freedom in Late Modernity*. Princeton, NJ: Princeton University Press, 1995.

Childs, Peter, et al. *The Routledge Dictionary of Literary Terms*. New York: Routledge, 2006.

Dalrymple, William. *Nine Lives: In Search of the Sacred in Modern India*. New Delhi: Bloomsbury, 2013.

Ghosh, Amitav. *In an Antique Land*. New Delhi: Ravi Dayal, 1992.

Ghoshal, Somak. "Tabish Khair's New Novel Takes a Chilling Look at Trauma and Muslim Lives in India." *Livemint Mint-Lounge Features*, July 27, 2018.

Guha, Keshava. "Review of Tabish Khair's 'Night of Happiness': In the House of Inversions." *The Hindu*, May 12, 2018.

Haddad, Yvonne Yazbeck, and Tyler Golson. "Overhauling Islam: Representation, Construction, and Cooption of 'Moderate Islam' in Western Europe." *Journal of Church and State* 49:3 (2007): 487–515. JSTOR, www.jstor.org/stable/23921517. Accessed Mar.14, 2021.

Herrero, Dolores. "Tabish Khair's *Just Another Jihadi Jane*: Western Civilization and 'War on Terror' Versus Islamist Terrorism as the Two Sides of the Globalization Coin." *Societies*, Oct. 2018.

Karnor, Maithreyi. "Gujarat Riot Literature: The Narrative Tool of Surveillance and Its Mystical Aftermath." *The Wire Books*, June 2, 2018. https://thewire.in/books/gujarat-riots-night-of-happiness-tabish-khair.

Keyes, Claire. *The Aesthetics of Power: The Poetry of Adrienne Rich*. Athens: The University of Georgia Press, 2008.

Khair, Tabish. *Just Another Jihadi Jane*. Gurgaon, India: Penguin Random House, 2016.

———. *The New Xenophobia*. New Delhi: Oxford University Press, 2016.

———. *Night of Happiness*. New Delhi: Picador, 2018.

Nussbaum, Martha. *The New Religious Intolerance*. Cambridge, MA: Harvard University Press, 2012.

Zamindar, Vazira. *The Long Partition and the Making of Modern South Asia: Refugees, Boundaries, Histories*. New York: Columbia University Press, 2010.

2

KURUKSHETRA AND KARBALA

Mahabharata in Intizar Hussain's[1] fiction

Haris Qadeer

> the lives of Muslims and Hindus in the subcontinent are so
> deeply enmeshed that the two cannot be separated.[2]
> > – Intizar Hussain

> We speak so much of memory because there is so little of it left.[3]
> > – Pierre Nora

In an interview with Asif Farrukhi, Intizar Hussain (1925–2016), an icon of modern Urdu fiction, comments on the amalgamation of different mythologies and cultures in his writing and explains how the culture of Muslims of the Indian subcontinent is different from the cultures of Muslims of the other parts of the world. While referring to the lived Islam in the subcontinent, he condemns the idea of pure and monolithic Islam in an anti-puritanical tone: "I have no idea what a purely Islamic culture is" (Bhalla 2015: vii). The culture, as he believes, is 'Indian Islamic culture,' – a culture which is a product of the natural confluence of different cultures and religions in the subcontinent. Hussain attempts to debunk the myth of monolithic Muslim identity and embraces the existence of multiculturalism among Muslim communities. His understanding of this unique and multilayered Muslim identity in the subcontinent has deep cultural roots, he, like many other Muslims of the subcontinent, celebrates the influences of different cultures and traditions on Muslim lives in the region. He states:

> Our Islam, our culture, is an Indian Islamic culture. I don't know where
> a purely Muslim culture took birth in the world. It didn't take birth in
> Iran, and the Arabs' tradition was the Arabs' own culture; Islam came
> and mixed into it; while our culture is an Indian Islamic culture.
> > (Farrukhi 2005: 07)

In his interviews and writings, he vociferously articulates his belief in multicultural identity and pluralistic societies of the Indian subcontinent. It

DOI: 10.4324/9781003158424-4

would not be an exaggeration that Hussain's fictional world is a microcosm of the composite culture of the subcontinent and is crowded with characters from different mythologies and cultures (Islamic, Buddhist, and Hindu). Scholars and critics such as Menon, Bhalla, Farrukhi, Zaidi, Jalil, and others have also emphasized the various beliefs of the author. His writing can be read as an archive of cultural memory of the people of the Indian subcontinent, and through it, he delves deeply into the pluralist culture of the past by populating his canvas with real and imagined characters from different histories and mythologies and also by bringing together the human and the non-human world. He deploys narrative techniques that draw together different modes of narration, and his stories, as Daruwala notes, are woven on an oriental loom; they "often tread that twilight zone between fable and parable" (Daruwala *The Hindu* 2 March 2003). Confluences of cultures, amalgamations of traditions, and recollections of multicultural memories are the ingredients of Hussain's narratives. He blends personal, mythical, historical, and political and recreates a world where the "*Ramayana* and the *Mahabharata*, the Buddha and the *Jatakas*, Meerabai and Tulsidas," are "as much a part of the literary, moral, and religious habitat of the Muslims as Nizamuddin Auliya and Amir Khusrau, Baba Farid and Ghalib, the azan and the Koran were of the Hindus" (Bhalla 2015: ix). Though he migrated to Pakistan in the wake of the 1947 partition of India and Pakistan, his writings continue to draw upon the pluralistic traditions of the subcontinent. Aijaz Ahmad, in *In Mirror of Urdu: Recompositions of Nation and Community, 1947–1965*, argues that at the time of partition, a bulk of Urdu writers constituted a community, and "a secularist belief in the composite culture of Hindus and Muslims in India was the predominant ideological position" (1993: 11) of the community. Further, he notes that even the partition "did not decisively break up emotional structure" (1993: 11) of the community. Hussain could also be regarded as one of the authors from the community. Syncretism is an aesthetic marker in Husain's literary world, and in it, he focuses upon, as Mayaram (2004) would put, "a border zone where cultures get blurred but a space of immense cultural creativity."

The chapter seeks to study how Hussain's writings foreground the epic, the mythic, and the historic by focusing on the deployment of *Mahabharata* in short stories such as '*Daira*' (Circle), '*Morenama*' (A Chronicle of Peacock), '*Ek Binlikhi Razmiya*' (An Unwritten Epic), 'Rishi aur Qasai' (The Sage and the Butcher), and his non-fiction, *Dilli tha Jiska Naam* (Once There Was a City Named Dilli). This chapter, however, does not attempt to do a close reading of the previously mentioned texts; it rather attempts to explore: How does Hussain meditate on the contours of syncretic culture and pluralistic traditions of the past? How does his oeuvre move beyond the logic of national citizenship? In what ways does his fiction debunk the myth of monolithic Muslim cultural identity in South Asia? Given the fact that Hussain was not the first Muslim writer from South Asia to engage with *Mahabharata*, the chapter begins with a brief but important note on *Mahabharata* and Muslims of the Indian subcontinent and attempts to locate Hussain's writing in the tradition.

Mahabharata and Indo-Muslim Traditions

For centuries, the imagination of several poets, authors, artists, and connoisseurs of art of the Indian subcontinent, who can be identified as Muslims, has been preoccupied with *Mahabharata*, a sacred ancient text. The Persian translation[4] of the *Mahabharata* as *Razmnama* (The Book of War) in the sixteenth century is the first documented evidence of the engagement of Muslims of the subcontinent with the epic. Commissioned by the Mughal emperor Akbar, the translation was the result of "a lengthy collaboration between Muslim Nobles and learned Brahmans" (Rice 2010: 127) who worked together in the *Maktabkhana* (translation bureau) established by the emperor to promote interreligious understanding. The book was "meant to be a bridge between Hindus and Muslims, and to address Akbar's goal of minimizing religious factionalism" (Rice 2010: 126) by focusing on the sectarian commonalities between both the Hindus and the Muslims. One of the illustrations of *Razmnama* depicts both Hindu as well Muslim scholars working together on the translation project.[5] The lavishly illustrated book was the first pictorial representation of the *Mahabharata* and is an important milestone in the history of visual cultures in South Asia. In the Mughal school of painting, a considerable amalgamation between the Hindu devotional themes and Persian-style illustrations took place. A famous miniature painting known as *Krishna Govardhana*[6] (1595), attributed to the painter Miskin and commissioned by Akbar (1556–1605), depicts Lord Krishna lifting the mountain Govardhana to protect the villagers of Braj and their herds against the torrential rain sent by the god Indra. As far as twentieth century is concerned, the mention of two artists is indispensable: Rahi Masoom Raza (1927–1992), the Hindi novelist, wrote the script and dialogue for a television adaptation of *Mahabharata* (1988–1990). In the series of *Mahabharata* paintings (1971–1990), the famous Indian artist MF Hussain (1915–2011) emphasizes the universal importance of the epic.

It is interesting to note that among all the characters of *Mahabharata*, Krishna holds a special place in the hearts and minds of Muslim authors and poets. Various strands of Krishna devotionalism can be found in the works of Muslim poets from the thirteenth century. Numerous Hindi and Urdu poets such as Amir Khusrau (1253–1325), Sayyad Ibrahim Khan alias Ras Khan (1548–1628), Nazeer Akbarabadi (1735–1830), Syed Fazlul Hasan Hasrat Mohani (1875–1951), Ashiq Husain Siddiqui alias Seemab Akbarabadi (1882–1951), Josh Malihabadi (1894–1982), Abdul Hayee alias Sahir Ludhianvi (1921–1980), and Nida Fazli (1938–2016) wrote poems in praise of Krishna. In an interesting article, 'The Maulana who loved Krishna,' Naim discusses the maverick poet Hasrat Mohani's profound love for Krishna and notes, "Hasrat did not view Krishna as a deity, but did regard him as imbued with some grace of the Divine" (2013: 41). In his Urdu poems, Mohani referred to Krishna as 'Hazrat Srī Krishna Alaihi-Rahma' and 'Hazrat Krishna.' In Muslim culture, the honorific 'Hazrat' is generally used before the name of a revered and pious personality. It may also "include all prophets, including the Prophet of Islam, the latter's 'Companions' and all Sufi saints, religious savants and martyrs. Its use, therefore, places Krishna in a most august company, though in a somewhat generic manner" (Naim 2013: 41). Similar honorifics for Krishna are also found in various Urdu translations of *Mahabharata* and *Gita*. An interesting intervention in the tradition of Krishna Bhakti literature by Muslim authors of the subcontinent is Raihana Tyabji's *The Heart of a Gopi*, a devotional text written in 1924. In this small book of Bhakti devotionalism, Tyabji, a Muslim woman of the Bohra community and an associate of Gandhi, demonstrates Sharmila's unconditional devoutness to Krishna in the *gopi* tradition. In most writings by Muslim authors, the figure of Krishna evoked is not a political figure or a warrior. These authors appear to be more enchanted with Krishna's avatar and his philosophy of love and compassion, as depicted in *Harivamsa Purana* (the lineage of Hari), a work that is believed to be a supplement to the *Mahabharata*.

An eighteenth-century musical retelling of *Mahabharata*, composed by Muslim poet Saadullah Khan, known as 'Padun ka Kada' (Pandava's couplet) is popular in the Mewat region of India. The epic is performed in the Mewati dialect, primarily by Muslim Mirasi or Muslim jogis who trace their origin to the Rajputs and claim to be the descendants of Rama, Krishna, and Arjun. The unique version of *Mahabharata* does not begin with an evocation of Hindu gods but with a brief ode in praise of the Prophet Muhammad and the Sufi saint Khwaja. For Shail Mayaram (2004), the Meo version of *Mahabharata* is an example of "Hindu-Muslim cultural encounter," and the folk epic "is far more than mere myth" and is central to "the cultural identity of the Meo Muslims." Her comment is noteworthy, as it demonstrates how a Hindu text becomes "central" to the cultural identity of Muslims of the region. The Indo-Muslim traditions of *Mahabharata* are cultural spaces of amalgamation and immense creativity: Krishna is addressed as 'Hazrat Krishna' by North Indian Muslim Krishna Bhakts; Salabega, a seventeenth-century Odia poet, composed *bhajans* depicting scenes of *Mahabharata*; and Muttal Ravattan, a Muslim character, becomes a devoted battle-companion of Hindus in a South Indian folk epic of the Draupdati cult.[7] These cults have, down the ages, created their own narratives based on *Mahabharata*.

Intizar Hussain has adopted and adapted various ancient narratives in his stories. By adopting *Mahabharata* as his frame of reference in many of his narratives, he carries forward the Indo-Muslim tradition of the epic. He presents himself as well acquainted with the epic's sacrosanct position

within the cultures of the Indian subcontinent and utilizes themes, characters, and plots of the epic to depict the political, historical, and social complexities of the past as well as the present of the subcontinent.

Syncretic past and multicultural memories

Edward Said, in *Invention, Memory, and Place*, argues that memory and its
representations "touch very significantly upon questions of identity" (2000:
176). He further demonstrates how

> memories of the past are shaped in accordance with a certain notion
> of what "we" or, for that matter, "they" really are. National iden-
> tity always involves narratives – of the nation's past, its founding
> fathers and documents, seminal events, and so on.
>
> (2000: 177)

How does Hussain shape memories of the past in his fiction? How does he
navigate through the memories of the nation that he left? Although Hussain opted for a new nation for various personal reasons, he neither shuns
the memories of the nation that he left, nor does he bifurcate them on the
basis of geographical boundaries. In his recollection of the past, the two
nation-states become one multi-cultural civilization space, and through
his art of writing, he meditates on the syncretic cultural heritage of pre-
partition India. Even after he migrates to Pakistan after the 1947 partition,
he continues to yearn for the formative years that he spent in India. Umar
Menon, the renowned Urdu critic, claims that Hussain's world "is devoted
to the remembrance of things past, moments gone, and faces dissolved by
time" (1981: 73). In Pakistan, being an author from the community of
muhajirs, Hussain understood the vital role that memory plays in "insider's understanding of one's country, tradition, and faith" (Said 2000: 176).
While constructing the past, he does not confine himself to the geographical
boundaries of Pakistan; rather, he embraces multicultural memory of the
combined past of both countries, as it gives him a sense of belonging and a
sense of cultural identity. Hussain belongs to, as Said would say, "an era of
a search for roots" (2000: 177), with "people trying to discover in the collective memory of their race, religion, community, and family a past that is
entirely their own, secure from the ravages of history and a turbulent time"
(2000: 177). In his search, Hussain revisits his past; his nostalgic revisits to
his personal past as well as historical/mythical past in his fiction speak of his
diasporic desires and are akin to what Tololyan calls a "re-turn, a repeated
turning to the concept and/or the reality of the homeland – rather than a
desire for a literal return" (1996: 15).

Hussain incorporates vivid images, myths, and tales from Islamic,
Hindu, and Buddhist cultures and weaves together the different threads

37

of his narrative. Apart from *Jataka Tales, Ramayana, Panchtantra, Katha Sarit Sagar, Thousand and One Nights*, and Sufi lore, *Mahabharata* is also utilized as a frame of reference in many of his narratives. The trans-Islamic tropes in his writings indicate his desire to remain connected to a cultural tradition that has had a formative influence on his writings. Unlike various South Asian authors who are known for their modern retellings of *Mahabharata*, Hussain's treatment of the epic is different. He borrows specific episodes and characters of the epic, and weaves his stories around them – often, characters are resurrected from the epic and situated in contemporary times. His preoccupation with epics can be traced back to his childhood days in Dibai, a small town, where he was born in pre-partition India. In the opening pages of his magnum opus, *Basti* (1979), he depicts a prelapsarian world of the pre-partition India of his childhood days. Perhaps this harmonious society, "the parallel worlds of Bhagat-ji and Abba Jan, of Hindu mythology and Muslim legend and lore" (Menon 2007: Introduction) had a seminal influence on his personality, and he often recreates the bygone era of harmony and peaceful coexistence of Hindus and Muslims. In the fictional town of Rupnagar, Bhagat-ji, the knowledgeable and devout Hindu with "his sacred thread around his neck, his caste-mark on his forehead, his whole head shaved except for one tuft" (Husain 2007: 01) sat in his shop and narrated wise stories from *Ramayana* and *Mahabharata*, and in the same town, Abba Jan, the narrator's father, a Muslim scholar, explained how "God Most High make the earth" (Husain: 2007: 02). The different stories of the creation of the universe by Bhagat-ji and Abba Jan, and how these very different stories had an everlasting effect on the narrator, may remind one of Barthes' comment:

> narrative starts with the very history of mankind; there is not, there has never been anywhere, any people without narrative; all classes, all human groups have their stories, and very often these stories are enjoyed by men of different and even opposite cultural backgrounds.
>
> (1975: 273)

In an attempt to trace the civilizational history of the subcontinent, Hussain is persuaded to search for how different histories, cultures, and literature interact with each other and result in a pluralistic civilization. He once translated a section of the *Mahabharata* into Urdu for publication in a journal. Masud Ashar, the editor of the journal, enquired about the reasons for Hussain's choice of the fragment of the epic. The question persuades Hussain to ponder over the tradition of mourning and lamentation associated with Karbala. He finds many connections between the war of Mahabharata and the battle of Karbala. Hussain read similarities between the human tragedies of Karbala and Kurukshetra and between the martyrdoms of Ali and Abhimanyu. He states:

> I remembered all that whole tradition of mourning and lamentation when Ali Asghar been martyred and his mother is mourning and lamenting, or his aunt, or his sister. The mourning, the grief of Abhimanyu's mother – I saw so much similarity to the lamentation of Karbala that I was astonished. Had the marsiyah tradition been influenced by this kind of expression in the Mahabharata?
>
> (Farrukhi 2005: 08)

Apart from drawing a parallel between the human tragedies at Kurukshetra and Karbala, Hussain's comment demonstrates how art and literature evolve and how they are influenced by other cultures. However, in the interview, Hussain does not substantiate his speculations about the influence of *Mahabharata* on the genre of Marsiya.[8] It can be inferred that Hussain was only speculating on the marsiya tradition in the subcontinent, not on the entire genre of marsiya, which originated in Pre-Islamic Arabia and traveled to the other parts of the world, including the subcontinent. However, one can build upon Hussain's questions and find similarities between the texts, especially how these texts move beyond a mere narration of the tragedies and deal with provoking questions of humane and inhumane, good and evil, and the notion of *deen* and *dharm*.

Hussain's short story 'The Sage and the Butcher' deals with the question of *Dharm* (righteousness) and *Karma* (action). Like many of the retellings of *Jataka Tales*, such as *Kachhwe* (Tortoise) and *Patte* (Leaves), Hussain retells a story of *Vyadha Gita* from *Vana Parva* (Book of Forest) of the *Mahabharata*. The section of the epic destabilizes the power structure of society. In this section, a sage named Markandeya narrates the story of a butcher and brahman to Yudhishthira, one of the Pandavas. The arrogant sannyasi, in the story, is humbled by a butcher. The focus of the story is on the idea of *Karma*, and in his retelling, Hussain appears to be preaching dignity of labor.

The cultural geography of Hussain's writings

There is a strong "sense of place"[9] in Hussain's writing. In his fiction, he visits villages, cities, and towns, but these are not merely nostalgic returns to the past. Each place he visits is inextricably tied to a specific memory, and the tangled relationship is crucial, as Nathan Wachtel states: "the preservation of recollections rests on their anchorage in space" (Wachtel 1986: 216). Whether they are actual places like Qayyuma's shop, Karbala ground, the deserted temple in *Daira*, or the half-imaginary towns such as Rupnagar and Vyasnagar in *Basti*, the specificity of geographical location plays important role in Hussain's oeuvre.

In narratives dealing with *Mahabharata*, Hussain refers to actual cities such as Delhi, Jaipur, and Vrindavan, and links them with the epic. The depiction of specific locations in these cities could be read as what Pierre Nora calls the "sites of memory" or "*lieux de mémoire*" – physical and concrete places such as buildings, churches, and museums as well as non-material sites such as celebrations and rituals. These are the sites where "memory crystallizes and secretes itself" (Nora 1989: 07). The constitutive relationship between memory and place forms the background of his narratives dealing with *Mahabharata*. In *Once There Was a City Named Dilli*, written in the form of a cultural biography of the city, Hussain performs a literary excavation of the city to documents its multi-layered history. To trace the origin of the city, he exhorts his readers to read the *Mahabharata*, as he regards the text as an authentic source of the past. Blurring the boundary between history and mythology, he informs the reader that the city was called Inderprasth, Inderpuri, or Inderpat during ancient times and explains how the Pandavas, who were asked to leave Hastinapur by King Dhritrashtra, settled in Khandoban, a wilderness. The forest of Khandoban was cleared, and Indraprasth, a new town, was founded and later became a lively city. For Hussain, the city was not invaded or destroyed, as all the enemies had already been defeated and destroyed in Kurukshetra; the city was abandoned by all the Pandava brothers and Draupadi. Hussain admits that there is no historical record of the era, but there are legends, and the legends about Delhi, for him, are as authentic as historical records. He believes that any investigation would merely reproduce what has already been said. Menon is not off the mark when he comments: "the power of mythology and sacred history does not depend on the verifiability of the events they recount, but on their symbolic meanings and emotional truths" (Menon 1981: 76). Hussain's depiction of geographical locations focuses on the symbolic meanings and emotional truths of *Mahabharata*.

Apart from Delhi, Hussain also depicts other Indian cities such as Vrindavan, Kurukshetra, and Jaipur in his writings. In *A Chronicle of Peacock*, Hussain borrows a character from *Mahabharata* to link the present to the past and to demonstrate the futility of war. On a visit to Jaipur, India, Hussain is followed by Ashwatthama of *Mahabharata*, who fought in the battle of Kurukshetra, on the side of Kaurava against Pandava. In the epic, Ashwatthama received the curse of immortality for misusing his celestial weapon, Bharmastra. Hussain recalls the similarities between the destruction that was caused in the mythic past due to the use of Bharmastra by Ashwatthama and foresees the destruction that would be caused by the use of nuclear weapons in contemporary times. Ashwatthama, who could be seen as an epitome of evil forces as well as an extension of the past, comes back to haunt the narrator throughout the narrative. In the opening lines of the story, Hussain informs the readers that an evil spirit got hold of him when he went to inquire about the well-being of the peacocks of Jaipur. A small note in a newspaper on how the explosion of atomic bomb testing (Pokhran II) by India had frightened the peacocks of Jaipur, Rajasthan, persuades Hussain to rethink his duties and obligations as a writer. In response to the explosion, he wrote a column expressing his sympathies for the birds, and the "insignificant piece of information" (Husain 2015b: 105) brings back the memories of his visit to Jaipur, but now, the author, who is known for resurrecting memories, is neither able to reimagine the city nor hear the songs of peacocks – all he can visualize is desolateness and destruction. All the peacocks, except one lonely, bruised, and battered peacock, have fled the city. Peacocks for Hussain are not just beautiful birds; they are also "a link between the past and the present" (2015b: 107). As a binding symbol and metaphor of timelessness and beauty and an emblem of cultural continuity, Hussain links different times and cultures to peacocks. They are an integral part of both his personal as well as mythical memory; they remind him of his childhood days and of his grandmother, who believed that peacocks were exiled from paradise, and as the living witnesses of Indian civilization, they are part of different historical and mythological sites: they cried in Kurukshetra when Bhramastra was used; they cried in Jaipur when nuclear weapons were tested. They were present at the garden of Indraprastha, the city of Pandavas; they are the survivors from Buddha's times and are an indispensable part of the landscape of Buddha's Sravasthi. Hussain also finds them near Nizamuddin during his visit to Delhi. He writes: "I have travelled far and long. I have seen peacocks – peacocks from different ages and lands. I have heard their song. Now, it is time for me to write my *Morenama* – my Chronicle of the Peacocks" (2015b: 109).

Hussain summons the past to bear witness to the present and uses the war of *Mahabharata* to make an anti-war statement against nuclear weaponry as well as against contemporary wars between various nation-states. Through the narrative, he raises crucial questions regarding human loss, destruction of nature, exile, and borders. The repercussions of atomic explosions on nature are demonstrated through the example of the physical (bruised and battered) as well as psychological (frightened) state of the peacocks. He shows how "war transforms men utterly" (2015b: 109) by alluding to the important episode about the use of Bharmastra by Ashwatthama, the cursed warrior and "the great criminal of Kurukshetra" (2015b: 109) who has been wandering since the war of *Mahabharata*. While Hussain was traveling between times and cultures, Ashwatthama "attached himself" (2015b: 109) to the author and followed him like a shadow through different cities, even across the border of India and Pakistan. Hussain suggests that the culture and memories of the people of the sub-continent cannot be divided by geographical borders. The story is exemplary of Hussain's syncretic narratives: it starts with an invocation to Allah, refers to the Hindu myth of Manuji and fish and to *Mahabharata*, and narrates the author's visits to the shrines of Sufi saint, Moin-uddin Chishti, and the Bhakti poet Meerabai.

41

In his attempt to depict memories of the cartographic cracking of the Indian sub-continent in 1947, Hussain, like many other authors, such as Dharamveer Bharti (1926–1997) and Sunil Gangopadhyay (1934–2012), utilizes the complex narrative of *Mahabharata*. In her reading of Gangopadhayay's use of the epic in the Bengali novel *Arjun*, Debali Mookerjea-Leonard notes how the epic can serve "as a guide for India's long past to its uncertain present" (2008: 50) and how the epic "relates the dissolution of human bonds, contestations over territory, and a massive and senseless loss of human life" (50). Her observation stands valid for Hussain's writing on the 1947 partition. In an interview with Meena Menon, Hussain states: "The first partition was in Mahabharata" (*The Hindu*, 05 July 2014). In the same interview, he compares the pain of his own migration to the exile of Pandava. Hussain's understanding of the epic and his use of familial metaphors for the event of partition is akin to Gandhi's reading of the partition. Like Gandhi, Hussain understood that the narrative crust of the epic lies in a heinous act of violence against familial relations. *Mahabharata*, for Gandhi and Hussain, was not only a book of deception, betrayal, and violence but also a book that demonstrates the futility of war. Gandhi referred to the epic to spread his message of love and non-violence. He regarded the partition as a tragic sequel to *Mahabharata*:

> They all fought – the Pandavas and the Kauravas – blood-brothers, and what was the result? While evil was certainly defeated, only seven of the victors remained to tell the tale. This was the state of the country today.
>
> (Tendulkar 1953: 496)

The analogy between the partition and *Mahabharata* also resonates with Ashis Nandy's reading of the partition (Mittal 2003: 94); he argued that the epic violence is the violence between intimates, and he compares the war of *Mahabharata* between cousins to the violence and bloodshed of the 1947 partition. In Hussain's *An Unwritten Epic*, referring to the large-scale violence and upheaval of the partition of India and Pakistan, the narrator explains the reasons for not writing a prose epic on the subject. The character Pichwa of Qadirpur, "who confronted the riot with his own body" (Husain 1983: 11), has some heroic characteristics like dignity and greatness, but he only remains an insignificant character in the narrator's "two penny stories" (1983: 11). The narrator wanted him to be cast as "a twentieth-century Tipu Sultan" (1983: 12), but Pichwa's arrival in Pakistan deprives him of all the greatness and grandeur. In the newly created Pakistan, Pichwa is unable to make ends meet without a job and shelter. Unlike his epic prototype (Arjun of Vyasa's *Mahabharata*), Pichwa, the Arjun of Qadirpur, is not a courageous and intelligent warrior but the "real problem" (1983: 14) in

Pakistan: "The Arjuna of this *Mahabharata* is now the picture of failure and he wanders around the street and lanes of Pakistan looking for a house and a job. He doesn't get these two things and he continues falling from his true place" (1983: 14). Hussain's "Mahabharata of Qadirpur" is deprived of any epic grandeur, and his Arjun is neither an epic hero and nor bears any similarity to his namesake. He is "the vanquished Arjun" (1983: 14) of the Mahabharata of Qadirpur, and through him, Hussain brings forth the plight of muhajirs in Pakistan. Like many other muhajirs, Pichwa is an ordinary man struggling hard to adjust himself in a new nation. Hussain locates the notion of *Hijrat* (both religious and political), a crucial event in the history of Islam, within the narrative framework of *Mahabharata*. Hussain's localization of the epic by scaling down sublimity implies the relevance of the epic in modern times.

Zaidi, in her introduction to her English translation of Hussain's *Day and Dastaan* (2018), explains how the art of storytelling, for Hussain, was a journey and spiritual experience – Sufi traditions, or *Varidat*, as Hussain himself would use. In many of his stories, he describes the process of creation of a story, and in the process, the figure of storyteller or narrator gains prominence. In *An Unwritten Epic*, the heterodiegetic narrator informs the reader about his inability to produce a prose epic and his failure to create an epic hero; similarly, in *Daira*, the narrator explains the dilemma of rewriting an old story. *Daira* was written fifty years after his first story 'Qaiyyuma ki Dukan,' a story that Hussain thinks was not written the way it should have been written, as the main character, Qaiyyuma, was absent in the story. In an attempt to complete the story, Hussain returns to his familiar world of pre-partition India in *Daira*, but the task of rewriting the story is not simple as it may seem. The narrator is faced with a dilemma: "Should I write the story that I had written fifty years ago" (Husain 2015a: 89). The predicament of the storyteller is explained with an example of Karn's dilemma from *Mahabharata*:

> But Karan said he did not believe in re-using an arrow that had once left his bow. If the arrow was wasted, then so be it; it was destined to go waste. I am lost in thought . . . should I attempt to rewrite the story that has been squandered away. After much dilly-dallying, I make up my mind. Karan's words went away with him. I must attempt to write that story once again.
>
> (2015a: 89–90)

The narrator in the story ponders the question of rewriting a story that has already been told. The act of retelling a story initially becomes 'Karn's arrow' that he "did not believe in re-using" (2015a: 89), but for continuity, a story needs to be told multiple times. The storyteller finally makes up his mind, and the words of Karn fade away.

Stories from *Mahabharata* have been told many times, but Hussain's retelling of the episodes of the epic is unique. It is his craft of storytelling that draws the readers into the stories. In his purposeful revival of the ancient epic, he can be regarded "as a qissa-khvān or katha-vacak – a teller of stories that exist in their own worlds, and that keep a fascinated audience wondering, 'Then when what happened?'" (Pritchett 1983: 198). Hussain's writings depict how different communities in India have shared the same spaces and cultures and have more in common than differences. His idea of homeland, as Bhalla explains, "is not merely defined by the territory within which he now claimed his rightful citizenship" (Bhalla 2015: x). It was also "the larger civilizational space from which he derived his imaginative strength" (x). He identified himself as a wanderer between Karbala and Ayodhya, and both the cities in his works are not only actual places but also symbolic sites of memories. In his fiction, often the real is presented as imaginary, and the imaginary is depicted as real, and both the real and imagined spaces become sites of cultural memory. Hussain also demonstrates awareness of the course of Muslim history in many of his writings and expands the cultural geography of his writings by including references to significant places and histories of the broader Islamic world, such as the bygone Islamic kingdom of Al-Andalus and the tragedy of Karbala in Iraq. It may be read as Hussain's attempt to understand his own cultural identity in the subcontinent as well as beyond it. However, this doesn't stop him from alluding to other histories and mythologies of the subcontinent. He appears to be a custodian of the vanishing cultural geography of his youth.

Hussain never wrote a full-length retelling of *Mahabharata* and alludes to the epic only indirectly and tangentially. He re-situates certain episodes of the epic in the present and resurrects specific characters of the epic. Through the use of *Mahabharata*, he conveys that the syncretic heritage and pluralist past of the Indian subcontinent cannot be confined to various borders and boundaries built by modern nation-states. One of the major themes in Hussain's writings is the indelibility of memories and of the past, and he, often, uses stories from the epic to depict the past of the Indian subcontinent. Though he celebrates syncretic cultures, at times, it is done through the idealization and mythification of the past. In much of his fiction, he depicts different communities living together harmoniously in pre-partition India. Such depictions are based on, as Amir Mufti would put it, "a nostalgic notion of the syncretic nature of traditional Indian religious life, a syncretism that is then understood as the basis for indigenous forms of religious tolerance and coexistence" (2011: 124). By amalgamating both Islamic and trans-Islamic frameworks in his oeuvre, Hussain proposes religious syncretism as a solution for religious separatism.

Notes

1 Scholars have used both 'Husain' and 'Hussain' for Intizar's surname.
2 See Bhalla, Alok. "In Conversation with Intizar Husain: Some Remembered, Some Imagined." *Mānoa* 27:1, Story Is a Vagabond: Fiction, Essays, and Drama (2015): 245–256.
3 See Nora, Pierre. "Between Memory and History: Les Lieux de Mémoire." *Representations*, No. 26, Special Issue: Memory and Counter Memory (Spring, 1989), p. 07.
4 It was an abridgement rather than a faithful translation of the entire text. For more details on *Razmnama*; see Rice, Yael. "A Persian Mahabharata: The 1598–1599 Razmnama." *Mānoa* 22:1, Andha Yug: The Age of Darkness (Summer, 2010): 125–131.
5 A digitalized copy of the illustration is available on https://libwww.freelibrary.org/digital/item/38973 Accessed on 15 June 2020.
6 A digitalized copy of the miniature is available on: www.columbia.edu/itc/mealac/pritchett/00routesdata/1500_1599/akbar/krishnapainting/krishnapainting.html Accessed on 15 June 2020.
7 For details on the Draupdati cult among Muslims, see Hiltebeitel, Alf. *Rethinking India's Oral and Classical Epics Draupadi among Rajputs, Muslims, and Dalits.* Chicago: The University of Chicago Press, 1999.
8 Elegiac poems recited to commemorate the martyrdom of Hussain and his companion at the battle of Karbala.
9 The term, as used in Human geography, refers to the emotional bonds and attachments people develop or experience in particular locations and environments.

Works cited

Ahmad, Aijaz. *In the Mirror of Urdu: Recompositions of Nation and Community, 1947–1965.* Shimla: IIAS, 1993.
Barthes, Roland. "An Introduction to the Structure of Narrative." *New Literary History* 6:2, On Narrative and Narratives (Winter, 1975): 237–272.
Bhalla, Alok. "Introduction." *Mānoa* 27:1, Story Is a Vagabond: Fiction, Essays, and Drama (2015): vii–xv.
Daruwala, Keki, N. "Narratives from an Oriental Loom." Review of *A Chronicle of the Peacocks: Stories of Partition, Exile and Lost Memories.* Translated from Urdu by Alok Bhalla and Vishwamitter Adil. *The Hindu*, March 2, 2003. http://www.thehindu.com/lr/2003/03/02/stories/2003030200420700.htm. Accessed Feb. 18, 2020.
Farrukhi, Asif. "Talking about Basti: Intizar Husain in Conversation with Asif Farrukhi, Lahore, July 2005." Translated by Frances W. Pritchett. www.columbia.edu/itc/mealac/pritchett/00litlinks/basti/txt_intizar_asif_2005.pdf. Accessed Jan. 15, 2020.
Hiltebeitel, Alf. *Rethinking India's Oral and Classical Epics Draupadi among Rajputs, Muslims, and Dalits.* Chicago: The University of Chicago Press, 1999.
Husain, Intizar. *Basti.* Translated by Frances W. Pritchett. New Delhi: Oxford University Press, 2007.
_____."Daira." In *The Death of Sheherzad.* Translated by Rakshanda Jalil. New Delhi: Harper Collins, 2015a.

————. "The Sage and the Butcher." In *The Death of Sheherzad*. Translated by Rakhshanda Jalil. New Delhi: Harper Collins, 2015.

————. *Once There Was a City Named Dilli*. Translated by Ghazala Jamil and Faiz Ullah. New Delhi: Yoda Press, 2017.

————. "A Chronicle of the Peacocks." Translated by Alok Bhalla and Vishwamitter Adil, *Mānoa* 27:1, Story Is a Vagabond: Fiction, Essays, and Drama (2015b): 105–112.

————. "An Unwritten Epic." Translated by Leslie A Flemming and Muhammad Umar Menon. *Journal of South Asian Literature* 18:2, The Writings of Intizar Husain Summer (1983): 6–19.

Mayaram, Shail. "Meos of Mewat: Synthesising Hindu-Muslim Identities." *Debating India*(2004). https://india.eu.org/spip.php?article1227. Accessed July 10, 2020.

Menon, Meena. "Writing in Exile." *The Hindu*, July 5, 2014. www.thehindu.com/ books/literary-review/writing-in-exile/article6180409.ece. Accessed July 25, 2020.

Menon, Muhammad Umar. "Reclamation of Memory, Fall, and the Death of the Creative Self: Three Moments in the Fiction of Intizar Husain." *International Journal of Middle East Studies* 13:1 (1981): 73–91.

————. "Introduction." In *Basti*. Translated by Frances W. Pritchett. New York: NYRB, 1995. http://www.columbia.edu/itc/mealac/pritchett/00litlinks/basti/00_ intmemon.html. Accessed on January 15, 2020.

Mittal, Sushil. *Surprising Bedfellows: Hindus and Muslims in Medieval and Early Modern India*. Lanham, MD: Lexington Books, 2003.

Mookerjea-Leonard, Debali. "The Diminished Man: Partition and Transcendental Homelessness." In *Narratives of Home, Displacement, and Resettlement*, edited by Anjali Gera Roy and Nandi Bhatia. New Delhi: Pearson Longman, 2008, 50–64.

Mufti, Aamir. "Auerbach in Istanbul Edward Said, Secular Criticism, and the Question of Minority Culture." In *The Indian Postcolonial: A Critical Reader*, edited by Elleke Boehmer and Rosinka Chaudhuri. London: Routledge, 2011, 107–137.

Naim, C. M. "Maulana Who Loved Krishna." *Economic and Political Weekly* 48:17 (Apr. 27, 2013): 37–44.

Nora, Pierre. "Between Memory and History: Les Lieux de Mémoire." *Representations*, No. 26, Special Issue: Memory and Counter Memory (Spring, 1989): 7–24.

Pritchett, Frances W. "Narrative Modes in Intizar Hussain's Short Stories." *Journal of South Asian Literature* 18:2, The Writings of Intizar Hussain (Summer, Fall, 1983): 192–199.

Rice, Yael. "A Persian Mahabharata: The 1598–1599 *Razmnama*." *Mānoa* 22:1, Andha Yug: The Age of Darkness (Summer, 2010): 125–131.

Said, Edward. "Invention, Memory, and Place." *Critical Inquiry*. Vol. 26 No. 2 (Winter 2000) 175–192.

Tendulkar, D. G. *Mahatma Vol.7 (1945–1947)*. New Delhi: The Publications Division Ministry of Information and Broadcasting Government of India, Patiala House, 1953.

Tololyan, Khachig. "Rethinking Diaspora (s): Stateless Power in the Transnational Moment." *Diaspora: A Journal of Transnational Studies* 5:1 (Spring, 1996): 3–36.

Tyabji, Raihana. *The Heart of Gopi*. Delhi: Motilal Banarsidas Publisher, 1936.

Wachtel, Nathan. "Memory and History: Introduction." *History and Anthropology* 12 (1986):207–224.

Zaidi, Nishat, and Alok Bhalla. "Introduction." In *Day and Dastan: Two Novella by Intizar Hussain*. New Delhi: Niyogi Book, 2018.

3

THE RETURN OF THE GODDESS

Amitav Ghosh's *Gun Island* and the *Manasamangal*

Swati Moitra

Introduction

Shiva, Shiva, I set out on a journey and you took me off my path, – you destroyed my house, – you destroyed everything. I thought that I would wear these wounds as ornaments and stand before you at the end of my life, your earnest follower. That day I would say – you gave me these wounds – . But that too is gone, because Chand will worship Manasa. Stay witness, Shiva, your mad devotee Chand worshipped Manasa today. Take this, o dark Manasa-serpent, Chand Sadagar worships you with his left hand. Shiva, Shiva, witness me, Chand bows to Manasa.

(Mitra 1978: 124)

In the much-acclaimed play *Chand Baniker Pala* (1978), Sombhu Mitra (1915–1997) re-imagines the conflict between Chand Sadagar and the serpent goddess, Manasa, as a conflict between reason and unreason, between the spirit of inquiry and blind, stultifying faith. In this retelling of the medieval *Manasamangal*, Mitra represents "Manasa and her female worshipper Sanaka [Chand's wife] as symbols of darkness, of the womb, of power-hunger, and of the absence of *yukti*/reason, as opposed to the 'enlightened' male merchant Chand" (Banerjee 2017: 190). In the last monologues of the play, a section of which is quoted previously, Chand's surrender to Manasa – as opposed to his true devotion to Shiva – marks a tragedy, as reason makes way for the irrational and light succumbs to darkness. In the final lines of the play, Chand finds out that his surrender has meant nothing, since Manasa has not prevented the resuscitated Lakhinder and Behula from taking their lives by suicide. He is left rambling like a maddened Ulysses, dreaming of another journey to the seas in the company of long-dead sailors, "The endless depths – keep sailing – In this darkness, Champaknagari still sails in the search of Shiva – keep sailing, keep sailing – " (Mitra 1978: 125).

DOI: 10.4324/9781003158424-5

Mitra's influential retelling of the *Manasamangal* poems, as Milinda Banerjee argues, represents an 'ambivalence' (Banerjee 2017: 190) characteristic of the reception of the *mangalkabyas* among the Bengali literary elite in the nineteenth and twentieth centuries. *Chand Baniker Pala*, thus, repeatedly and uncritically refers to Manasa as *'chyangmuri kani'* (the low-caste one-eyed one) in an epithet drawn from the medieval *Manasamangal* poems. Its critique of the Brahminical order – one that repeatedly interferes in Chand's voyages and asks him to abandon his ideals – sees no conflict in the glorification of Shiva as the representative of rationality, enlightenment, and the spirit of inquiry in opposition to the 'low-caste one-eyed' goddess. "For Mitra," as Banerjee points out, "Manasa heralded the fury of a pre-state (female) nature, which robbed the universe of (male) order" (Banerjee: 190). In Jibanananda Das' (1899–1954) more celebratory references to the *mangalkabyas* in his poetry, the world of the *mangalkabyas* and characters like Behula and Dhanapati Sadagar (of the *Chandimangal*) represent a pre-lapsarian pre-colonial Bengal. In a poem like "Ekhane Akash Neel" (The Sky is Blue Here), the cuckoo's call connects the modern poet with the sixteenth-century poet Mukundaram Chakrabarti, composer of the *Chandimangal*, and with Behula's voyage in the *Manasamangal*, thereby "carving out a nostalgic *mangalkabya*-defined poetic nation" (Banerjee 2017: 188). As David L. Curley has pointed out,

> the very definition of mangal-kabya as a genre was shaped by the nationalist context of its discovery, and by the way, that discovery looked at the past with an emotional valence of present loss, and with the project of recovering works of an authentic, traditional folk art.
>
> (Curley 2008: 14)

The fortunes of the *mangalkabyas* have continued to be defined by this 'ambivalence' (Banerjee 2017: 190) well into the twenty-first century. Their inclusion in school syllabi has accompanied periodic revisits, such as Ramkumar Mukhopadhyay's Ananda Purashkar-winning book, *Dhanapatir Sinhalyatra* (2010), wherein the *mangalkabya* narrative allows for a return to pre-colonial authenticity. The legend of Manasa has been reimagined on the television screen in kitschy soap operas such *Behula* (2010–11) and *Manasa* (2018–19), where the vitality of the medieval *Manasamangal* poems finds itself flattened into melodramatic representations of wifely devotion and divine retribution that resonate with contemporary television audiences.

The 'ambivalence' (Banerjee 2017: 190) – or the outright hostility, such as in *Chand Baniker Pala* – that marks the modern literary reception of the *mangalkabya* narratives and the goddess cults like those of Chandi, Sitala, or Manasa in West Bengal, has had little to do with the practices of veneration of the aforementioned goddesses, which continue to flourish across present-day Bihar, West Bengal, Bangladesh, Odisha, and Assam. This chapter is concerned in particular with the cult of Manasa and the *Manasamangal*, relegated to the domain of unreason and darkness in influential retellings like Sombhu Mitra's play or celebrated as a narrative of domestic devotion in soap operas. The chapter will concern itself with the works of Amitav Ghosh, in whose novels such as *The Hungry Tide* (2004) and *Gun Island* (2019), Anglophone literary fiction can claim to have found its own chronicler of the goddess cults of Bengal. Ghosh has often explored the contours of the modern secular imagination in his writing and in recent times has turned to the 'uncanny' to speak of climate change and the limits of human reason. In the words of Stark, Schlunke, and Edmonds,

> Taking the notion of the uncanny from Freud's *unheimlich*, that which is unhomely or unfamiliar (4), Ghosh here evokes the idea of a strange yet familiar haunting of the present by that which has previously been repressed. 'No other word', Ghosh writes, 'comes close to expressing the strangeness of what is unfolding around us. For these changes are not merely strange in the sense of being unknown or alien; their uncanniness lies precisely in the fact that in these encounters we recognize something we had turned away from: that is to say, the presence and proximity of non-human interlocutors' (40).
>
> (2018: 23)

In *Gun Island* (2019), Ghosh turns to *Manasamangal*, offering a retelling of sorts through the story of the Bonduki Sagar. This chapter seeks to study Ghosh's interrogation of the secular and the uncanny and his engagement with the cult of the serpent goddess, Manasa, in the liminal lands of the Sunderbans. To this end, it will at first address Ghosh's exploration of the limits of the secular imagination in novels like *The Shadow Lines* (1998) and *The Hungry Tide* (2004). The chapter will, thereafter, go on to address the history of the *mangalkabyas* and locate the *Manasamangal* poems in the same. In the final section, the chapter will address *Gun Island* (2019) and its entanglement with the *Manasamangal*, testing the limits of reason and unreason, of the possible and impossibility.

Interrogating the secular in Amitav Ghosh's novels

In recent years, the concept of the 'secular' has come under fire from more than one quarter in India, including from an assertive religious right that deems the concept of secularism a Nehruvian construction, deliberately designed to deny India's link to its Hindu past and future. The political debate over Nehruvian secularism, however, is quite beyond the scope of this chapter. The chapter will concern itself with critiques that trace the contours of the secular liberal project of the modern state and the idealized visions of the same. To draw upon the work of Saba Mahmood (2001), it is important to recognize that state secularism does not necessarily mean a banishment of religion from the public sphere. On the contrary, it marks the sanction of the state in favor of certain forms of religious expression, even as other forms of religious expression might confront barriers in the shape of the law and legal authorities. In Mahmood's words,

> To say that a society is secular does not mean that "religion" is banished from its politics, law, and forms of association. Rather, religion is admitted into these domains on the condition that it takes particular forms; when it departs from these forms it confronts a set of regulatory barriers.
>
> (2001: 226)

Needham and Sunder Rajan, in their interrogation of secularism in the context of postcolonial India, point out that religion serves "as the basis of identity and identitarian cultural practices [in modern societies] – with co-religionists constituting a community, nation, or "civilization" – that comes to be the ground of difference and hence conflict" (2003: 3). The idea of secularism in a postcolonial nation like India, they argue, has been "called on to perform multiple functions in the service of nation-building" (Needham and Sunder Rajan 2009: 3). It has been entangled with questions about the peaceful coexistence of communities and religious violence, with the notion of national unity and democratic ideals for a postcolonial nation-state. Secularism, therefore, must be considered in terms of these multiple registers, and not simply as religion's Other.

The Partition of India in 1947 is often imagined in postcolonial India as the originary moment for the secular Indian state *vis-à-vis* its Other, the theocratic state of Pakistan. *The Shadow Lines* (1998), set in the aftermath of the Partition and the violence that followed the disappearance of a relic associated with Prophet Mohammed from the Hazratbal shrine in Kashmir in 1963, asks urgent questions about the nature of the same and the careful omissions and silences that mark the existence of the secular Indian state. In the riots of 1964, rioters in East Pakistan killed and evicted Hindus and indigenous communities such as Garos, Dulas, and Hajongs, while retaliatory riots in Calcutta killed at least 100 people. In *The Shadow Lines*, Tridib's self-sacrifice in the Dhaka riots of 1964 marks an incomparable loss for the narrator, who idolized him. In the process, Ghosh's narrator muses on the nature of cartography and lived experience,

> I had to remind myself that they [cartographers] were not to be blamed for believing that there was something admirable in moving violence to the borders and dealing with it through science and factories, for that was the pattern of the world. They had drawn

their borders, believing in that pattern, in the enchantment of lines, hoping perhaps that once they had etched their borders upon the map, the two bits of land would sail away from each other like the shifting tectonic plates of the prehistoric Gondwanaland.

(1998: 233)

The narrator, who "struggles with silence" (Ghosh 1998: 218), learns to reimagine the national borders – once envisioned as immutable entities that could resolve the crisis of communalism and religious violence in postcolonial India and Pakistan – as shadowy, fluid entities through their experience of violence and loss. Manav Ratti (2015) reads the aforementioned passage as a critique of state secularism, which assumes that the state's ability to physically disentangle warring communities by placing them on separate tracts of land can resolve the problem of communal violence. Ratti writes,

> In the above passage, Ghosh also suggests that violence is a physical object, one that can be moved safely out of sight onto the margins of borders. We can induce from this the metaphor of violence and religion as physical objects that state secularism attempts to separate from one another (and, concomitantly, for the state to "distance" itself, in however a principled a fashion, from religion). Yet the shadows of the lines challenge the lines themselves.
>
> (2015: 66)

Priya Kumar (2008) argues that the riots of 1964, as Ghosh depicts them in *The Shadow Lines*, lay bare the fantasies of separation that the "enchantment of lines" might have suggested to the policymakers during the Partition of India. The new nation-states of India and Pakistan remain entangled nonetheless, through the bonds of shared history and violence. As Kumar writes, "*The Shadow Lines* thus reveals the futility of any attempt to grapple with contemporary Hindu–Muslim violence in India in isolation from the shadow of Pakistan" (108). Pakistan, in postcolonial India, has historically been envisioned as secular India's Other – representing everything that India claims it is not. As Calcutta and Dhaka mirror each other in 1964, Ghosh's narrator begins to understand that such claims can only be sustained by silence and looking away from events that undermine said claims. Priya Kumar thus points out, "Only by undoing narratives of essentialized differences between a "secular" India and a rabidly 'fundamentalist' Islamic Pakistan, as the narrator learns, can we begin to think about possibilities of multireligious coexistence in the subcontinent" (2008: 108).

The Hungry Tide (2004), set in the littoral communities of the Sunderbans and featuring the liminal lives of humans and animals who populate the region, pushes Ghosh's interrogation of the secular paradigm to another dimension. The haunting shadow of the Partition looms large in this novel as well as Ghosh breaks the silence on the Marichjhapi massacre (which took place on 24 January 1979) and the state's betrayal of the Dalit refugees who were promised the right to live in secular India. Alongside, Ghosh draws upon the *Raymangal* and *Banabibi'r Palagaan* (see Mandal 2017), centering on the figures of Dakshin Rai, the tiger god (or demon, in some versions of the narrative) and Banabibi, the goddess of the forest. Venerated by Hindus and Muslims alike, Banabibi stands as the protector of all humans who enter the forests for their livelihoods. For Ghosh, the tiger god represents the non-human world of the forest, while the Lady of the Forest represents humanity. In the pre-colonial narratives of conflict and eventual resolution between the two gods, "Ghosh locates a model of environmental preservation embedded in the normatively sanctioned control of human greed (to prevent over-exploitation of forest resources)" (Banerjee 2017: 193). The structure of shared authority, as decided upon by Dakshin Rai and Banabibi, offers a solution for the survival of the littoral communities of the Sundarbans in the era of rapid climate change.

Much of the novel's narrative marks the "moral re-education" (Mukherjee: 128) of the elite protagonists like Kanai and Piya, who must unlearn their

> privileged normative cosmopolitan or metropolitan point of view in the novel to that of the local or provincial, mirrored in the formal mixture of psychological realism (as in the passage above) and the highly melodramatic and theatrical [represented by the *jatra* performances of the Banabibi legend.
>
> (Mukherjee 2010: 129)

The 'local or provincial' – represented here by Fokir's unflinching faith in Banabibi as the interlocutor between the human and the non-human – can only be comprehended when Kanai and Piya learn to embrace the non-secular and the uncanny, "their uncanniness [lying] precisely in the fact that in these encounters [they] recognize something [they] had turned away from: that is to say, the presence and proximity of non-human interlocutors" (Ghosh, qt. in Stark et al. 2018: 23).

The "moral re-education" of the elite protagonist takes on an even more urgent turn in *Gun Island* (2019), where the *Manasamangal* and the cult of the serpent goddess become Ghosh's conduits for exploring the allegedly non-modern and decidedly non-secular world of Manasa and the Bonduki Sadagar. The following section of this chapter will discuss the *Manasamangal* poems in brief before going on to address *Gun Island* in the final section.

Manasamangal and the cult of Manasa

The *Manasamangal* poems are the oldest among the Bengali *mangalkabyas*, with the oldest extant versions of the poem (by Hari Dutta, whose fragments alone survive) dating back to the thirteenth century. There is considerable scholarly dispute over the origins of Manasa. Ashutosh Bhattacharya (1958) argues that Manasa is a non-Vedic, non-Aryan goddess, whose origins might lie in southern India (in the goddess Manchamma, who is associated with snakes), while Sukumar Sen (1940) is of the opinion that there is considerable evidence to connect Manasa to the Vedic tradition. Sister Nivedita and Ananda K. Coomaraswamy (1967; originally published in 1913), in their commentary on the legend surrounding Manasa in the Bengal region, write,

> This legend of Manasā Devī, the goddess of snakes, who must be as old as the Mykenean stratum in Asiatic culture, reflects the conflict between the religion of Shiva and that of feminine local deities in Bengal. Afterward Manasā or Padmā was recognized as a form of *Shakti* (does it not say in the Mahābhārata that all that is feminine is a part of Umā?), and her worship accepted by the Shaivas.
>
> (1967: 330)

Dimock, drawing upon a vast body of work including that of Bhattacharya and Sen, traces Manasa's ancestry from the Buddhist serpent goddess, Janguli. Dimock argues that Manasa's contradictory powers of destruction and regeneration can be understood in the context of this ancestry. Regardless of the scholarly debates over the origins of serpent-worship in Bengal and Manasa's complex heredity, her cult continues to thrive to date. This is despite her relative insignificance in the broader Brahminical pantheon or her absence in the public sphere alongside gods like Rama or Hanuman, who have been at the center of vociferous public debate in recent times.

Speaking of the *mangalkabyas* as a genre, Dimock has pointed out that

> [as] oral and non-canonical literature, the mangal songs are not of fixed form. Over the centuries, they have been modified or expanded according to the currency of myth and legend, the concern of the individual poet, and social forces and events.
>
> (Dimock 1962: 309)

Indeed, poets from the same period in history have also produced *mangalkabya* texts with marked differences. The *Manasamangal* is no exception to this norm. Ashutosh Bhattacharya lists the names of seventy-eight known poets of the *Manasamangal*, cautioning his readers that it is impossible to tell which of the poets were composers themselves and which of them were *gayens* (singer-performers) who did not compose on their own. Despite the many differences, however, "there is a basic story frame which remains constant" (Ibid.: 309).

In the *Manasamangal*, this 'story frame' is the tale of Manasa's conflict with Chand Sadagar, the merchant-king of Champaknagari. The wealthy and powerful Chand Sadagar, who also possesses divine knowledge, is a devout worshipper of Shiva. He refuses to worship Manasa on the grounds of her low caste origins and her physical disability (she loses an eye courtesy of the actions of her step-mother, the goddess Chandi) and insults her in response. This leads to a battle that has Manasa destroy Chand's garden, take his divine knowledge, kill his six youthful sons, drown his fourteen ships and accumulated goods in the Kalidaha, and eventually reduce him to penury, to the point where most people fail to recognize him. Despite this suffering, Chand refuses to bow down to Manasa. Manasa thus takes the life of his seventh son, Lakhinder, who was born as a result of Manasa's boon to Chand's wife, Sanaka. Lakhinder's death on his wedding night sets his newlywed bride, Behula, on an epic voyage of her own to the abode of the gods. Behula, after many trials and tribulations, eventually reaches the gods and dances to please Shiva, who then summons Manasa and requests she fulfill Behula's wishes. Through Behula's intervention, thus, the Chand–Manasa conflict is resolved. Manasa restores the lives of all seven sons and restores Chand's wealth and his ships, and in return, Chand consents to worship Manasa, albeit with his left hand. With Chand's surrender to her authority, the worship of Manasa spreads far and wide in the world.

A simple narration of the 'story frame,' however, does not do justice to the complexity of the *Manasamangal* narratives. As Milinda Banerjee points out,

> Between the fifteenth and the eighteenth centuries, the *mangalkabyas* opened up new spaces of reflection on issues of power and authority: about the transition from forest/nature to state society; about the relation between state, market, and just price of goods; about the relationship between merchants and rulers; about the status of human women and female goddesses in society; about the relative position of upper caste and lower caste devotees and deities.
>
> (2017: 186)

The *Manasamangal* is no exception in its depiction of the 'low-caste one-eyed' goddess's battle for recognition by Chand Sadagar. Saumitra Chakravarty (2012), in an insightful analysis of Manasa's narrative, argues that Manasa "strikes at the threefold foundations of patriarchy in the text – the androcentric Hindu pantheon of gods, the Brahminical priestly power and the wealthy merchant community that controlled the economy of contemporary society" (Web). Far from the force of darkness and unreason in *Chand Baniker Pala*, Manasa in the late medieval/early modern *Manasamangal* poems allows for explorations of power and accountability, including her own. It is this complexity, this potential for 'political thought' (Curley 2011), that draws Ghosh to the *Manasamangal* in *Gun Island*, wherein he locates himself in sharp opposition to the interpretation offered by *Chand Baniker Pala*. The following section of the chapter will seek to engage with the same.

The gun merchant's saga

The 'story frame' that Amitav Ghosh employs for his Bonduki Sadagar or gun merchant/merchant of Venice is roughly similar to the familiar saga of Chand Sadagar and Manasa. Ghosh's narrator calls it a seventeenth-century 'local' legend specific to the Sunderbans, tied to a forgotten shrine in the depths of the forests. The merchant, much like Chand, runs afoul of the goddess Manasa and sets out on a voyage that soon runs into misfortune. He is kidnapped by Portuguese pirates and sold to a ship captain (*nakhoda*) named Ilyas, who recognizes his learning and frees him. Together, they travel to strange lands such as the Sugar Candy Land, the Land of Kerchieves, the Island of Chains, and the Gun Island. Misfortune and curious accidents follow wherever they travel. At the Gun Island, eventually, Manasa finds him, and the Bonduki Sadagar relents, agreeing to worship Manasa at last. The shrine, it is said, was built by none other than the merchant himself.

Deen, the narrator – a merchant in his own right, dealing in rare books – confronts this fable with the pedantry of an academic. Like the merchants of the fables before him, Deen has his own brand of arrogance: he takes pride in his rationality and his ability to tease out 'meaning' out of a seemingly incoherent fable. He speaks frequently of his academic past, and the thesis he wrote on the *Manasamangal*. Deen's "moral re-education" (Mukherjee 128) in *Gun Island*, much like that of Piya and Kanai in *The Hungry Tide* (Piya is also a character in *Gun Island*), demands not only an abandonment of his metropolitan world-view but also a re-evaluation of his much-vaunted rationality. Deen, the rare books merchant, is a characteristic Ghosh protagonist. In Ghosh's own words, spoken in an interview, "All my life I have been writing about merchants. . . . At the heart of *In An Antique Land* is a merchant, the figure of the merchant also looms over the entire Ibis trilogy" (qt. in Roy 2019, Web). Cinta, Deen's mentor and guide, is the scholar – another figure that persists in much of Ghosh's writing, as Rituparna Roy (2019) has pointed out.

Cinta, whose experience of grief and loss has opened her up to the uncanny and the non-rational, stands in contrast to Deen, who scoffs at the fable of the gun merchant and resists ideas such as demonic possession or visions. While Cinta challenges him through her erudition, young Tipu – son of the late Fokir and Moyna – challenges him through his insouciance as he speaks casually of his involvement with the business of trafficking desperate migrants to Europe for a cost. Eventually, it is Deen's journey to Venice that begins to yield answers as he learns to open up to the uncanny, marked by visions of a spider and a dreamlike experience at the Querini Stampalia Library. Alessandro Vescovi (2017), speaking of the uncanny episodes in *The Hungry*

Tide, argues that these episodes are an attempt at "moving beyond the scientific discourse and beyond the human vs non-human dichotomy" (Web) that defines discourse about conservation in the Sunderbans. In Vescovi's words,

> Far from being literary embellishments, these elements must be interpreted as a way of moving the boundaries of the secular novel into the realm of the non-secular, in other words, from the modes of knowledge of colonizers to the modes of knowledge that are deeply embedded in the Indian culture that the novel describes, where everything is interconnected.
>
> (Web)

It is in Venice that Deen stumbles upon a moment of epiphany, that the serpent goddess must be understood as a 'negotiator' or a 'translator',

> [Manasa] was in effect a negotiator, a translator – or better still a *portavoce* – as the Italians say, 'a voice-carrier' between two species that had no language in common and no shared means of communication. Without her mediation there could be no relationship between animal and human except hatred and aggression.
>
> (Ghosh 2019, "The Ghetto", para. 8)

Far from being an agent of darkness, as imagined in an influential modern text like *Chand Baniker Pala*, Manasa becomes the crucial link between worlds, that of humans and the non-human. "How can a translator do her job if one side chooses to ignore her?" (Ghosh 2019, "The Ghetto", para. 9), Deen asks himself and concludes that Manasa's urgent pursuit of the gun merchant stemmed from her need to uphold the "unseen boundaries" (Ghosh 2019, "The Ghetto", para. 9) between the human and the non-human world. Should the "unseen boundaries" vanish, "humans – driven, as was the Merchant, by the quest for profit – would recognize no restraint in relation to other living things" (Ghosh 2019, "The Ghetto", para. 9). The seventeenth century, after all, marked the beginning of the capitalist expansion and ocean-oriented globalized trade, driven by an endless need to consume and accumulate. It marked the beginning of the great European empires that would reshape the world order and the balance of power in it. In opening himself up to the uncanny and to Manasa's urgent attempts to communicate, the rare books merchant – much like the gun merchant before him – is able to witness the final miracle that marks the climax of the book, featuring the refugee boat with Tipu in it. Manasa, one must remember, has powers of destruction as well as of regeneration. In Dimock's words,

> She destroys ruthlessly and wantonly, the innocent with the guilty, to demonstrate her might. She is full of wrath and violence. But she

has a strange and equally wanton compassion. She has the power to bring her victims back to life, and this she often does once she has conquered them. She herself is like a snake, now striking out randomly and angrily, now spreading its hood over the face of a sleeping child.

(1962: 317)

Tipu, once bitten by a cobra at the gun merchant's shrine and blessed with Manasa's visions, becomes subject to the final storm,

"Time itself is in ecstasy," said Cinta softly. "I had never thought I would witness this joy with my own eyes, pouring over the horizon."

And then there they were, millions of birds, circling above us, while below, in the waters around the Blue Boat, schools of dolphins somersaulted and whales slapped their tails on the waves.

(Ghosh 2019, "The Storm", para. 86)

With Manasa's mediation, the non-human world comes to the aid of desperate, persecuted humans like in an animal fable of the past or a miracle, offering hope for a future where balance might be restored again.

Conclusion

As this chapter has argued, the complex political thought of the *mangalkabyas* and their "multi-vocal mode of questioning of authority" (Banerjee 2017: 186) defines their appeal for Amitav Ghosh. If earlier novels such as *The Shadow Lines* and *The Hungry Tide* questioned the logic of the modern secular state and the secular liberal project – a strand of thought that persists in *Gun Island* – Ghosh's latest novel pushes further into the territory of the non-secular and the non-modern. Much like the *mangalkabyas*, it is an intensely political novel – Ghosh has never shied away from controversial political issues, and here he wades into questions about borders and refugees, about regular and irregular migration, with aplomb. Tipu and Rafi's journey, moving beyond boundaries of religious difference and normative sexuality, represents a vision of a more egalitarian future.

Gun Island, furthermore, is a novel about climate change and climate justice, which "resists literary fiction" because of "its resistance to language itself" (Ghosh 2016, "Chapter 18", para. 12). In *The Great Derangement* (2016), Ghosh had spoken the emergence of "new, hybrid forms" that *can* make climate change representable, even as "the act of reading itself will change once again, as it has many times before." (Ghosh 2016, "Chapter 18", para. 12) *Gun Island* turns to the complex and poly-vocal *mangalkabyas* to push literary fiction further in that direction. Even as he takes a stand against the doyens of Bengali modernity to mark a triumphant return to the serpent goddess and the non-modern, non-secular worldview that venerates her, Ghosh's use of the *Manasamangal* molds the modern novel itself into a model of storytelling that can embrace the uncanny and speak the truth of climate justice.

Works cited

Banerjee, Milinda. "Gods in a Democracy: State of Nature, Postcolonial Politics, and Bengali Mangalkabyas." In *The Postcolonial World*, edited by Jyotsna G. Singh and David D. Kim. Abingdon: Routledge, 2017, 184–205.

Bhattacharya, Ashutosh. *Bangla Mangalkabyer Itihash*. Kolkata: Kolkata Book House, 1958.

Chakravarty, Saumitra. "Defeating Patriarchal Politics: The Snake Woman as Goddess: A Study of the Manasa Mangal Kavya of Bengal." *Intersections: Gender and Sexuality in Asia and the Pacific* 30 (2012). Curley, David L. *Poetry and History: Bengali Mangal-kābya and Social Change in Precolonial Bengal*. New Delhi: Chronicle Books, 2008. Collection of Open Access Books and Monographs, 5. https://cedar.wwu.edu/cedarbooks/5.

———. "The 'World of the Text' and Political Thought in Bengali Mangal-Kāvya, c. 1500–1750." *The Medieval History Journal* 14:2 (Oct. 1, 2011): 183–211.

Dimock, Edward C. "The Goddess of Snakes in Medieval Bengali Literature." *History of Religions*, 1:2 (1962): 307–321.

Ghosh, Amitav. *The Shadow Lines*. New Delhi: Ravi Dayal, 1998.

———. *The Hungry Tide*. London:Harper Collins Publishers, 2004.

———. *The Great Derangement: Climate Change and the Unthinkable*. Chicago: The University of Chicago Press, 2016.

———. *Gun Island*. London: John Murray, 2019.

Kumar, Priya. *Limiting Secularism: The Ethics of Coexistence in Indian Literature and Film*. Minneapolis: University of Minnesota Press, 2008.

Mahmood, Saba. "Feminist Theory, Embodiment, and the Docile Agent: Some Reflections on the Egyptian Islamic Revival." *Cultural Anthropology* 16:2 (2001): 202–236.

Mandal, Mousumi. "Bonbibi-r Palagaan: Tradition, History and Performance." *Sahapedia*, Sahapedia, Mar. 17, 2017. www.sahapedia.org/bonbibi-r-palagaan-tradition-history-and-performance.

Mitra, Sombhu. *Chand Baniker Pala*. Kolkata: M.C. Sarkar & Sons Pvt. Ltd., 1978.

Mukherjee, Upamanyu Pablo. *Postcolonial Environments: Nature, Culture and the Contemporary Indian Novel in English*. Basingstoke, England: Palgrave Macmillan, 2010.

Needham, Anuradha Dingwaney, and Rajeswari Sunder Rajan. *The Crisis of Secularism in India*. New Delhi: Permanent Black, 2009.

Nivedita, Sister, and Ananda K. Coomaraswamy. *Myths of the Hindus & Buddhists*. New York: Dover, 1967.

Ratti, Manav. "Rethinking Postsecularism through Postcolonialism." *Interdisciplinary Journal for Religion and Transformation in Contemporary Society – J-RaT* 1:1 (2015): 57–71.

Roy, Rituparna. "Gun Island: Climate Change & Refugees." *The Punch Magazine*, Sept. 22, 2019. www.thepunchmagazine.com/the-byword/review/gun-island-climate-change-amp-amp-refugees.

Sen, Sukumar. *Bangla Sahityer Itihash*. Kolkata: Modern Book Agency, 1940.

Stark, Hannah, et al. "Introduction: Uncanny Objects in the Anthropocene." *Australian Humanities Review* 63 (2018): 22–30.

Vescovi, Alessandro. "The Uncanny and the Secular in Amitav Ghosh's *The Great Derangement* and *The Hungry Tide*." *Le Simplegadi* 17 (2017): 212–222.

4

"ALL TRUE BELIEVERS HAVE GOOD REASONS FOR DISBELIEVING IN EVERY GOD EXCEPT THEIR OWN"

Faith, doubt, and poetics of secularism in *The Enchantress of Florence*

Sk Sagir Ali

Timothy Fitzgerald, in *Discourse of Civility and Barbarity*, opines that religion is a modern-day development that naturalizes and authorizes a structure of Euro-American secular nationality. This putative secular position, in turn, authorizes and shapes its "other" religion and religions. (Fitzgerald 2009: 6) Borrowing Robert Gleave's words in "Should We Teach Islam as a Religion or as a Civilisation?", it can be said that in contemporary times, we can see a movement "from an uncritical acceptance of the category of 'religion,' towards a critical interrogation of 'religion' as a category" (Gleave 2010: NP). From the post-Rushdie affair to the wake of 9/11 and the war on terror, religion, culture, race, and representation run the risk of being employed in disloyalty, threat, or artistic compromise. This chapter looks at the overlapping parameters of religion, representation, recognition, and secularism that distinguish between Islam as a religion and Islam as a culture in Salman Rushdie's *The Enchantress of Florence*. It also explores the tensions between an individualistic subjectivity and a communitarian adherence to culture and faith that manifest themselves in the narrative as they negotiate between the pull of a liberal individualist lifestyle and that of family, community, and religion, between speaking as an "I" and a collective "self."

There are two important narratives in Salman Rushdie's novel, *The Enchantress of Florence*, that happen during the late fifteenth to the late sixteenth century. The novel begins with the advent of an enigmatic, blond-haired visitor to Sikri, the home of the Mughal emperor, Akbar the Great. The man of manifold names – Mogor dell'Amore, the Uccello di Firenze, Niccolò Antonio Vespucci – aims to take pains to disclose to the emperor a secret that will either cost him his life or secure his fortune. The plot revolves around Vespucci, and Emperor Akbar is mesmerized by the former's ability

DOI: 10.4324/9781003158424-6

of storytelling, and, on being aware of the performative of Scheherazade, he fends off possible execution by clubbing together his marvelous tales. The second plot of *The Enchantress of Florence*, one of the most significant of these stories, features the novel's namesake, the enchantress Angelica, who is discovered, later on, to be Akbar's deceased great-aunt, Qara Köz. Two generations before Vespucci's appearance at Akbar's court, the Mughal princess was coerced to abandon her home as her brother handed her over to another ruler as spoils of war. It follows a flow of events, as she falls in love with an Ottoman janissary, Argalia, who takes her along on a tour of the West. At the end of the novel, these two narratives coincide when Qara Köz surprisingly comes back home to Akbar at a time when he is under a crisis of religious faith in his life and mourns the loss of religious toleration. Akbar argues that the future will not be as he has desired and hoped for; rather it will be a hostile, dry, ill-disposed habitation where people live on in the best possible way they can with profound hate and animosity. They will kill one another and destroy their places of worship once again in the renewed heat of the "great quarrel" he had sought to end forever, the "quarrel over God." It is not civilization but harshness that will rule (Rushdie 2008: 435). The very word "quarrel" is a term that signifies an amicable and discursively productive disagreement of principles rather than a violent clash. Emperor Akbar describes religious differences that direct us into the contemporary polity of religiously inflected violence. He assumes that the future will not be a peaceful one; instead, it will be a place where communities will be filled with hate mongers and "quarrel over God" (Tate and Bradley 2010: 94). The word "quarrel" implies disagreement with the non-believers in terms of principles or attitudes towards God in depicting religious differences without the avenues of aggression taken for granted. In this novel, in wake of the fatwa against Rushdie in 1989 by Ayatollah Khomeini, 9/11, and the subsequent war on terror, the issues of religious conflicts, the question of religious belief and disbelief, and the collision between faith and secular rationalism in the polarized worldviews are explored within the ambit of secular freedoms. Though there are other aspects in *The Enchantress of Florence*, this chapter focuses only on what it takes to be a person of religious faith and a secular one and how one can negotiate the structures of religious faith and faithlessness in a multicultural society in the wake of 9/11 and the subsequent war on terror.

In *The Enchantress of Florence*, Rushdie's questions about God can be inquired into without the structure of aggression. Rushdie probes a religious conflict – the relationship between monotheism and power. Akbar, despite being religious in his private life, has considerable doubts about religion which, he contends, is not a body of truth but a set of habit formations based on powerful, familial practices that might be misplaced when mankind finally usurps the place of God. He contemplates that there is no true religion and is suspicious that men make their own gods, and it is man, not God, at the heart of all things –

> man the angel and the devil, the miracle and the sin, man and always man, and let us henceforth have no other temples but those dedicated to mankind. This was his most unspeakable ambition: to found the religion of man.
>
> (Rushdie 2008: 100)

Rushdie's gradual fascination with the "quarrel over God" is evident when the emperor Akbar would materialize a new world in Sikri beyond region, rank, religion, and tribe (51), and it would be a human habitation of adoration – a place of disputation where "everything could be said to everyone by anyone on any subject, including the non-existence of God and the abolition of kings" (Ibid.: 46). The slain ruler opines that "in Paradise the words worship and argument mean the same thing" and also declares that "the Almighty is not a tyrant," and in "the House of God all voices are free to speak as they choose, and that is the form of their devotion" (Ibid.: 44–45). To the historical emperor Akbar, this new house of adoration is a badge of serious concern with an aesthetico-political commitment to hybridism, difference, and pluralism, and this utopian space is a locus in the form of "Republic of Heaven" (Pullman 2001: 548) with a continuing engagement with serious faith in the (im-)possibility of godless liberalism. Emperor Akbar's idealistic pluralism is placed against religious authoritarianism. Akbar's secularist faith with tolerant beliefs has a strong aversion to religion in the public sphere and to the privatization of religion. The confinement of religion to the private sphere becomes the litmus test of whether societies are modern. Rushdie, in his polemical essay entitled "Yes, This Is about Islam," rejects the contemporary responses to 9/11 and seeks to claim that the attacks had nothing to do with Islam. He argues that all Muslim societies must grasp private faith with "the restoration of religion to the sphere of the personal, its depoliticization" in order to become modern. Terrorists are interested in technology, the only aspect where they find a weapon that can be turned against its makers. The world of Islam, according to Rushdie, should take on board the principles of secularist-humanist approaches on which the idea of being is based and without which freedom of these countries will remain a distant dream if terrorism is to be defeated (2001). The being of being modern in this context refers to the ability to exercise rationality and cogitative criticality both within the realm of the private sphere and the public sphere of policy-making. He further opines that, this "paranoid Islam" that holds the outsiders, "infidels," responsible for all the ills of Muslim societies and whose suggested cure is the shutting of those societies to the "rival project of modernity" presently is the fastest-growing version of Islam in the world (Ibid.). Rushdie takes a dig at radical

Islam and its twentieth-century founding fathers, such as Sayyid Qutb and Abdullah Azam (Osama Bin Laden's mentor) as antithetical to the post-Enlightenment ideal of a universal civilization based on reason and secular belief. In *The Enchantress of Florence*, it is the secular-as-modern versus religion as a soothing but corruptible form of irrationality and the reality of singularly subjective emotional inspiration versus the veneer of collectivist political rhetoric that shape the propounded views of Rushdie. Akbar, who was gradually losing faith in religion, "trusted dogs, music, poetry, a witty courtier and a wife he had created out of nothing. He trusted beauty, painting, and the wisdom of his forebears. In other things, however, he was losing confidence; in, for example, religious faith" (Ibid.: 69–70). He wishes to hold a debate on the subject of religious faith in his Tent of the New Worship

> to investigate why one should hold fast to a religion not because it was true but because it was the faith of one's fathers. Was faith not faith but simple family habit? May be there was no true religion but this eternal handing down. And error could be handed down as easily as virtue.
>
> (Ibid.: 100)

Akbar's dilemma raises a serious question: "Was faith no more than an error of our ancestors?" (Ibid.). The emperor's modern rational individualism along the parlance of a renaissance humanism provides a new perspective to evaluate the role and function of religious faith that presents a lack of privileging faith as the important and dominant determinant of identity in a society where "difference" has tended to be subsumed by ethnicity. Akbar, being a "Muslim," has given himself a selection of identitarian choices that are fixed formatively in Islam, a worldview that includes miscellaneous patterns of interpellation and critical engagement. Here, Akeel Bilgrami's argument is pertinent:

> There may be some for whom Islam is nothing short of a monolithic commitment, overriding all other commitments, whenever history or personal encounter poses a conflict. But I think it is safe to say, despite a familiar tradition of colonial and postcolonial caricature in Western representations of Islam, that such an absolutist project is the exception in a highly diverse and internally conflicted religious community.
>
> (1992: 823)

We can also recall Paul Berman in *Terror and Liberalism* (2004) and, especially, his critical discussion with Tariq Ramadan's argument about faith and doubt in his book, *Islam, the West, and the Challenges of Modernity* (2001).

Berman refers to Ramadan's interest in the story that is common to both the Bible and the Quran about God's command to Abraham to sacrifice his son, Issac. In *Islam, the West, and the Challenges of Modernity* (2001), Berman alludes to Tariq Ramadan's view that room for doubt within Western Enlightenment is symbolically ushered in the dilemma as mediated by God's order to Abraham, whereas the Quranic revelation articulates unquestioning compliance with God's will. Berman says:

> In Western religious tradition, there is a space for skepticism and doubt. These two attitudes, skepticism and doubt, are elements of faith – the elements that prove the authenticity of belief in God. . . . The God of the *Old Testament* instructs Abraham to sacrifice his son, Isaac, and Abraham doubts the instruction and struggles to resist it, for a little while – and Abraham's doubt and struggle testify to the sincerity of his belief.
>
> (2004: 26)

There is no dilemma articulated in the Biblical version between submission and disobedience. Abraham honestly follows the instructions by taking Isaac to the chosen place and makes a fire to burn the offering as well as preparing the knife. Berman and Ramadan attempt to categorize several types of religiosity – a Judeo-Christian practice where doubt that is nuclear to philosophical thought gets historical acceptance and validation and *ijtihad* or independent reasoning and questioning in the Islamic system holds a crux within a discourse of deep religious faith. Ramadan's analysis of Islamic faith, contrary to doubt and suspicion, rather seems to analyze the hegemonic structure that finds its interpretation in certain ways since all his contentions and claims define a presumably universal experience for believers. For Paul Berman, doubt, questioning, and reasoning are the quintessence that presumably make the West different from Islam. Ramadan deciphers Danish philosopher, theologian, and existentialist philosopher Søren Kierkegaard's seminal reading of Abraham and Isaac in *Fear and Trembling* which

> shows that the story of Abraham carries, in itself, Christianity's fundamental message concerning the existence of man who is subjected to the sense of sin, suffering, anguish and fear. Faith is, at best, the assumed test of anguish and inward conflict.
>
> (2001: 212)

Akbar, in *The Enchantress of Florence*, "wanted to be able to tell someone of his suspicion that man had made their gods and not the other way around. He wanted to be able to say, it is man at the center of things, not God" (Rushdie 2008: 100). Palpably, these words from the emperor are obvious in a critical postmodernist term about the construction of the concept of God, and its aberrant identification as a transcendental signified needs to be deconstructed. Akbar's train of thought passes from a position of the new critical intentional fallacy towards, in a way, that of the post-structuralist stance:

> If man had created God then man could uncreate him too. Or was it possible for a creation to escape the power of the creator? Could a god, once created, become impossible to destroy? Did such fictions acquire autonomy of the will that made them immortal?
>
> (Ibid.)

Akbar also finds that sometimes religion's power and potentiality lead to violence. Suicidal deaths of two girls, Tana and Riri, who had fundamentalist leanings, pain the king. Akbar, who has always fervently sought religious tolerance, states, "If there had never been a God . . . it might have been easier to work out what goodness was" (Ibid.: 381). The emperor did not have the answer to "an autonomy of the will" of God (God has been identified as a fiction) "that made them immortal" as he departs from Sikri. Freedom and the desire to transcend beyond the belief of God are necessarily the constituent parts of his desire for liberation from the tyranny of logos, monolithic truths, and the hegemonic authorizations that silence the freedom of an artist and even throttle the freedom of speech of individuals. To him, "discord, difference, disobedience, disagreement, irreverence, iconoclasm, impudence, even insolence might be the wellsprings of the good" (Ibid.: 382) – that, in a certain sense, attests to a Bakhtinian sense of grotesque realism. It can be argued that Akbar's liberal humanism is coterminous with the ethics of Bakhtiniandialogism insofar as it insists upon an openness towards a teleologically indeterminate alterity and an aversion towards parochial monisms of any kind.

There is the concept of the sacred to uphold a society rooted in the emergence of individualism, secularization, and cultural pluralism. Religion and religious experience are based in terms of belief and religious faith. For all people of faith, faith is something that defines them. Talal Asad has critiqued the claims of Rushdie that the very idea of "religion" itself is an aftereffect of secularism that has profoundly changed the understandings of what being "religious" is and a shift to a secular "knowledge" where "religiosity" develops less as a discourse of disciplinary codes and practices that showcases the socio-political authority of the medieval church and more a set of "propositions" for believers. It is attended by a shift in authority far from the institutions, where disciplinary practices were deep seated towards the supremacy of personal "conscience" with the event of creating a "cognitivist" comprehension of religion where religious experience is fundamentally "about" what one believes (Asad 2003: 13). Eventually, "religion" appears with "rationalism," the philosophical idealism of modern liberalism; the new idea of religion came together to develop dialectically with collective construction in relation to post-Reformation and post-Enlightenment advancement in the secular formation of thoughts. Tariq Modood, however, has upheld that the division between beliefs and the people who may or may not find these beliefs fundamental and functional, which shapes the self-definition of a group; there cannot be "membership of a group without some idea of the relevant groupness" – at least, the one type of belief where it does not hold. Modood further says a group only lives while some people recognize themselves and others in certain ways, and this cannot be done without beliefs (2005: 120–121). People should be inspired to think about their beliefs if they are the result of rational enquiry or the effect of careful consideration, not the consequence of animosity or bigotry, tradition, or mere emotion. To say that: values and beliefs – religious or secular – are voluntarily chosen and readily abandoned following "a strong sense in which what we are given rather than chosen," and, like our racial, ethnic, or gender identities, "moral and religious belief/s . . . are equally incapable of being given up simply by an act of will or on the basis of rational deliberation" (Ibid.: 15). In the novel, Akbar, a renaissance humanist and precursor to a postmodern agnostic, wishes to place man at the center of all things and dreams of a world free from the monotheistic idea of God. When Mogor is attracted to

> the great polytheist pantheons because the stories are better, more numerous, more dramatic, more humorous, more marvelous; and because the gods do not set us good examples, they are interfering, vain, petulant and badly behaved, which is, I confess, quite appealing
>
> (Rushdie 2008: 168)

Akbar confesses, "we have the same feeling, And yet we must be what we are. The million gods are not our gods; the austere religion of our father will always be ours, just as the carpenter's creed is yours" (Ibid.). To the emperor, identity and culture are as much objects of individual choice and perception as they are about the composite idea of the sacred, secularized or not.

Debates about cultural differences, religious plurality, and existential conflicts are recurrent in literature and society since the publication of *The Satanic Verses*, which foregrounds the (transcendental) textuality of a sacred text and brings together the religious and the secular in a way that challenges the severe frameworks of religious identity. Engaging himself with the distinctly post-9/11 themes of terror and religious fundamentalism, Rushdie attempts to confront the real through an inversion of the Huntingtonian "clash of civilizations" thesis which can be traced back to the 1988 Rushdie Affair itself. Samuel P. Huntington's crude neo-orientalist "clash of civilization" thesis rewrites the transcendental kernel of Western secular modernity as a redemptive ideological counter to the religious revivalist project of the Middle East. To Rushdie, there is no means to challenge terror in the present without simultaneously confronting terror in the past (Malik 2009: 155). Rushdie, in *The Enchantress of Florence*, walks on a metaphorical tightrope between and across varied entities: personal and political, religious and secular, past and present, and attempts to deconstruct difference through the representation of secularism and fundamentalism and its tryst with the historical construction of the East and the West in the sixteenth-century Florence and India. He employs the inherent "passe-partout" (Rushdie 2008: 32) quality of magical realism, a metaphorical device that blurs the borderline between the real, unreal, and the epistemic frameworks. Set in the sixteenth century, the novel's action is split between Florence and the Mughal city of Fatehpur Sikri, with some historical figures like Niccolò Machiavelli and the Mughal Emperor Akbar, who is famous for his liberal style of despotism. Narratives in the novel take their engagement between the worlds of fact and fiction in the form of a story narrated to Akbar by a mysterious Florentine traveler named Niccolò Vespucci, also called Morgordell' Amore (or "the Mughal of Love"). Rushdie, perhaps, has in mind the character of Jean Passepartout from Jules Verne's *Around the World in Eighty Days* when he coins the term "passe-partout." It is also the name given to the piece of card that is placed between a painting and its frame, a "frame within a frame" – an interstitial state between the artwork and the external world that adheres entirely to no one.

For Derrida, the "passe-partout" can be perceived as a type of transmutational "slash" – or "trait" – between the artistry and the external surroundings:

> One space remains to be broached . . . in order to give place to the truth in painting. Neither inside nor outside, it spaces itself without letting itself be framed but it does not stand outside the frame. It works the frame, makes it work, gives it work to do.
>
> (1987: 11–12)

It is the "partition of the edge" – that sets up a liminal space to make us think exactly where a work of art ends and the outer world starts in. It is the fissiparous nature of the borderline between the reality of the self and the other that resonates Derrida's work on "différance" through the deferral of "truth" or "meaning" from one signifier to another in Rushdie's portrayal of cultural relativism and relations between the discourses of the East and the West. Rushdie, in this novel, intends to do away with the importance of Said's Orientalism. Edward Said finds that the epistemological framework of "Othering" in Huntington ambiguous. He argues that the act of recognizing the "Other" is a kind of "threat" and arrogance of the West rather than Western hegemony over the Orient. The "clash of civilizations" is a "manufactured" one, and we need to focus on the slow working together of cultures which borrow from and overlap with each other and live together in far more gripping manner than any inauthentic or abridged mode of understanding can allow (Said 1977: xxii). The actual clash is not between the civilizations but the "discriminations between elites and the masses" (Ibid.) over the definition of factuality. Said calls it the "Western ignorance" (Ibid.). Vassilena Parashkevova opines that the novel attempts to posit alternatives to the neoliberal thesis of the present association between West and East as a clash between the West and Islam and the representation of sword-wielding Islam in its encounter with Hinduism on the site of what is now the Indian subcontinent (2012: 179). *The Enchantress of Florence* examines the extent to which such an Orientalism can be defined in its epistemic totality that determines the kind of inverted, left-leaning perspective which can often merely aggravate the perceived fundamental differences between the "East" and the "West" with the re-arrival of the dominating frameworks – "us and them" binaries. Rushdie ostensibly foregrounds the East-West binary by highlighting the presence of difference with the Orientalist stereotypes in the formation of identity and history. Listening to Morgor's dialogue, Akbar reflects on the "fabulous Western climes" of fifteenth-century Europe, as he perceived that the lands of the West were surreal and exotic to a degree unfathomable to the "humdrum people of the East" (Rushdie 2008: 409). He is also surprised by the apparent proneness of the Western people to a special type of extreme hysteria in the worshipping of gold. In his mind's eye, Akbar draws Western temples made of gold and golden worshippers and priests inside, bringing offerings of gold to appease their golden god. On the other hand, Akbar continues with the ideas of fantastical "Eastern wisdom":

> In the East, men and women worked hard, lived well or badly, died noble or ignoble deaths, believed in faiths that engendered great art, great poetry, great music, some consolation and much confusion.
>
> (Ibid.)

Rushdie's proximity to difference in *The Enchantress of Florence* figuratively disrupts the space between the "everywhere" of the present and the "everywhere else" of the past in a manner that intertwines the present-day framing of secular and fundamentalist identity and disrupts the mapping of the contemporary dichotomy of the East and the West in identitarian terms. Following Neelam Srivastava, Vassilena Parashkevova argues:

> In Sikri, Rushdie locates a nascent, if historically isolated, form of Indian secularism that will be drowned in sectarian violence centuries later. In Akbar's vision, the future is a 'dry hostile antagonistic place' where people 'hate their neighbours and smash their places

of worship and kill one another' in the 'quarrel over God'. . . . The world of Sikri is not imagined within the parameters of secularism as equated with the contemporary Western state, tolerant of religious voices, whilst concealing an anti-Muslim bias. Political and religious tolerance precedes and feeds into a secular vision, and as the novel suggests, it has Eastern origins unparalleled in the West at the time.

(2012: 191)

What is noteworthy in *The Enchantress of Florence* is that Rushdie shows established religion as a "circle" – an "encircling" force with a rigid and collective narrowing of thought in the manner of a passe-partout that overtly collapses the "us" and "them" binary. Akbar says, "Could foreigners grasp what his countrymen could not? If he, Akbar, stepped outside the circle, could he live without its comforting circularity, in the terrifying strangeness of a new thought?" (Rushdie 2008: 100–101). Akbar's idea of fundamentalist thought as a kind of "circle" resembles Anshuman Mondal's critique about the postmodern secularism of *The Satanic Verses*:

"[t]he radical excess of cultural difference, as represented by Islam, is encircled and domesticated by a secular skepticism, the dominance of which is insistently reasserted over its efforts to empathetically represent the experience of religious belief" (2013: 71). Rushdie, by stepping out of the "circle" of fundamentalist thought towards a secular and state of plurality, ironically accepts the choice of others to continue encircling themselves from plurality, if they wish, by "divid[ing] the unity" of its interstitial space. In a socio-political context, Elizabeth Shakman Hurd opines, secularism has taken two distinct paths – a laicist trajectory where religion is viewed as an impediment and rival to modern politics and a Judeo-Christian secularist trajectory where religion is perceived as an origin of identity and unity that entails a conflict in modern international politics (2008: 23). Rushdie in *The Enchantress of Florence* adheres to the "laicist" path and plays down the physical and epistemic violence that "dominating frameworks" of nineteenth-century imperialism have inflicted upon the lives of millions over the centuries. In the course of his narrative, Morgor advises Akbar that "this may be the curse of the human race. . . . Not that we are so different from one another, but that we are so alike" (Rushdie 2008: 382), and the enchantress of Florence, QaraKöz's, supposed disenchantment of Eastern "enchantment" – of both an Orientalist and an "anti-Orientalist" is remarkable when she says to Argalia that "all human beings are foolish to the same degree" (Ibid.: 349). Rushdie, in a post-9/11 context, presumably reinforces Judith Butler's contention that "thinking through the problem of temporality and politics . . . may open up a different approach to cultural difference, one that eludes the claims of pluralism and intersectionality alike"

(2009: 103). The frivolity of religious faith is revealed in the episode of the children's prison camp at Usküb, where

> there were many tongues but only one God. Each year the press gangs roamed the expanding empire to levy the devshirmé tax, the child tribute, and took the strongest, cleverest, best-looking boys into slavery, to be changed into instruments of the Sultan's will. The principle of the Sultanate was governance by metamorphosis. . . . Then Christianity was taken from him as well and he was obliged to put on Islam like a new pair of pajamas.
>
> (Rushdie 2008: 213)

At the end, the satirical picture of the holy man with his long beard – a dervish of the Bektashi order, who had come to convert them to Islam and the white hat converting the young minds poignantly portrays fundamentalist movements and also all processes of ideological indoctrination (Rushdie 2008: 214). The metamorphosis of the boys begins, and in their many accents, the frightened, angry boys parrot the necessary Arabic sentence about his Prophet and the one God. The fundamentalism of the Mughal East offers the rise of a kind of separatism spawned by the fetishization of cultural and religious identity in the process of wrestling with the challenges to identify a search for an authentic self in the power dynamics of the freedom-versus-restraint binary. It also affirms what Homi Bhabha has described as the real blasphemy of *The Satanic Verses*. Bhabha contends that blasphemy is not only a "misrepresentation of the sacred by the secular" but rather the content of a cultural tradition or subject matter that is being alienated in the act of translation. "Secular blasphemy" releases a temporality that uncovers the contingencies concerned with the process of social transformation into the "assorted authenticity or continuity of tradition" (1994: 323). The "perspective of historical and cultural relativism" and the subsequent "act of cultural translation" are the essential understanding of blasphemy that necessarily entails the emphasis on the multiplicity of differences, such as between East and West, "fundamentalist" and "secular," and "us" and "them" (Ibid.).

Salman Rushdie's work hinges on the impossibility of cultural relativism, the (in)compatibility of Islam in a more or less cohesive multicultural society. His portrayal of the fragmentation of religion in literature shows the porous border of faith and ideology as a refuge in the discursive encounter of secularism. The uncritical acceptance of stereotyped imbrications of distinct religious and non-religious identifications should be engaged in what Aamir Mufti has termed "critical secularism" (2007: 13) that is accessible through the oppositional feasibility and positionalities of literary interpretations with manifold modes of secularism.

Works cited

Asad, Talal. *Formations of the Secular: Christianity, Islam, and Modernity*. Stanford, CA: Stanford University Press, 2003.

Berman, Paul. *Terror and Liberalism*. New York: Norton, 2004.

Bhabha, Homi K. *The Location of Culture*. London: Routledge, 1994.

Bilgrami, Akeel. "What Is a Muslim? Fundamental Commitment and Cultural Identity." *Critical Inquiry* 18:4 (Summer, 1992).

Butler, Judith. *Frames of War: When Is Life Grievable?* London: Verso, 2009.

Derrida, Jacques. *The Truth in Painting*. Translated by Geoff Bennington and Ian McLeod. Chicago: University of Chicago Press, 1987.

Fitzgerald, Timothy. *Discourse of Civility and Barbarity: A Critical History of Religion and Related Catgories*. Oxford: Oxford University Press, 2009.

Gleave, Robert. "Should We Teach Islam as a Religion or as a Civilisation?" Unpublished Paper, Islamic Studies Network: Perspectives on Islamic Studies in Higher Education, Aston University, May 2010. www.heacademy.ac.uk/assets/York/multimedia/audio/islamic_studies/Professor_Ron_Geaves.mp.

Hurd, Elizabeth Shakman. *The Politics of Secularism in International Relations*. Princeton, NJ: Princeton University Press, 2008.

Malik, Kenan. *From Fatwa to Jihad: The Rushdie Affair and Its Legacy*. London: Atlantic Books, 2009.

Modood, Tariq. *Multicultural Politics: Racism, Ethnicity, and Muslims in Britain*. Minneapolis: University of Minnesota Press, 2005.

Mondal, Anshuman A. "Revisiting the Satanic Verses: The Fatwa and Its Legacies." In *Salman Rushdie: Contemporary Critical Perspectives*, edited by Robert Eaglestone and Martin McQuillan. London and New York: Bloomsbury, 2013.

Mufti, Aamir R. *Enlightenment in the Colony: The Jewish Question and the Crisis of Postcolonial Culture*. Princeton, NJ and Oxford: Princeton University Press, 2007.

Parashkevova, Vassilena. *Salman Rushdie's Cities: Reconfigurational Politics and the Contemporary Urban Imagination*. London and New York: Continuum, 2012.

Pullman, Philip. *The Amber Spyglass*. London: Scholastic, 2001.

Ramadan, Tariq. *Islam, the West, and the Challenges of Modernity*. Markfield, Leicester: Islamic Foundation, 2001.

Rushdie, Salman. "Yes, This Is about Islam." *New York Times*, November 2, 2001.

———. *The Enchantress of Florence*. New York: Random House, 2008.

Said, Edward. *Orientalism*. London: Penguin, 1977.

Tate, Andrew, and Arthur Bradley. *The New Atheist Novel: Philosophy, Fiction, and Polemic after 9/11*. London and New York: Continuum, 2010.

Part 2

ETHNICITY, MYTH, CASTE, AND CENSORSHIP

5

THE POETICS AND THE POLITICS OF KASHMIRIYAT

A study of Mirza Waheed's *The Collaborator* and *The Book of Gold Leaves*

Somjyoti Mridha

Kashmiri nationalists claim that Kashmiri nationalism is based on Kashmiriyat, a concept which is a veritable semantic explosion, primarily signifying religious bonhomie as well as shared cultural values based on Kashmiri ethnicity, yet for practical purposes, it primarily privileges the Kashmiri Muslim community residing in the valley. Kashmiriyat is one of the most frequently used terms in the volatile political landscape of Kashmir. In the sphere of literary imagination, the term 'Kashmiriyat' is sprinkled generously across contemporary Anglophone literary narratives, both fictional and autobiographical. While most literary narratives follow the principles of erasure and obfuscation so prevalent in the political domain when referring to the Jammu or Ladakh regions and the Kashmiri Pandit community in Kashmir, there is a tendency to claim the politics of Kashmiriyat as a defense against the hegemonic political narrative of the Indian state. This chapter will primarily deal with Mirza Waheed's engagement with Kashmiriyat as represented in his novels.

There was a spout in literary creativity among Kashmiris in the aftermath of the armed resistance. An avalanche of life writings and fictional narratives by Kashmiri authors came in quick succession since the publication of Basharat Peer's *Curfewed Nights* (2008).[1] Mirza Waheed is one of the most profound literary voices among the Kashmiri pro-azadi[2] authors. A journalist by profession, Mirza Waheed inaugurated his literary career with *The Collaborator* (2011), followed by *The Book of Gold Leaves* (2014) and *Tell Her Everything* (2019). His characteristic poetic rendition of the brutal realities of Kashmir and his formidable grasp of political events is unparalleled among the new corpus of Anglophone Kashmiri pro-azadi literature. This chapter will primarily focus on *The Collaborator* and *The Book of Gold Leaves*, both novels representing the heady days of armed resistance in Kashmir valley of the 1990s.

DOI: 10.4324/9781003158424-8

Like most brands of nationalism, Kashmiri nationalism is also exclusion-ary in its ideology and praxis. The nature of exclusion is not only restricted to regional bias but also includes religious bias. While the regions of Jammu and Ladakh are primarily non-existent from the discourse of Kashmiri nationalism, they are routinely co-opted within the geographical contours of the putative Kashmiri nation. Kashmiri nationalists also imagine Kashmir as an Islamic nation, thereby making the position of the minority Kashmiri Pandit community of the valley tenuous within the precincts of the putative Kashmiri nation. Balraj Puri rightly comments,

> Pakistan and Islamist ideology championed the same urge for Kash-miri identity. In this context the role of the Muslim aspect of Kash-miri identity cannot be ignored. Kashmiri Muslims have, in fact, never been quite isolated from the universal identity of Muslim *umma*.
>
> (Puri 2010: 33)

The metaphors and slogans used in protests and processions are over-whelmingly Islamic. Hence, Kashmiri nationalism may be considered religious nationalism, where a common religion, usually the religion of the majority community, in this case, Islam, is regarded as the basis of national identity. Slogans like 'Pakistan se rishta kya? La illaha Illallah' (What is our bond with Pakistan? There is no God but Allah) or 'Azadi ka matlab kya? La illaha Illallah' (What does freedom mean? There is no God but Allah) leave little doubt regarding the religious character of nationalist resistance in Kashmir. All other communities are marginalized in such a religiously determined nationalist sentiment. In the context of sub-continental history, where religious antagonism forms the basis of nation-building exercises, Kashmiri nationalism is no exception. As Peter van der Veer writes:

> From its very beginning in the nineteenth century nationalism in India has fed upon religious identifications . . . . In all these cases nation building is directly dependent on religious antagonism, between Hindus and Muslims, between Sikhs and Hindus, between Buddhists and Hindus. At Independence this antagonism led to the most important political event of twentieth-century South Asian his-tory, the formation of Pakistan as a homeland for Indian Muslims.
>
> (Veer 1994: 2)

In the context of Kashmiri nationalism, antagonism between the Kashmiri Pandits and Kashmiri Muslims within Kashmir has also given rise to the overwhelmingly Muslim-dominated Kashmir valley's antagonism towards the Hindu majoritarian Indian state. This straightforward religious/political contestation in Kashmir is also complicated by the presence of Kashmiri nationalists like Prem Nath Bazaz of the earlier period and Nitasha Kaul or Mona Bhan of the contemporary era, wherein lies the significance of Kashmiriyat.

Kashmiriyat

Kashmiriyat refers to the shared socio-cultural ethos specific to the geo-political and cultural space of Kashmir which transcends religious and other affiliations. Although communal relations in Kashmir followed the overarching pattern of sub-continental politics on the axis of majority and minority, it was also guided by the discourse of Kashmiriyat. Various scholars have engaged with the concept of Kashmiriyat, for example, Mridu Rai, Chitralekha Zutshi, Manisha Gangahar, Ananya Jahanara Kabir, Mohammad Ishaq Khan, Rattan Lal Hangloo, and Neil Aggarwal. This section will deal with their ideas about Kashmiriyat. Manisha Gangahar rightly pointed out in the introduction to her book,

> While it is hard to arrive at a precise definition of *Kashmiriyat*, it is also essential to note that no matter how trivial a role, the idea of *Kashmiriyat* being a distinct socio-cultural space has contributed to the sense of unease among Kashmiris when they step into the outside world.
>
> (Gangahar 2013: 3)

At the mundane level, Kashmiriyat is supposed to bind Kashmiris together irrespective of other differences. Historically speaking, the term had ambivalent, rather contradictory political and cultural resonance. Gangahar stresses the semantic fluidity of the term 'Kashmiriyat' in the political and cultural contours of Kashmir in different historical epochs. According to Gangahar, Prem Nath Bazaz, the Kashmiri Pandit intellectual, coined the term 'Kashmiriyat' to project cultural commonality among Hindus and Muslims of Kashmir. Engaging with the concept, Gangahar tries to dissect 'Kashmiriyat,' pointing out the long-standing contribution of various cultural streams that united on the fertile cultural landscape of the Kashmir valley across the centuries, like Sanskrit learning, Persian language, Shaivism, Sufism, and Buddhism (103). According to her, Kashmiriyat refers to the century-long traditions that characterized the people of Kashmir. Theoretically, Kashmiriyat refers to the ethos of religious harmony and social cohesion. This idea was conveniently adopted by the Muslim/National Conference during the early twentieth century to further its political demands from the discriminatory Hindu Dogra state. The term 'Kashmiriyat' emerged as an ambiguous, frequently articulated, and hugely contested idiom in the political discourse of Kashmir starting in the early twentieth century.

At times, it refers to the real or supposed secular underpinnings of Kashmiri society since time immemorial where people of different religions and sects co-existed harmoniously. Though narratives of persecution of the Kashmiri Pandit community since the early medieval period seek to challenge any notion of harmonious co-existence, the discourse surrounding Kashmiriyat is extremely popular and remains politically expedient. The discourse was primarily popularized by the National Conference spearheaded by Sheikh Abdullah in order to build up a secular front against the Dogra state. In fact, secular overtures of the National Conference were primarily notional since Kashmiri Muslim political discourse was essentially directed against the socio-economic inequities in Kashmiri society institutionalized by the Dogra regime. In real political terms, Kashmiriyat became a thinly veiled political rhetoric to legitimize the agitations against the preponderance of the Kashmiri Pandits in every sphere of Kashmiri society and the politically Hindu Dogra state. In fact, Sheikh Abdullah repeatedly mentions the preferential treatment accorded to the Pandits by the Dogra state, which he states as the raison d'être for spearheading agitations against the Dogra state in his memoir. According to him, religious prejudice was palpable in all spheres of governance in Kashmir:

> I started to question why Muslims were singled out for such treatment? We constituted the majority, and contributed the most towards the State's revenues, still we were continuously oppressed. Why? How long would we put up with it? Was it because a majority of government servants were non Muslims, or because most of the lower grade officers who dealt with the public were Kashmiri Pandits? I concluded that the ill-treatment of the Muslims was an outcome of religious prejudice.
>
> (Abdullah 1993: 13)

Abdullah is one of the most vocal proponents of Kashmiriyat and also the precursor of government policies which eventually marginalized the Pandits in Kashmiri society. Rhetorical co-option of Kashmiriyat facilitated his self-projection as the most popular leader of Kashmir. Yet his government undertook policies which privileged the majority community in every sphere of public life, thereby reversing the relations of power in Kashmiri society. While there was lip service to social justice for undertaking 'Naya Kashmir' reforms, most Pandit narratives state that the real socio-political aim was perhaps to marginalize the Kashmiri Pandit community. As eminent scholar of Kashmir Chitralekha Zutshi writes:

> the narrative on *Kashmiriyat* ignores the contradiction that forms the substance of Kashmiri nationalist movement: this movement, which supposedly rescued *Kashmiriyat* from the jaws of the Dogra

regime, based its demands squarely on the socio-economic distinctions between the two main religious communities in Kashmir, Pandits and Muslims. This contradiction is rooted in the story of the
political, social and economic transformations introduced on to the
Kashmiri landscape during the Dogra period.

(Zutshi 2003: 47)

Occasionally, Kashmiriyat also meant claiming a distinct identity for Kashmiris *vis-à-vis* Jammu-based Dogras and Punjabis and political independence
from the Dogra State and subsequently from the Indian Union. Sometimes it
referred to retaining autonomy within the political fold of the Indian Union,
as stated by eminent scholar Victoria Schofield, while in various instances,
it meant fighting for the sanctity of Article 370, which guarantees manifold
autonomous powers of the state of Jammu and Kashmir and its legislative
assembly. This particular semantic possibility has become all the more relevant after the abrogation of Article 370 by the government of India on the
5th of August, 2019.

While this chapter broadly engages with Rai, Zutshi, and Gangahar's
ideas about Kashmiriyat, it is imperative to engage with Mohammad Ishaq
Khan's and Rattan Lal Hangloo's conception of Kashmiriyat, primarily
because of their location and position as resident Muslim Kashmiri and
migrant Kashmiri Pandit, respectively. While most scholars refute the existence of communal bonhomie among the different communities of Kashmir
commonly referred to as Kashmiriyat, both Hangloo and Khan vehemently
argue in favor of the existence of Kashmiriyat in the social life of Kashmir valley. According to M. I. Khan, Kashmiriyat does not merely refer to
religious tolerance but broader ideals of 'nationality, intercommunity life,
international life and inter-religious life' (22). Yet Khan's conception of
Kashmiriyat is primarily based on Islamic theology, which makes any claims
towards religious syncretism a little suspect. He writes:

> Kashmiriyat, therefore, rests on Koranic egalitarianism and plu-
> ralism rather than on a shallow synthesis of Hindu-Buddhist and
> Islamic mystic ideas. It was this spiritual and social base of Islam in
> the valley that stood as a bulwark against the post-partition Hindu
> communalist frenzy of Jammuites. While the later phenomenon led
> to the massacre of thousands of Muslims in Jammu, not a drop of
> blood was shed in Kashmir, thanks to the real spirit of Kashmiriyat.
>
> (Khan 2015: 24)

Such a conception of Kashmiriyat denies the Kashmiri Pandits and the Sikhs
of Kashmir valley any agency, positing Islam as a religion and the Kashmiri Muslims as community on a superior plane. In fact, Khan refers to
the idea of synthesis of Hindu-Buddhist elements and the Islamic elements

as "shallow," thereby negating any possibility of long-standing harmony between the three most prominent religious groups within the state of Jammu and Kashmir. Hangloo broadens the concept of Kashmiriyat. According to him, Kashmiriyat encompasses all the cultural, socio-economic processes Kashmiris underwent across the centuries. In his essay, "Kashmiriyat: The Voice of the Past Misconstrued," he writes:

> Kashmiriyat . . . is far wider concept that has grown over centuries of historical processes that the region of Kashmir has embraced, both in peace and turmoil. Kashmiriyat is not a mere concept but an institution with societal, political, economic and cultural currents and under-currents. Kashmiriyat is unique to Kashmir, and this specificity of Kashmir has evolved as a result of special circumstances rooted in the centrality of Kashmir's topography/geography, ecology, religious ethos, and cultural moorings.
>
> (Hangloo 2015: 43)

Quite interestingly, Hangloo also associates the right to dissent without fear with the semantic possibilities of Kashmiriyat (53). He blames the nation-states of India and Pakistan, the religious organization of Jamaat-i-Islami, and the lack of political acumen of Kashmiris for the erosion of Kashmiriyat from the public life of Kashmir valley. The problem with his understanding of Kashmiriyat is that it is broadened to the level of encompassing everything that influenced Kashmir and its people since time immemorial, thereby diluting the core issue of communal relationships within the valley. Besides, Hangloo is extremely cautious about not blaming the pro-Azadi factions among the majority Kashmiri Muslim community for the atrocities committed against the Kashmiri Pandit community. The overwhelming support of the Kashmiri Muslim community for the armed militants, their political aspirations to either join Pakistan or become independent from India, and their tacit complicity towards selective victimization of the Pandit community is never mentioned. Hangloo constructs the Kashmiri Muslim community as passive subjects of international political events with no agency of their own. He goes on to say that, "The Indian state repetitively invoked Kashmiriyat even though the migration of Hindus had nothing to do with any communalism, because the contemporary crisis in a great measure stemmed from the residue of Cold War Politics" (59). This assumption is questionable primarily because armed resistance in Kashmir did not lead to the exodus of Kashmiri Muslims, even though a significant section of the Kashmiri Muslim community was not equally enthusiastic about azadi, which loudly proclaimed the formation of Nizam-e-Mustapha as its goal.

The Kashmiri Pandit narratives written and published in the aftermath of the Kashmiri Pandit exodus of the 1990s not only refer to the discrimination against them institutionalized by the state of Jammu and Kashmir but also point out sporadic instances of communal violence directed against them. In his narrative of Pandit persecution, *Under the Shadows of Militancy*, Tej N. Dhar refers to the preferential treatment accorded to Muslims in securing government jobs since the dawn of independence. This kind of preferential treatment on the basis of religious affiliation had its precedent in Kashmiri society, since the Kashmiri Pandits were privileged by the Dogra regime. Pandit perception of discrimination has to be refracted through a historical prism. The Kashmiri Pandit community compensated for their demographic disadvantage through their disproportional influence in every sphere of Kashmiri society, especially in the administration. They were co-opted by most regimes for the smooth functioning of the state. The Dogra state was particularly interested in co-opting the Hindu minority of Kashmir in order to legitimize its rule over Kashmir as well as to establish its character as a Hindu state. The Pandit community was "critically sought after by the Dogras. . . . Forming at best a mere 5 percent of the population of Kashmir, this community exerted influence out of all proportion to its numbers" (Rai 2004: 9). This undue influence of the Kashmiri Pandits was primarily due to their high levels of literacy, proficiency in languages like Sanskrit and Persian, and traditional knowledge base about the administration of Kashmir. With the dissolution of the Dogra Raj, democracy and majoritarianism flourished in the valley through the effective implementation of the 'Naya Kashmir' agendas promised by Sheikh Abdullah. Reforms carried forward by the state government destroyed the predominance of the Pandit community and brought about the dominance of Muslims in the government sector. The Kashmiri Pandit perception of discrimination may also be attributed to their loss of traditional privileges. The majoritarian nature of Indian democracy, which privileged the Hindu community in most parts of India, backfired on the Kashmiri Pandit community in the valley since they were a privileged minority community in a Muslim-majority state. It is evident through the narratives that there was simmering discontent among the Pandit segment of the population regarding the structural changes in governance of Kashmir since their interests were not properly catered to.

Notions of regional affiliation or Kashmiriyat functioned effectively during socio-political considerations outside the valley. Within the Kashmir valley, religious affiliation plays a much more potent factor in the creation of horizontal solidarity among the populace than regional affiliation. Superficial rhetorical discourse like that of Kashmiriyat, occasionally articulated by opportunistic politicians, seems to have limited social base in Kashmiri society. In this aspect, Kashmiri society seems to echo religious contestation that has been part and parcel of sub-continental history and politics since the late medieval era. As Mridu Rai succinctly states, Hindu-Muslim strife in Kashmir did not always take the shape of riots in Kashmir like it did in other parts of north India, but communal discord was by no means absent or superseded by regional considerations (42–43). Kashmiriyat was primarily valorized to legitimize the inclusion of Kashmir in the Indian Union and also to contribute to the pan-Indian political discourse of secularism in times of great communal discord:

> Indeed, as many modern ideologues of Kashmiriyat also remind us, when north India was rocked by religious violence surrounding the trauma of partition, Gandhi looked northwards to Kashmir as a 'ray of hope' and a source of inspiration. As such, this vision of a timeless Kashmir of communal euphony represented, at least to mainstream Indian nationalism, a better past and the prospect that this cherished society had a future in the subcontinent. But this is to make Kashmiris and their history hostages to an Indian national- ism that was working out its own paradoxes from having grown increasingly exclusionary in practice, not least by espousing a uni- tary national identity intolerant of assertions of religious or cultural difference while holding on to its original language of inclusion.
>
> (Rai 2004: 43)

Literary narratives written by Kashmiri Pandit authors in the aftermath of their mass exodus to Jammu negates the existence of Kashmiriyat in the public sphere of Kashmir. There are references to historical events in the Pandit narratives that dispel any notion of the existence of Kashmiriyat or communal bonhomie since the 1930s. With the onset of armed resistance in the 1990s, communal relations in the Kashmir valley reached its nadir with the selective brutalization of the Kashmiri Pandit community and their subsequent exodus to Jammu. It may be safely assumed that commu- nal relations in the Kashmir valley had been deteriorating for decades with- out any check either from state institutions or civil society. The recent turn of events since the 1990s has prompted some scholars like Neil Aggarwal to consider Kashmiriyat as an 'empty signifier' (Aggarwal 2008: 229). But to say that Pandits and Muslim Kashmiris have been living for centuries without any instance of communal bonhomie would be far from the truth. Apart from the much-propagated syncretic traditions of Nund Rishi and Habba Khatoon, which have attained mythical proportions, there are fig- ures like Maqbool Sherwani and scholars like Prem Nath Bazaz or Rugho- nath Vaishnavi from the recent past who are revered by both communities and contemporary scholars like Neerja Matto, Suvir Kaul, and Nitasha Kaul or politicians like Farooq Abdullah who are respected across the religious divide and are known for pursuing common Kashmiri ethos and political goals. To a certain extent, Sheikh Abdullah was also revered by most Kashmiris in the early period of his political career. Rahul Pandita, the most virulent critique of Kashmiriyat, celebrates the role of Maqbool Sherwani during the Kabaili invasion of 1948. The history of the Indian sub-continent is replete with instances of persecution as well as exceptional communal bonhomie in different historical epochs, and the Kashmir valley is no exception.

Kashmiriyat and its relation to Indian secularism

The preamble to the Indian constitution declared the Indian state a secular nation-state. In spite of the fact that secularism and Indian nationalism had been intertwined since the onset of nationalist resistance, the word 'secular' was added to the preamble in 1976. Secularism is a much-debated and discussed issue in the country. The word 'secular' refers to anything that is non-religious. In the western political tradition, 'secularism' refers to the

> ideology that people should confine their beliefs to what they can observe in the material world, or that to have a secular outlook, including the belief that state and religion should be separate, is to be modern, progressive, and rational.
>
> (Ratti 2013: 5)

While in the west, secularism is practically tantamount to equidistance from all religions, the Indian state follows a policy of promotion of all religions without any preferential treatment to any. Within the political structures established under the aegis of Nehru and the Congress party, secularism basically meant that,

> The state can intervene in different religious communities through law and policy, but although that treatment of people and communities might be differential – allowing religion to enter the public sphere – the state must be guided by non-sectarian values of freedom and equality.
>
> (Ratti 11)

There has been a characteristic shift in the secular credentials of Indian polity since the upsurge in the electoral predicament of Hindu nationalist parties, the Bharatiya Janata Party (BJP) being the foremost, yet in matters of principle, the Indian state continues to follow the principles of 'Nehruvian Secularism.' Since the late nineteenth century, nationalist resistance was organized under the leadership of upper-caste Hindu men; therefore, the idea of India and Indian identity heavily draws from ideas and tenets associated with Hinduism. Indian nationalism, though self-avowedly secular, was majoritarian for all practical purposes (Tejani 2007; Ratti 2013). In recent years, Indian polity, though secular in principle, seems to be sliding towards a Hindu majoritarian polity. The division of the Indian populace into majority and minority communities, a consequence of the decadal census introduced by the colonial rulers, privileges the Hindu majority population across the length and breadth of the country, barring the state of Jammu and Kashmir and the North East, which have Muslim and Christian majorities, respectively. The state of Jammu and Kashmir is the only Muslim-majority province in the Indian union, and its inclusion in the Indian union bolstered the secular credentials of the Indian state.

The Kashmir valley, with its unique history of anti-feudal, anti-monarchical resistance against the Dogra regime, devised the political ideology of Kashmiriyat. In the post-independence period, the ideology of Kashmiriyat was conveniently adopted and popularized by both the Indian state and Kashmiri politicians like Sheikh Abdullah in order to merge with the Indian national ethos of secularism. The state of Jammu and Kashmir tried to merge with the Indian national narrative through the discourse of Kashmiriyat. Conscious overtures towards notional secularism by Sheikh Abdullah were also a way of differentiating themselves from the avowedly Islamic political discourse of Pakistan:

> In the case of Kashmir, Indian and Kashmiri nationalist discourses have both converged to define Kashmiri history and cultural identity in terms of a concept widely known as Kashmiriyat. Akin to its Indian cousin, Kashmiri nationalism's memory of the past is refracted through rose-tinted glass, in which Kashmir appears as a unique region where religious communities lived in harmony since time immemorial and differences in religion did not translate into acrimonious conflict until external intervention.
>
> (Zutshi 2003: 2)

Indian politicians like Gandhi and Jawaharlal Nehru also referred to Kashmir as a secular heaven imbued with the values of Kashmiriyat, primarily to legitimize Indian claim over the territory of Jammu and Kashmir. Their claims did not take into account the existential realities of the minority community of the Hindu Kashmiri Pandits and the Sikhs. The stress on Kashmiriyat, that is, the secular credentials of Kashmiri society, was valorized to provide a counternarrative to Pakistani claims over the state of Jammu and Kashmir on account of it being a Muslim-majority area. Kashmiriyat as a discourse is projected as a regional variant of the larger rubric of Indian secularism signifying social and communal harmony within the state of Jammu and Kashmir. At the ideological level, various permutations and combinations are carried out, and the strands of meaning uncomfortable to the stakeholders, that is, the Indian state and the pro-India factions within the Kashmir valley, are erased, while the discourse of Kashmiriyat is given legitimacy by all stakeholders. The appropriation of Kashmiriyat as an ideological tool by the Indian state and pro-India political parties led to its abandonment by pro-azadi factions in the Kashmir valley.

Kashmiriyat in the fictions of Mirza Waheed

Representing Kashmir is a highly problematic endeavor in the aftermath of the armed resistance against the Indian state. The recent corpus of Anglophone Kashmiri literature is saddled with the demanding task of representing a conflict in medias res catering to both readers from within Kashmir, non-Kashmiri Indians, and a global readership. Along with a conflict in medias res involving multiple stakeholders with conflicting interests, there is also the issue of censorship and the difficulty of finding a publisher for a literary rendition of politically volatile reality. Literary representation of the Kashmir conflict not only depicts the conflict but also constructs various strands of 'Kashmiriness' depending on the ideological/political predilections of the author. Mirza Waheed's literary imagination is unique among the recent corpus of pro-azadi Kashmiri literature since it is considerably more attentive towards erasures and aporias within Kashmiri society and critiques the dominant strands of majoritarian conservative Islamic culture. All pro-Azadi narratives refer to the gradual Islamization of the Kashmiri nationalist movement and subsequent polarization of Kashmiri society. But none critiques this social development through their literary endeavors as scathingly as Waheed. He succinctly portrays the all-pervasive Islamization of Kashmir in *The Collaborator*:

> When we were mosque-less and imam-less, people seldom prayed, some almost never did ('these Kafir Gujjars, they don't even know their namaz' was the taunt often tossed in our direction by many a townsfolk); but now, everyone seemed to be in a rush to make up for a lifetime of lost blessings, to catch up with divinity. Very soon . . . sincere religious devotion became a priority occupation for many in the village.
>
> (Waheed 2011: 30)

The overtly Islamist nature of the movement for azadi has been elaborately critiqued by Kashmiri Pandit writers. Though pro-azadi writers refer to the Islamization of Kashmiri society and the movement for azadi, they do not provide a sustained critique of the same. The green flag of Islam and occasionally of Pakistan as well as the call for Nizame-e-Mustafa excludes and marginalizes the minorities within the putative Kashmiri nation. While the Kashmiri Pandits in the valley were 'otherized,' labeled as 'informers' of the Indian state machinery, and projected as hostile to Kashmiri nationalism, minorities from other regions within the putative Kashmiri nation were erased from the Kashmiri nationalist discourses, though the regions they inhabited were incorporated within the precincts of the imagined national territory. Even among the Kashmiri Muslims, the Shia community is considerably marginalized within Kashmiri society. Waheed portrays vivid details of Kashmiri Shia life and the influence of Persian in Kashmiri culture through the representation of the Shahmir family and their lifestyle in *The Book of Gold Leaves*. Waheed also stresses the importance of cultural nationalism along with armed resistance against the Indian state that has become the hallmark of Kashmiri literature and nationalism since the onset of armed conflict. The character of Faiz in *The Book of Gold Leaves* embodies the twin dimensions of Kashmiri resistance against India as conceptualized by Waheed. His goals are to revive Kashmiri papier-mâché art and to drive away Indian soldiers from the streets of Srinagar.

The victimization and subsequent exodus of the Kashmiri Pandit community is cursorily mentioned in most pro-Azadi narratives without elaborating on the circumstances. Marginal narrative space accorded to Pandit predicament in the aftermath of the armed rebellion is a synecdochic representation of the marginalization of Kashmiri Pandit community within the discourse of Kashmiri nationalism. Apart from Mirza Waheed's *The Book of Gold Leaves*, none of the pro-Azadi narratives devote significant narrative space to the predicament of the Pandits in the context of the armed resistance against the Indian state. Waheed delves deep into the quiet lives of revered Kashmiri Pandit educationists Madan Koul and Shanta Koul, unsuspectingly caught up in a volatile armed conflict. The reference to Neel Chacha and his voluntary abdication of land rights in the context of mid-twentieth century Kashmir complicates the monochromatic socio-political narrative peddled by the pro-azadi Kashmiri nationalist discourses portraying Kashmiri Pandits as oppressive feudal lords and agents of the Dogra regime. The complex history of Kashmir with members of both the Kashmiri Pandits and Kashmiri Muslim community contributing towards the welfare of common Kashmiris has been projected in the novel. Though there is a tremendous sense of euphoria about the impending freedom to be wrested by the militants from the Indian state, Waheed also represents how the armed conflict victimized the Kashmiri Pandits, leading to their exodus. In a crucial way, Waheed represents the devolution of Kashmiriyat in the wake of armed resistance.

Despite mild criticism from various quarters, including literary authors, there seems to be an easy acceptance of Islamic discourses, frequently bordering on Islamic fundamentalism, embedded within nationalist discourses in Kashmir. Literary authors from both the Kashmiri Pandit and Muslim communities barring Waheed contribute to exclusivist visions of Kashmir and its society. Gowhar Fazili historicizes the use of Islamic discourses but presents them as the inevitable choice for emergent Kashmiri nationalism. Kashmiri nationalism primarily presents an ideology of resistance against Indian nationalist discourses, which in turn tries to subsume Kashmiri subnationalism within its fold. In a bid to project an oppositional stance against Indian nationalism that espouses secularism and appropriates the discourse of Kashmiriyat in the context of Kashmir, Kashmiri nationalism adopts

86

Islamic religious discourses. Kashmiri nationalist resistance is projected as Jihad against the Indian state, which is perceived as un-Islamic by certain sections of Kashmiri nationalists. While Islamized discourses and rhetoric are legitimized as the only mode of presenting a counter-hegemonic discourse to that of the secular discourses of Kashmiriyat, now appropriated by the pro-India factions in Kashmir in sync with pan-Indian nationalist discourses, what remains unacknowledged is the selective victimization of minority communities in general and the Kashmiri Pandit community in particular. Though exclusion in terms of religious affiliation has been voiced by the Kashmiri Pandit community and occasionally acknowledged by Kashmiri nationalists as well as Kashmiri literary authors, there is absolute silence about regional exclusions. The simmering discontent of the people of Ladakh and Jammu against the hegemony of the Kashmir valley and the detrimental impact of the movement for azadi in these regions has never been acknowledged by Kashmiri nationalists and literary authors, including Waheed. In his essay, "Kashmiri Marginalities: Construction, Nature and Response," Gowhar Fazili rightly captured the different shades of political objectives encompassed within Kashmiri nationalism:

> Kashmiris have also produced a wide range of political, intellectual and strategic responses that range over many categories: separatists, autonomists, Islamists, secularists, loyalists, anarchists, humanists, spiritualists, apologists, radical, pacifists, and a myriad other responses (including self-loathing) and many still nascent and yet to be born.
>
> (Fazili 2011: 222)

Even Kashmiri tribal communities like the Gujjars and Bakarwals are somewhat dispassionate about the movement for self-determination and are consequently marginalized within the Kashmiri nationalist discourses. The tribal communities of Kashmir are not regarded as proper 'Kashmiris,' and most of the recent corpus of literature is silent about their status in the context of the armed resistance since the 1990s. In *The Collaborator*, Mirza Waheed represents the predicament of a Muslim Gujjar village near the Line of Control after the outbreak of militancy and massive militarization along the border areas. In fact, most of the important Gujjar characters in the novel remain anonymous and are hence depicted as representative of the community rather than as individuals. It is crucial that Waheed is the only literary voice among Anglophone Kashmiri authors to represent rural Kashmir bordering the Line of Control (LoC) far away from the centrality of Srinagar. The recent corpus of Anglophone pro-azadi narratives focus on Srinagar and its suburbs. While describing the political situation in the state and parental anxiety about the repercussions of the movement for azadi, the anonymous central protagonist states that "valley people didn't think of us as Kashmiris anyway" (Waheed 26). The ambiguous political positioning of the Gujjar community caught in the midst of an armed resistance they were forced to participate in is palpable through his musings in the course of the novel. A pro-azadi militant organization reaches the Gujjar village and recruits from among the Gujjar youth in the novel, their incomplete incorporation within the 'Kashmiri' nation and continuation of prejudices portrayed through the cruelty meted out to Shaban Khatana and his family on the pretext of betrayal. Waheed is the only author representing the ambiguous incorporation of the tribal communities of Kashmir within Kashmiri nationalist discourses.

The reference to various erasures and aporias within Kashmiri society does not necessarily blunt the emancipatory potential of Waheed's literary imagination. Though Waheed's politics is guided by principles of Kashmiriyat, it has absolutely no allegiance whatsoever to the Indian state or its official discourse about Kashmir. Therein lies his difference with the pro-India factions of Kashmiri society, which believe in Kashmir's political union with the Indian state. The Indian state has been conceptualized as a monster in Waheed's novels. Kadian, an Indian army officer in *The Collaborator*, describes India thus:

> India, my dear, is a sisterfucking giant, a colossus with countless arms and limbs and tongues and claws and hands and mouths and fucking everything else. . . . Even if you have these small ulcers festering in various places and crevices, they don't matter to it; it uses one of its many hands or claws to scratch at the sore, soothing the irritation, and then waits until the ulcer dies on its own, or just plucks it off and throws it away. It is a huge fucking jinn.
>
> (Waheed 2011: 278)

It is highly improbable that an Indian army officer will conceptualize India as a monster like hydra, given the high-voltage Indian nationalistic discourses they are ensconced in. In the popular Indian imagination, including in the army, the Indian nation is conceptualized as a nourishing mother, Bharat Mata or Mother India. In *The Book of Gold Leaves*, Waheed describes, almost in a magic-realist fashion, a monstrous machine being unleashed on the streets of Srinagar to trap young Kashmiri boys considered potential militants. He describes it as 'Yes, it is a Zaal. A dangerous, perfect trap' (Waheed 103). Waheed's narratives are staunchly critical of the army's brutality in Kashmir, and the representation of Indian army officers is somewhat stereotypical, though Major Sumit Gupta in *The Book of Gold Leaves* remains the only 'round' character among all the literary representations of army officers in the context of Kashmir. Waheed not only depicts the brutal repression of the pro-Azadi movement by the army but also provides a glimpse of the travails experienced by Indian soldiers posted in a hostile environment. The military heavy-handedness exercised by the Indian state in order to curb the nationalist/secessionist movement during the 90s has resulted in the negative portrayal of the Indian armed forces. The literary rendition of military ruthlessness is determined both by the pro-Azadi politics of the authors as well as the lived reality of Kashmiris since the onset of armed rebellion against the Indian state.

In *The Collaborator*, Waheed goes on to enumerate the governor's speech, presumably Jagmohan Malhotra, considering the period depicted in the novel in Nowgam, which articulates the official Indian discourse about Kashmir:

> 'My dear brothers and sisters, let me tell you something . . . . The bond between Kashmir and Mother India is based not just on your king Maharaja Hari Singh's Instrument of Accession and the articles and clauses of India's great constitution; it is held together by far more tenacious and lasting forces that neither the convulsions, tribulations and tremors of history, nor the anarchy and cynicism of contemporary politics, can break up! . . . It is a bond of soul and spirit that has survived for millennia and found demonstration in shared emotional and intellectual output, art and literature, metaphysics and worldview, clothing and, hmm . . . food!'
>
> (Waheed 2011: 232–233)

This rehearsed political speech is an attempt at irony which alternately appeals to the emotional attachment of the Kashmiris to their land, which is then projected as Indian soil. The novel depicts massive military deployment along the Line of Control, which is presented as the mainstay of Indian state's power in Kashmir. It also represents the military oppression of the villagers as part and parcel of the official policy of the Indian state. Unlike in most pro-Azadi narratives, Waheed does not resort to straitjacketing the discourse of 'azadi' and its hegemony over the Kashmiri populace. Though Waheed certainly believes in a separate Kashmiri nation and a distinct Kashmiri identity, *The Collaborator* and *The Book of Gold Leaves* depict the collusion of Kashmiris with the political agenda of both the Indian and Pakistani states either through force or volition. Both novels portray collaborators of the Indian state among Kashmiris, actively engaged in sabotaging the movement for azadi, thereby representing those sections of the Kashmiri populace who have allegiance towards the Indian state. Thus, Waheed represents the spectrum of political allegiance in contemporary Kashmiri society.

Conclusion

Kashmiriyat is a nebulous concept that supposedly guides the public life of the Kashmir valley. There are multiple registers of meaning associated with this oft-quoted and politically overloaded term. Waheed's literary imaginary and politics has a significant bearing on the principles of Kashmiriyat. His imagination of the putative Kashmiri nation is inclusive and heterogeneous, encompassing the Kashmiri Muslim Shia community, Kashmiri tribal communities like the Gujjars and Bakherwals, and the Hindu minority Kashmiri Pandit community. There is a critique of the majoritarian cultural monochrome propagated by the pro-azadi factions in the novels of Mirza Waheed. Yet his critique of internal hierarchy and majoritarian Islamist impulses of Kashmiri society does not dilute the emancipatory potential of his novels with respect to the movement for azadi. *The Collaborator* is the only Anglophone Kashmiri novel that represents the predicament of the Kashmiri tribal Gujjar community along the Line of Control away from the spotlight of Srinagar. *The Book of Gold Leaves* is the only pro-azadi novel written by a Kashmiri Muslim author that provides significant narrative space to the marginalization of Kashmiri Pandits within the ambit of Kashmiri resistance against the Indian state.

Notes

1 While the publication of pro-azadi fictional narratives and life writings by Kashmiri Muslim authors began with Basharat Peer's *Curfewed Nights* (2008), there were a few Kashmiri Pandit life writings published since 2002, like Tej N. Dhar's *Under the Shadow of Militancy: The Diary of an Unknown Kashmiri* (2002) and Sudha Koul's *The Tiger Ladies: A Memoir* (2002). Anglophone poetry was published about the conflict situation much before prose narratives were published. H.K. Kaul's *Firdaus in Flames* (1995) and Agha Shahid Ali's *The Country without a Post Office: Poems 1991–1995* (2000) were the inaugural poetry volumes about the Kashmir conflict.
2 The term pro-azadi signifies narratives primarily supporting the movement for azadi in Kashmir. The term was coined by the author. Most Kashmiri Muslim Anglophone literary authors have political allegiance to the movement for azadi, along with a few Kashmiri Pandit authors like Nitasha Kaul.

Works cited

Abdullah, Sheikh Mohammad. *Flames of the Chinar: An Autobiography*. Abridged and Translated by Khushwant Singh. New Delhi: Viking, 1993.

Aggarwal, Neil. "Kashmiriyat as Empty Signifier." *Interventions* 10:2 (July 4, 2008): 222–235.

Dhar, Tej N. *Under the Shadows of Militancy: The Diary of an Unknown Kashmiri*. New Delhi: Rupa and Co, 2002.

Fazili, Gowhar. "Kashmiri Marginalities: Construction, Nature and Response." In *Until My Freedom Has Come: The New Intifada in Kashmir*, edited by Sanjay Kak. New Delhi: Penguin Books, 2011.

Gangahar, Manisha. *Kashmir's Narratives of Conflict: Identity Lost in Time and Space*. Shimla: Indian Institute of Advanced Studies, 2013.

Hangloo, Rattan Lal. "Kashmiriyat: The Voice of the Past Misconstrued." In *The Parchment of Kashmir:History, Society, and Polity*, edited by Nyla Ali Khan. New York: Palgrave Macmillan, 2015.

Khan, Mohammad Ishaq. "Evolution of My Identity *vis-à-vis* Islam and Kashmir." In *The Parchmentof Kashmir: History, Society, and Polity*, edited by Nyla Ali Khan. New Delhi: Palgrave Macmillan, 2015.

Puri, Balraj. "Identities, Ideologies and Politics." In *Identity Politics in Jammu and Kashmir*, edited by Rekha Chowdhury. New Delhi: Vitasta Publishing, 2010.

Rai, Mridu. *Hindu Rulers, Muslim Subjects: Islam, Rights, and the History of Kashmir*. New Delhi: Permanent Black, 2004.

Ratti, Manav. *The Postsecular Imagination: Postcolonialism, Religion, and Literature*. New York and London: Routledge, 2013.

Tejani, Shabnum. *Indian Secularism: A Social and Intellectual History 1890–1950*. New Delhi: Permanent Black, 2007.

Veer, Peter Van Der. *Religious Nationalism: Hindus and Muslims in India*. Berkeley and Los Angeles: University of California Press, 1994.

Waheed, Mirza. *The Collaborator*. London: Penguin Books, 2011.

———. *The Book of Gold Leaves*. New Delhi: Penguin/Viking, 2014.

Zutshi, Chitralekha. *Languages of Belonging: Islam, Regional Identity, and the Making of Kashmir*. New Delhi: Permanent Black, 2003.

6

THINKING THE BODY, FIGURING (THE) WOMAN

Religion, caste, gender, and identity in literary representations

Arunima Ray

Caste is an all-pervasive aspect of South Asian life, especially that of India. Hinduism is followed by the majority in India, and caste is the defining feature of Hinduism as a religion. Interestingly, the caste system has affected even the non-Hindus in India. It has affected Christianity and even Islam in many parts of India. The origin of caste can be found in ancient religious texts which tell us how it evolved as a religio-social conception to control and maintain society as a hierarchic order. However, caste as a fluid concept has developed over the centuries, often being treated as an interchangeable term with *varna*. Anthropologists and sociologists have reconstructed the story of the origin and the development of caste in varied ways, and hence, there is no dearth of competing theories and explanations about its origin and development in India.

It is in the *Vedas*, supposed to have been compiled between 1500 and 1000 BC, that we find the earliest formulation of caste to shape and conduct society. It was the *Rig Veda* which was accepted as the determining core of Hindu faith and worship. As Susan Bayly has it, in one of its most famous sections, the *Rig Veda* has a description of the primordial act of blood sacrifice from which the gods created the four human *varnas* (Bayly 1999: 13). It refers to the creation story of the thousand-eyed Purusa, the first created man, from whose dismembered body each of the four *varnas* came into being:

> When they divided the Purusa, into how many parts did they arrange him? What was his mouth? What his two arms? What are his thighs [loins] and feet called? The brahmin was his mouth, his two arms were made the rajanya [kshatriya, king and warrior], his two thighs [loins] the vaisya, from his feet the sudra [servile class] was born.
>
> (*Rig Veda* 2.2.1.1, qt. in Bayly 1999: 13–14)

DOI: 10.4324/9781003158424-9

The sacredness of caste is also endorsed in the *Bhagavad Gita*. Without caste, says the *Gita*, there would be a corruption of humanity's most precious standards of domestic honor and sexual propriety. Especially talking about the relationship between gender and caste, and how the sexuality of a woman should be controlled to maintain caste purity, the *Bhagavad Gita* has something very serious to say:

> when lawlessness prevails . . . the women of the family become corrupted, and when women are corrupted confusion of castes arises. And to hell does this confusion bring the family itself as well as those who have destroyed it. . . . By the misdeeds of those who destroy a family and create confusion of *varnas* [castes], the immemorial laws of the race and the family are destroyed.
>
> (Bayly 1999: 13–14)

The *Manusmriti* is another text and perhaps the most important one where the principles of caste as the basis of social conduct, morality, and sacred obligations have been further enjoined. This work is said to have been written by Manu, the mythical sage and lawgiver, around the first century AD. Drawing on Susan Bayly's *The Cambridge History of India: Caste, Society, and Politics in India*, we can sum up that the focus of both the *Bhagavad Gita* and the *Manusmriti* is the concept of *dharma*, the key principle propounding for the caste Hindu the code of duty, religious law, and right human conduct leading to spiritual fulfillment. Each of the four *varnas* has a distinct moral quality and a calling to follow. God is believed to have made separate innate activities for the different orders of humanity for the wellbeing of all; indeed, it depended upon this stratified ordering of caste (Bayly 1999: 14).

It is intriguing to see how these ancient scriptural codes have affected the everyday life of the Hindu caste and society at large. Lots of theorization have happened about its workings and how it has been used by the powers that be. The French sociologist Louis Dumont specified that underlying this stratification that remained predominant and stringently imposed were the opposing conceptual categories of purity and pollution. This, he claimed, pervades the conscious or unconscious thought processes of all the Hindus. Dumont held it to be unique to caste; it is observed both in scriptural formulations and in everyday life and worship. The difference between high and low castes consists not merely in the ability to command material resources. According to Dumont, more important in this respect is the question of purity and pollution, which provides socio-religious measurements of rank and status for the caste Hindu. "Preoccupation with the pure and the impure is constant in Hindu life," Dumont declares (Dumont 1970: 44). Dumont's Brahmin-centered understanding of caste has been questioned by many sociologists. Nicholas Dirks and Gloria Goodwin Raheja say that there is strong evidence that proves that all of India is not ruled by the Brahmin-centered values of caste, as claimed by Dumont. The plurality and multiplicity of Indian life are such that no ideology can be all pervasive at any point in time. However, despite such criticisms, it can be said that Dumont touches on the crux of the problem in the Hindu view of social and religious life. Recurrent protests down the ages at both micro and macro levels by both men and women have evinced the fact of casteism being ruled basically by the binary of the pure and the impure. Counter-positions from religions like Buddhism make it all the more glaring. Ambedkar, himself a Dalit and a dissident intellectual, had spent the best part of his life fighting this issue through his immense writings and activism. He also considered this order of precedence not merely conventional but "spiritual, moral and legal." It is "a principle of graded inequality" (Ambedkar 2002: 84) that, he says, regulates the whole sphere of Hindu life. Its roots being deep in religion, people observe caste because they are deeply religious, and they are not wrong there. "In my view," as Ambedkar says,

> what is wrong is their religion, which has inculcated this notion of caste. If this is correct, then obviously the enemy, you must grapple with, is not the people who observe caste, but the *Shastras* which teach them this religion of caste.
>
> (Ambedkar 2002: 102)

No wonder Ambedkar burned the *Manusmriti* in 1927 during the Mahad Satyagraha and, as he had promised, converted to Buddhism a few months before his death. Similarly, in questioning this division that has been created between the four upper castes and the untouchables, and with special reference to his untouchable character Yellana, G. Kalyana Rao, in his celebrated book *Untouchable Spring*, says:

> Who is that half-man who drew the line on Yellana's forehead and on his life? Who is that half-animal? What must be the name of the awesome, distorted one? The answer is clear. It is in the shape of papers. The term *smriti* is also appended to his name . . . . That half-animal is Manu. That terribly distorted Manu. He expounded the *dharmas*, special dharmas, expounded the principles of the caste system.
>
> (Rao 2000: 15)

In fact, all the three texts that I have taken up for discussion in this chapter will prove this point. In each case, the male protagonist in Anantha Murthy's *Samskara* or the female protagonists in Mahasweta Devi's "Bayen" and Hariharan's "The Remains of the Feast", the individual will emerge by achieving an identity only when he or she resists, transgresses, and subverts the all-pervasive caste laws, especially their controlling concept of the binary of purity and pollution.

If casteism legitimizes itself in terms of the binary of purity and pollution, creating in the process the fifth varna, the "untouchables" of the society as its far-reaching effect, then the other section of society suffering long-drawn-out discrimination on this score is women. Women suffer under all patriarchies but suffer the most under the Brahmin patriarchy, where the Brahmins, as male Brahmins, are the law-givers who would see to it that marriage of the proper kind takes place so that *varnashankara* does not corrupt the society. More to that purpose is the control of the sexuality of women who are the reproducers and have leaky bodies and hence are more the victims of the binary of purity and pollution. We have already referred to the *Gita* in this regard. Uma Chakravarty refers to the other texts that have similar observations on the "innate" nature of women as sinful and impure:

> At the time of creation, the original Manu (IX, 17) allotted to women the habit of lying, wasting time, an indiscriminate love of ornaments, anger, meanness and treachery, and bad conduct. As early as the *Satapatha Brahmana* it was held that a woman, a sudra, and a crow are the embodiments of untruth, sin, and darkness.
>
> (Chakravarty 2003: 70)

Hence, as Chakravarty has it, upper-caste dominance and male dominance have not only a common lineage but are closely linked (Chakravarty 2003: 37). The site of this domination is the body, and the legitimizing discourse is that of a ritual division of purity and pollution. As casteism has it, the so-called untouchables and women suffer discrimination and segregation on this very score as being "em-bodied."

Since my specific object of study is the caste and gender relationship in a specific religious perspective bedeviling identity, let me start by mapping the caste and gender relationship in brief in this respect. We have already observed how upper-caste domination and male domination are linked together, segregating people on the basis of caste at birth, in general, and subjugating women, in particular. It was carried on ritualistically, economically, socially, and otherwise. Being the means of reproduction, women are made to be the reproducers of the system. The control is effected through a whole host of social restrictions, religious rituals, and cultural ideologies. It, however, concerns mainly the upper-caste women, and gender inscription is especially glaring in the fact that while their sexuality is stringently controlled, the upper-caste male's sexuality is not similarly controlled. In patriarchy, it is men's prerogative to control female sexuality and thereby effect women's complete subordination. As casteism works through the ritual division of purity and pollution, women, by virtue of being women in terms of reproduction and the periodic menstrual cycle, are already considered polluted,

95

and like the Sudras in the caste system are excluded from rites, rituals, and yajnas, while their male counterparts are absolutely free. Women have to be devoid of sexuality to be pure and chaste. The ideology of womanhood, or *pativrata*, as it is called, is also a form of coercion by men to keep upper-caste women in compliance with caste ideology. Dalit women are also charged with an excess of sexuality. While on that score they are assumed to be easily accessible and become victims of sexual violence at the hands of upper-caste masters, they are, of course, no less victims of patriarchy within their own caste on various grounds, especially age-old superstitious practices. They are thus exposed to double jeopardy because of the complicity between caste and gender. The system is often challenged through transgressions and disruptions, and it has to relegitimize itself through negotiations, violence, and coercive actions. In such cases, again, women have to bear the brunt. They are punished in various ways. In other words, it is the body of a woman on which these practices and discourses are played out, sometimes making her asexual and sometimes libidinal. The Body itself has always been suspect. It is dubbed unruly and unsettling in terms of excess of passion and appetite and hence considered disruptive of the pursuit of truth and knowledge. It is more the case when it comes to the woman's body. But this mind-body split happened to be not only gendered in its resonances, but, as Shildrik and Price remark, "the association of the body with gross, unthinking physicality marks a further set of linkages – to the black people, to the working-class people, to animals and to slaves" (Price and Shildrik 1999: 2). I would like to add to the list the Indian Dalits, the Tribals, or the so-called lower castes. While all these groups suffer discrimination and domination on this score, women specifically have to suffer most because the female body, as observed previously, is supposedly intrinsically unpredictable and leaky (because it menstruates, gives birth to another body, lactates, and so on). Not surprisingly, to quote Shildrik and Price again,

> then, the ability to effect transcendence and exercise rationality has been gender marked as an attribute of man alone – and further of only some men, i.e. those who are white, middle/upper class, healthy and heterosexual – such that women remain rooted within their bodies, held back by their supposedly natural biological processes.
>
> (Price and Shildrik 1999: 2)

In contrast to the supposedly embodied emotional chaos that a woman is, the male body is considered one of ordered self-containment and disembodied rationality. Hence the need for control and surveillance over women's bodies through a whole array of discourses, regulations, and rituals to preclude possibilities of deviations and aberrant pleasures counter to the norms of the patriarchal society and the economy of reproduction. But

this form of the family and its organization and rituals hide the power relations whose marks of injustice and oppression on the bodies of the women
remain discursively naturalized. But, despite this inscription for contain-
ment, or because of it, a woman as a sexual body remains an ambiguous
and conflicting site within the domain of the family and society. This situation constitutes a process of psychic violence that Julia Kristeva, the feminist psychoanalyst, calls 'abjection.' The abject, as she maintains, is always
ambiguous: desirable and terrifying, nourishing, and murderous; it does not
simply involve repudiation: "It is something rejected from which one does
not part" (Kristeva 1982: 4). Women, as "em-bodied," are thus looked upon
both as dangerous and excluded 'others' but remain, as it were, an original
presence. No wonder much literary representation builds on this, trying to
expose the subtext underlying women's so-called naturalized roles in society in whatever garb, gender, race, class, culture, and so on. If, in one case,
the subtext is "de-sexualization" of women to ensure purity, chastity, and
divinity, necessary to preserve culture as something spiritual, in another, it
is "demonization" whenever "transgressions" and "deviations" threaten the
socius. It is carried on in terms of many garbs; one of the garbs is the gender-
caste nexus. Though caste is being used here as a specificity to understand
women's discrimination in specific locations in society, it falls within the
same patriarchal ideology of heterosexual normativity. If it is given to controlling women's sexuality, it also paradoxically represses the male body,
which, as the recent unsettling excesses expose, is not "dis-embodied" but is
equally em-bodied and, hence, plural. In this respect, Spivak is worth quoting. She says: "There are thinkings of the systematicity of the body. There
are value codings of the body. The body as such cannot be thought" (quoted
in Price and Shildrik 8). It means that there are only multiple bodies marked
by quite an array of differences – race, class, sexuality, age, mobility, and
so on. In such a circumstance, the masculinist discourse of dis-embodiment
gets challenged and has to give way to the Foucauldian discourse in favour
of plural and open embodiment. That this should be the right approach is
also suggested in the critiques inscribed in the literary representations that
I am going to look at. I have chosen the three texts, as mentioned, for brief
discussions to show how the texts inscribe in them the debilitating effect of
the caste-gender nexus on the formation of subjectivity and identity, pointing out at the same time how transgressions and subversions take place.

Let me begin with *Samskara* (1976) by Anantha Murthy. *Samskara* works
on these two binaries: the asexual Brahmin women and the libidinal lower-
caste women, whose subjectivities are erased for the construction of the
subjectivity of Praneshacharya, the protagonist of the novel. It is primarily
Praneshacharya's story, his movement from the traditional self to a more
modern one. It is about his search for truth and selfhood. The women are
just a site on which this whole experiment is done. Praneshacharya, the
most respected Brahmin of the *agrahara* (a locality exclusively inhabited by

the Brahmins), is shown as an androgynous figure who has renounced all desires to make himself ready for the attainment of salvation. He has also married an invalid wife with whom no sexual relationship is possible. In other words, he has made his whole life into a veritable penance. He does everything for her, from bathing her to feeding her. As the text has it, his wife represents all other Brahmin women in general, who are emaciated, shrunken, and unattractive. If this happens due to the deliberate ritualized quotidian life that emphasizes bodily purity, then, as Nalini Natarajan points out, it can be assigned to the inevitable connection here "between a ritual economy and a money economy" because "in the ritual economy women's impurity directly affects their husbands' livelihood. That is, if women are impure their men may find no way to survive, to feed themselves or their families" (Natarajan 1999: 158). Hence the scenario of the Brahmin wives' constant washing of clothes, of floors, and of observing all the rituals – ritual fasting, ritual purification after casual contact with "impure" things or castes, or such rites related to childbirth or deaths – bespeaks women's erasure and de-sexualization.

In the same agrahara lives Naranappa, who has rejected his wife for Chandri, a beautiful prostitute. Naranappa has broken all the rules of the Brahmins and has done all things forbidden. In the text, the dilemma begins when Naranappa is dead and the question arises as to who will cremate him and whether he remains a Brahmin at all. Praneshacharya's scriptures give him no answer, but on his way back from the Maruti temple where he goes to seek guidance from the god, he has a sexual encounter with Chandri, the prostitute with whom the deceased Naranappa was living. His sexual encounter with the beautiful prostitute, Chandri, who can only give pleasure, shatters his own Brahminhood. The foundation on which his whole idea of Brahminhood, penance, and salvation was built is shattered at once. His idea of the truth is shaken. Hereafter, he leaves the agrahara in search of the real truth. He does everything that a Brahmin cannot do. He drinks coffee at a common coffee shop; he is still in mourning for his dead wife but enters the temple to eat food; he even visits a prostitute called Padmavati and looks at her lustfully. At the end, he decides that real freedom can come only if he sleeps with Chandri of his own volition. So, at the end of the novel, he is shown to move towards Chandri's village.

In short, this is the story. But, if one thinks carefully, it is all about the body and its positioning *vis-à-vis* various caste dynamics. If it is the body of an upper-caste chaste woman, it has to be asexual and devoid of any positive sexuality. Asexuality is emphasized because of the fear of excess, transgressiveness, deviation, the multiplicity of a woman's body, making it suspect, impure in the Brahminic ritual economy as well as in the patriarchal economy of reproduction. The excess goes against chastity, thereby denying her acceptable identity as a woman in society. She is thus male identified, the second sex, without a subjectivity of her own. The labour of a Brahmin woman is crucial in the maintenance of the ritual purity of the household and thereby the economy of the Brahmins, as discussed previously. But she stands erased both socially and sexually. The text also shows that even amongst the Brahmins a group is valued more if it represses its women more. The lower categories even amongst Brahmins follow less stringent rules. A fallen Brahmin woman can bring disrepute to the whole village. The whole line of Brahmins can be considered mixed if a mistake is made by a Brahmin woman. In this regime of strict surveillance, what is paradoxically interesting is that male Brahmins constantly have an eye on the more beautiful and sexually attractive lower-caste women. Praneshacharya, who rendered himself asexual, an androgynous figure, has been serving and cleaning his invalid wife for the last twenty years. But, this lacks spontaneity and represents the sterility of the lives of the Brahmins, while others around the agrahara can be cunning, disgraceful, and constantly eyeing Chandri and Belli, the prostitutes. This constant hankering for the so-called lower but sexually more attractive women shows not only the hypocrisy but also the unnaturalness in the very living mode of the agrahara. In the same manner, the other extreme is the representation of the lower-caste woman as the excluded other, excluded from rituals, and is dubbed an embodiment of libidinality, a very reductive representation by all means. It can be said that both Naranappa and Praneshacharya appear to be subversive in their breaking of caste rules and by their cohabiting with a prostitute as they break caste identities. The total impact speaks volumes, especially the way Naranappa's death makes his ritual cremation problematic, and Praneshacharya, at the end, assumes a more modern subjectivity. He says, "This is me, the new truth I create, the new person I make" (Murthy 1976: 98). The binary of purity–pollution gets jolted at the site of a woman's body beyond the question of caste hierarchy. But the woman gets erased. In its bid to give a more modern subjectivity to its protagonist Praneshacharya, the text erases the subjectivity of both his wife and the prostitute. However, what the text achieves so successfully is to articulate these very important questions in terms of their inherent contradictions and ironies, thereby clearing a space for a critique. It shows the orthodox Hindu culture in fracture and transition.

"The Remains of the Feast" by Githa Hariharan (1993) offers a different representation in terms of a different problematic. This is the story of a Hindu Brahmin widow who is on the verge of death and who suddenly becomes greedy and develops a ravenous appetite. Suddenly, she desires everything that widowhood has not allowed her throughout her life when she is going to die because of cancer. Stringent rules have been laid down to control the figure of a widow. A widow cannot be a desiring subject, and she is generally kept under surveillance to maintain that. But, in this story, the upper-caste Hindu Brahmin suddenly cannot control her desires anymore at death. She wants to eat cake bought from a Christian's shop and prepared by a Muslim baker, which might have eggs in it; Coca-Cola that she imagines may have alcohol in it and may taste alcoholic; *bhelpuri* from the bazaar, possibly touched by anyone from any other caste, including the untouchables; and finally, she asks for a red bridal sari with a gold border just before her death. This is the result of years of deprivation and a need for the fulfillment of desires that is necessary before death. The flesh, the body, and the primal instincts seem to be reasserting themselves. The effect of the repression of even the usual desires of life at the end of life proves terrible, rendering her crazy, grotesque, and witchlike.

She is the typical widow, tonsured; wearing white; eating sparsely, or only what is strictly prescribed. But, with this sudden upsurge of the body, she becomes, as Susie Tharu succinctly coins the term, a "body-personhood" (Tharu 1999: 190) that is unable to follow discipline. The deprived body seems to be celebrating itself with a vengeance, even going to the extent of being indecorous by farting at will and laughing. In the face of death, most of her desires have to be fulfilled. She laughs at and ridicules the very authorities who want to control her. Her ally is her great grand-daughter who indulges her and gets all these forbidden things, even though being disapproved of by her parents. At her death, the widow, clad in a red sari with golden border to look like a new bride, an act which appears almost to have given her a new life, proves the most desperate and grotesque sight. This attempt to fulfill herself at the last moment is represented as a severe critique of society by the author. It seems to tell us how the body ultimately defies the order that has hitherto disciplined and deprived her. This is the body of the defiant modern widow who indulges in excesses and eats her way to freedom. Her body is tough and resilient. It has not only accepted extreme repression and deprivation but also demonstrates, even at ninety, extreme defiance to the point of being grotesque and abject. She dies indulging in excess. Death is almost like a celebration for her. Interestingly, what *Samskara*'s creator could not achieve could be achieved here by a woman writer. However, "The Remains of the Feast" and *Samskara* have a similar message. Susie Tharu puts it very aptly in her essay "The Impossible Subject: Caste and Desire in the Scene of the Family": the main thrust of the narrative of "The Remains of the Feast" is "the claim of a natural appetite for life – be it male or female – against an order which seeks to deprive or discipline it" (Tharu 1999: 192). It is a statement that also applies equally to *Samskara* as its inscribed problematic. In this context, it is important to note the transition that has been meanwhile happening in India at the advent of modernity. The change has been made noticeable in the text. This upper-caste old Brahmin woman is, of course, affected by the caste system and the control and deprivation that it has caused her. Yet modernity in the family (the conduit here being the great grand-daughter) allows her to transcend all these even at her death. Given the change that has meanwhile infiltrated the socius, the prohibition is not here as important as the mind that is capable of shaking off inhibitions, usually developed through long internalization, and becomes the real hurdle. If modernity makes it possible here for the old Brahmin woman to turn "deviation" into "defiance" and breach of rules into the rule itself, then the same could not happen for the female figures of *Samskara*. However, the transgression of Praneshacharya as shown in the text is no less significant. It suggests an emancipation on his part in that his prioritization of the soul over the body in terms of a self-imposed androgynous state breaks down here, releasing the male body from imprisonment.

My last example of literary representation, however, concerns the body of a so-called lower-caste woman. As is usually looked upon, it is always either in excess or always deficient. She is like a terror and abjection. "Bayen" by Mahasweta Devi illustrates this well. In fact, the body as a site of subversion is an important theme in nearly all of Mahasweta's stories: "Breast-Giver," "Draupadi," "Douloti the Bountiful," to name a few. Though most women represented in the stories are not always intentional subjects of resistance, these stories disturb our ease and effectively alter our assumptions and perceptions. In most of her stories, Mahasweta makes it a point of her attack that decolonization in the true sense of the term did not reach certain peripheries of the nation, in her case, mostly the tribal people of India. Her absolute devotion to understanding that life and to work towards a possible change for it, both in terms of organization and writing, was highly acclaimed at home and abroad and inspired Gayatri Spivak to translate her and use the term "ethical singularity" (Spivak 2001: xix) to describe her.

"Bayen" tells us how the bodies of women are perceived as abject, unsettling, and suspect. The various fluids that come out of a woman's body at different times, like during menstruation, lactation, childbirth, and so on, are seen as inauspicious. Chandidasi, the protagonist in the story, has passed through this lactating phase at the time of giving birth to her son, Bhagirath. But she is branded a witch for this very fact of lactating, unacceptable at other times. Chandidasi is from the untouchable 'Dom' community. Her job is to bury dead children in the morgue. She does her work well until she becomes a mother herself. When she buries Tukni, the last child, her breasts start oozing milk. The villagers observe this strange phenomenon with superstition. The people believe that she is a witch and probably breastfeeds dead children. She appears to them grotesque and a witch figure. Such is the power of superstitious beliefs that even her husband, Malindar, starts believing that she is a witch. Most importantly, she has broken caste rules, for which she will not be forgiven. She has refused to bury dead children any more thereafter.

A witch cult is a violent system where one has no escape from social ostracization once she is declared a witch. Even today, witch-hunting is practiced in around twelve states, out of which only seven have laws criminalizing the practice – Jharkhand, Bihar, Chhattisgarh, Maharashtra, Rajasthan, and Assam. Jharkhand ranks highest in these crimes against women. Branding one as a witch is a way of punishing one, especially when the person is from a lower caste. Violence in the form of rape, molestation, and social ostracization is a part of the caste system. Chandidasi is not only branded a witch and punished but also separated from her son. As time passes, Chandidasi too believes that she is a witch and is very concerned when her son goes to meet her one day on the sly. She is going to see her husband Malindar regarding the unwanted visit of the son. On the way, she finds that people from her community are trying to derail a train and rob it. At the sight of the witch, they run away. Chandidasi gives up her life in trying to prevent the accident. The government declares that she will be given an award for bravery. The point is once again the body. Everybody thinks she a witch because her body lactates out of season, an ominous thing. Nobody takes the "mother" in her into account, the mother that responds to a child. Mahasweta Devi shows how this body that was responsible for her ostracization can be valorized through the use of the body in sacrifice for a greater cause to win recognition and identity back. If the body is the site of discrimination and subjugation, Mahasweta's representation shows how the subaltern can resist or, for that matter, speak with her body to earn identity, especially when the dominant discourse to which she has no entry erases her or even demonizes her.

To conclude, we can say that the body–soul, female–male, homosexual–heterosexual, upper–lower castes, purity–pollution, and such other tenacious binaries have always proved disciplinary and oppressive against the plural potentials of an individual and her identity in society. The caste–gender nexus has been the most pernicious in this respect. The inherent logic of social mobility, however, proves that there takes place a blurring of the boundaries that vested interests raise for subjugation and domination. The so-called "deviations" in many basic social practices as much as in sexuality and gender practices do look forward to a freer temporality beyond a religion-, caste- and class-bound regime. It is an exercise of a power relation that, in the name of maintaining social stability, property relations, nation, and community, would rather enforce the binary as a necessary part of its politics of domination. The divide created by the use of binary opposition is hierarchic and, hence, discriminatory. It is true in the case of gender and sexuality as much as of caste and caste–gender relationships. Feminist voices and social activists as well as intellectuals have paved the way for emancipation and identity by exposing the socio-religious politics behind the straitjacket of the so-called binaries, thereby destabilizing the accepted categories of religion, class and caste divisions, caste–gender practices, sexuality, and so on.

Works cited

Ambedkar, B. R. "Caste in India." In *Caste and Democratic Politics in India*, edited by Ghanashyam Shah. Delhi: Permanent Black, 2002.
Bayly, Susan. *The New Cambridge History of India*, IV, 3. Cambridge: Cambridge University Press, 1999.

Chakravarty, Uma. *Gendering Caste: Through a Feminist Lens*. Kolkata: Stree, 2003.

Devi, Mahasweta. "Bayen". Translated by Mahua Bhattacharya. In *Translating Caste*, edited by Tapan Basu. New Delhi: Katha, 2002.

Dumont, Louis. *Homo Hierarchicus*. Chicago: University of Chicago Press, 1970.

Hariharan, Githa. *The Art of Dying*. New Delhi: Penguin, 1993.

Kristeva, Julia. *Powers of Horrors: An Essay on Abjection*. New York: Columbia University Press, 1982.

Murthy, U. R. Anantha. *Samskara*. Translated by A. K. Ramanujan. Oxford: Oxford University Press, 1976.

Natarajan, Nalini. "Gender, Caste and Modernity: A Reading of U. R. Anantha Murthy's *Samskara* in Its Intellectual Context." In *Signposts: Gender Issues in Post-Independence India*, edited by Rajeswari Sundar Rajan. New Delhi: Kali for Women, 1999.

Price, Janet, and Margrit Shildrik, eds. *Feminist Theory and the Body*. New York: Routledge, 1999.

Rao, G. Kalyana. *Untouchable Spring*. Hyderabad: Orient BlackSwan, 2000.

Spivak, Gayatri Chakravorty. "Translator's Preface." In *Imaginary Maps*. Calcutta: Thema, 2001.

Tharu, Susie. "The Impossible Subject: Caste and Desire in the Scene of the Family." In *Signposts: Gender Issues in Post-Independence India*, edited by Rajeswari Sundar Rajan. New Delhi: Kali for Women, 1999.

7

DEATH OF AN AUTHOR

Dissecting the notion of religious hurt
sentiment *vis-à-vis* literary-political
censorship in India through *One Part Woman*

Nasima Islam

In this chapter, I would like to take up and analyze the debate that sur-
rounded the Indian novel *One Part Woman* written by the Tamil writer
Perumal Murugan. As one knows, a section of people and a few religious
groups held massive protests against the novel, apparently on the grounds
that it "hurt" their religio-cultural sentiments and insulted their deities, their
women, and their community as a whole. The protest and the ensuing events
became so serious in nature that the poor author had to literally declare his
abrupt leave from the world of writing. He declared to the world that his
writer self is no more. He lamented this death of his author-self in the most
sophisticated way, along with a self-written virtual obituary that he posted
on his social media wall.

Now, before I begin to map out the conceptual schema of this chapter,
let me draw the reader's attention to two of the specific titular words that I
have deliberately used not only because they produce an alliterative effect
but also because of their significance at a conceptual level. These two words
are 'death' and 'dissection.' However, one may notice that I have used the
verb 'dissect' while lending it quite an irrelevant object, which is *not* the
"dead body" of the author but the notion of religious "hurt sentiment." In
other words, the aim of this chapter is not to investigate the "death" of the
author of the concerned novel per se, which is anyway a metaphorical death.
Rather, the scalpel of the chapter's criticality would endeavor to cut open an
engineered idea. It attempts to un-layer the constructed notion of sentiment
which is 'injured' or 'hurt' – another notion that makes the medical metaphor for my discussion more suitable. Bio-medically speaking, the concept
of "hurt" is premised on "an aggravated pathology of being" (Ramdev et
al. 2016: xxvi). It is a "symptom-begging-cure" which, at a very experiential level, is "part of the inner life of an individual" that is recognized only
when "it renders itself susceptible to the eye of the diagnostic apparatus"

DOI: 10.4324/9781003158424-10

(Ibid.: xxvi–xxvii). Also, it can claim healing "only when it gains in bodily aspect and visibility" (Ibid.: xxvii). Therefore, the chapter intends to understand the symptoms and nature of injured or hurt religio-cultural sentiments in this particular case that were hailed as the reason for the demand to ban the aforementioned novel.

To give a quick overview, as one knows, Perumal Murugan hails from India's southern state of Tamil Nadu and is a critically acclaimed writer of several fictions, non-fictions, short stories, and anthologies of poems. His book *Madhorubhagan* or *One Part Woman* (*OPW* from now onward) is an excellent critique of the contemporary Tamil society. As Murugan has been a professor of Tamil for around two decades, the book is a result of his long years of sincere investment into researching the indigenous Tamil language, folklore, folk deities, and several Tamil classic texts. Such authority on his part over indigenous community lifeworld(s) obtained him a prestigious grant from the India Foundation of the Arts, Bangalore, to further his research on folklore "surrounding the temple town of Tiruchengodu, a town that he knew very well from his childhood but, in a sense, did not know at all" (Raman 2015). However, this unknowability on his part did not cause him to shy away from depicting the complex lifeworlds of his own people but actually injected an honest endeavor to portray the full spectrum of their complex lived realities where intersections of caste, class, gender, hetero-patriarchal feudal family structures, and resistance to all of it coalesce unapologetically. *OPW* is set during the colonial era of Tamil Nadu and is a saga of a married couple of two passionate lovers, Kali and Ponna, who finally fall prey to the societal pressure of begetting a child of their own, leading to the falling apart of their otherwise happy marriage. The storyline offers poignant critique of the patriarchal conspiracy to reduce women to their uterine space and discipline their bodies. It also critiques the deeply entrenched caste system *vis-à-vis* a compartmentalized hetero-patriarchal socio-cultural feudal fabric of India. In such an India, two things are of utmost priority: land and an heir (preferably a cis-heterosexual, masculine male) to inherit it. However, it takes the readers by surprise, introducing them to an age-old indigenous chariot festival at Tiruchengode where a carnivalesque liberty of sexual indulgence is afforded to men and women for a specific night of the year. At this specific night, they can mate with anybody and even conceive a child out of this mating – precisely the route our female protagonist Ponna ventures into, angering her husband as well as the protesting Hindutva cadres of certain groups post-publication of the book.

The book caused a huge sensation because it allegedly hurt the religious and community sentiments of a specific group of people. On this ground, a fierce smear campaign against the author was launched and mobilized, threatening him with dire consequences. According to a *The Hindu* editorial entitled "Resurrecting the author" (dated Sept. 18, 2016), in the wake of this manufactured campaign against Murugan by conservative religious and caste Hindu groups that demanded a ban on his novel and his prosecution, apparently a "peace meeting" was organized by the local officials at Namakkal that forced Murugan to agree to write an "unconditional apology." Per another article in *The Guardian* entitled "Indian Judges Rules Novelist Silenced by Nationalist Pressure 'Be Resurrected'" (dated July 7, 2016), protests that went on for a course of a long 18 days in 2015 against Murugan and his novel were coordinated by the president of the Tiruchengode's Hindu extremist group *Rashtriya Swayamsevak Sangh* (RSS). Its members contended that the novel misrepresented the Hindu scripture and insulted the Hindu deity honored in the fertility ritual, which apparently offended their sentiment. The article further wrote quoting a close friend of Murugan saying "one of them (the RSS members) threatened to cut off (Murugan's) hand in a public meeting," which established the immediate and real nature of the violent threats that Murugan received. In this context, the article refers to the act of "*award wapsi*" or returning the top national Sahitya Akademi awards conferred by the prestigious National Academy of Letters by 40 writers in the country in 2015 protesting the climate of intolerance under the regime of the *Bharatiya Janata* Party (BJP). The article further argued that Murugan's silence(-ing) can be seen as a part of a larger trend of censorship in India under the current political climate.

However, the RSS denied the allegations of its involvement in the issue. *The Indian Express*, in an article with the headline "No Role in Perumal Murugan Issue, Says RSS" (dated Feb. 1, 2015) quoted its leader Manmohan Vaidya's post in the organization's microblog page: "The RSS has already made it unequivocally clear that it has no role whatsoever in the issue that led to Sri Perumal Murugan to withdraw his books from the market." However, it is not always a real physical act of censoring that needs to be checked. One must also consider how a climate of intimidation of different kinds and threats from potential censors might generate severe self-censoring tendencies. After the Madras High Court judgment which went in favor of the author Murugan, he wrote, in his book of poetic anthology entitled, *Songs of a Coward: Poems of Exile*:

> A censor is seated inside me now. He is testing every word that is born within me. His constant caution that a word may be misunderstood so, or it may be interpreted thus, is a real bother. But I am unable to shake him off. If this is wrong let the Indian intellectual world forgive me.
>
> (2017)

Nonetheless, even if it were Murugan himself who withdrew his books from the bookshops and decided not to write again, one must analyze the circumstances and deep climate of insecurities and fear psychosis under which such acts must have had taken place. As Kaur and Mazzarella suggest, if we expand the category of censorship, we may have to take into consideration not only the operations of official regulatory authorities or bureaucratic orders which include the courts, the police, and the censor boards but also different extra-legal or extra-constitutional initiatives and interventions (2009: 5). They also hinted at the fact that in many cases, these forms of legal and extra-legal censorship may be intertwined (Ibid.). In the case of Murugan, the vitriolic hate campaign against him and his novel made him a target of open death threats that caused him immense public humiliation. It finally demoralized and overwhelmed him into subjugation. Subsequently, Murugan wrote a virtual obituary of his own death on his Facebook wall:

> Perumal Murugan, the writer is dead. As he is not god, he is not going to resurrect himself. He also has no faith in rebirth. An ordinary teacher, he will live as P. Murugan. Leave him alone.
>
> (Barry 2016)

This obituary is highly loaded and demands one's utmost attention. A close reading of this obituary and the entire phenomenon that prompted it would lead to some crucial realizations that seem noteworthy.

I

In the first place, it once again galvanized the classic tension between the notion of 'censorship' and the idea of 'freedom of expression.' On a very philosophical plane, the notions of 'censorship' and 'freedom of expression,' ontologically speaking, are co-constitutive and feed on each other. People tend to claim the latter only when they confront the former. Again, the advocates of censorship try to legitimize their demands, often drawing upon the potential "threat" a text poses to the harmony and health of society if it is allowed to enjoy freedom of expression. Many thinkers, while philosophizing on these notions, argued that we should refrain from justifying censorship, as it can never be an absolutely reliable answer to the "problems" that the unrestricted use of freedom of expression might engender. Rather, they point out quite persuasively that the technologies of censorship might run the risk of becoming very convenient tools at the hands of fascist/ic forces in a given society. Existing ideological regime(s), by monopolizing the power of censoring and evoking the mobilized sentiments of a select group of the masses, can actually muzzle any dissident voice of opposition and thus jeopardize the democratic fabric of society and polity.

Again, another important aspect is that between the tense coupling of censorship and freedom of expression, resides the third element – the element of 'sentiment,' which can take the form of 'harm,' 'hurt,' 'humiliation,' 'offence,' 'hate,' and so on. Therefore, this trio of censorship, freedom of expression, and the aspect of (hurt/humiliated/offended) sentiments has to be dealt with cautiously. Otherwise, there might always be a chance that cashing in on the mobilized and injured sentiments, any potential pressure group, person, or organization, that is, extra-state actors and/or even the state itself would resort to the censoring mechanisms at hand to gag the dissident voices of the opposition and their right to freedom of expression. This leads us to our next realization, which is how to analyze the idea of "hurt sentiments," especially when the hurt is claimed on the ground of something as sensitive in today's polity as "religion."

Broadly speaking, many scholars argue that we should refrain from demanding censoring of any ideas, texts, or speeches, no matter how controversial they are, provided they are not triggering or inciting direct, imminent forms of violence. Owing to censorship's inherent anti-democratic tendencies of repressing freedom of expression, instead of demanding censoring of any debatable texts or expressions, it seems more rational to desire that controversial or biased texts, speeches, or expressions should be contested with more speeches, more texts, and more expressions that would pose counter-arguments on the matter at issue. In this way, availability of all sorts of opinions – both popular and unpopular – would be ensured in the public sphere for the citizen-publics to be familiarized with and make informed choices of their own. It would also recognize and enable citizens' critical-cognitive and ethico-moral abilities to make their own opinions, which is something that the act of censorship, especially censorship with the aim of imposing prior restraints on texts or speeches, is antithetical to.

As Kevin McCormick, in his article "Censorship: Some Philosophical Issues," suggests, while talking about the "harm argument" of censorship, the logic of censorship presupposes that the censor would be a godly, paternalistic, authoritative entity who knows the best as to what to publish and what to ban (McCormick 1977: 32). It is afforded a hierarchically superior status over the masses who are infantilized and who supposedly cannot decide on their own what is bad and what is not for them to be exposed to (Ibid.). Also, McCormick critiques the logic of a censor board that might function discreetly without any public re/view and has an agenda of prior restraint on texts or expressions disobeying the rule of law (Ibid.: 36). Such measures pre-empt the space for certain expressions to have a public life. Such practices, we can say following McCormick, while being absolutely inconsiderate of the different public opinions and disregarding the option for democratic deliberations that texts and freedom of expressions generally deserve, can also give birth to malpractices of favoritism and corruption as well.

In this context, however, it is important to note that even the "rule of law" is not sacrosanct. It can be tweaked, exploited, and conveniently deployed in favor of the dominant power-brokers. As Ratna Kapur, in her article, "Who Draws the Line: Feminist Reflections on Speech and Censorship," argues, even the lines between what is usual freedom of speech and what is hate speech can be compromised given the interest of the majoritarian groups ruling a particular polity. She deals with what we may call "the normalisation" or even "normativisation" of certain kind of majoritarian hate speech *vis-à-vis* what we may call usual free speech (Kapur 1996: 19). She questions, "when hate speech itself becomes a part of a mainstream discourse that is, it becomes increasingly acceptable among a large section of the population, what is the function of such laws?" (Ibid.).

II

Second, coming back to the case of the kind of censorship that *OPW* as a novel faced, we must talk about different kinds of hurt that the entire incident gave birth to. For example, apart from the alleged hurt sentiment of a certain section of people, one cannot unsee how colossally hurt the author Murugan himself might have been. The fact that he had to resort to his metaphorical death, which marked, fortunately temporarily, cessation of his extremely fertile writing career points towards his experience of 'hurt" as well. It suggests that the way a particular group mobilized the ground of alleged hurt of sentiment of a community became the very site of production of more hurt for an individual, that is, the author and all those who shared the author's sentiments, by extension. From this circumstance, a debate between 'community hurt' versus 'individual hurt' can ensue. The rationale of the hurt taken by the community in this context is premised on the fact that the alleged hurter-individual (in this case, the author), despite sharing the same lifeworld within the community space, is projected as a threat to its (supposed) homogeneity because of the individual member's nonconformist position within it (Ramdev et al. 2016: xxxv). Therefore, to counter this (imagined/apprehended) moment of potential disintegration and "its own fear of the threat the community in turn attempts the marshalling of a thwartive, interventionist machinery to censor and censure the detractive agent" (Ibid.: xxxvi).

Again, in this context, one is provoked to contemplate a set of questions related to the very category of hurt and the normative aspect of claiming hurt which seems to have an in-built gradation as well. It deserves our attention also because no hurt-claim is apolitical and the claimants have specific locations within a given socio-political-economical and religio-cultural framework. Questions like who can claim hurt; what if the hurt person/ entity does not or cannot afford to claim the status of being hurt (Ramdev et al. 2016: 16); are all kinds of hurt visible; whose hurt deserves immediate redress; how do we hierarchize among different kinds of hurt-claims coming from different locations within a deeply unequal society like India which is conspicuously hierarchized across different markers of identity like class, caste, religion, gender, sexuality etc. – are too significant to miss. As Anup

Dhar, in his article entitled "What If the Hurt Is 'Real'? Psyche, Neighbor, and Intimate Violence," provocatively asks,

> Would the experience of (and response to) hurt be different in the case of the (purportedly) powerful and the (purportedly) powerless. Or, more radically, is hurt an experience that is limited to the powerless; because in the powerful hurt is perhaps a nascent state; it quickly turns to either hate or rage, geared at times to (retributive) action; while the experience of hurt in the powerless does not necessarily translate to action, to an undoing, but remains cocooned, and encrypted as a traumatic spur, a thorn stuck in the flesh, a thorn whose nature is perhaps unknown or not fully known but which is not or never unfelt.
>
> (16)

III

Third, the fact that Murugan was humbled into declaring his leave from the vocation of writing, a vocation that he had been dearly engaged in for decades, pointed towards his immense identitarian vulnerability not only as an author but also as a citizen. Keeping aside the hurt of author-Murugan for a moment, we must attend to the fact that his vulnerability also stems from his legitimate sense of insecurity as a citizen of a post-colonial, constitutionally declared democratic, secular republic. It was because not only his right to freedom of expression was at risk of getting censured/censored, but his right to safety was threatened as well. This makes the ontological vulnerability felt on his part two pronged. On one hand, this precarity of his identity as an author can be located at a philosophical level as his intentions, his ethics of representation, the hermeneutics of reading, and even the function of literature itself were misperceived and politicized. Again, on the other, his sense of immediate physical insecurity as a citizen of apparently the world's largest democracy, India, can be situated in a pragmatic, juridico-legal domain. It is so because the incident proved that even extra-state players are capable of acting as unavoidable censors, be it even temporarily, who can cow a respectable author like Murugan despite all the constitutional safeguards regarding the freedom of expression he as a citizen is entitled to.

However, thanks to the Madras High Court verdict that went in favor of the author, he was finally judicially resurrected. Upholding the author's freedom of expression, in his landmark judgment, Justice Sanjay Kishan Kaul of Madras High Court wrote,

> Perumal Murugan should not be under fear . . . . He should be able to write and advance the canvas of his writing. His writings would be a literary contribution, even if there were others who may differ with

the material and style of his expression . . . . We conclude by observing this: 'Let the author be resurrected to what he is best at. Write.'

(Joshi 2016)

Nonetheless, the entire phenomenon can be perceived as an entry point to the larger literary-political censorship regime of India that seems to share an unholy entente with politics or at least has a lot of political economy. Also, in the same judgment which otherwise championed the freedom of expression, a provision for the "expert body" was kept. Even if the provision was well intentioned and was for the purpose of resolving unreasonable disputes between different stakeholders, this seems problematic. It is so because the seed of existence of any such "expert body" may leave scope for politico-ideological bias.

Also, it leaves open the debates around the political resourcefulness of certain kinds of hurt within the market economy of identity politics given the deeply casteist and communal nature of Indian society and Indian polity that is divided across majoritarian and minoritarian lines. Ideological regimes might favor certain hurt-claims over others that would suit their agenda better. By weaponizing such hurt-claims, they might push for political mileage, keeping in mind their target vote bank and how to influence their ballot-box behavior.

IV

Another important aspect of the *OPW* controversy was that the conservative Hindutva ilk was angered that the novel portrayed the lead female protagonist Ponna's participation in a traditional temple chariot festival which apparently allowed her to have physical intercourse with anyone for a specific night and bear a child out of that encounter. One may speculate that here are at least two aspects that might scandalize a conservative worldview. First, here, a woman's sexual autonomy is highlighted, where she can choose anyone across the caste-class spectrum as her one-night sex partner outside the sanctity of marriage, and an alternative extra-marital eroticism is hinted at. Second, it was not something that she had to venture into by revolting against the societal order as a rebel. Rather, she was shown to be pushed into this carnivalesque play by her own community members, despite her husband's disapproval. This makes the existence of such a robust tradition within the universe of the community something legitimate and celebratory. However, in two possible sequels to the novel, Murugan later showed two alternative trajectories of Ponna's life after her participation in the chariot festival from which she returns pregnant. In one, Kali commits suicide, and in another, he develops deep rage and resentment for Ponna, his erstwhile beloved wife. Clearly, both ends ensure Ponna's suffering for the apparent 'crime' which at least partially threatened to subvert the hetero-patriarchal construction of the institution called "marriage" that is based on the idea of monogamy and absolute female submission of her agency – bodily and otherwise. However, as far as the present novel is concerned, the ritualistic tradition of the temple chariot festival could be read as a feminist moment within the novel that shows how indigenous prototypes of resistance from within a given community to its otherwise strictly hetero-patriarchal, casteist, and feudal societal structure can be imagined. It is these non-conformist moments within the text that caused such discomfort to a section of the public which turned into an over-jealous mob that sought to operate as self-styled censors.

Coming back to Murugan's ordeal, one may notice that instead of treating it as an isolated incident, one should locate it within the larger pattern of literary-cultural censorship. It directs our attention to enquire about the larger literary-cultural censorship regime in the country which has its own history of harassing and intimidating litterateurs and culture workers. And the fact that more often than not the rationale behind such acts of censorship has been religious hurt sentiment begs for critical academic attention to rethink our registers of hurt and religion, and their many ramifications.

Works cited

Barry, Ellen. "'A Censor Is Seated Inside Me Now': Hometown Wrath Tests a Novelist." *The New York Times*, August 22, 2016. www.nytimes.com/2016/08/23/books/indian-novelist-stages-a-comeback-after-threats-in-his-hometown.html.

Dhar, Anup. "What If the Hurt Is 'Real'." In *Sentiment, Politics, Censorship: The State of Hurt*, edited by Rina Ramdev, Sandhya D. Nambier and Debaditya Bhattacharya. New Delhi, India: Sage, 2016.

Joshi, Vidhi. "Indian Judge Rules Novelist Silenced by Nationalist Pressure 'Be Resurrected'." *The Guardian, Guardian News and Media*, July 7, 2016. www.theguardian.com/books/2016/jul/07/indian-judge-rules-novelist-nationalist-pressure-perumal-murugan.

Kapur, Ratna. "Who Draws the Line? Feminist Reflections on Speech and Censorship." *Economic and Political Weekly* 31:16/17 (Apr. 20–27, 1996).

Kaur, Raminder, and William Mazzarella. *Censorship in South Asia: Cultural Regulation from Sedition to Seduction*. Bloomington: Indiana University Press, 2009.

Mathew, Liz. "No Role in Perumal Murugan Issues, Says RSS." *The Indian Express*, Feb. 1, 2015. https://indianexpress.com/article/india/india-others/no-role-in-perumal-murugan-issues-says-rss/.

Mccormick, Kevin. "Censorship." *Index on Censorship* 6:2 (1977): 31–37.

Murugan, Perumal. *One Part Woman*. India: Penguin Random House, 2013. Kindle.

———. *Songs of a Coward: Poems of Exile*. India: Penguin Random House 2017. Kindle.

Raman, N. Kalyan. "Why Perumal Murugan's 'One Part Woman' Is Significant to the Debate on Freedom of Expression in India." *The Caravan*, Jan. 13, 2015. caravanmagazine.in/vantage/why-perumal-murugans-one-part-woman-significant-debate-freedom-expression-india.

Ramdev, Rina, Sandhya D. Nambiar, and Debaditya Bhattacharya. *Sentiment, Politics, Censorship: The State of Hurt*. New Delhi, India: Sage, 2016.

"Resurrecting the Author." *The Hindu*, Sept. 18, 2016. www.thehindu.com/opinion/editorial/Resurrecting-the-author/article14474599.ec.

8

RELIGIOUS HEGEMONY AND LITERATURE

Appropriation of subaltern parables in Amitav Ghosh's *The Hungry Tide*

Jai Singh

Since the dawn of consciousness in human beings, the spheres of literature and religion have overlapped. Religion and literature overlap in terms of subject matter, as they are inclined towards the imperceptible, ethereal, and abstract in contrast to science, history, and philosophy that deal with shreds of evidence and certifiable reality. Apparently they deal with human experience, existential truths, abstruse meanings, and spiritual and emotional well-being; however, they also form an integral part of hegemonic structures in a given society. Religion and literature draw their strength from imagination and intuition to nourish understanding of the human situation that leads either to creation and consolidation of existing hegemony or embarks on a mission to challenge the existing hegemony. In simple words, religion and mythology are not scientific; however, they can be studied by making use of natural sciences such as psychology and psychiatry, and this vital fact makes them no less scientific. As religious discourses emanate from the human psyche and, in return, shape the human psyche, it is pertinent to analyze how religious discourses, symbolism, and vocabulary enter into the novel and how they shape the psychological space of a reader.

One may doubt how literature in general and novels, in particular, can shape the psyche of the masses and hence shape society; however, it is a well-established fact because any change either in the structure or in the meaning of socio-linguistic genes changes the society and its structure as well as its perception of physical reality. At the same time, social structure on the one hand and economic and political circumstances on the other hand interact with socio-linguistic genes, and this interaction not only mutates the linguistic genes but also determines the dimensions of social, economic, and political

DOI: 10.4324/9781003158424-11

circumstances not just for the present but also for the future, as propounded by T. Deacon:

> [T]he ability to use language symbolically has phylogenetically affected the human brain, not in a direct cause and effect manner, but indirectly through its effects on human behaviour and on the changes that human behaviour brings about in the environment. Even though the ability to use language as a symbolic system doesn't bring about genetic changes in the nature of the human brain, the changes in environmental conditions brought about by human symbolic responses to that environment can, in the long run, bias natural selection and alter the selection of cognitive predispositions that will be favoured in the Future.
>
> (Kramsch 2006: 241)

Language, the ideology embedded in it, and the material reality for which it is constructed do not affect the biological structure of the human brain but rather affect and alter the software of the brain i.e. mind, which to a large extent is constituted of socio-linguistic genes. Any alteration at the level of linguistic genes brings out large-scale changes at the level of the perception of the outer world because we

> know no world that is not organized like a language, we operate with no other consciousness but one structured like a language – language that we cannot possess for we are operated by those languages as well. The category of language then embraces the category of world and consciousness as it is determined by them.
>
> (Spivak 1988: 77–78)

This predominance of linguistic construction of reality over real life suggests that it "is language which speaks, not the author" (Barthes 2001: 1467) and reduces the author's function significantly because the human subject is not taken as the creator of a work but rather as a space in which innumerable traces precipitate into a particular text or a site wherein the cultural constructs, discursive formations, and configurations of power, prevalent in a given cultural era or inherited from distant cultures both in time and space, congregate and are documented. These configurations of power are transferred from one space and time to another through language because a man "spins language out of himself, he spins himself into it" (Humboldt 1988: 60). However, the reduction of the author function of individual writers transforms them significantly, and they are located at the intersection of innumerable forces both known and unknown and cannot function independently, therefore "which other machine the literary machine can be plugged into, must be plugged into in order to work" (Deleuze 2005: 4).

114

The world and the text have a very complicated relationship and cannot exist without each other, as "any text, if it is not immediately destroyed, is a network of often colliding forces, but also that a text in its being a text is a being in the world" (Said 1975: 3). This chapter takes a slightly different position. Here, the text's very production is an amalgam of innumerable texts and forces. The world is located in the texts in the form of their internal structure – choice of subject matter, its treatment, linguistic choices, their arrangement; at the same time, texts are located in the world; that is, their success in outside society, such as the number of copies they sell, the number of awards they get, the social machine's adoption, and adaptation of the texts. Therefore, linguistic machines like writer, text, and reader and the organic machines like a human body, other organisms, and inorganic machines plugged into each other and innumerable other machines of past and present are creating new machines and being created by them simultaneously.

In the relationship between religion and literature in an Indian context when seen in the light of the Orientalist project started by Colonial Authorities, one thing becomes perceptible: Indian intelligentsia in general and a majority of creative writers are shaped by the oriental construction of Indianness and Hinduism, which have become synonymous to some extent, and Amitav Ghosh is no exception. In the novel *The Hungry Tide*, the orientalist construction of Hinduism as a synonym of Indianness is made to look natural aspect of life in India by the author. Before looking into the representation of Hinduism as a hegemonic construction used to colonize the alternative religious formation, it is required to understand oriental investment into the field of religion and culture.

The colonial machinery worked in a very subtle manner and evolved a new method of ruling over the Orient. On the one hand, it destroyed the peasantry and working class, and on the other hand, it funded the Orientalist project, which became the most powerful institution for ruling over the Orient. Warren Hastings, the viceroy responsible for atrocities on masses, summoned Brahmans versed in Shastras from all parts of India and paid each of them one rupee a day for teaching Sanskrit. The colonial authorities gave a fellowship for learning Sanskrit and Persian and established a committee that "layout above a lakh of rupees in printing Arabic and Sanscrit books" (Macaulay 2005: 128). This project increased the number of Orientalized Indians from amongst whom the intelligentsia emerged, and at the time of independence, the Indian nation-state was handed over to them, and they, as a product of colonialism, helped in the establishment of First World neo-colonialism and on their part extended internal colonialism (an extension of First World colonialism) to the marginal sections who were not contaminated by the colonial project.

In the fictional world of *The Hungry Tide*, Amitav Ghosh brings in two kinds of religious discourses and establishes hegemony of the one over the other. The local and non-hegemonic religious discourse belongs to the local inhabitants of the Sundarbans delta region and is rejected by the author through Nirmal Bose as superstition. After listening to the mythical story of Bon Bibi from Horen, who tells him that it is Bon Bibi who provides for him, along with other means of sustenance, Kanai, who is a child at that time, is curious to know more about Bon Bibi, to which Nilima says, "In these parts, people believe she rules over all the animals of the jungle" (Ghosh 2004: 28). The author takes up a rational position with regard to the mythology of marginalized sections and shows that a grown-up man like Horen should not entertain such a naïve and irrational attitude; that is why he makes Kanai, "unable to suppress the snort of laughter that rose to his lips" (Ibid.: 28).

On the one level, the author makes a child laugh at the myths and stories of socially, culturally, economically, and politically marginalized sections; on the other level, through the purportedly secular and supposedly Marxist scholar Nirmal, who is shown to have a highly scientific approach, he also rejects the local myth as superstition and false consciousness when he tells Kanai, "It's just a tale they tell around here. Don't bother yourself with it. It's just false consciousness, that's all it is" (Ibid.: 101). The subaltern is denied by the author to delineate their version of the myth; rather, Nirmal is made their spokesperson, who misrepresents their version as mere superstition when he says,

> he would tell you that Bon Bibi rules over the jungle, that the tigers, crocodiles, and other animals do her bidding . . . . You would think that in a place like this people would pay close attention to the true wonders of the reality around them. But no, they prefer the imaginary miracles of gods and saints.
>
> (Ibid.: 102)

The author makes fun of the myths and stories of socially, culturally, economically, and politically marginalized sections; on the other hand, the myths and stories of the hegemonic and homogenizing religion of India, that is, Hinduism, which are equally irrational and sources of superstition, are not problematized, and the same purportedly secular, rational, and supposedly Marxist Nirmal talks about the Brahmanical myths as universal truths and wants to adopt them as pedagogy for teaching schoolgoing children of vulnerable sections:

> *I would begin, "what do our old myths have in common with geology . . . . And then, of course, there is the scale of time – yugas and epochs, Kaliyuga and the Quaternary. And yet – mind this! – . . . Maybe I would start with the story of Vishnu, in his incarnation as a divine dwarf, measuring out the universe in three giant strides. I would tell them about the god's misstep and how an errant toenail on one of his feet created a tiny scratch on the fabric of creation. It*

was this pore, I'd tell them, that became the source of the immor-
tal and eternal Ganga that flows through the heavens, washing
away the sins of the universe . . . . "Look, comrades, look," I would
say. "This map shows that in geology, as in myth, there is a visible
Ganga and a hidden Ganga: one flows on land and one beneath the
water. Put them together and you have what is by far the greatest
of the earth's rivers."

(Ghosh 2004: 180–182; emphasis in the original)

To a purportedly secular writer who is writing history from below in his novels, the marginalized is only the Indian hegemonic sections *vis-à-vis* Western colonial powers, and he is not bothered about the same process of hegemonic and homogenizing presence of Hinduism. This particular position makes Horen's belief that Bon Bibi rules over the jungle and the wild creatures like the tigers, crocodiles, and other animals obey her become an example of irrationality and superstition, and it is supplemented by an example when Kusum's father is killed by a lion and Kusum, while witnessing the whole scene, prays to Bon Bibi to save her father, but no supernatural power comes to save him. At this juncture, the author criticizes these marginalized people for their superstitious nature and their belief in Bon Bibi and Shah Jongoli and also criticizes them for not paying attention to the accurate phenomena of the nature and reality around them. At this point, the author arouses hope that he is for inculcating a scientific temperament and hence against all superstitions; however, very surprisingly, the author replaces myths and superstitions with Brahmanical myths and superstitions, which happen to be the hegemonic and homogenizing force in India and undeclared national religion as well.

The author proves that myths of marginalized sections are full of superstition, however simultaneously he proves that Brahmanical myths are scientific, through Nirmal, the critic of Bon Bibi and Shah Jongoli, who equates Brahmanical myths with geology. He does not stop here and describes yugas and epochs, Kaliyuga and the Quaternary as history. He further includes history, geology, and astronomy in the mythical narrative on the incarnation of Vishnu as a Divine Dwarf who measured the universe in three giant strides. He projects a myth as the origin of geological phenomena and ascribes the origin of geographical creations to the Divine Dwarf incarnation of Vishnu when he says that a delinquent toenail on one of his feet produced a miniature abrasion in the cosmos and led to the descent of the river Ganga from heaven on Earth. Further, the river Ganga, which is a geographical reality, is mixed with mythology when he talks about two types of Ganga – one visible and another hidden.

Amitav Ghosh is seemingly a secular novelist who, to foreground his secularism, questions mythology and superstitions in his novel, but only the mythology and superstition of marginal sections, not of the hegemonic

117

group, which is proved scientific in its nature and scope. The author maintains his position of a secular author; however, a careful study of the novel reveals that the secular in this novel is synonymous with liberal Hinduism, which happens to be the unofficial religion of the state, irrespective of which party is in power. In this novel, Nirmal and Nilima are the representatives of the state's attitude, which happens to be the hegemonic castes' and classes' attitude towards the marginal sections of Indian society. Like Nirmal and Nilima, the state's definitions of rationality, scientific attitude, and superstition keep on changing. Brahmanical myths remain unquestioned or rather are affirmed as scientific and rational; the author, through the character of Nirmal, proves them scientific and hence an appropriate pedagogy to teach children in a school.

This particular dimension of the relationship between religion, literature, and state is foregrounded by Deleuze and Guattari while discussing religion's association with the state apparatus and war machine. According to them,

> Religion is in this sense a piece in the State apparatus (in both of its forms, the 'bond' and the 'pact or alliance'), even if it has within itself the power to elevate this model to the level of the universal or to constitute an absolute *Imperium*.
>
> (Deleuze 2005: 382)

Further, while treating religion like a war machine, they say,

> We are referring to religion as an element in a war machine and the idea of holy war as the motor of that machine . . . the war machine may very well favor the movement of migration and the ideal of the establishment; religion, in general, may very well compensate for its specific deterritorialization with a spiritual and even physical reterritorialization, which in the case of the holy war assumes the well-directed character of a conquest of the holy lands as the center of the world.
>
> (Deleuze 2005: 382)

Deleuze and Guattari's insight on the role of religion as a war machine is pertinent to understand its representation in literature in general and in Amitav Ghosh's *The Hungry Tide* in particular. It also sheds light on how hegemonic religion is represented as secular in literature and comes to be accepted as natural as against minority religious practices, which are seen as superstitious and unnatural. This theoretical framework focuses on religion's representation in Indian literature and foregrounds that religion and literature both turn out to be a kind of war machine, and in a very subtle manner, all religions except one are either erased or misrepresented.

118

The Hungry Tide by Amitav Ghosh on the surface level is about state atrocities on the lower-caste migrants who occupy the Sundarbans delta region;
however, in a very subtle manner, it is about establishing the hegemony of
the dominant religion over minority religions as found in the long discourse
of Nirmal on the Brahmanical idea of the Ganga and other rivers and the
appropriation of the Bon Bibi song within Brahmanism.

The mythical narratives of Bon Bibi and Shah Jongoli at one level try
to cope with the dangers of the Sundarbans delta region, especially tigers,
and at another level try to reject organized religions like Brahmanism and
Islam that require more devotion and put a monetary burden on their followers, which the people of the Sundarbans region cannot afford. Their
lives are full of hardships and risks, they have very little time to practice
religious rituals in routine life, and they hardly have any money to give. So,
they opt for a much simpler mythology and a simpler hybrid god that suits
their kind of life. Bon Bibi and Shah Jongoli are hybrid gods who do not fit
into any definition of organized religion. When Kanai, who subscribed to
Brahmanical mythology, watches the dramatic performance of the Bon Bibi
and Shah Jongoli story, he is surprised because this story did not start in the
conventional manner of any Brahmanical story in heaven or on the banks
of the Ganga. Rather, this story, as it is an amalgamation of diverse cultures, opens in Arabia against a backdrop of mosques and minarets. In this
story, the setting is the city of Medina, the holy place of Muslims, and the
story is about a man called Ibrahim who is a very religious-minded person
without children. With the blessings of the Archangel Gabriel, he becomes
the father of twins, Bon Bibi and Shah Jongoli. These two children possess
supernatural powers, and the Archangel assigns them the job of traveling
to the Sundarbans region, a place of eighteen tides, and transforming it for
human habitation. When they reach this place, they find that it is ruled by
Dokkhin Rai, a powerful demon-king who exercises command over every
being that lives here, even every phantom, ghost, and malevolent spirit.
Dokkhin Rai hates human beings, and if he spots any human being in his
realm, he kills and eats them. When Bon Bibi and Shah Jongoli reach this
realm and give *azán*, the Muslim call to prayer, Dokkhin Rai is alerted
and attacks them; however, as his opponents are stronger therefore he is
defeated. Once Bon Bibi and Shah Jongoli win the battle, they do not kill
him; rather, they spare his life and restore half of his kingdom, which is
prohibited for human beings, but another half is for human beings and
prohibited for Dokkhin Rai.

Unlike the Brahmanical story of the Divine Dwarf incarnation of Lord
Vishnu, which is pure mythology and created to establish a particular kind
of hegemonic ideology in society, this myth of Bon Bibi and Shah Jongoli is
a product of people's struggle with the world of nature, which is full of dangers. This myth is a kind of compromise between the world of nature and
the world of human beings; therefore, it is more scientific and rational in

its inception, though the believer of this myth understands it like a religious dictate. But the author rejects it as pure irrationality and regards the Divine Dwarf incarnation of Vishnu as scientific thing related to geology, history, and astronomy.

The accounts of Bon Bibi and Shah Jongoli on the one hand and Dokkhin Rai and his demon hordes on the other hand; their conflict; Bon Bibi's mercy on Dokkhin Rai; and the division of tide country into two parts, one for human beings and other for wildlife, are more scientific approaches to strike a balance between human civilization and ecology than either Islam or Brahmanism. It is true that the illiterate and ignorant people of this region believe in the miracles of Bon Bibi, and they seriously believe that she will save them whenever they need her. The author here takes a rational stance and busts the myth when Bon Bibi does not answer the prayers of Kusum, and her father is killed by a tiger:

> It was Kusum who spoke first. "I called her too," she said. "But she never came."
> "Who?"
> "Bon Bibi. The day my father died. I saw it all, it happened in front of me, and I called her again and again . . ."
>
> (Ibid.: 107)

It is always good for a writer not to stand with superstition, and Amitav Ghosh, through Nirmal, produces a strong critique of superstition and irrationality; however, only when they are harbored by a marginalized and minority section. The same secular author, through one of the most powerful characters, Nirmal, who is also projected as an embodiment of secularism and rationality, affirms the Brahmanical myths of Vishnu as a natural part of the Indian ethos. In this way, the novelist questions superstitions selectively. At every point, he questions the rationality of subalterns, even when they are fully rational, for instance, when Nirmal reads part of *Bernier's Travels* to Horen and Horen identifies certain phenomena as natural occurrences in this region, contrary to Berner's observation, who records them as supernatural, Nirmal suspects Horen's wisdom. In the following dialogue, when Horen identifies a particular geographical place and a natural phenomenon, Nirmal does not believe him:

> *When night approached, they took their boat into a "snug creek" and anchored it at a distance from the shore where they judged themselves to be safe from predators. But they took the additional precaution of maintaining a watch through the night and this proved lucky for the priest. When his turn came he was privileged to witness a truly amazing spectacle: a rainbow made by the moon.*

120

> *"Oh!" cried Horen. "I know where this happened: they must have been at Gerafitola."*
> *"Rubbish, Horen," I said. "How could you know such a thing? This happened over three hundred years ago."*
>
> (Ibid.: 146, emphasis in original)

Similarly, in *Bernier's Travels*, when glowworms are described as devils and Horen very clearly calls it a natural phenomenon, the so-called rationalist and anti-superstition character, Nirmal, does not praise him for a rational approach, as can be seen from the following dialogue:

> *Then all of a sudden the mangroves around the boat seemed to burst into flame as the greenery was invaded by great swarms of glowworms. These insects hovered in such a way as to give the impression that fires were dancing in the mangroves' roots and branches. This caused panic among the sailors, who, the Jesuit says, 'did not doubt that they were so many devils.'"*
> *"But Saar," said Horen with a puzzled look in my direction. "Why should they doubt it? What else could they be?"*
>
> (Ibid.: 146–147, emphasis in original)

This particular rejectionist attitude of Nirmal towards the scientific and rational understanding of natural phenomena which are described as supernatural events throws light on the close association between European colonizers, Indian upper-caste intelligentsia who are internal colonizers which becomes apparent in Deleuze and Guattari's views on the formation of state and the role of certain classes,

> It no longer of itself forms a ruling class or classes; it is itself formed by these classes, which have become independent and delegate it to serve their power and their contradictions, their struggles and their compromises with the dominated classes.
>
> (Deleuze 2000: 221)

In this novel, the state apparatus evicts the inhabitants from the delta region because it suspects their citizenship and wisdom and later on hands over the same region to a multinational company to develop as a tourist place. Similarly, the local representatives of the state's unofficial religion, Nirmal and Nilima, suspect the mythology of the natives, which is more eco-sensitive, is superstition and therefore evict minority religions from the psychological space of the characters from marginalized sections in the novel as well as from the psychological space of the readers from marginalized sections and hand it over to the hegemonic religion by projecting Brahmanical mythology as a pedagogy to teach natural sciences in the school.

Works cited

Barthes, Roland. "The Death of the Author." In *The Norton Anthology of Theory and Criticism*, edited by Vincent B. Leitch. New York: W. W. Norton & Company, Inc., 2001.

Deleuze, Gilles, and Felix Guattari. *Anti-Oedipus: Capitalism and Schizophrenia*, 1983. Translated by Robert Hurley, Mark Seem and Helen R. Lane. Minneapolis: University of Minnesota Press, 2000.

_____. *A Thousand Plateaus: Capitalism and Schizophrenia*, 1987. Translated by Brian Massumi. Minneapolis: University of Minnesota Press, 2005.

Ghosh, Amitav. *The Hungry Tide*. New Delhi: Harper Collins, 2004.

Humboldt, Wilhelm von. *On Language: The Diversity of Human Language Structure and Its Influence on the Mental Development of Mankind*, 1836. Translated by P. Heath. Cambridge: Cambridge University Press, 1988.

Kramsch, Claire. "Language, Thought, and Culture." In *The Handbook of Applied Linguistics*, edited by Alan Davies and Catherine Elder. Oxford: Blackwell, 2006.

Macaulay, Thomas Babington. "Minutes on Indian Education, February 2, 1835." In *Postcolonialisms: An Anthology of Cultural Theory and Criticism*, edited by Gaurav Desai and Supriya Nair. Oxford: Berg, 2005.

Said, Edward William. *Orientalism*, 1975. New York: Vintage Books, 1979.

Spivak, Gayatri Chakravorty. *In Other Worlds: Essays in Cultural Politics*. London: Routledge, 1988.

Part 3

WAR, TRAUMA, AND HISTORY

9

THE "LONG SHADOW" OF THE BANGLADESHI LIBERATION WAR

Religion and nationalism in Tahmima Anam's Bengal Trilogy

Rimi Nath

Introduction

This chapter is a tribute to a woman I met in an India-Bangladesh border district, Karimganj, of Assam, India. I call her grandmother, and her psyche, like that of millions of others – who have witnessed the brutalities of war, felt the deep pain of loss – is in a state of perpetual mourning. The call and plea for humanity and understanding are for them and for the subsequent generations of Indians, Pakistanis, and Bangladeshis who continue to feel and suffer the "long shadow" of Partition. Urvashi Butalia, in *Partition: The Long Shadow*, emphasizes this "long shadow that Partition cast" (Butalia 2015: xviii). The traumatic memories of war linger – the guilt, the loss, the vulnerability, the questions of justice – and are passed on to the next generation. India, Pakistan, and Bangladesh have witnessed the transformation of national identities over space and time with the Partition of 1947 where British India was divided into India and Pakistan and then with the emergence of East Pakistan as Bangladesh in 1971.

A nation is generally defined as a distinct group living in a demarcated sovereign territory with a common language, tradition, or religion (Kedourie 1994: 1; Smith 1999: 11). Anthony D. Smith argues that ethnic communities and their myths of collective memory give shape to the idea of nationalism, although nation and nationalism are considered modern concepts (1999: 1–19). In his book *National Identity*, Anthony D. Smith holds that according to the non-western concept of nation, "whether one belonged to a community or emigrated to another, one remained organically a member of the community of one's birth and one's identity was stamped by it" (1991: 11). Many theories of nation and nationalism do not hold true for South Asian nations like Pakistan or Bangladesh. There have been the

DOI: 10.4324/9781003158424-13

formation and de-formation of nations that contest the idea of a nation as a fixed entity, bounded by territory, tradition, collective memory, or birth. The multi-national character of some South Asian nations also contests the uniformity that one expects from a nation, as S. L. Sharma and T. K. Oommen, in *Nation and National Identity in South Asia*, put it – "South Asia provides a fascinating laboratory for the study of the national question, for testing the formulations derived from the West, and also for generating new formulations" (2000: ix).

Nationalism has been a source of integration as well as conflict. Religion and nationalism played an important role in the partition of the Indian subcontinent in 1947. The fear of alienation among the Muslim population was operational there, as it was in 1971 (with the economic disparity between West and East Pakistan and the question of state language).[1] South Asian nations like India, Pakistan, and Bangladesh showcase how the idea of a 'nation' can lead to animosity and violence. The history of the rise of these nations is a narrative of conflict. The creation of Pakistan with its two wings, East and West, which were territorially distant, also makes it a "psychic projection" (Devji 2013: 6). If a nation is seen as an ideology, it can be imagined in new ways, as Faisal Devji talks about "the paradox of rejecting nationalism while desiring it at the same time" (Ibid.: 4) in the context of Pakistan and Israel. The "long shadow" (Butalia 2015: vii) of the national question is still a cause of conflict among these South Asian nations. Tahmima Anam has often highlighted that she refutes the idea of borders, as they may not be sustainable in the long run, as Tagore refutes the idea of all nations.

Islamic and Bengali identities/cultures shape national identity in Bangladesh (Phadnis 1989: 108), although the constitution of Bangladesh formulated in 1971 mentions secularism as one of the principles. There has been a growing Islamic sensibility in the vernacular cultural model of Bangladesh; as Willem Van Schendel puts it,

> Officially Bangladesh is still a 'people's republic' but to most of the citizens, the old ideals sound pretty hollow. Only nationalism has withstood the ravages of time. Socialism and secularism were ditched in the mid-1970s, and democracy has had a chequered and interrupted career.
>
> (2009: 251)

For the growing Islamic sensibility, Schendel lists causes like a period of military rule, migrants to the Gulf bringing in notions of Islamic decorum, Islamic groups receiving financial aid from West Asia, insecurity of a lower middle class who fails to acquire 'bhodrolok' self-esteem and turn to Islam, and the quest for positive values/faith in people who are disgusted with the growing urban jungle and corruption (2009: 252). Tahmima Anam, in her Bengal trilogy, shows how a search for solace and purpose after one is touched by disturbing events (war or personal loss) can turn people towards religion.

Tahmima Anam's Bengal trilogy – *A Golden Age*, *The Good Muslim*, and *The Bones of Grace* – charts the lives of three generations of Bangladeshi characters and brings the lesser-known history of the Bangladeshi Liberation War into the global domain in an unprecedented way. There are, of course, Bangladeshi writers like Adib Khan, Shaheen Akhtar, or Mahmudul Haque who have written on the war. In Anam's novels, however, the past, present, and future – pre-war, war, and post-war scenarios – are highlighted in a complex trajectory of individual lives caught up in the whirlwind of time. This chapter intends to show how the past of conflicts, on religious and national grounds, casts a "long shadow" upon the subsequent generations as depicted in the novels. The chapter, while interrogating the mutability of national identity, seeks to highlight how political events before, during, and after the 1971 War of Independence altered/politicized individual relationships and the dynamics of conflict in Bangladesh. Tahmima Anam questions the fundamental positions on war, conflict, religion, and nationalism. Anam believes that writing fiction is an act of protest for her. In an interview with Amy Finnerty, Tahmima Anam opines on protest and politics:

> I am unapologetically and emphatically interested in politics. I believe writing is an act of protest, in that we are asked to question our fundamental positions by entering into the point of view of another person. This act of stepping outside of ourselves and into the lives of others is a radical and radically political act. Having said that we need to expand our notion of the political. It isn't just writing about revolutions or armed struggles, it can also be about the politics of the family or relationships.
>
> (2015: 45–46)

Anam suggests that one can expand one's notion of the political by extending it to the politics of family and relationships, and this chapter seeks to explore this facet of politics in relation to the war, religion, and the national question.

A Golden Age: "my golden Bengal, how I adore you"

Tahmima Anam's *A Golden Age* explores love, nationalism, sacrifice and chronicles the events from March 1971 to December 1971, the nine months of struggle which led to the emergence of an independent nation, Bangladesh, keeping the Haque family at its center. The novel is narrated from Rehana's point of view. The main thread of the novel is woven against the backdrop of the armed struggle between the Pakistani armed forces and the East Bengali nationalists. The nature of conflict in Bangladesh is multi-layered, and Tahmima Anam deals with many of these issues – communalism, the plight of minorities, women as victims, the question of sacrifice, and the geopolitical games.

'The Prologue,' set in March 1959, carries a sense of loss (in Rehana's separation from her children, who, according to court orders, would remain in the custody of her brother-in-law and thus were taken to Lahore) as Rehana's voice, talking to her dead husband, sets the tone of mutability: "Dear Husband,/I lost our children today" (Anam 2012a: 3). This separation of Rehana and her children, Sohail and Maya, where the children are taken to West Pakistan (in Lahore) and Rehana stays back in East Pakistan (in Dhaka), marks the symbolic breach of relationship or distance between the two wings of Pakistan. Rehana's sisters are married, and they are all settled in West Pakistan. Rehana has not seen her sisters for years. Rehana, with her decision to stay in East Pakistan after her husband's death, offends her family, who expect her to be in Karachi. Her sisters see it as an act of betrayal, just as the "war is generally viewed as an act of 'betrayal' by Bengalis" (Saikia 2011: 4). Rehana holds her sisters "by a loose bit of feeling, not fully connected, not entirely severed" (Anam 2012a: 19), like how the two wings of Pakistan are held together. Her parents, who lived in India (Calcutta), are no more. The familial relationships and the geographical areas they navigate weave India, Pakistan, and Bangladesh together – all parts of the millennia-old civilization. During the civil war, Rehana finds herself siding with the revolutionaries, drawing a line between herself and her sisters or her brothers-in-law. Anam explores this politics of relationships in all her novels together with the politics of the nation, which seems to work on the principle of inclusion and exclusion.

The tales of 1971 begin with Rehana's annual party to mark the day she brought back her children to Dhaka. The house, 'Shona,' which she builds and rents out, gives her the necessary means to bring her children back. Her children, Sohail and Maya, are now nineteen and seventeen, respectively. They wait for Mujib to be declared the prime minister. The youth is swayed by the revolutionary spirit. Sohail and Maya are no exceptions. The Assembly gets postponed indefinitely, as "Bhutto's convinced Yahya there can't be a Bengali running Pakistan" (Anam 2012a: 44). On 7 March 1971, Mujib calls a meeting and Sohail insists that his mother should attend the meeting. Mujib is loved "the way orphans dream of their lost parents: without promise, only hope" (Ibid.: 51), and the citizens of East Pakistan can be seen as orphans in their sense of not belonging to a nation and in their desire for a yet-to-be nation. As Rehana attends the public meeting, she feels convinced in the idea of a new nation. She sees new possibilities.

When the cyclone hits Bangladesh in 1970, Sohail and Maya join the rescue operations and are disappointed to see no help coming from the Pakistani government. Maya then joins the student Communist party and, to Rehana's dismay, she starts wearing only white saris. Sohail, on the other hand, refuses to join any of the student movements, "claiming he couldn't be swayed by one faction or another" (35). Sohail is popular in his university, and everyone knows how committed he is to the cause. He loves Bengal and everything Bengali. His love for Urdu poetry, which he has inherited from his mother, poses no threat or contradiction. After Silvi, the girl whom Sohail loves, gets married to Sabeer, an army officer, and his friends join the liberation war, Sohail too joins the war. On the fateful day of 25 March 1971, Pakistan's dictator, Yahya Khan, in his bid to assert dominance and quell Bengali nationalism, orders a military attack led by General Tikka Khan, the Butcher of Bengal, on East Pakistani citizens. Attempts are made to crush the police and the paramilitary East Pakistan Rifles. The army also targets the slums and Dhaka University, attacks Hindu citizens, razes the Shahid Minar (symbol of the Language Movement), and arrests Sheikh Mujibur Rahman (67). As the military crackdown Operation Searchlight happens, Silvi's mother becomes hysterical and arranges the marriage of her daughter to Sabeer. Lieutenant Sabeer (an officer of the Pakistani army turned revolutionary whom Rehana later brings back from the cell for Sohail's sake, as he believes that it will melt Silvi's heart) is in a fix when the crackdown happens, and later we see him as a prisoner of the Pakistani army after he joins the Liberation war. The next evening, the commander-in-chief of the Bangladesh Liberation Army makes an announcement on the radio that he, on behalf of Mujib, proclaims the independence of Bangladesh. Many people take refuge in villages, and many cross the border to India. Rehana's tenants Mr. Sengupta and his family decide to move to their village in Pabna, as "it's not safe for Hindus in the city" (74). (Later, Rehana finds Mrs. Sengupta at a refugee camp in Calcutta, while there is no trace of Mr. Sengupta and their child.) The young are leaving their houses and joining the resistance. Thus, Sohail's doubts about becoming a soldier slowly disappear, and he embraces the war with a sense of devotion – "So this was it: a war had come to find them. Whatever was going to happen had already happened; now they would have to live in its shadow" (68).

The novel dwells on the identity of the Urdu-speaking Haque family in East Pakistan as the loyalty of Rehana Haque is tested. Rehana suffers from a sense of guilt for letting her children go to Lahore, and that guilt constantly nudges her to prove her loyalty to her children and to the cause of the nation they are fighting for. Rehana believes that she does not have the "proper trappings of a nationalist" – youth, appearance, words. There is ambiguity in her sense of nationalism. Urdu and Bengali give Rehana a "mixed tongue" (49). Later, as Sohail warns her to watch out for the Urdu-speaking[2] butchers, Urdu-speaking Biharis who are rumored to have sided with the army, Rehana sees how Urdu has become the language of her enemy. However, she cannot imagine home as anywhere other than East Pakistan. After the military crackdown, when the nationalist fervor reaches its peak and Rehana worries about the safety of her children, Maya challenges Rehana's loyalty to Bengal. In the heat of the moment, Maya blurts out, "Sohail . . . where is he now? Probably dead, killed by one of your Pak soldiers!" (92). Rehana, in order to prove her loyalty, donates all her expensive saris to make *kathas* (blankets) for the soldiers and refugees. She forms a sewing group and announces, "I'm doing something. Making blankets for the refugees . . . . Everyone has to make sacrifices, why not me? It's my country too" (95). Resistance becomes more organized after a government-in-exile is formed in India and more and more young men and women join the *Mukti Bahini* (Freedom Fighters). Those who are unable to join the *Mukti Bahini* directly help the fighters by giving them food and shelter. Rehana's house, Shona, becomes a hideout for guerillas and their weapons. She also gives shelter to and nurses a wounded major with whom she eventually falls in love, and the major, too, demonstrates his love through his final act of sacrifice – protecting Sohail and surrendering himself to the army.

Tahmima Anam also brings in the predicament of women, the victims of war, through the character of Sharmeen, Maya's closest friend. Anam, however, explores the women's question at length in her next novel, *The Good Muslim*. Maya is shaken as her friend Sharmeen, a sturdy young girl, is raped by Tikka Khan's soldiers, becomes pregnant, and dies. Sohail and Rehana, who are concerned about Maya, eventually send her to Calcutta. Maya attempts to help the government in exile there; she writes press statements and does her bit for her friend. Anam raises her voice of dissent against waging war in the name of religion in the novel. She describes the Pakistani soldiers as "explorers, pioneers of cruelty, every day out doing their own brutality, every day feeling closer to divinity because they were told they were saving Pakistan, and Islam, maybe even the Almighty himself, from the depravity of the Bengalis" (133). Anam also makes a critique of religion through the character Silvi, who suddenly turns to religion and conservatism and thinks that there is no reason to condemn the genocide, as it is a sin to sever a Muslim homeland. She says, "Pakistan should stay together. That's why it was conceived. To keep the Ummah united. To separate the wings is a sin against your religion" (260). However, on 16 December 1971, the Pakistani army is forced to surrender, leading to the emergence of an independent Bangladesh. 1971 suddenly becomes the focal point of the delta's national history, cutting off its national history linked to 1947. Anam explores and questions this hope for a golden Bengal in her subsequent novels.

The Good Muslim: questioning radical Islam

While in 1947, the Islamic notion fuels a sense of belongingness to a new nation for the people of the delta, a regional identity emerges later. They are now Bengalis first and Muslims later – "Islam was important as part of the majority culture and as a matter of personal faith, but it was not part of national identity" (Schendel 2009: 183). This change of identity from Bengali *Muslims* to Muslim *Bengalis* has been possible because "a dual Bengali-Islamic identity had roots going back centuries in the Bengal delta" (Ibid.: 183). However, with the country's independence and subsequent military rule, Islam replaces secularism and the 'Bengali' national identity. The nation's transformation is reflected in the personal transformation of Sohail. *The Good Muslim* is narrated from Maya's perspective. The novel's plot moves between the 1970s and the 80s. The 'Prologue' is set in 1971 and the 'Epilogue' in 1992. In 1972–73, people are seen in a state of euphoria, ready to brush away the past. While people are busy designing their future, Sohail and Maya struggle to come out of the shadows of the past.

Schendel highlights how "by 1974 the dream of a Golden Bengal had turned out to be a chimera" (Ibid.: 180), with floods and famine hitting the population of Bangladesh along with the failure of the government to resolve any socio-economic-political issue of the land. In January 1972, when Sheikh Mujibur Rahman is released from Pakistani captivity, he takes on the leadership and forms a parliamentary government, the constitution of which asserts that the republic is based on the principles of 'nationalism, socialism, democracy, and secularism' (*Gonoprojatontri Bangladesher Shongbidhan* 1972: 12). There are three immediate concerns of the young state – dealing with the collaborators of war, the war victims, and developing the nation. However, Bangladesh's economy falls like never before. Corruption and coercion emerge and lead to dissatisfaction and unrest. In 1975, the government introduces a single-party presidential system, and in the same year, with the assassination of Sheikh Mujibur Rahman, the country is taken over by military rule. After Mujib's assassination, the people of Bangladesh remain in the political hands of the military-backed government. Major-General Ziaur Rahman (Zia) (1975–81) emerges as a ruler after the first military coup, and the second military coup sees Hussain Muhammad Ershad (1982–90) as the ruler. Bangladesh was under military rule from 1975 to 1990. Widespread agitation in 1990 finally manages to topple military rule in favor of parliamentary democracy. During military rule, basic/civil rights are much more curtailed than in the initial year. Schendel says that this truth is hardly accepted by a large number of people in Bangladesh (Schendel 2009: 197). However, Tahmima Anam raises her voice of protest through the novel. Towards the end of the novel, we find that Maya's article, where she calls the dictator a "war criminal" (Anam 2012b: 285), lands her in prison. Tahmima Anam highlights the growing tendency towards Islamization and the rise of Islamic politics during military rule. In politics, Islamic symbols are reintroduced by Zia as "he purged secularism from the Bangladesh constitution, instead of inserting Islam in its preamble" (Schendel 2009: 203), and this trend further escalates with Ershad, who abandons secularism and declares Islam the state religion. Maya's aversion to the state of affairs in Bangladesh is obvious:

> On Independence Day, Maya switched on the television and saw the Dictator laying wreaths at Shaheed Minar, the Martyrs'Memorial . . . . Last month he had tried to change the name of the country to the Islamic Republic of Bangladesh . . . . Now, on the anniversary of the day the Pakistani Army ran its tanks over Dhaka, he was making a speech about the war. Eager to befriend the old enemy, he said nothing about the killings. He praised the importance of regional unity. All Muslims are Brothers, he repeated. She couldn't bear to listen.
>
> (Anam 2012b: 42)

Maya finds it difficult to grasp how people – the local vendors, her friends – have changed their vocabulary. Saima's "Alhamdulillah" bothers her, as does the vegetable man's "Allah Hafez." Women increasingly embrace 'Purdah.'

The protagonist of Adib Khan's novel, *Spiral Road*, rightly highlights, "You can create illusions of nobility and great deeds, and hide behind them. But recollections and the guilt surface later" (Khan 2008: 121). Sohail is deeply disturbed after the war. He has killed an innocent man. He keeps thinking of all the people who have died. The specter of the war keeps haunting him, in dreams "that have him pacing the hallway at night, the ones that leave his pillows wet and his mouth frozen stiffly" (Anam 2012b: 92). His mother gives him the Book, and when he refuses to take it, she starts reading passages from it to console him. Later, it hurts Rehana to see the transformation in her son, and she blames herself for it. Rehana, though deeply religious, resists fundamentalism. When the children have been given into the custody of her brother-in-law, the judge also mentions how Rehana "had not taught them the proper lessons about Jannat and the afterlife" (Anam 2012a: 5). After Sohail survives the war, he clings to religion, believing that God loves him and that he lives on for a purpose. Sohail becomes popular for his *bayaan*, his sermons. He builds a completely different world and leads a detached life, drowning the voices of the war, as Andreas Huyssen rightly points out, "every act of memory carries with it a dimension of betrayal, forgetting, and absence" (Huyssen 2003: 4). The afterlife that is promised in the book becomes more important for him. He goes through stages of transformation. His sermons begin with recitations from "the *Torah*, the *Gita*, the *Bible*," and then his worldview narrows down to the "only one" (Anam 2012b: 179) – the *Qur'an*.

Maya, on the other hand, returns home in 1984 after seven years of staying away from Sohail's transformed self. In those years, she has served as a country doctor, helping women deliver their babies. Silvi's death perhaps makes her return possible. She takes her time to get adjusted to the changed city and the changed circumstances of her house. On her return, she remembers how much she has always loved her brother, "how fiercely she needed him to be like her, how she had turned away when he had leaned towards God, taken it personally, as though he had done it to offend her" (17). Maya has always blamed Silvi for filling her brother's mind with weird ideas, and now Silvi, the widow of Sabeer, wife of Sohail, and mother of Zaid is no more. Zaid is a neglected child who steals and lies, and Maya now wants to take Zaid under her wing. However, Sohail is reluctant to send his son to school – secular education and the comforts of living being prohibited. His son is packed off to a madrasa, where, along with physical and emotional hardships, he is also subjected to sexual abuse. Only when Rehana is ill with cancer does Maya try to seek solace in religion. It is a moment of weakness, and Maya tries to shake it off to find momentary solace in it again in accepting forgiveness for herself when Zaid dies during her attempts to save him from the huzoor of the madrasa. A secular point of view is, therefore, expressed through the character of Maya whose concerns, on the other hand, revolve around poverty, filth, and corruption in the new nation; the 'birangonas,' as she realizes that "calling them heroines erases what really happened to them" (123); the discrimination against the tribal population of the land, the Garo and the Chakma, who are neither Bengalis nor Muslim and are asked "to become Bengalis, to forget the colonial past and join the Bengali culture" (Schendel 2009: 186); and discrimination against non-Bengali Muslims. The successive governments have also discouraged examination or scrutiny of the war. The plights of the freedom fighters and the victims of war are brushed aside. However, some groups have tried to build up a platform to address grievances. The novel shows Maya's encounter with Jahanara Imam, who forms the Nirmul Committee, and how emotionally charged she feels attending the meetings, sometimes questioning them and at times letting out tears of joy and sorrow on hearing the testimonies and seeing that a public platform is at last given to them.

The epilogue of the novel is set in 1992, and we find that Maya is married to Joy, a freedom fighter, the younger brother of Sohail's best friend, who has died in the war. After the second dictator is overthrown with a popular uprising and civilian government (parliamentary democracy) comes into power, the 'people's court' is staged by Jahanara Imam's Nirmul Committee to get "the people's verdict on the leader of Jamaat-e-Islami, whom they accused of war crimes and treason" (Schendel 2009: 217). They try to bring the prosecution of war criminals into the political agenda.[3] Maya's five-year-old adopted daughter, Zubaida, named after Zaid, accompanies her. Piya, a victim of war, is seen narrating her war testimony. Piya names her son, whom she has refused to abort, Sohail, after the man who saved her life. Maya realizes that her heart will break every time she thinks of her brother's transformed self – a self she doesn't recognize. Anam also tries to understand this process of transformation – a strategy for survival that many have adopted, and through Maya, she shows a sense of acceptance. It is an attempt at understanding a particular personal history, as Anam says – her response to Islam is 'one at a time.'

The Bones of Grace: coming to terms with the "long shadow"

The Bones of Grace is narrated through Zubeida. Zubeida, who represents the third generation of the Haque family, is aware of the "long shadow" of war that frames her parents' life and hers. She shows her understanding of the past when she writes, "what I was in thrall to was the past. This had to do with my parents and the war they had been in, and, as a model for love, for what was possible between two people" (Anam 2016: 13). Zubeida goes to an elite college in America and then to Harvard. It is important to note that international migration in Bangladesh has had a long tradition. By the 1990s, the migration trend had increased manyfold, with the national elites coveting higher education abroad as a status symbol (Schendel 2009: 225–227). However, for Zubeida, living in America has never held charm as it did for many others from her country. Her father, Joy, lived in New York once. He returns to Bangladesh after he has tamed his memories of war, divorcing the woman he has been married to in order to settle there. Zubeida knows the socio-political and economic scenario of her country and understands why everyone wants to escape the country. She sometimes wishes to hate her country but is forced to love it because of her parents' love for the country. Unlike Zubeida, her parents, Joy and Maya, are rooted in the soil of the country. The war is fundamental to their existence, and every time the country falters, Maya and Joy take it personally.

Maya keeps herself busy with the lawyers and the trials of men who aided and abetted the army. She tries to help the Birangonas, many of whom, in their sixties now, still live in the camps set up for them just after independence. The given name becomes a "label for life" (Anam 2016: 311) for all sorts of discrimination. Maya dwells in those dark spaces, guilt haunting her being (as she was a part of Mujib's campaign once). However, Zubeida, who represents the third generation, is unsure of her position. She is confronted with questions of loyalty, "I knew my parents questioned whether I cared about the country as much as they did, and I had never really felt the need, or had the courage, to confess that I did not" (325). She admits – "I seek the connection, but resist when the opportunity is offered. My heart is a nomad, still, after so many years of being in this country, child to these parents" (84). Zubeida, however, is aware of the importance of national consciousness in their lives. She comes from a family of skeptics, and she claims – "Nationalism is the religion in our household" (31). Zubeida cannot ward off the long shadow of war from her psyche, as she sometimes imagines herself as an outcome of rape. She resents the space that war occupies in her life and she fears that she might end up doing nothing significant when compared to her parents. The long shadow of war follows her and "the children of the people who survived, all of us burdened with what we couldn't do" (326). Maya and her friend, Dolly, plot the coming together of Zubeida and Rashid (Dolly's son) for years "because together they formed a single set of hopes" (112). The war lurks in Zubeida's personal space because this marriage is for the mothers "an erasure of history as much as a mark of history" (112).

One can find a sense of diasporic 'inbetweenness' in Zubeida. Zubeida and her friends in America, who come from other countries, refer to themselves as amphibians in America, and it is interesting to note that Zubeida, for her PhD, looks for the bones of an amphibian, "a creature embracing its duality, its attraction to both the lure of the seas and the comforts of the land" (20). The bones' potential to rewrite the history of mankind and Zubeida's quest for her personal history are a journey towards discovery. She was adopted by Joy and Maya two years after their marriage and "fifteen years after the war" (5). The novel is written in the form of a letter that Zubeida addresses to Elijah – an American she first meets as she prepares to leave for Dera Bugti to find a complete skeleton of the ancient whale *Ambulocetus natans*. This meeting is significant as she seriously thinks about her adoption for the first time, and the course of her future is guided by that. The idea of a 'nation' (Bangladesh) has been adopted by the East Pakistani population, and these adoptions (the nation's and Zubeida's) are outcomes of a desire. Zubeida's adoption and her quest for belongingness or rootedness can be seen as symbolic of the nation's quest.

Zubeida's renewed contact with Elijah in Bangladesh is significant because it takes her further into that quest. This is after her miscarriage and strained relationship with Rashid. Zubeida invites Elijah to check out a piano aboard the ship, *Grace*, at the "Prosperity Shipbreaking" (125) in Chittagong where she is offered a job, and he comes. Elijah and Zubeida, in their intimacy, realize how fragile they are. They understand how easily they can be destroyed, just like the ship that is being taken apart. Zubeida finally does not acknowledge her relationship with Elijah in front of her husband, Rashid, as Elijah leaves for America, and she is determined more than ever to know about her adoption, which culminates in her tracing the remnants of the past in the form of discovering the traumatized daughter of her dead twin sister, Megna. In the midst of that, Zubeida walks out of Rashid's life. This discovery of the past – her history – makes her free, and "released me from all the things I believed I couldn't do, wasn't entitled to because my past was a mystery" (54).

The bones she has been looking for and has abandoned become her saving grace, and they take Zubeida again to America as she finds herself putting the pieces of Diana together. Zamzam, who has been in the expedition with her at Dera Bugti and is later arrested, manages to instruct someone to carry forward his last wish before he dies – to send the pieces of Diana (*Ambulocetus natans*) to Zubeida. Now that she has pieced together not just the fossil but herself, Zubeida, along with Prof. Bart and Jimmy, plans to display *Ambulocetus natans* at the Natural History Museum. She hopes that Elijah will come and they will walk hand in hand "past Diana and the glass flowers and Zamzam and Megna and the war my parents fought, all of our ghosts behind us, and before us the terrible, dark world – belonging only to each other" (407). The novel ends with the hope of togetherness, where Zubeida, like the nation (Bangladesh), seeks to leave the ghosts of the past behind.

Conclusion

Bangladesh's history of fragmented, multiple, and ever-changing frontiers eludes any singular identity. Its ideology varies from secular and modern to orthodox and conservative. The personal is, of course, political, as "every hiccup of the political landscape made its way to their door" (Anam 2012a: 134). However, the separation or negotiation of religion and nationalism seems difficult (taking into account the power politics that is involved in the process), as Talal Asad highlights, "in a sense what many would anachronistically call 'religion' was always involved in the world of power" (Asad 2003: 200). There is a long tradition that equates nationalism with religion, where nationalism is sometimes seen as the religion of a nation-state, given its power to unite people, as emphasized by Carlton Hayes, Huxley, Margaret Jacob, and Clifford Geertz, among others. However, Talal Asad, in *Formations of the Secular: Christianity, Islam, Modernity*, questions this association and emphasizes the need to think about what is meant by religion or the secular. Taslima Nasrin, in *Lajja: Shame*, makes a plea to replace religion with humanism, as it is a national shame "if we allow ourselves to be ruled by religious extremism" (Nasrin 1994: ix). To conclude, I would like to emphasize that the voice of protest, coming from these writers, becomes relevant because it comes from the much-coveted domain of 'freedom' – of speech and expression, which is often under censorship, and for protest against ideological violence, religion-induced aggression, or discrimination on communal grounds to be more effective, it is important that it comes from within – the insiders.

Notes

1 The 1952 movement to have Bengali recognized as a state language alongside Urdu after Mohammed Ali Jinnah "declared at the gathering at Dhaka University that Urdu would be the sole state language" (Haq 2015: 3) can be seen as the first step towards self-determination or the beginning of the national struggle of the Eastern Wing of Pakistan. The government was forced to accept the demand, and the Bengalis who sacrificed their lives came to be known as the 'language martyrs.' Their death anniversary (21 Feb) is now recognized as International Mother Language Day.

2 Non-Bengali Muslims (who had migrated after 1947 and who were then wel-
comed as Muhajirs) were looked at with suspicion. Many were Urdu-speaking
Muslims, and they sided with the Pakistani authorities. Bengalis referred to them
as 'Biharis', although not all of them were from Bihar (Schendel 2009: 173). Many
lost their lives at the hands of nationalist mobs.

3 The government did not take this step in good spirits and charged Jahanara
Imam's Nirmul Committee with treason. The committee stands for and has be-
come "an important rallying point for secular and anti-fundamentalist forces in
Bangladesh" (Schendel 2009: 217).

Works cited

Anam, Tahmima. *A Golden Age, 2007.* Edinburgh: Canongate Books, 2012a.

———. *The Good Muslim,* 2011. New Delhi: Penguin, 2012b.

———, Interview by Amy Finnerty. "An Interview with Tahmima Anam." *Wasafiri*
30:4 (Dec., 2015).

———. *The Bones of Grace.* Gurgaon: Hamish Hamilton (Penguin), 2016.

Asad, Talal. *Formations of the Secular: Christianity, Islam, Modernity.* Stanford:
Stanford University Press, 2003.

Butalia, Urvashi, ed. *Partition: The Long Shadow.* New Delhi: Zubaan, 2015.

Devji, Faisal. *Muslim Zion: Pakistan as a Political Idea.* Cambridge, MA: Harvard
University Press, 2013.

Gonoprojatontri Bangladesher Shongbidhan (Constitution of the People's Republic
of Bangladesh). Dhaka: Bangladesh Gonoporishod, 1972.

Haq, Kaiser. "The Hijra Comes in from the Heat and Dust: Notes Towards a Definition of Bangladeshi Writing in English." *Wasafiri* 30:4 (2015).

Huyssen, Andreas. *Present Pasts: Urban Palimpsests and the Politics of Memory.*
Stanford: Stanford University Press, 2003.

Kedourie, Elie. *Nationalism.* Oxford: Basil Blackwell, 1994.

Khan, Adib. *Spiral Road,* 2007. Noida: Harper Collins, 2008.

Nasrin, Taslima. *Lajja: Shame,* 1993. New Delhi: Penguin, 1994.

Phadnis, Urmila. *Ethnicity and Nation-Building in South Asia.* New Delhi: Sage,
1989.

Saikia, Yasmin. *Women, War and the Making of Bangladesh: Remembering 1971.*
Karachi: Oxford University Press, 2011.

Schendel, Willem Van. *A History of Bangladesh.* London: Cambridge University
Press, 2009.

Sharma, S. L., and T. K. Oommen, eds. *Nation and National Identity in South Asia.*
New Delhi: Orient Longman, 2000.

Smith, Anthony D. *National Identity.* London: Penguin Books, 1991.

———. *Myths and Memories of the Nation.* Oxford: Oxford University Press, 1999.

10

SITUATING RELIGIOSITY IN NINETEENTH-CENTURY ASSAM

Reading Tilottama Misra's *Swarnalata*

Sibsankar Majumdar

One of the most prominent phenomena associated with the social-cultural reformation in nineteenth-century Bengal is the Brahmo Movement, which emerged in Calcutta in 1828, and by the mid-eighteenth century, the Brahmos had made considerable progress within the upper echelon of natives in colonial society. The primary objective of prominent Brahmo Samajists like Ramohan Roy, Dwarkanath Tagore, Devendranath Tagore, Keshav Chandra Sen, and others was to reform Hindu society by coalescing the sensibilities of Vedic spiritualism with rational thinking. As this influence gradually extended past the periphery of Bengal, it inspired young people from the neighboring regions to visit Calcutta, the second-largest city of the British Empire, which was gradually transforming itself into the greatest destination for Western education in the East. These young people desired to seek and share the progressive humanitarian spirit of science, culture, and literature. The youth of Assam, the frontier province of the British-Indian empire, were not an exception in this regard. The biographies, memoires, letters, and correspondence of nineteenth-century Assamese literary-cultural icons like Anandaram Dhekiyal Phukan, Gunabhiram Barua, Lakshminath Bezbaroa, Padmanath Gohain Barua, Benudhar Rajkhowa, and Manikchandra Barua are rich in references to years spent in Calcutta in an atmosphere of intellectual exuberance. Of the pioneering Assamese intellectuals, on whom the impact of the Bengal Renaissance was most visible, Gunabhiram Barua turns out to be one of the most prominent. Ideas of socio-cultural reformation advocated by Raja Rammohan Roy, Iswar Chandra Vidyasagar, and Keshav Chandra Sen had a profound impact on Gunabhiram. He was inspired to embrace the Brahmo faith. Later, he played a crucial role in "sowing the seeds" of socio-religious and cultural reforms of the Brahmo Samaj in Assam (Chattopadhyay 1998: 621). By the time of his return to Assam, he was quintessentially saturated in the ideas of resistance to Brahminical hegemony and widow remarriage, which found a powerful expression in *Ram-Navami Natak*, a play Gunabhiram wrote during a week-long passage from Calcutta to Nagaon in the

DOI: 10.4324/9781003158424-14

winter of 1857. *Ram-Navami Natak* showcases the deplorable condition of Hindu widows in Assamese society during the first part of the nineteenth century. Its passionate justification for widow remarriage outraged Assamese Brahmins, but his next course of action, marrying a widow called Bishnupriya, made him an outright object of hatred for the orthodox Hindus of nineteenth-century Assam. Gunabhiram's family was ostracized and branded as *mlechhas* (i.e. untouchable).

The intellectual class of late nineteenth-century Assam can be broadly classified into two groups – the first group includes Calcutta-educated emancipatory idealists like Jagnaram Khargaria Phukan, Anadaram Dhekial Phukan, Padmanath Gohain Barua, Manik Chandra Barua, Laxminath Bezbaruah, Jagannath Barua, Kalicharan Mech, and so on, and another group includes individuals like Padmahash Goswami, Kamala Kanta Bhattacharya, Hem Chandra Barua, and Braja Sundari Devi, who received most of their education in Assam. Luminaries from both these factions actively participated in a series of reformative activities:

> opening schools for the education of both boys and girls, supporting widow remarriage and opposing polygamy. They submitted memorandums to the government to lighten the tax burden, change the opium policy, increase the number of law courts and give due recognition to the Assamese language.
>
> (Banerjee 2006: 23)

By the 1870, the first groups of Brahmo emissaries from Bengal started undertaking travels to Assam to propagate their faith among the natives of this hilly region. It was a time of significant socio-cultural transformation in the frontier region, where the Brahmo movement was slated to play the role of a catalyst. Accounts of caste prejudice and other forms of socio-cultural superstitions prevalent among Assamese people can be found in the correspondence of Pandit Shibanath Shastri, eminent Brahmo litterateur of nineteenth-century Bengal, who visited Assam in 1981 with his friend Ramkumar Vidyaratna. Shastri describes an incident in Nagaon which might shed some light on the social customs of the common people of Assam:

> We were very thirsty . . . . Soon we spied the Government inspection bunglow on a little mound close to us. We went there and asked the Assamese servant there for water. He had a little glass which he refused to lend us. He did not agree to pour water on our hands lest the pitcher should get touched by us. Mr. Ganguly (one of Shastri's companions) went in search of some big leaves to make cup-shaped thing. While he was away I began to preach to this man. I said the same God has created both you and me. In

His eyes we are brothers. We are dying from thirst and you have the water, yet you cannot give it to us in the time of dire need. Are you not ashamed that you refuse to give us the water He has given freely to all? Perhaps my reproaches touched his heart; he gave me his glass to drink from.

(Ray 1988: 165)

Tilottama Misra's *Swarnalata*, a fictional biography of the famous Barua family, represents a composite picture of life and times in Eastern India during the nineteenth century by comparing and contrasting domestic and social realities between the greatest city of the British Empire, Calcutta, and Nagaon, a mofussil town in Assam. The novel highlights the zeal of Brahmo Samajists to take the light of reform into the farthest corners of Assam, especially among the disadvantaged people from the hills and forests of this region who were caught in the web of age-old ignorance and superstitions. At the heart of this narrative also lies the issue of the rise of 'new women,' resisting and challenging the dictates of patriarchy in colonial Assamese society. Misra's motive behind writing this novel can be perceived from her observation, "the complacence and obscurantism of ages summed up as tradition was beginning to be questioned by new ideas based on reason and tolerance" (2001: v). Her portrayal of the ideological conflicts within the Brahmo Samaj and personality clashes among the Samajists in colonial Calcutta constitutes one of the principal attractions of this novel. At the same time, Misra provides us a glimpse of a small group of Assamese students and professionals from Calcutta who started viewing this newfound reformative zeal "with growing apprehension" (Misra 2007: 39). Especially the progress made by women's education in Bengal made this faction very restless. There was also a strong sense of apprehension within the native Assamese society that "if this tendency to give masculine education to women is encouraged in Assam, the result may be disastrous for traditional hierarchical social structure" (39). My objective in this chapter is to offer a few observations on the contemporary milieu of Assamese society by highlighting the paradoxical impulses of fear and apprehension coupled with robust optimism in the spirit of reformation through a minute reading of Tilottama Misra's *Swarnalata*.

Towards the end of the novel, there is a small passage in which Tilottama Misra describes Gunabhiram's great interest in ideas of emancipation and empowerment of women espoused by Michael Madhusudan Dutt, an iconic non-conformist Bengali litterateur. Swarnalata Barua, Gunabhiram's daughter, finds a copy of Michael's *Birangana Kabya* in a book shop. She presents it to her father:

That evening, much like earlier days, Gunabhiram was seen passionately reading poetry. Reciting Madhusudhan's verse in a full-throated manner, he explained to his daughter the significance of

140

women's liberation. Swarna was simply enraptured and a surge of self-confidence swept over her.

(Misra 2001: 265)

Set against the backdrop of a fundamentally conservative and the backward society where "forces of traditions were being challenged by the new concepts of modernity," Tilottama Misra presents a realistic picture of life and times in Assam under the colonial regime by juxtaposing it against the spirit of Enlightenment, which was swaying the society of *bhdraloks* in Calcutta. As the title suggests, *Swarnalata* revolves around the life of its eponymous character, who is the only child of a colonial official-cum-social reformer, Gunabhiram Baruah. The novel brings to life a host of eminent historical personalities of Bengal and Assam like Laxminath Bezbaruah, Devendranath Tagore, Rabindranath Tagore, and so on, along with a few fictional characters. Misra's dexterous handling of the narrative through a skilful blending of facts and fiction makes it one of the best specimens of historical fiction. *Swarnalata* begins on an arresting note as the narrator provides us a glimpse into the arduousness of the journey from Calcutta to Nagaon by road and partly on steamers through the waterways. However, in spite of the hazardous transportation, Calcutta retained a great fascination in the minds of upper-class Assamese natives, especially its educated section, as an epicenter of enlightenment:

> Though the journey between Nagaon and Calcutta had been considerably reduced after the introduction of the steamer service on the Brahmaputra, yet it still took some nine to ten days to make the journey. But despite its geographical distance, Calcutta was not very far from the Brahmos of Nagaon. They would be posted with news about the metropolis, from the letters, papers and journals that kept coming from Calcutta at regular intervals.
>
> (Misra 2001: 80)

The plot of *Swarnalata* is based on the intertwined lives of three women, Swarnalata, Tora, and Lakhipriya, who belong to different social strata of colonial Assamese society. These three women are caught in a whirlwind of socio-cultural transformation, desperately trying to decode a future course of life. Fearlessly facing the odd limitations and challenges in their individual circumstances, these three women continue their struggle to break free from confinement. Swarnalata turns out to be lucky, since she is the daughter of a liberal social reformer. Her parents decide to "shape her as an ideal of the new age" (Misra 2001: 71). She is indoctrinated in the values of western enlightenment, civil liberty, and religious tolerance by her parents. Gunabhiram appoints Panchanan Sharma, a lawyer and the father of Lakhipriya, as a private tutor for Swarnalata before sending her to Calcutta for further studies. He has a firm conviction in the ancient principles of Hinduism and believes

141

that for "shedding one's petty prejudices" and "learning to view the world in the light of modern liberal ideas brought in by western education," one does not "need to give up his Hindu faith" (Misra 2001: 12). For Gunabhiram, "the Brahmo faith" is "a higher stage of Hinduism" which represents "a unique synthesis of ancient Vedic beliefs and modern rationalist views" (12).

Unlike Swarnalata's refined Brahmo upbringing, Tora, the daughter of Golapi, grows up in a family of Christian converts. She receives her basic education from missionaries. From early childhood, she shows an ambitious spirit, and due to her upbringing with Christian missionaries, she imbibes liberal values. Characteristically, she is a very ambitious girl, who is admired by Swarnalata for her psychological attributes. Swarna envisions Tora growing up as a girl of superlative capabilities unparalleled in studies as well as in "singing, sewing, knitting" (Misra 2001: 34). Gunabhiram is also greatly impressed by this little girl and observes in an interesting context that, "If only our girls have similar aims in life, then our society would have prospered fast" (72). Of these three women, it is Lakhipriya who struggles the most in life. Her father, Panchanan Sharma, who is a considerably educated person, does not show any real concern for Lakhipriya's education. It is only when he begins providing tuition to Swarnalata that he decides to take Lakhipriya with him to the Barua household. But before long, Lakhipriya's marriage is fixed, and then an unthinkable tragedy occurs – Lakhipriya becomes a widow even before entering her husband's home. She is compelled to lead a life of complete austerity following the conservative customs of Hindu society prescribed for widows. Lakhipriya puts up a stiff fight against her own family as well as the rest of the society to pursue further education. She has to be admitted to a boy's school, as there is no school for girls in Nagaon at the time. She is routinely tormented and humiliated by the boys at school. In spite of all these hardships, she excels in studies and becomes a teacher. Her marriage to Dharmakanta sends "shock waves throughout Nagaon," and as a result, the family members of the bride and the groom do not attend the marriage ceremony (236).

The leading female characters in *Swarnalata* represent the 'new women' of Gunabhiram's Brahmo vision. It portrays the growth of the three leading female characters after the manner of a *bildungsroman*. Their struggle echoes the struggle of progressive Indian women in the nineteenth century who were attempting to break free from the shackles of social taboos and constraints. Interestingly, unlike Tora or Lakhipriya, the character of Swarnalata, the protagonist of the novel, can't be seen undergoing any significant transformation. More than an agent, she is rather a 'product' of reformist activities. She dutifully follows the wishes and advice of her parents and does whatever is expected of her. Her parents have molded her nature perfectly to present her as an 'ideal modern women,' an embodiment of superlative Victorian virtues. From early childhood, she has been taught ideal table manners. She is always expected to act according to societal norms and be a "good girl" and keep her voice subdued and not disturb her father during his study time, but there are occasions in the novel when she dares to raise her voice to show her resentment against the orthodox norms of Hindu society:

> To hide a face behind the veil is not bashful. The meaning of bashful is the fear to do anything wrong who fearlessly goes ahead and distances from wrong-doings is bashful. Those memsahibs who do good work are all coy, even if they never wear veils and move around together with men. That is the real meaning of a woman's independence.
>
> (Misra 2001: 195)

This statement shows the rebellious aspect of her character. Unlike, Swarnalata, Lakhipriya has a voice of her own. She does not shy away from fighting with her own family and relatives for her rights. Lakhi is rather ahead of her time. Dharmakanta admires Lakhipriya for her strong determination and liberal views. She supports him and inspires him to work for the country. While engaging in a conversation with a distant relative of her first husband, Lakheswar, she innocently asks, "If there is no harm in a man marrying a second time, what is wrong if a woman does it?" (2001: 207) Tora is also very passionate and full of zeal. She belongs to the lower strata of society where female education is a taboo, but through her grit and passion, she overcomes these odds and fulfils her dreams. She dedicates her life to the cause of society and also inspires others to do the same. After marriage, she supports her husband to continue with his education. As a supreme example of bravery, she sacrifices her life while trying to save a little boy. It is chiefly through these three characters that the novelist portrays the predicament of Assamese women caught in the quagmire of orthodoxy and parochialism.

Along with the depiction of the struggles of women against different kinds of prohibitions, another major preoccupation of Misra has been to expose the patriarchal hypocrisy in Assamese society. *Swarnalata* exposes the attitude of Assamese elites caught in the web of deep-rooted customs, strange rituals supporting orthodoxy in the name of tradition. Through the character of Panchanan Sharma, Misra hits the hardest at the heart of the patriarchal hypocrisy. Though Panchanan is a regular visitor to Bilwa Kutir, that is, the Barua household, he steadfastly refuses to accept their food. He also sternly instructs his daughter to do the same. Moreover, he dutifully carries his mat to Bilwa Kutir every day, and his daughter brings it back home after the tutorial is over. Lakhipriya can only enter home after a ritual bath each time she returns from Bilwa Kutir. Baruahs are considered *mleccha* by the Brahmins; however, the conservative headmen refrain from openly exhibiting their resentment against the family members because of Gunabhiram's high position under the colonial government. However, the Barua family continues to be a hot topic of gossip and object of ridicule among other families of their neighborhood. Outwardly, these people respect Gunabhiram and Bishnupriya,

143

but they are never invited to religious gatherings and social functions. The orthodox Assamese Hindus of nineteenth-century Assam practiced social distancing not only from Christians but also from Brahmos, which would be clear from Pandit Ramtanu Lahiri's letter quoted previously. Moreover, Gunabhiram did something which was considered a great sin by the Hindu priestly class. His act of marrying a Brahmin widow, Bishnupriya, was singled out as a definite attempt to undermine the Hindu socio-religious structure by a man who apparently had sold his soul to Christian foreigners. That the influential sections of the society of Assamese Hindus were not ready to accept him becomes evident during Lakhipriya's marriage. Panchanan is categorically warned by the orthodox priestly class that they cannot dine with Bishnupriya and Swarnalata since they consider them *mlechhas*. Even Lakheswar, Lakhipriya's husband, who harbors emancipatory sensibilities, considers widow marriage an obscene act and advises his wife not to read *Ram-Navami Natak*, a play based on the theme of widow remarriage, written by Gunabhiram Baruah.

Nineteenth-century Assamese society hardly exhibited any genuine concern for female education. In his autobiography titled *Mor Jivan-Xuoron*, Laxminath Bezbarua mentions that his mother (his father had two wives) could only read a few select episodes from Kashiram Das's *Mahabharata*, but she did not know how to write (Bezbarua 56). Patriarchs in traditional Assamese families did not show much concern for educating their womenfolk until the mid-twentieth century. In *Swarnalata*, Panchanan is rudely shocked when Gunabhiram asks him to educate his daughters. On hearing his proposal, Panchanan's elder brother starts quoting all the relevant sections from Hindu scriptures to convince Panchanan that "the true meaning of women's education lay in their doing their household duties well and in providing succor and satisfaction to the husband at all times" (Misra 2001: 28). Most importantly, he mentions that educated women are "by and large thought to be women of ill repute," since they are in the habit of spending their leisure time reading bad books (28). Tilottama Misra draws our attention to this issue through the portrayal of the character of Lakhipriya:

[Lakhipriya's] struggle to educate herself, the rather unexpected support that she receives from a conservative and tradition-bound father, the humiliations that she faces and her eventual triumph in securing a job as a teacher and marrying the man of her choice makes for absorbing reading and effectively throws light on one of the major social issues of the nineteenth century.

(Misra 2001: v–vi)

Ironically, some of the reformers of the Brahmo Samaj themselves did not seem to have been very confident on the question of female education, uncomfortably caught, as they were, in a conflict between traditional value systems versus modern ideologies. Ramkumar Bidyaratna was sent to Assam in 1878 immediately after the inception of Sadharan Brahmo Samaj for propagating the novel principles of Brahmo philosophy. He undertakes an extensive trip from Dhubri to Goalpara, Barpeta, Guwahati, Nagaon, Jorhat, and Shivsagar before moving on to Shillong eventually. Detailed accounts of this trip are available in his *Udasin Satyasrabar Assam Bhraman* (1881), a travelogue which he published after his return to Bengal. In different sections of this travelogue, he laments the absence of basic education among the women of Assamese society. Like most other chief Brahmo ideologues, he also suggests that some elementary knowledge of science should be imparted to women, but the larger focus of female education should be on molding them as ideal wives and mothers in order to secure the domestic sphere. More importantly, he also writes that ideal Brahmo women must educate their children and help them become responsible citizens. The prominent Brahmo ideologues of nineteenth-century Bengal, steeped in Victorian modernity, "drew upon notions of bourgeois domesticity and the ideals of Victorian womanhood introduced via British rule in India" (Sinha 2007: 217). The zeal of Brahmos in Assam, as far as female emancipation is concerned, however, was limited within the narrow confines of domestic sphere. The Victorian model of female modernity, which the Brahmos institutionalized in Bengal, could not make much headway in frontier regions like Assam by the late nineteenth century. Nevertheless, Tilottama Misra argues that this Victorian 'modernity' also appealed to a section of Assamese intellectuals:

> The Victorian concept of domestic bliss centered round neatly organized small households with a wife who is an efficient manager as well as proficient in feminine accomplishments like needle works, painting, singing, and reading caught the imagination of a section of the educated Assamese men of the nineteenth century who had come into contact with the urban life of Calcutta.
>
> (2007: 39–40)

In spite of considerable critique written and preached by eminent Brahmo reformers on widow burning, child marriage, and other evil customs associated with orthodox Hindu society, some of them were succumbing to the quagmire of those very sins. Already Brahmos were taking flak from different sections of society for Keshav Chandra Sen's decision to marry his daughter Suniti to Nripendra Narayan, the Hindu prince of Coochbehar. Since the bride and the groom were below the age of consent when the marriage was to be solemnized, Keshav Chandra was not only flouting Brahmo morality but was also found guilty of violating the provisions of the Native Marriage Act of 1872, which the Brahmos themselves were instrumental in getting enacted after a lot of effort. From all conceivable angles, this marriage stood against the cherished ideals of Brahmos. Even Gunabhiram's noble act of marrying a Brahmin widow was later criticized by a few Samajists because at the time of the marriage, Bishnupriya was still a minor. Though Gunabhiram was a firm believer in Brahmo principles in most social matters, he did follow certain practices which were quite unlike those of the Brahmos. Because of his wife's insistence, who refused to take food prepared by non-Brahmins, Gunabhiram appointed a Brahmin cook, who used to accompany them whenever they traveled to Calcutta. However, one of the most anticlimactic aspects of the impact of Brahmo reformation in Assam can be found in Lakhinath Bezbaruah's autobiography, where he mentions that after sincerely preaching Brahmo ideals in different parts of Assam over many years, Ramkumar Bidyaratna returned to the fold of Hinduism and established a minor sect of his own after his return to Bengal (Bezbarua 76).

Towards the end of the novel, Gunabhiram begins searching for a respectable groom for Swarnalata when she is barely twelve years old. He feels very excited at the prospect of a marriage proposal for Swarnalata from Rabindranath Tagore, the poet, completely disregarding the fact that at that time, she is still a minor. Rather ironically, Maharshi Devendranath Tagore, the father of Rabindranath, refuses the marriage proposal not because the bride is a minor but because Swarnalata's mother is a widow who was remarried to Gunabhiram. As a result of this.

> every now and then Bishnupriya, unseen by anyone, would heave a deep sigh. She had always wished to see Swarna married to a boy from a respectable Assamese family. But Bishnupriya's illusions were shattered when she found that even a leading Brahmo of Bengal like Maharshi Devendranath Tagore had refused to accept Swarna as a daughter-in-law.
>
> (2001: 229)

In hindsight, it feels rather ironic that certain prominent Bengali as well as Assamese Brahmo could not completely rise beyond prejudice and the trap of social ostracism and petty materialistic concerns. Misra highlights this paradox with one of the final realizations of Bishnupriya:

> She realized then that there are times when even highly educated people shrink from adopting a liberal approach.
>
> (2001: 229)

Swarnalata justifies its status as fictional biography, a genre of writing which is very popular in the West, to re-present a crucial phase of our colonial modernity by successfully juxtaposing a host of historical personae with fictional characters and religious orthodoxy with cultural modernity and, most importantly, an illuminating portrayal of a 'new woman' of India.

Works Cited

Banerjee, Dipankar. *Brahmo Samaj and North – East India*. New Delhi: Anamika Publishers, 2006.

Bezbarua, Laxminath. *Mor Jivan-Xuoron*. Guwahati: Lawyer's Book Stall, 2010 (1999).

Chattopadhyay, Kanai Lal. *"Brahmo Movement in Assam"*. Proceedings of the Indian History Congress Vol 59 (1998). 621–628. https://www.jstor.org/stable 10/03/2020.

Misra, Tillotama. *Swarnalata*. Trns by Udayan Misra. Delhi: Zubaan, 2001.

———. "Introduction". Gunabhiram Baruah's *Ramnabami Natak: A Story of Ram and Nabami*. New Delhi: OUP, 2007.

Ray, Nisith R. (Ed.). *Atmacarit: Autobiography of Sivnath Sastri*. (trns.) Suniti Devi. Calcutta: Riddhi India, 1988.

Sinha, Mrinalini. "Gender in the Critiques of Colonialism and Nationalism: Locating the 'Indian Woman'". Sumit Sarkar and Tanika Sarkas ed. *Women and Social Reform in Modern India: A Reader* Vol. II. Ranikhet: Permanent Black, 2015 (2007).

11

A HISTORIAN UNDER SIEGE

Rethinking secular historiography

Kaushani Mondal

The conditions that determine the relationship between secularism and its historiographical discursivity are more than a mere negotiation. Secularism determines what religion is and must be; it determines the place of religion within the statist machinery. This is problematic in that secularism becomes as institutionalized as any theocentric system. Principles matter, as do categories of understanding. Questions are raised as to the conditions of choice, preferences, and, ultimately, freedom. Further questions build up around the non-religious public sphere, private domains of belief, ministrations of mythic identities, and dogmatic institutional structures. Secularism and its counterpart, principled religion, build hierarchic structures where the less mighty fall victim to the relatively powerful. In such a framework, the notion of history is under siege because outside its own disciplinary impartiality and objectivity, history has to keep emphasizing its political legitimacy. This is the failure of history that troubles the discipline and its protectors and practitioners. When Juergen Habermas emphasizes the public use of reason, he looks beyond the instrumentalist paradigm of understanding into a world of knowledge where arguments and analysis matter. When reason has public use, we encounter questions and debate as to the legitimacy and validation of reason leading to perspectives that may not be in sync with each other. So dissensus and consensus form a legitimate dialectical reason that we can come to call 'secular,' which is distinguished from secularism and religion as institutionalized formations and polarizations. The fraught connections between secular reason and historical thinking become a case in point when religious affiliation informs how we narrate our past, most specifically our cultural past. The public use of secular reason brings ethics into the heart of all historical representation, although multiplicities of understanding are a reality that cannot be ignored. History, thus, owes its expression to regimens of a totalitarian state and often submits to the governance of a particular ideology and statist rationale. Modern democracy is not without historians who are victims of political religion and sharp cultural reclamation. Within the instrumentalist reason of the state machinery, historical narration is largely besotted by statist lobbying, corporate

DOI: 10.4324/9781003158424-15

power flexing, political game-matching, self-protective nationalist blarney, and different forms of misrepresentations. History is closely connected with what religion is and what it does. And the historian, often, becomes an actor within certain tested discourses of power, legitimacies of expression, and collective reason of authenticity. Public history and popular conscious-ness are vexatiously connected, leading to structural argumentation across communities of power and schools of belief. The problematic of historical performance, then, is in mooting the preemption of ideological approval before epistemological authenticity and objectivity. Orality, popular imagi-nation, and history, as tales in circulation, memorialization, inauthenticity of sources, and non-veridic discourses, put historians in several categories with separate sets of belongings. It is on such belongings that the crisis of secular reason in historiography lies.

I

Before we unravel the intricacies and ramifications of the issues raised, it is wise to settle on an early 'interpretive' date with Githa Hariharan's *In Times of Siege* as our immediate case study. The novel highlights the vexa-tious intersection between religious bigotry and historical representation and, consequently, raises issues as to the status of the historian and the his-torian-intellectual within the pulls and pushes of institutional democracy. In recent times India has faced opprobrium from all over the world for being discriminatory towards academia, media houses, filmmakers, and art-ists, forcing several meaningful and constructive voices to compromise with their freedom. Be it Wendy Doniger's *The Hindus: An Alternative History* (2009) or Sanjay Leela Bhansali's *Padmavaat* (2018), every word of a book or every piece of art is under unqualified surveillance and knee-jerk scrutiny. Religious fanatics and fundamentalists like Shiksha Bachao Andolan Samiti and Rajput Karni Sena have taken upon themselves the self-authorized job to protect the history and culture of a Hindu India so that the aura of Hin-duism stays vigorously afloat. Such figures abound in Hariharan's novel, as we find extremist vigilantes taking recourse to violence and vandalism to suppress secular voices. The public space is also under seizure.

The novel begins with a controversy surrounding a course written by Shiv Murthy, a fifty-two-year-old history professor at Kasturba Gandhi Central University. Unlike regular universities, KGU is an open university where "only teachers are visible"; "the students are names, addresses, postmarks"; and where lessons, modules, and courses are prepared for registered stu-dents (Hariharan 2003: 3). Shiv is accused by 'Hindu watchdog group' Itihas Suraksha Manch of "distorting history and historical figures" in one of the BA courses he has written on Basavanna or Basava, a twelfth-century poet and social reformer (Ibid.: 53). The allegations are that the lessons have con-flicting narratives and provide contradictory accounts of Basava's life. This does not go down well with the ideology of the Manch – the self-styled 'protectors' of 'history.' The immediate question here is about the 'owning' and 'possessing' of history, the accounts from the past. Fredric Jameson points out that "history is not a text" (Jameson 2002: 14): it is non-narrative and non-representational; ironically, history is "inaccessible" to us except in the textual form (Ibid.: 20). This inaccessibility has pushed historians to question the past and its objectivity. Therefore, history becomes predominantly "an imaginary horizon of what is possible," and what comes to us as history textbooks and lessons is a result of a historian's reinterpretation, reimagination, and representation of the past without certain bones and marrow of objectivity (Ghosh 2012: 2). Shiv, while writing on Basava, assumed the role of a time-traveler, a meta-historical narrator who went back and forth in time, got engaged in a dialogue with the past, negotiated with the aporias, and restructured the past with all the historical facts and sources at hand. Shiv's Basava "is so many things, so many people rolled into one – poet and mystic, finance minister and political activist, man of the people and man of god" (Hariharan 2003: 67). Shiv traces the life of Basava – from the growth of his radical ideas and his struggle against caste divisions and the temple establishment to the tensions that grew between the court, the Brahmins, the merchants, the low-caste artisans, and the untouchables. The lesson narrates a violent clash between these groups that did not end well for anyone in Kalyana, leading to the dispersal of Basava's followers, his own departure from the kingdom, and his death shortly after at Kudalasangama. Shiv's historical position in writing the lesson was neither monolithic nor hagiographic; he followed a method that was dialogic and objective.

However, such historicalities and Shiv's creation of historical spaces of intervention through method and interpretation land the university in a controversy. The head of the department disapprovingly points out that Shiv has exaggerated "the problem of caste and written in a very biased way about the Brahmins and temple priests" and failed to make "it clear enough that Basavanna was much more than an ordinary human being" (Ibid.: 54). The university decides to have no part in this; rather, it suggests an apology or retraction from Shiv to pacify the Manch; it also hints at the discontinuance of the booklet that contains the module so that the controversy around the institution can be averted. But Shiv emphasizes that the lessons don't distort history and refuses to apologize to people who, he thinks, have no sense of history and are not recognized as historians. History demands methodological training and critical understanding; having a sense of history comes with a background, learning, and consciousness. Hence, Shiv considers institutional complacency seriously disconcerting even in the wake of such infringement and rabid surveillance and more so when history has become the handmaiden of political ideology and mobilization.

It is here that secular historiography takes its first body blow. Recognizing India as a secular country becomes problematic because "the normative idea of the modern nation as a secular institution is a European one," and in the post-independence era, the word 'secular' has been primarily used to promote national unification (Needham and Rajan 2007: 6). Hinduism may be the only religion in the world today that does not have a 'left':

> The secular leftism in India contributed to a process of constructing all things Hindu as inherently backward and regressive, thus pushing reformist, originally left-of-center Hindu organizations such as the Ramkrishna Mission and Arya Samaj into the arms of the Hindu right.
>
> (Menon 2007: 137)

On the performative and pedagogical levels, the syncretic culture of India is integral to its becoming. Armed with secular syncretism, the fabric of the Indian subcontinent is multi-discursive and polyvalent both in faith and systems of belief. But this coexistence of belief was not given enough cognizance under the aegis of Sangh Parivar's Hindutva ideologues. It was controlled and disseminated as a singular sacred narrative of prodigious goodness and greatness, conveniently erasing anything that is tantamount to weakness. This goes against the foundation of secularism that India is built on. The drawback here is the indifference to 'dharma.' There is a

> contradiction between *dharma-nirpekshata* (neutrality to religion) and *sarvadharma-samabhava* (harmony of religions). . . . It is *sarvadharma-samabhava* which has constituted an essential feature of Hinduism and of Indian culture as a whole and not *dharma-nirpekshata*, which is utterly foreign to it.
>
> (Ghosh 2013: 3)

Ranjan Ghosh argues,

> In countries such as India where secular power is under the sign of theological power (not in the sense of a theocratic state, though), where decisions based on secularism are somewhat contaminated by 'hurting religious sentiments' syndrome, secularism can hardly do away with the sacred. It becomes imposingly difficult to neutralize this relationship, and, thus, the profanisation of the secular does not happen.
>
> (2013: 8)

When such hardwired instructions cripple secular historical thinking, the 'sacred' dominates the nationalist consciousness, and history and myth are aggregated into a bolus with no secular reason to separate and analyze them.

Nationalist historiography tries, unfortunately, to erase the subaltern modes of historical writing and thinking. The nationalist consciousness of an Indian is fixated on an image of land built through selective narratives of the past, disregarding the heterogeneity of the populace of the Republic. Suffocated by Brahmanical historiography, all secular politics come under the hammer, with accusations ranging from distraction to communalization. Githa Hariharan builds anti-elite historiography through the rise of Veerashaivas in the kingdom of Kalyana when the ruler was King Bijjala. Basava, despite being the treasurer of Kalyana and a friend of the king, took on the caste system that existed in the society. He followed his egalitarian dream and formed "a community that sought to exclude no one – not women, not the lowest, most polluting castes" (Hariharan 2003: 60). In fact, "poets, potters, reformers, washermen, philosophers, prostitutes, learned Brahmins, housewives, tanners, ferrymen – all were equal part of the brief burst of Kalyana's glory' who called themselves *Veerashaivas* – warriors of Siva" (Ibid.: 60). This made people become a "movement" that "swelled and surged" and transformed into a "wave that threatened to swallow social conventions and religious ritual, staple diet of tradition" (Ibid.: 61). Here, Ghosh observes:

> Legend has it that a misalliance between a Veerashaiva couple – a Brahmin bride with a bridegroom who was the son of a cobbler – ignited an unruly row. Traduced and tried, Basava saw his mission falling apart with the moderates and the extremists tearing into each other. The great moment of pushing for social change was over. 'What began as a critique of the status quo would be absorbed, bit by bit, into the sponge-like body of tradition and convention. But Basava and his companions left a legacy: a vision consisting of vigorous, modern thought; poetry of tremendous beauty and depth, images that couple the radical and the mystical. Most of all, Basava's passionate questions would remain relevant more than eight hundred years later'.
>
> (2009: 196)

What Shiv wrote of Basava was a result of his genuine interest and historical curiosity. This position owes to the interpretation of history as dependent on facts and not merely subservient to a myth, philosophy, popular imagination, and experience. Ghosh's observations are pertinent:

> Hindus revere the past but not always in the religious sense; the past has come down to them as inspiration and prescription of social and personal conduct. . . . . Hindus know the subtle art of mixing fact with myth, unlike their Western counterparts; Hindus choose to revel in diverse meanings and compose meaning out of

their rather "affect" relations with the past. . . . Reconstruction-ism leaves enough room for "presences" to keep crawling in and debouch in ways that take the narrative by ideological twists, bias and inventive bursts of historical interpretation. . . . Different ver-sions of ancient texts exist, and different texts always tell slightly altered accounts of particular events. Such accomodationist tenden-cies and maneuverability challenge our understanding of the mental constructions of the Hindus.

(2012: 14–15)

Historical reconstructionism, hence, has its own perils and fallacies. Ver-sions of history are not easy passports to relativism. It is here that the impor-tance of a 'trained' historian comes into full power and effect.

The novel narrates a similar incident that occurred in 1994. A Kannada play on Basava that had won a state award and was later prescribed as a textbook in a couple of universities was banned after eight years of pub-lication. A group of protestors accused the play of portraying Basava as a coward and implied that he had committed suicide. The play allegedly raised questions on the chastity of some Veerashaivas; it used obscene lan-guage, too. Copies of the play and the effigy of the playwright were burnt; there were rallies, protests, fasts, and attempted self-immolation. It became a convenient election issue, and soon the book was withdrawn from the university syllabus in 1995 by a government order to mollify the religious maximalists. This controlling of narratives to forward the agenda of the right-wing party has trammeled the academic freedom of the historians and academic institutions. There has been a continuous attempt at homogenizing education through Hindutva versions of history. Syllabi have been altered, chapters have been either edited or deleted, and history as a discipline has been reduced to a glorification of Hindu ideologies undergirded by fantasy and myth.

The Itihas Suraksha Manch justifies their allegations by saying that texts which 'overemphasize caste divisions' and project Hindu religion and cul-ture in poor light should be kept out of circulation. The Manch ideology circumscribed by V.D. Savarkar's *Who Is a Hindu?* and Madhav Sadashiv Golwalker's *We, or the Nationhood Defined* envisions a 'Hindu Rashtra' for India. Romila Thapar emphasizes that they have been instrumental in converting "'Hindutva' into a political slogan encapsulating an aggressive Hinduism" that protects the Hindu Golden age (Thapar 2007: 195); all other religions come next to Hinduism. Thapar further points out:

The Hindutva version of history was written and expounded gener-ally by nonhistorians – by engineers and computer specialists and by religious organizations. So there has been little understanding of historical method and the complications in handling source material or the theories of historical explanation . . . the Hindutva version of history is a sledgehammer history reducing everything to a single reading, narrowly defined according to its own choice. The teaching of this history, therefore, takes on the form of a kind of catechism, as is evident from the history textbooks used in schools in Gujrat and in the schools run by RSS – the Shishu Mandirs. Questions and answers are dictated and there is no deviation from either.

(2007: 197, 202–203)

Shiv's position resonates with such ideas. He opposes this sledgehammering of history into a certain template of understanding and courts the ire of the Manch for refusing to apologize. Unpleasantness piles on him: a colleague assaults him in a meeting, and his office in the university is vandalized by a group of unidentified rioters and supporters of the Manch. What ensues is a deluge of accusations and attacks by newspapers, media, articles, and academicians. Twisted journalism spares no effort to give this event a nationalist color, and, expectedly the academics, protestors, and common citizens choose their sides and stripes. Traditional historians accuse Shiv of being a secular academic who is trying to appropriate foreign ideas about Hinduism; he is compared to Muslim invaders and Pakistanis. The university, too, retracts the lesson without consulting Shiv – the institution allows only "a sanitized Basava," a "saint-singer," to feature in the curriculum (Hariharan 2003: 86). The 'only' way to keep Basava in society is to turn him into a saint-poet, someone floating in a heavenly limbo or to turn a leader into a "minor god; the man into a saint" (Ibid.: 92). That's the only way to make him safely untouchable.

> For the purveyors of magic (and their subject of zealots) Basava's life unfolds in a haze of legend. It was Lord Siva who sent him down to earth. The usual birth legends have been fabricated; the usual precociousness lore and self-sufficiency tales proliferate. Demi-gods are easier to co-opt into the pantheon of gods once they die. (Demi-gods do not end up as political prisoners; they do not end their lives in broken, disillusioned exile.) For the detractors and demonizers, Basava was nothing more (and nothing less villainous) than a bigoted revolutionary. A man obsessed with upsetting tradition. A dangerous man, a threat to structure, stability, religion.
>
> (Ibid.: 87)

One of the hate mails blurts:

> This Professor Murthy has made the great Basavanna a mere politician, appealing to caste and dividing society like Mandal did some years back. . . . Our misled historians and other troublemakers

criticize Hinduism for its caste system and pull our saints off their pedestals. But they keep quiet about Christianity or Islam. The truth is that these minorities will be safe in India only if they share our vision of our country and culture. Then, we won't mind accommodating two more gods (Allah and Christ) along with our thirty-three crore gods and goddesses.

(Hariharan 2003: 117–118)

Here, history comes to haunt and hound when Shiv's secular-rationalist views on the Basava-history come under much vitriol and brimstone – a clear assault on the principles of historical representation, truth and objectivity. Shiv argues:

Is there a single image, a simple one that will hold his knowledge of Basava? Shiv imagines a hospitable tree, the kind that attracts all sorts of vines and creepers. It is impossible to look at this tree, visualize it in all its wealth of detail, if the vines and creepers are cut out of the picture. But what happens when the parasites grow too thick and lush, when they rob the tree of all nourishment? The tree sickens; it dies a lingering death. The hagiographies – the creepers – are an inevitable part of any reconstruction, historical or literary, of Basava's life. . . . They use the creepers to prettify the picture; whitewash it; or even better, use them like brushes dipped in magic paint.

(Hariharan 2003: 91–92)

History cannot be a singular narrative of truth, shrinking all forms of expression and possibilities of reflection and understanding under a grand old banyan tree. Reducing history to a point is choking knowledge into a bolus. There cannot be one way to remember a man and one great way to consider a man as great. So when the Manch and its cohorts are clamoring that 'there is only one way to remember a great man, *their* way' and 'only one way to remember the past' (Hariharan 2003: 110), should we accept history as singular, monolithic, unilinear, unchangeable? Is it a fixed spot in time, an immutable event? Is Shiv speaking as a historian with a biased perspective and ideology? What happens to the sacred, secular, and historical thinking when the majority influences the axis and needle of historical truth making? Is history only about ideologizing the past, or does it encourage making sense of the past, too?

II

What makes a historian come under siege? How is history under siege where cabalistic historiography tries to determine the historical consciousness of a nation? What kind of secularity does history generate to achieve a kind of reason that enables objectivity, truth, and contexts of understanding? Is history secular by its formations, or does history by itself in its affinities to ideology and emotions provide a space for assault on what it chooses to defend and establish? The professor-historian enables a 'historical thinking' that opens more questions than it answers.

The idea of a historian in the period after the 1850s was associated with a "substantial philosophy of history" – Historia Magistra Vitae – and also with "nationalist or otherwise politically inspired grant narratives" (Froeyman 2016: 219). However, the concept of history and historians underwent significant changes after the mid-twentieth century based on objectivity that drew its inspiration from scientific enquiry dominated by historiographical principles of understanding. Historians were expected to be non-ideological and devotees of objectivity and factuality. What kind of truth are we expecting the historians to be devoted to? A school of historians spearheaded by Lynn Hunt would consider objective truth as a commonly agreed-upon program where differences come to be erased and more and more ideological and cultural issues are discounted and obviated. A historian is expected to bring the 'truth' to society. However, deconstructive historiography, as advocated by Alun Munslow and Keith Jenkins, considers truth anything but totalitarian and organic. Being objective with the past is asking for an unachievable reality. History can fact-check and objectify, but its analysis brings with it, to an extent, a figural understanding of truth and historical representation. In that light, Shiv's understanding of history may not be closer to an uncontestable objective truth. Truth is narrative, epistemological, and discursive. This makes Shiv's interpretation of history different and differential. Perhaps extremist historiography fails to appreciate the 'differential' in historical understanding. Extremism considers truth totalitarian and, hence, apodictic. The historian graduates to a level of historian-intellectual in the Edward Saidian sense where, keeping the 'political' in mind, alternative narratives and 'perspectives on history' are sought to be investigated. The political is a composite of national identity, agenda, 'carpentered history' (in the words of Amartya Sen), official memory, and myth.

Expatiating the historian-intellectual, something that I argue Shiv to be, Ghosh notes:

> The intellectual, for Said, is not a hero but a person who knows what it takes to 'speak', what makes articulation compelling, what it is that draws 'others to listen'. A historian must train himself to know that there is a 'matter of knowing how to read' which is allied with the 'issue of knowing what to read'. Reading the past or the text does not necessarily produce finished objects or projects.
>
> (2009: 196)

Emphasizing the social function of history and considering history as often a part of an unfinished project of enquiry:

> Shiv avoids slithering into hermetic monocausal explanations and the banalities of the antiquarian for whom reading the 'past' is scrubbing the dusty visage of time. He makes a call on the deeper structures of analysis directing our attention to the central function of history which is to explain social development. Like Said's secular intellectual, he '*invents* goals abductively', reading out a 'better situation from the known historical and social facts'. . . . For Said, a historian – intellectual functions as a major force when he stays within the 'area of historical restitution and reparation'.
>
> (Ibid.: 196–197)

Shiv resists and desists all "invidious disfiguring, dismembering, and disremembering of significant historical experiences" sponsored by politicized lobbies – history, as it were, a classroom for lobbyists. Shiv vouchsafes for "deintoxicated, sober histories" that make allowance for patience and sensitivity; he expects intense purveying of the complexities of history as a narrative and discourse. History cannot be a prefiguration because some historical narratives come with reflective judgment while others figure as teleological.

> A 'secular historian' knows what it means to preserve the fragile bond between ethics and knowledge, cultivate the balance between historical enquiry and the public use of history; this space is also the zone of 'supervision' for Said, a stretch where 'dissent' cannot be encouraged to run amuck much in the same way institutionalised knowledge cannot be allowed to be tutelary and, thus, exempted from censure in a metatopical space.
>
> (Ibid.: 197)

History demands to be known in ways that broaden our horizons of thinking and reflection. Objectivity cannot promise inflexibility; it has to breed historical consciousness founded on certain principles of knowing and rationale of analysis. History cannot become pedagogical through an extremist devotion to a certain arc of truth because methodology is a key to certain spaces and zones of understanding. I am tempted to believe that over-historicization can undo all the good faith in knowing the past. The life lived is both historical and existential. Basava is historical and also circumscribed in conditions of human consciousness and life-experiences. He cannot be a figure with only historical points to join in the formation of a broad and clear outline. Basava is an 'experience,' and a historian is expected to analyze the intricacies of the experience alongside the documentary support that his historicality has. Basava lived unhistorically in a Nietzschean way with an affective force; this assimilates in its development and does not become a concatenation of singular events that can be put into a formal order of understanding. The unhistorical here is the limit phenomenon, and monumentality is limiting to the nature of our historical being. So, Hans Ruin observes,

> as historical beings, we are involved in and claimed by the past toward which we constantly find ourselves having to respond, not only to what has been, but to who has been. History is not just a reservoir of facts to be learned, but an ethical entanglement to which we always already belong. This is our historical condition, our facticity and our vulnerability, or in existential-phenomenological terms: our 'historicity'.
>
> (2019: 802)

It is dangerous to make the past serviceable to the present for a 'particular' brand of future. The fundamentalists hectoring Shiv have their own monuments to promote and preserve. It is history without 'hunger,' a culture without 'cultured decisions.' Ruin argues further:

> What is it that historical knowledge is meant to serve? And what is the relation between the ethos of a spontaneous use of history and a research-based approach to the past? And perhaps most importantly: what do we need to understand about the inner pathology of historical existence, in order to truly respond to its various manifestations in the present? By contrasting them so sharply, Nietzsche provokes the historical educator up until this day to reflect on the meaning of her task. The core of his critical challenge lies in what he has to say about the relation between historical truth and justice. History can be reduced to the learning and remembrance of stories, for the sake of knowledge and education. But then it is no longer operative, since it ceases to have a connection to the capacity to exist and act in the present. It is, as he writes, as if 'the task were to guard history so that nothing could come of it but stories'. But to really confront the past, to engage in what has been, is to force oneself to confront what is difficult and demanding, both psychologically and morally. This is why he can also state that 'only strong personalities can endure history: the weak are completely extinguished by it'. To really engage in historical learning and understanding is not just to note and interiorize facts of the past, but to confront the moral and political reality of that past, and to try to judge it adequately as also a way of shaping a response to it.
>
> (Ibid.: 804)

Shiv cannot produce objective history as much as his detractors cannot lay claim to a singular, partisan version of understanding the past. The past, in fact, is exposed to 'interpretation' (in the Nietzschean sense). Also, Foucault sees 'effective history' as not strictly 'objective knowledge': this is 'affirmation of knowledge as perspective.' Keith Windschuttle is right to argue that

> Nietzsche's version of historical sense is explicit in its perspective and acknowledges its system of injustice. Its perception is slanted, being a deliberate appraisal, affirmation, or negation; it reaches the lingering and poisonous traces in order to prescribe the best antidote. In other words, objectivity is impossible, so historians should be deliberately biased in their interpretations. However, if one takes this view, where does this leave the pursuit of the truth about what happened in the past? Foucault is quite explicit: everything that happened in history has to be seen from a perspective. Even what most people would regard as fairly basic historic facts should not be seen as standing on their own.
>
> (1998: 9)

This encourages me to argue that Shiv's version of Basava was perspective. And secular historiography must acknowledge its investments in 'interpretation' and perspectives. However, would that mean that historical understanding is relativistic, and all versions of history are vulnerable to deconstructive angst? It is here that 'secular reason' demands a common agreement based on principles of methodological investigations and verificatory discourses that are settled on principles of objectivity, sequential discourse, and epistemological consensus. Interpretation of history cannot be free floating and amenable to partisan interests of the present; it is difficult, as well, to see history as emerging from "a bedrock body of unshakeable evidence" (Ghosh 2012: 85). Controversy forms an important thread of history, a compelling thread, to be precise. However, epistemic agreement installs order into the heart of historical discourse and understanding of historiographies. The historian becomes the intellectual here – argumentative, interpretive, investigative, and methodically discursive. Shiv knows that secular historiography is built not only through contestation but also clearly through an inheritance that cannot be ambiguous forever. The secret from the past cannot stay fully secretive even though some units of our inheritance can stay under recurrent argumentation. Shiv belongs to a category of historians who appreciate the sensitive association between research and reconstruction. He knows the 'limits' of relativism and reconstructionism. As a historian under fire and whose profession is threatened to be beleaguered, Shiv declares "an engagement with some unassailed historical truths alongside a wise relaxation to accept some possible failures in his historical understanding" (Ibid.: 87). Agent-intentionality, empathy with the past, self-implication, and empiricity come to contest with each other within a secular historical consciousness.

The past is malleable but not at the expense of sectarian manipulation. It is not always an incontrovertible reality; rather, past invites a dissenting congregation, a revisionist reception, as Romilar Thapar, in her narration of the history of the Somnath temple, shows us. Representative narrative history cannot be overdetermined, either. There are some issues that stay as prisoners of the past whose uncaging can let a whole new debate on secular reason in historical thinking loose. If the dead are buried, how long can they stay dead? How much do the ghosts of the dead come to speak out? Rigidifying the past is immunization against historical revisionism that can keep disciplines of thinking alive. Past is applicative; can be duplicative; is reflective and objective, too. Shiv is under ideological barricade; critical rationality is under attack, and with it the whole institution of historical thinking and performance is immune from assault. Postmodern historiography sees such a 'seige' as the breath of history, the promise of history to flourish with more meaning and significance. The fight is, thus, always between the predators and protectors of history. Shiv challenges the predators by daring to think discriminatively and with a promise for alternative voices; he wants history to survive as a different mode of reading, more secular in its renditions and understanding. Perhaps the debate centers on 'practical past' with 'historical past,' the 'contrived past,' and the 'investigated past.' However, the neutrality of the historian is debatable; one cannot deny the bias towards historical representation that comes from documentary, subjective, and hence strategic arrangement of facts and other ideological determinants. Dissension enlivens history; extremism sounds its death knell. Secular historiography is restless, always under siege in a good way, in productive ways of knowledge generation. The historian has always been under siege, and history, fortunately, has never been a calm endgame.

Works cited

Froeyman, Anton. "The Ideal of Objectivity and the Public Role of the Historian: Some Lessons from the *Historikerstreit*, and the History Wars." *Rethinking History* 20:2 (2016): 217–234.

Ghosh, Ranjan, ed. *Edward Said and the Literary, Social, and Political World*. New York and London: Routledge, 2009.

———. *A Lover's Quarrel with the Past*. Oxford and New York: Berghahn Books, 2012.

———, ed. *Making Sense of the Secular*. New York and London: Routledge, 2013.

Hariharan, Githa. *In Times of Siege*. New Delhi: Penguin Books, 2003.

Jameson, Fredric. *The Political Unconscious: Narrative as a Socially Symbolic Act*. London: Routledge, 2002.

Menon, Nivedita. "Living with Secularism." In *The Crisis of Secularism in India*, edited by Anuradha Dingwaney Needham and Rajeswari Sunder Rajan. Ranikhet, India: Permanent Black, 2007, 118–140.

Needham, Anuradha Dingwaney, and Rajeswari Sunder Rajan, eds. *The Crisis of Secularism in India.* Ranikhet, India: Permanent Black, 2007.

Ruin, Hans. "The Claim of the Past – Historical Consciousness as Memory, Haunting, and Responsibility in Nietzsche and Beyond." *Journal of Curriculum Studies* 51:6 (2019): 798–813.

Thapar, Romila. "Secularism, History and Contemporary Politics in India." In *The Crisis of Secularism in India,* edited by Anuradha Dingwaney Needham and Rajeswari Sunder Rajan. Ranikhet, India: Permanent Black, 2007, 191–207.

Windschuttle, Keith. "Foucault as Historian." *Critical Review of International Society and Political Philosophy* 1:2 (1998): 5.

12

"FIRST A FRIEND AND THEN AN ENEMY"

Trauma, fetish, and binary politics
in *The Black Coat*

Avijit Basak

The Black Coat (2013) by Neamat Imam hinges on the speech Sheikh Mujibur Rahman delivered on 7 March 1971, a few months before Bangladesh
got its independence on 16 December of the same year. In that speech, he
talked about the series of sacrifices made for Bangladesh by its people;
how they were betrayed by the Pakistani government, which cruelly killed
Bengalis, their own brothers; and how Pakistanis ruthlessly oppressed the
poor people of Bangladesh. The speech demanded accountability from the
Pakistani militia and was a clarion call for resistance against an oppressive
regime, leading to freedom and democracy. The speech became the "seed"
of Bangladeshi independence (Imam 29) inspiring people to fight against the
Pakistani soldiers. Imam's text critically engages with the promises made by
Mujib in that speech, and with his, rule exposing the cynicism with which
Mujib and his followers handled his failures as a ruler. Through a number of
characters, representing different socio-political aspects of the newly born
country, Imam tries to critically engage with the history of a country which
represses the vast tragedy of its internal fractures to promote a redemptive
narrative of hero-worshipping. Imam chooses the 1974 famine of Bangladesh to scrutinize the regime of Awami League, since this dark period in
their history is repressed to construct celebratory image of Mujib, and Imam
imaginatively recreates the period to question the authorized narrative of
the nation. In this chapter, I shall focus on the fate of the unrecognized
minority of unorganized migrants who form world's largest vulnerable
group, the precariats, and shall try to discuss how politically vested interests
manipulate them for vote politics, as Imam does not shy away from showing
in *The Black Coat*. In doing so, I shall engage with Western philosophical
thoughts, borrowing insights from ethical philosophy and trauma theory,
and taking cues from the multidirectionality of memory,[1] where one tragedy
of great magnitude might invoke the memory of another tragedy of similar

DOI: 10.4324/9781003158424-16

gravity. The bureaucratic indifference with which Mujib's cabinet and army handled the migrant question vividly invokes the memory of the banality of evil that plagued Europe in the 1940s. My aim shall be to analyze the text to highlight the politics of cynical treatment of the "minority" (in this case, poor migrants), something the political theology of Mujibism concocted, which is symptomatic of the failure of ethical demands of democratic praxis.

In 1974, within a couple of years of its birth, Bangladesh went through a massive famine, caused by erratic weather and the denial of the administration to admit that there was a famine. Amartya Sen, in his book *Poverty and Famines* (1981), has conclusively shown how the "food availability decline" or the FAD approach "provides no explanation of the Bangladesh famine, and that a better understanding of the famine can be found through the entitlement approach" (153). What Sen believes is that famines can be caused by the selective distribution of materials, where "if we look at the food going to *particular* groups" (154), then the cause of starvation becomes more evident. He prefers an "entitlement" approach, which leads to deprivation of any group that is not entitled. Sen's thesis[2] is an important intervention for an understanding of the deprived precariat class and how this minority group is exploited by influential and affluent elites. Imam's book, in excruciating detail, shows the deteriorating condition of the refugees and probes the limit of bureaucratic apathy in the wake of the famine. The narrator of the book, Khaleque Biswas, sees around him people coming to Dhaka in search of a better opportunity, because they do not have any future in villages already destroyed by the famine. For them, a shoe has more monetary value than the constitution (167). They live in squalor, in an atmosphere of chaos and extreme deprivation. Not only that, since they do not have enough resources to support their living, they start to cook and defecate openly. The government fails to address their demands, causing a threat to Dhaka's eco-system. Gradually they learn to steal and fight with each other in filthy language, and things often take violent turn (73–74). They would even throw their baby away for food (163). They get cholera drinking foul water (236). Imam is acutely aware of how such a condition oppresses women, who are doubly marginalized, the most. Refugee women try to steal from others and start using their bodies as a last resort to protest (135) or earn money for food (73–74). Bangladesh, Khaleque observes, has turned into a hell (127). Graffiti artists start to protest, asking the famished to eat Awami League leaders and asking for the death of the dictator (71). Disconsolate people, with or without political affiliations, start to rebel against the government and choose violent means (69–70), leading to bloodshed, destruction of property, and physical harm. In this dystopian situation, everyone needs to be assured of a strong democratic government that would look after its people, take care of them, and recognize their demands, precisely what Mujib promised in his 7 March speech.

At the beginning, we are introduced to Mujib's Bangladesh from the perspective of Khaleque Biswas. Khaleque is a journalist who overcompensated for his failure to fight for his country by creating an atmosphere of Bengali nationalism around *Muktijuddha*, the war for liberation, and Sheikh Mujib. Through his columns, he frequently criticized the Pakistani government, comparing the Pakistani army to beasts and Nazis, defining them as CIA, Jews, and the likes and demanding their murder. His columns particularly targeted the *Razakars*, the corroborators, who, he believes, should be killed twice. When the war was won, with others, he also became ecstatic with new hopes for their country. However, noting the gradual increase in the number of refugees in his neighborhood, it becomes impossible for him not to see the problem with the Mujib government. Khaleque reflects:

> Too many people had moved to Dhaka after the war: those that were directly affected by the war; those that could not find any employment in their villages, like Nur Hussain. . . . The homeless made up the largest group among them.
>
> (23)

Watching their miserable conditions, he grows critical of the Mujib government, and he asks his editor, Lutfuzzaman Babul, to help him out. Consequently, he is fired from his job. Khaleque dryly observes that now there is no difference between Nur and him. He starts looking for a job and fails repeatedly. During this period, however, he discovers Nur's remarkable capacity to mimic Sheikh Mujib's 7 March speech, and decides to monetize it by creating a "charade" out of it, which proves a very successful enterprise. Poor people, deprived of government's direct intervention to make their lives better, start paying them handsomely for the hope the "speech" offers. As Khaleque observes, they are manufacturing and selling dreams to an ideologically engineered society, based on nationalism (52, 55). Immediately they grab the attention of powerful people like Moina Mia, an Awami League leader, who decides to cash in on the propagandist power of Nur's performances and buys their service. Afraid of living the way the refugees are living in front of him, Khaleque decides to defect to the Mujib camp, to turn coat, because during a famine, a time of desperation, the value of money grows (122).

Nur's recruitment is purely based on exploitation, where everything from his hair to his shoes has ideological significance. He is the symbol of the fact that "sooner or later all Bangladeshis must become Sheikh Mujib; that was the only way to show him our sincerest appreciation for his leadership" (59). The idea behind's Nur's recruitment, as Khaleque learns and acquiesces to, is to "bring people under the control of the Awami League" (68), to put people under the spell of Mujibist ideology. Ideology is defined by Zizek not as a 'false consciousness' but as "an illusory representation of reality, it is rather this reality itself which is already to be conceived as 'ideological' ... 'a formation whose very consistency implies a certain no-knowledge on the part of the subject'" (21). Zizek implies that the subject is not aware of the fact that

> their social reality itself, their activity, is guided by an illusion, by a fetishistic inversion. What they overlook, what they misrecognize, is not the reality but the illusion which is structuring their reality, their social activity. They know very well how things really are, but still they are doing it as if they did not know.
>
> (2008: 32)

But that is how hegemony works – it slowly forces us to be in denial, and we tacitly agree with the status quo and gradually accept the leading ideology as normal. Khaleque is as aware of the condition of the refugees as he is aware of the charm of the Mujib coat, a symbol of the camp a Mujibist belongs to. The coat lets people who were once freedom fighters loot the very country and country people they freed; they chant *Joy Bangla* and then indulge in rampant corruption. They behave like Pakistani soldiers, and Mujib deliberately covers for them, since his existence depends on nepotism. The development measures he has introduced are insufficient for ordinary people (65), still, Khaleque comes under the thrall of this charming figure (103). When he meets Mujib, he fails to ask him the uncomfortable question has long planned to, since a

> man wearing a Mujib coat could not charge Mujib with any wrongdoing; a man wearing a Mujib coat could not object to anything said or done by any other man wearing a Mujib coat, not even when he saw people dying.
>
> (103)

Incidentally, the word "fetish" comes from the word *fétiche*, which means "charm," supernatural magic, and Khaleque, who hates his father (Imam 152), is transfixed by the overwhelming figure of Sheikh Mujib, the "Father of the Bengali nation" (1), immediately in denial of the entropy he sees around him. Even though Zizek believes that the "only real obedience ... is an 'external' one," unmediated by the self, he contrasts it with "obedience out of conviction," which is mediated by a faith of the subject himself on the benevolent aspect of the ruler, where the subject exercises his choice and uses his agency as a rational being (Zizek 37). The long dialogues Khaleque often engages in with himself, chastising his transformations, are an act of intellectual defense working towards self-righteousness – a parapraxis impeding the act of working through the trauma.

A democracy is by definition a fractured body, a dis-organized, disincorporated body, where no one has absolute power. A people's representative is elected, but he is replaceable; democracy, as Critchley notes in *The Ethics of Deconstruction* following Bataille, is a "headless community" always facing the risk of collapse being characterized by "competition, struggle, and antagonism" (209). Precisely for these internal fractures, democracy always runs the risk of lapsing into totalitarianism (Critchley 2014: 240), an incorporated, centralized, body organized and headed by a charming totalitarian. As Critchley argues, democracy "is the politics of ethical difference, political wisdom at the service of ethical love" (240). Totalitarian government does not have such a commitment; it is controlled by an egocrat who would do anything to retain his power. A totalitarian government feeds on the fear of its followers for an imaginary enemy, and it is possible because the very essence of community is imagined. The very "founding trauma," to borrow a term from Dominick LaCapra's *Writing History, Writing Trauma* (2001: 161), of the liberation war gives rise to the identitarian politics of Bengali nationalism, a hierarchy within Bengalis, where an Awami League member is more Bengali than other Bengalis. But, whereas with the end of the war, this kind of rhetoric should have been excised in favor of inclusive policies, Mujib's followers start creating imaginary enemies. LaCapra discusses how Nazis created an imagined distance between them and very assimilated, very German Jewish people so that "a pure divide" could be created, but at the centre of this divide, there is an anxiety; the binarization is marked by shared affinities (149). Similarly, here Khaleque suffers from such an anxiety, but he avoids the refugees and their touch, as if they are "pollutants" (LaCapra 165) and often exercises violence (Imam 54). Khaleque starts identifying himself with the refugees since he lost his job (55), but the very identification reduces him to a "pathological state of numbness" (56), which marks the beginning of his pathological self-justification to defect to the other side of the pole. Refugees are "extra trouble" (77), out of their minds (181), unreasonably violent (70), thieves, and destroyers of properties (73). Their condition disgusts Khaleque (163) – and apart from Shah Abdul Karim, whose company Nur enjoys, he does not seem to care much for them (52) and is often sadistically violent towards them (145–146). He is afraid of being contaminated by the "sick fantasies" of the penniless people (215). Once, when he decides to help them, it is only to please Nur (169). He believes famine is going to give birth to a new religion of the fittest with the survivors of the calamity, while the weak ones must die (164). Famine is a trial of dignity (179); it has increased the value of money (122) and those who have it are going to survive. Survival is the key, and Khaleque has survived, because he has kept his cool and has not indulged in undignified activities like the weaker section of society (118). This meritocratic argument effaces the fact that meritocracy comes with the baggage of privilege – the privilege of the right connections and right resources at the right time, and not everyone has access to them. Similarly, Moina Mia tries hard to eliminate this ideological other through a "scapegoat mechanism" (LaCapra 166) and to remove this "horror of contamination" (LaCapra 167) by often getting rid of them – remove the poor instead of poverty, so to speak. Basu, Gesu, and the screw eater are only few examples of such removal. His threat to Khaleque and Nur, when he learns of Nur's disloyalty, is also full of sinister obloquy. Not only that, Mujib's private militia, "a tough, formidable, totalitarian-minded armed force" (62), sets fire to the refugee slum only because some of them tried to resist Awami League members (172). These incidents are not important or shocking to people like Moina. Instead, he takes the deaths of people in the famine around him as normal

> There were deaths, Sheikh Mujib had acknowledged that. Those deaths were caused by natural calamities. Sheikh Mujib had admitted that too. It was expected that some people would die in the new country because some people always died in a new country. If it was expected, it should not come as a shock.
>
> (181)

With the increasing impact of the famine, the propaganda machine of Mujibism starts to gather power, with two pronged intentions: highlighting the good works done by the Awami League and showing how the ideological opponents of Mujibism are the agents of anti-Bangladeshi activities. Ideology thrives on its capacity to enfold everyone susceptible enough to believe it; Moina Mia knows it, and by hiring Nur, a precariat working for Mujib, he wants to show that the government of the Awami League empowers everyone in the country (63), which implies that if someone is not feeling empowered enough they are working at vested interest. This "ideological quilting," to borrow a term from Zizek's *The Sublime Object of Ideology*, "totalizes" (95) the "floating crowds" (Imam 55),[3] ideologically identified with migrants and refugees. Needless to say, this quilting is also a step towards ideological interpellation, a construction of a "symbolic and imaginary identification" (Zizek 123). The purpose of those meetings in which Nur speaks, Khaleque Biswas lets us know, is to "communicate the very important fact that Sheikh Mujib is not sitting inactive" and doing his very best to address the issue (75). Even though in "1974 alone over one and half a million people died in Sheikh Mujib's liberated Bangladesh" (90–91), which is five times higher than the total casualties of the liberation war, "Sheikh Mujib was far from admitting it" (73). Khaleque tries to exculpate Mujib of his responsibility when he tells Nur that it is "no good blaming Mujib for all the starvation and death" (178). Zizek's observation is particularly helpful here when he says that an "ideology really succeeds when even the acts which at first sight contradict it start to function as arguments in its favour" (50).

Zizek, in *The Sublime Object of Ideology*, following Peter Sloterdijk, talks of *kynicism*, which subverts the "pathetic phrases of the ruling official ideology" by "exposing behind the sublime *noblesse* of the ideological phrases the egotistical interests, the violence, the brutal claims to power" (26). Nur's ideological turn to use the platform provided by the Awami League to decimate the empty rhetoric of the 7 March speech resembles Slotjerdik's idea of *kynicism*. Violence seems to be an expected counter to such an action. As Nur refuses to do his bidding, stops delivering his "speech," and starts exposing Mujibism with bitter critique, Khaleque starts punishing him with brutal violence. The ideological scotoma of Khaleque exposes him for what he is. Derrida, in *Specters of Marx*, explores the word "spectre" in its many forms in his book, but locates it in the dialectic of visibility and invisibility. The root word for "spectators" and "spectre" is *specere*, meaning "to look." Khaleque constantly feels under the gaze of this spectre whom he neglected and punished violently; the spirit of Nur transmogrifies into the many spectres of those refugees who return to haunt Khaleque in their "frequentation"; the spectre "re(pays) us a visit" (*Specters* 2006: 125–126). That Khaleque's vision needs to be corrected is made clear in the very beginning of the book when he goes to buy prop glasses for Nur. The shopkeeper tries to pitch him by explaining that glasses would help him to "see clearly," to protect what he was "left with" (Imam 47), almost predicting Abdul Ali and Shah Abdul Karim's suggestions to him. Similarly, the unknown girl who comes to visit Nur during his lockdown tells Khaleque: "You do not believe what you see" (212); Khaleque "will suffer for a long, long time," she professes (213). Tragically, Khaleque sees better in darkness, whenever he has one of those self-scrutinizing conversations with his past self, or with spectral images. In a haunted dream, he talks to the spectre of Mustafa Kamal, a martyr of the liberation war, and he asks for his guidance. Instead, Kamal points out how Khaleque is unable to accept his limitations, and he is not alone in his confusion; along with millions of Bengalis, he is forced to love Mujib (209). The spectre departs with the suggestion to kill Nur. Khaleque, in his Hamletian dilemma of to do or not to do, chooses to do; unable to punish the real culprit, he kills the "other". Like Obiajulu in *No Longer at Ease*, whose career graph resembles his, Khaleque forgets the meaning of his name, his roots – hating everything about it due to culture bomb, as Thiong'o proposes in *Decolonizing the Mind* (1994: 3). The Urdu word *Khalique* means "creator," another name for god. Khaleque truly believes that by tutoring Nur, he has become a *murshid*, teacher, and Nur must behave like his *ghulam*, assistant, and devote his life in his service. The fake Mujib is his creation. In Nur's disobedience, he sees the intolerable seed of *jahala*, an act of stupidity, which must be punished accordingly. Yet, as a last resort, he asks Nur to forget everything, to act as a *nur*, light, and lead him (224). But when Nur, still adamant not to serve the cause of Mujib, calls Khaleque, "Little Sheikh Mujib" (227) who has betrayed "us" – the migrants – he ends up killing him, outraged at the notion. Khaleque repeatedly attacks his face, Nur's disobedient, indifferent, silent face, because it refused to serve him. By sacrificing himself, Nur realizes the true essence of "gift," as Derrida explains in *The Gift of Death*, which would "transform the gift into an economy of sacrifice" (1995: 31), and Khaleque undergoes a transformation that changes his life forever. The face of Nur, effaced and terrifying to face, demands loyalty to responsibility to respond to the call of the neighbor. Critchley, in a reading of Lacan and Levinas in *Infinitely Demanding*, says that for "both of them, ethical experience begins with a heteronomous demand, the infinite demand of the other's face in Levinas, the demand of the fellow human being who stands in the place of the real in Lacan" (2007: 66). Face is where otherness resides, as Critchley points out following Levinas (*Ethics* 134), and the "point of exteriority is located in the face" (6); "the face is the condition of possibility for ethics," and this ethical face is the location of alterity; "the exteriority which cannot be reduced to the Same" (5). But this distance between exteriority and interiority, between two neighbors, Lacan corroborates in *The Ethics of Psychoanalysis*, is not "complete; it is a distance that is called proximity, which is not identical to the subject, which is literally close to it" (76). The other is the object of desire, Critchley further adds, and the subject is related to the face of the other, of *autrui*, which "refers to the other human being, whom I cannot evade, comprehend, or kill and before whom I am called to justice, to justify myself" (*Ethics* 5).

Nur gifted Khaleque with death, indebting him further. When Khaleque repeatedly sold Nur, first to Moina Mia, and then to Mujib, he failed to realize that by exchanging Nur's gift, he is corrupting himself. A gift altered by calculation, by knowledge, or by recognition, even when it earns money, causes a change in its essence, is destroyed "as if from the inside," as Derrida argues (*Gift* 112). Not only that, for Khaleque, nationalism is a product which can be exchanged with money (132). Nur's decision not to comply with Khaleque's demand is his way to pay back the people who paid to listen to him, and he dutifully executes his performance. He acts upon his faith by not yielding to the ideological power of charm, to act on the infinite gift, which is pure goodness (Derrida, *Gift* 113). While talking to Abdul Ali in private, he discusses his discomfort at watching his neighbors suffering from hunger. He knows the potential of such a scene to cause trouble for the smug government; only one man with faith, with courage, with the power to tolerate enough hunger could decimate the rhetoric of status quo (Imam 138). In his disobedience, Nur marries his faith with responsibility, to borrow from Derrida (*Gift* 6), and donates death, sacrifice, to put Khaleque in debt, indebted, to pay by relinquishing further calculative manipulations; Nur goes "beyond duty as a form of debt" (*Gift* 63).

Nur's "imaginary identification" with Mujib throughout the text remains an extimate one; the way he delivers the 7 March speech without its immediate context; he also wears the coat only as a prop, devoid of its ideological significations. Nur resists any attempt at "symbolic identification"[4] to perform Mujib in his inimitability. Even in the midst of ideological interpellation of Nur as Sheikh Mujib, especially by Moina Mia (Imam 62), verging on a parody of ritualism, Nur maintains his indifference. In his stony silence, his refusal to express his opinion, in his deliberate avoidance of (69, 82) and indifference to Khaleque Biswas, we see the emergence of a rebellious spirit. He is what Lacan calls *das ding*, the undefinable thing whose very presence symbolizes a gap in the transference where traumatic kernel resists integration; it is "the impossible – real object of desire" (Zizek 221), "the real traumatic kernel in the midst of symbolic order (Zizek 150). Lacan explains that

> there is another register of morality that takes its direction from that which is to be found on the level of *das Ding*; it is the register that makes the subject hesitate when he is on the point of bearing a false witness against das ding, that is to say, the place of desire, whether it be perverse or sublimated.
>
> (Lacan 1992: 109–110)

Critchley glosses *das Ding*, or the Thing, as the representation of real, and ethics is a relation to this real (*Infinitely* 63). This real is not the ideological real; this is a non-integrated traumatic real which works as a moral compass. Nur is not only a traumatized figure, but he is also incomprehensible. Khaleque Biswas is jealous of Shah Abdul Karim with whom Nur seems to be more comfortable than he is with him. What Khaleque does not realize is that both these precariats are not only traumatized, but they are haunted and haunting, moving among the ghosts. If Mujib's appeal is in his *fétiche*, or charm, both Shah and Nur retain what Badiou in *Saint Paul* calls, following the eponymous saint, *charis* or grace and stand sharply against the disgrace (180) named Mujib. Critchley reads this as an ethical turn; grace is to be found in an act of faith, which Badiou calls the "coming forth" of the subject, which is complemented by the "practical labour of the subject" (Critchley, *Infinitely* 46), namely love. Shah and Nur are practically inseparable, whispering to each other, communicating what they have in their hearts. Their conversations are almost always about the conditions of the refugees, of the starving populace of Bangladesh with whom Shah Karim had direct contact (Imam 187). This ethical touch is what is missing in Khaleque. According to Lacan, *das ding* is not only real; it can also be defined by what Freud called a *nebenmensch* (Critchley, *Infinitely* 64), a neighbor, a near man (Lacan 187). As Shah Abdul points out: "No man is more of a stranger to you than you are to him" (85). However, Shah Abdul's message of humanity, of looking "beyond your self-importance" (85), or Nur's idea of protecting one's heart (93) is lost on Khaleque. Nur's decision to repeatedly help his neighbors, the slum dwellers living near the flat, baffles Khaleque, who has already decided that he is individually incapable of helping them. Yet Nur does not hesitate to strip down, first by not wearing the new of pair of shoes Khaleque bought for him, which he presumably donated (Imam 167); then he puts on his original cloth while giving away the Mujib coat, along with other household items, including food, to pursue "economic justice" (Derrida *Gift*, 96). In doing so, Nur justifies his *charis*, his *kharisma*, which means, as Badiou reminds us, "granting of a gift" (Badiou 77). However, in Mujib's Bangladesh, one cannot donate the black coat (182) an act that identifies one as an enemy of the nation. His final gift, his life, symbolizing "protest of corpses"[5] compels Khaleque to change his life: Khaleque's life in exchange for an easily replaceable precariat's life (Imam 232).

In *Writing and Difference*, Derrida describes "the responsibility of *angustia*: the necessarily restricted passageway of speech against which all possible meanings push each other, preventing each other's emergence," as characterizing the anguish of writing (2001: 8). Writing itself is the anguish of *ruah*, "experienced in solitude by human responsibility" (Derrida, *Writing* 9). In the same book, Derrida talks of palintropic writing (*Writing* 76), which, as Sean Gaston notes in *Starting with Derrida* "starts differently, with a start, it *startles* itself as it starts again" (2008: vii). Through this startling, palintropic writing loses logos "in the necessary violence of its disruption" (Derrida, *Writing* 76). In this startled starting, we can also trace elements of the uncanny, as Gaston notes, following Nicholas Royle (169). The uncanny returns, re-traces, and startles; a book which talks of a turn coat who converts himself in the etymological sense of *convertere*, "turns about" (Derrida, *Gift* 8), the re-turning to his previous life starts with a reminder of times gone by. In the prologue of the book, the pre-logos of what is to come, Khaleque watches as enthusiastic Awami League party workers try to control by means of violence the crowd gathered to celebrate the birthday of Sheikh Mujib. His mind goes back to a time when Nur accused him of betraying his people – however, the text does not begin with the accusation; it goes further back to a time when the spectral presence of Nur was yet to pay him a visit. When his narrative ends, it does so with this startling revelation: "By destroying Nur Hussain, I have only destroyed myself" (Imam 240). Judith Butler's reading of Levinas, in *Precarious Life* (136), helps us to understand the "misery" and "anxiety" (Imam 40) Khaleque talks about in the epilogue of *The Black Coat*; Khaleque at first is anxious to justify the murder of Nur as self-preservation, because otherwise Moina Mia would take the matter in hand. But this justification is utterly unjustifiable; the face of the other, as Butler notes, commands us not to kill – it "comes to me from outside and . . . calls me out of narcissism towards something . . . more important" (138). This "something more important" is the realization, as Butler quotes from Levinas, that the Other is the only being which the subject fails to kill, and when this wish to kill the other is realized, it escapes the grasp of the subject. Levinas adds that to be "in relation with the other face to face is to be unable to kill. It is also the situation of discourse" (Butler 2004: 138). Discourse "makes an ethical claim on us," Butler corroborates (138), and

Khaleque seconds when he says, "Growing up is a curse, if one fails to grow a sense of responsibility as well" (Imam 238). Feeling miserable with the recognition of the death he has caused with his "misjudgement" he chooses to be a gravedigger in an attempt at self-chastisement. Every dead body would remind him of Nur,[6] and the haunting would not stop until he confessed his crime, in the body of Imam's text. If historiography could be considered an act of sepulchre, as Ricoeur calls it in *History, Memory, Forgetting* (365), Khaleque's grave digging is an act of historiography, of raising the dead and their memory, since death means burying the trace of the person. Ricoeur adds

> The sepulcher remains because the gesture of burying remains; its path is the very path of mourning that transforms the physical absence of the lost object into an inner presence. The sepulchre as the material place thus becomes the enduring mark of mourning, the memory-aid of the act of sepulcher.
>
> It is this act of sepulcher that historiography turns into writing.
>
> (2006: 366)

Khaleque's confession is intended to be a lesson for the future generation, who must learn from past mistakes "to avoid them in future" (234), to raise the spectre of past so that the "guilt for the dead" is "reflected in our national conscience" (237).

By uncloseting the buried memory of Nur, Khaleque also bares the failure of Mujib, the great revolutionary leader, as an incompetent administrator who smugly finds it possible to not recognize, and therefore to not dignify, the deaths his government has caused during the famine (Imam 239). The 1974 famine and the liberation war cannot be seen separately, since one thing led to the other, but it is an exercise of brutal discursive violence that the narratives of millions of hungry rootless refugees, of fragile minorities, do not find their proper place in the official narratives of Bangladesh, being reduced mostly to footnotes or glossed-over summarization. This is precisely the ethical duty of historiography; by revisioning and relocating the founding trauma in the 1974 famine, in exploring the "relation between politics and paranoia" (Imam 65) leading to genocide and fratricide, and highlighting the damage done by a dictatorship, *The Black Coat* becomes an important text in historiography and does not offer a redemptive narrative even while being a cautionary tale.

Notes

1 See, for example, Michael Rothberg's book *Multidirectional Memory: Remembering the Holocaust in the Age of Decolonization*, Stanford U.P. (2009), for a succinct formulation of how we can evoke the Holocaust to find an apt analogy for the heinous acts perpetrated in the name of colonization.

2 Amartya Sen authoritatively case studies the Bangladeshi famine of 1974 in Chapter 9 of his book, and in the following chapter, he elaborates on his idea of "entitlement and deprivation".

3 Interestingly, Zizek himself uses "floating" to mean the diversity which ideological quilting totalizes: "The 'quilting' performs the totalization by means of which this free floating of ideological elements is halted, fixed – that is to say, by means of which they become parts of the structured network of meaning" (95–96).

4 Zizek defines: "in imaginary identification we imitate the other at the level of resemblance – we identify ourselves with the image of the other inasmuch as we are 'like him', while in symbolic identification we identify ourselves with the other precisely at a point at which he is inimitable, at the point which eludes resemblance" (121).

5 As Derrida quotes from Hugo's *Les Misérables* in *Specters of Marx* (119).

6 *The Black Coat* talks about the haunts of migrants and refugees, like Shaheed Minar, as "ghostly places" (176, 188) and compares Nur Hussain to a ghost many times (225, 238, 130), while Khaleque himself believes to be haunted by ghosts (127). Khaleque calls one migrant a "spectre of evil" (164). Most of Shah Abdul Karim's stories revolve around "starvation, disease, death, burial" (187).

Works cited

Badiou, Alain. *Saint Paul: The Foundation of Universalism.* Translated by Ray Brassier. Stanford: Stanford University Press, 2003.

Butler, Judith. *Precarious Life: The Power of Mourning and Violence.* London: Verso, 2004.

Critchley, Simon. *Infinitely Demanding: Ethics of Commitment, Politics of Resistance.* London: Verso, 2007.

———. *The Ethics of Deconstruction: Derrida and Levinas*, 3rd ed. Edinburgh: Edinburgh University Press, 2014.

Derrida, Jacques. *The Gift of Death.* Translated by David Wills. Chicago: Chicago University Press, 1995.

———. *Writing and Difference.* Translated by Alan Bass. New York: Routledge, 2001.

———. *Specters of Marx: The State of the Debt, the Work of Mourning and the New International.* Translated by Peggy Kamuf. New York: Routledge, 2006.

Gaston, Sean. *Starting with Derrida: Plato, Aristotle and Hegel.* New York: Continuum, 2008.

Imam, Neamat. *The Black Coat.* New Delhi: Hamish Hamilton, 2013.

Lacan, Jacques. *The Ethics of Psychoanalysis 1959–60: The Seminar of Jacques Lacan Book VII.* Translated by Dennis Porter. New York: W W Norton & Company, 1992.

LaCapra, Dominick. *Writing History, Writing Trauma.* Baltimore: The Johns Hopkins University Press, 2001.

Ricoeur, Paul. *Memory, History, Forgetting.* Translated by Kathleen Blamey and David Pellauer. Chicago: Chicago University Press, 2006.

Sen, Amartya. *Poverty and Famines: An Essay on Entitlement and Deprivation.* Oxford: Clarendon Press, 1981.

Thiong'o, Ngugi wa. *Decolonising the Mind: The Politics of Language in African Literature.* Harare: Zimbabwe Publishing House, 1994.

Zizek, Sloavoj. *The Sublime Object of Ideology*, 1989, 2nd ed. London: Verso, 2008.

13

RELIGION AS THE MESSIANIC "OTHER" OF SECULAR MODERNITY

Locating Habermas' post-secular society in Michael Ondaatje's *Anil's Ghost*

Swayamdipta Das

According to Jürgen Habermas, the post-secular world order moves beyond the constricting ideologies of the Enlightenment currency of "secularism" or religious tolerance and accepts the blind spots and ideological aporias that such a political arrangement often conceals. The intrinsic violence of secularism lies in its relentless peddling of an assimilative community identity wherein the identity differences of the minorities are often co-opted in lieu of a larger communal whole on the basis of shared citizenship. According to Jürgen Habermas in "Notes on Post-Secular Society",

> The secularists fight for a colorblind inclusion of all citizens, irrespective of their cultural origin and religious belonging. This side warns against the consequences of a 'politics of identity' that goes too far in adapting the legal system to the claims of preserving the intrinsic characteristics of minority cultures. From this 'laicistic' viewpoint, religion must remain an exclusively private matter.
>
> (2008: 25)

The exclusion of religion from the public domain into the private spaces also entails that in a secularist society, the state and the institution of religion must remain separate domains and that the realm of religion must remain trans-political. The secularization thesis insists upon a connection between the "modernization" of the post-industrial world and the gradual secularization of faith and religion. In this schemata, according to Habermas, the twentieth-century empirical world of anthropocentric footnotes leads to a decline in the religious macro-narratives, and second, the shift from agrarian to post-industrial society with heightened welfare and health

 DOI: 10.4324/9781003158424-17

benefits leads to a general decline in existential crises – thus preempting the need for the social role earlier played by religion. However, the secularization thesis that foresees the gradual death of religion in the public sphere with the rise of the modernization project witnesses a reality in the twenty-first century that is in stark opposition to its assumptions. The rise of religious institutions as a pervasive interpretive community that has formidable influence in public, social and political policies can be witnessed in the United States, Europe, and many South Asian countries like India in recent years. The rise of right-wing ideologues and a concomitant rise of religious influences in the corridors of statist power not only defeats the secularization thesis of post-industrial modernity but also asks important questions about the very complicity of the secular ideologies in the rise of the religious right in modern democracies of the twenty-first century. Political thinkers like John Rawls, who advocate the laicistic state, miss the entire point about the origins and the reiteration of the theologico-political order as delineated by both Jacques Derrida and Habermas. The secularization thesis, by relegating religion and faith to the realm of a private affair, retroactively instills it with the epoch of the "sacred" and the trans-political. This myopic and misleading understanding of religion often makes it immune to political and ideological questioning and thus prepares the conditions for a rise of a political order that endlessly peddles the "sacred" and the "trans-political" kernel of religion as the highest forms of ethical and moral justice. The strategic aim of this chapter is to dismantle the secularization thesis by reading the religious order as being always already co-existent with sovereign power and thus reclaiming it from the private kernel of the trans-political and the sacred. Subsequently, the chapter shall attempt to understand Ondaatje's text as reinstating the religious back into the public domain, albeit in a differential manner, away from the tokenistic representations of faith and religion in secularist political culture. *Anil's Ghost* has been widely read as a novel that upholds the altruistic values of religious secularism *vis-à-vis* Buddhism in civil-war-torn Sri Lanka. However, a close reading of the novel offers us a scathing critique of the secularism thesis and an indictment of the secularistic eulogization of Buddhism as a trans-political faith system.

The thematic conflict in the Buddhist faith regarding the dual forces determining the direction of the wheel of life is introduced at the very beginning of the novel through the popular miner's folk song: "Blessed be the scaffolding deep down in the shaft/Blessed be the life wheel on the mine's pit head/Blessed be the chain attached to the life wheel" (Ondaatje 2011: 1). In Theravada Buddhism, the primary ethical conflict is between the wheel of power and the wheel of righteousness. The wheel of power must sustain the wheel of righteousness by providing the ethico-material conditions required for pursuing the right religious path of the citizens. These two power matrices, though in perpetual conflict, are intricately linked to each other. Not only is the righteous king the supreme upholder of the wheel of power, very

often it is the monastic order itself which dictates the contours and direc-
tions of the wheel of power so as to sustain and reiterate the wheel of collective righteousness. The "life wheel" alluded to in the miner's song at the very
beginning of the novel thus echoes the terms of a social order wherein the
temporal and the material kernel of political power and its effective fields
(the wheel of power symbolized by the mine's pit head) are chained to the
"life wheel," and the discursive difference between the temporal aspects of
power and the transcendental project of the Buddhist idea of salvation are
erased. Derrida's reworking of the French idea of the Laicite (or the modern
secular state) in terms of a more radical secularism initiates itself by understanding the theological origins of the very idea of sovereignty:

> Today, the great question is indeed, everywhere, that of sovereignty.
> Omnipresent in our discourses and in our axioms, under its own
> name or another, literally or figuratively, this concept has a theo-
> logical origin: the true sovereign is God. The concept of this author-
> ity or of this power was transferred to the monarch, said to have
> a 'divine right'. Sovereignty was then delegated to the people, in
> the form of democracy, or to the nation, with the same theological
> attributes as those attributed to the king and to God.
> (Derrida and Roudinesco 2004: 91–92)

The rest of the novel shows how intricately Buddhism is intertwined with the
questions and issues of sovereign power and how an understanding of their
past relationship becomes instrumental in redeeming the secularist project
of its misleading solutions regarding the ethical conflicts in Sri Lanka.

Palipana highlights the intricate ways in which the realm of Buddhist faith
has never been able to transcend the politics and the corridors of power.
He cites an ancient chronicle in Pali to Sarath and Anil wherein a group of
Buddhist monks flee the court of king Udayana in order to escape the wrath
of the angry king. However, the king and his troops follow them wherever
they go and eventually cut their heads off. The populist version of Buddhism
that offers a transcendentalist and sanitized approach to salvation and righteousness is undercut by this particular tale, which shows us how religion is
intricately linked to political power and the ways in which power permeates
the bodily sites of religion. Palipana's approach to Buddhist historiography
and the archaeological sites of the sacred religion undermines the manner in
which secularism has approached the kernel of religion and state authority
post-enlightenment. What Palipana disrupts is not only the accepted version of Buddhism and religiosity in general but also the Rawlsian idea of
the duty of public reason, which must exclude the kernel of religiosity in
order to gain legitimacy of the post-rationalist public sphere. John Rawls'
idea of a liberal democracy rests upon a separation between the church and
the state and the exclusivist nature of public reason that must emanate from

this separation between these two spheres. In *Political Liberalism*, Rawls sees the politics *vis-à-vis* the standpoint of post-metaphysical secularism as a "free-standing view":

> A political conception tries to elaborate a reasonable conception for the basic structure alone and involves, so far as possible, no wider commitment to any other doctrine. . . . This means that it can be presented without saying, or knowing, or hazarding a conjecture about, what such doctrines it may belong to, or be supported by.
>
> (2005: 13)

The Rawlsian concept of public reason, which is premised upon this idea of political secularism, implies that the threshold of political power can successfully transcend the ambiguities of religious doctrines and can translate them into a secular language which ultimately bears no trace of the kernel of religious faith. According to Habermas, the post-secular society can accept the ideological blind spot of the Rawlsian idea of separatism and be aware that only religious views that have been successfully translated into a secular language can eventually pass the 'filter' of the institutional threshold. In other words, they have to respect the "institutional translation proviso" (Habermas 2006b: 10). Ondaatje's text, through the character of Palipana, questions the terms and constative of this "institutional translation proviso" that render the religious and the theological neutral and passive determinants in the origins and sustenance of the ethico-political matrices of the nation-state.

Anil Tissera, the forensic expert from abroad, who has been sent by the Centre for Human Rights in Geneva to report on the violation of human rights on the island, is a strong representative of the Enlightenment truth-machinery, with its insistence upon positivist and rationalist frameworks and episteme. Unlike Sarath and Palipana, she believes in the scientific traces of history and discards anything that has no positivist evidence. Anil's gaze is predominantly invested in the modernist pro-enlightenment order of knowledge, which, in turn, influences the secularism thesis of Rawls, which calls for a strict division between the scientific public domain of knowledge and policy-making and the private realm of mystic religious truths. Anil's mission *vis-à-vis* the neo-colonialist gaze is to implicate the former in terms of an internal discrepancy within it without probing into the nexus formed with the latter, that is, the realm of religion and its relation to politics. The ethical obligation of Anil to name the victim and thus make him a representative of all the "unhistorical dead" is implicated in the paradigm of Rawlsian positivist secularism. "The ethical obligation to name is part of Anil's scrupulous sense that 'permanent truths, the same for Colombo as Troy' lurks in knowable details, and that such truths 'set you free'" (Scanlan 2004: 307). Anil wishes to legitimize the question of human rights in Sri Lanka by pinpointing the role of the current government in the violence on the island. For Anil, the government's role in siding with one particular ethnoreligious identity kernel (the fallout of the Rawlsian order) is responsible for the human atrocities and the ailments of the nation-state. She wishes to reinforce the fact through the scientific evidence that the skeleton found in one of the ancient Buddhist sites is actually a recent one. By doing so, she wishes to stress the secularism thesis that the modern nation-state, when implicated in any theological ideology, leads to a breakdown of the social and political order of justice and consequently violates the condition of human rights. Her insistence on the skeleton being that of a recent murder would further redeem the age-old sites of the Buddhist sacred order of their involvement in political violence. However, both Palipana and Sarath disagree on the overall insistence upon the here and the now of the murder. At one point, Sarath tells Anil: "I want you to understand the archaeological surround of a fact. Or you'll be like one of those journalists who file reports about flies and scabs while staying at the Galle Face Hotel. That false empathy and blame" (Ondaatje 2011: 44).

Anil, by separating Sailor, the skeleton from the ancient Buddhist site of the Bandarawela caves, intends to retroactively keep intact the trans-political paradigm of the sacred order of Buddhism. She concurs that the political murder of Sailor occurred somewhere else, beyond the religious order, and that his skeletal remains were transposed later to this Buddhist site:

> It's likely he was buried twice. . . . I know that murders are sometimes committed during a war for personal reasons, but I don't think a murderer would have the luxury of burying a victim twice. The skeleton this head is part of was found by us in a cave in Bandarawela. We need to discover if we're talking about a murder committed by the government.
>
> (Ondaatje 2011: 53)

The indictment of the current state machinery in the murder of Sailor is a ruse used by Anil to establish that the ancient sites of Buddhist sacred places bear no witness to political excesses such as murders and therefore reiterate the secularist thesis that the separation of the two realms (the religious and the political) as it existed in the originary stages of the society *vis-à-vis* the Lockean thesis could redeem the modern nation-state and that public justice could be served when bio-political life is de-linked from the inter-linking overtures of the theologico-political nation-state. Even when Sailor is ultimately established to have been killed in recent times by elements in the government, Anil wishes to use this particular instance as an exemplar to decode the truth about all the dead bodies that have been found in the ancient religious sites. "And who was this skeleton? . . . Who was he? This representative of all those lost voices. To give him a name would name the rest" (Ondaatje

178

2011: 33–34). She wants to establish that, like Sailor, all the other dead bodies found in the sacred sites of Buddhism were in fact remnants of the current state regime, and thereby the cult of the sacrosanct ancient religious order had no role to play in these juridico-political excesses – their later transposition in these religious spaces being indicative of the failure of the nation-state to live up to the ideals of enlightenment secularism.

Anil's secularist approach to the problem of civil strife in Sri Lanka encapsulates the political approach of John Rawls on public reason and the need for secular government. In "Priority of the Right and Ideas of the Good," Rawls opines that ideal public reason entails a principle of "freestanding" political positioning. "According to Rawls, the reasons acceptable in public deliberations are freestanding if they do not presuppose the acceptance of a particular comprehensive doctrine in order to have forced" (Yates 2007: 3). The "comprehensive doctrines" mostly refer to religious ideologues which, according to Rawls, should not interfere with the trans-religious voice of public reasoning. The secularist vision of a public voice and governmentality envisaged by Rawls underplays the role of religion in shaping the very idea of the political sphere and the realm of sovereignty. According to Rawls, "How is it possible for citizens of faith to be wholehearted members of a democratic society who endorse society's intrinsic political ideals and values and do not simply acquiesce in the balance of political and social forces?" (1997: 781) Rawls' idea of political citizens and the agents of statist powers being able to split consciously between the public realm of objective and secular reasoning and the private realm of religious and other comprehensive doctrines takes for granted the idea that these two spheres originate and operate separately. In "Faith and Knowledge", Habermas argues, "The boundaries between secular and religious reasons are fluid. Determining these disputed boundaries should therefore be seen as a cooperative task which requires both sides to take on the perspective of the other one" (2005: 332). For Habermas, the secular and the religious must become co-legislators in determining the contours of justice in the public sphere. The task of self-critical splitting must occur symmetrically among the secular and religious citizens. He opines,

> To date, only citizens committed to religious beliefs are required to split their identities, as it were, into their public and private elements. . . . But only if the secular side, too, remains sensitive to the force of articulation inherent in religious languages will the search for reasons that aim at universal acceptability not lead to an unfair exclusion of religions from the public sphere, nor sever secular society from important resources of meaning.
>
> (Ibid.)

In other words, Habermas' idea of a post-secular public realm gestures towards a cognitive syncretism in which the scientific realm of secular reason has a dialectic relationship with religion and its deeper recesses of meaning. According to Anil, the uncanny coupling of the religious and the sovereign in the transposed body of Sailor is symptomatic of the decline of justice and democracy in Sri Lanka. However, she is unable to decipher the truth behind Sailor's history through her hackneyed tools of knowledge and expertise. The intervention of Palipana and, later on, of Ananda become crucial not only to ascertain the truth of Sailor but also to understand how an insular vision like that of secularism would be too myopic to provide a solution to war-stricken Sri Lanka.

Palipana, who was once regarded as one of the finest epigraphists of his generation, has fallen out of favor with the establishment in his later years. An important feature of his work was the manner in which he resurrected the historiography of the island from the specters of colonial knowledge and triggered a renewed interest in the island and its remaining historical edifices. Palipana made his name by leading an ethnocentric and nationalist interpretation of Sri Lanka's history which countered some of the claims made by the Europeans and was key to the Sinhala movement. However, at the pinnacle of his career, he offered a radical interpretation of an ancient Buddhist scripture that turned the establishment against him.

> And as he grew older he linked himself less and less with the secular world. . . . During these years Palipana had been turned gracelessly out of the establishment. This began with his publication of a series of inter-pretations of rock graffiti that stunned archaeologists and historians. He had discovered and translated a linguistic subtext that explained the political tides and royal eddies of the island in the sixth century.
>
> (Ondaatje 2011: 48)

Although Ondaatje never goes on to explain what these inconvenient truths might have been, the text is replete with suggestions that Palipana might have decoded the ancient political nexus between the sacred order of Buddhism and the royal eddies of the island:

> In the last few years he had found the hidden histories, intentionally lost, that altered the perspective and knowledge of earlier times. It was how one hid or wrote the truth when it was necessary to lie . . . an epigraphist studying the specific style of a chisel-cut from the fourth century, then coming across an illegal story, one banned by kings and state and priests, in the interlinear texts. These verses contained the darker proof.
>
> (Ibid.: 63–64)

Although never made explicit, the intertwining of the religious and the polit-ical is revealed through many anecdotes which Palipana shares with Anil and Sarath. Palipana recounts how his brother, a member of the Buddhist monkhood, was subjected to a political killing by his own co-brethren and how the sacred grove of ascetics was never able to escape from the sovereign political gaze, even during the reign of Udaya the Third. According to Marlene Goldman, "Ondaatje reinforces further in his novel the connection between Buddhism and earthly politics by fashioning striking parallels between its portrait of Palipana and the real-life eminent Sri Lankan epigraphist Senerat Paranavitana, the first Sinhala commissioner of archaeology" (Goldman 2004: 5). Like Palipana, Senerat Paranavitana faced a similar predicament when he offered a highly contentious reading of the gold foil Vallipuram inscription. According to Raṇavīra Gunavardana, Paranavitana's readings led to "the premise that conditions prevalent eighteen centuries ago were germane to the political issue of their own times" (Gunavardana 1995: 16). The discovery that ancient Buddhist faith in its initial years too was intricately linked with the political and the sovereign affairs of the state just as in the present was something that led to the statist ostracism of both Paranavitana and the fictional Palipana from the annals of official historiography. As Palipana himself notes, "I'm erased from the new one [the Sinhala encyclopedia]" (Ondaatje 2011: 57). Palipana's belief in the theologico-political roots of ancient Buddhism and the fact that "Buddhism has never stood outside the dynamics of power" (Kapferer 1988: 108) refute Anil's secularist thesis that the ancient sacred sites of Buddhism were outside the contours of statist power and that a historiographic separation between the two could lead to the location of the aporias tormenting the nation-state at the present.

When Anil and Sarath bring the skeleton of Sailor to Palipana to ascertain its identity, Palipana doesn't tread the path of forensic truth-mechanisms or evidential historiography to claim the truth. Instead, he draws a reference to the Buddhist ritual of *netra-mangala* that could bring life and truth to the banal and the material:

> Netra means 'eye'. It is a ritual of the eyes. A special artist is needed to paint eyes on a holy figure. It is always the last thing done. It is what gives the image life. Like a fuse. The eyes are a fuse. It has to happen before a statue or a painting in a vihara can become a holy thing.
>
> (Ondaatje 2011: 58)

According to Palipana, the ritual of *netra-mangala* would aid in reconfiguring the face of the anonymous "Sailor." For a historian who had indulged his entire life in reconfiguring the smallest details of the past through concrete evidence and facts, the act of suggesting *netra-mangala* as a way to recover the truth about the past is contradictory. Yet Palipana's act of turning towards the religious ritual as the only solution to the problem of Sri

Lanka *vis-à-vis* the truth regarding Sailor becomes emblematic of the ethical leap from the position of scientistic secularism to the post-secular truth archives of Habermas that must reinstate the role of religion in solving the problems that afflict the nation-state and contemporary democracy.

Ondaatje uses Sailor as a metaphor for the contemporary nation-state whose redemption could only be possible through tracing of the truth of its history. Anil's attempt to arrive at the monolithic truth of Sailor's predicament by alienating the scenes of his murder from the place where he was found (the ancient Buddhist sacred caves of Bandarawela) is symptomatic of the secularist ideology of Rawls regarding the importance of separating the theological and the corridors of public reason and governmentality to arrive at the objective truth. However, Palipana discards Anil's notion of the monolithic construct of objective truth that could be termed redemptive for the nation-state: Anil says, "We use the bone to search for it. 'The truth shall set you free.' I believe that", to which Palipana replies, "We have never had the truth. Not even with your work on bones. . . . Most of the time in our world, truth is just opinion" (Ondaatje 2011: 61). Palipana asserts the role of religion as one of the important "communities of interpretation" (Habermas 2008: 20) in reclaiming the public sphere on the issues of moral and ethical importance. Palipana's insistence on the kernel of the religious as an argumentative "surplus" in understanding a key issue that torments the affairs of the public sphere and the nation-state at large opens up the ethical imperative to question the limits of the enlightenment self (the position of Anil) and thus reach a dialectic space that doesn't reach a cognitive saturation point. The counter-intuitive methods suggested by Palipana to reconfigure the face of Sailor also metaphorically suggest the need to look beyond the constrictive ideologies of the Kantian liberal polity premised on the supremacy of positivist "reason." According to Habermas,

> Reason, reflecting upon its most basic foundation, discovers that its origin lies in an Other; and it must recognize the fateful power of this Other if it is not to lose its rational orientation in an impasse of hybrid self-empowerment.
>
> (2006a: 256)

Palipana's insistence on this counter-positivist extraneous kernel of religion as a significant intervention to break the monadic structure of Enlightenment and categorical imperatives of rationality and empiricism, signifies the need to have alternative communities of interpretation to aid the idea of justice in the public sphere and the realm of governmentality. However, Palipana's position must not be understood as right-wing reclamation of the more Puritanical and sacrosanct contours of religious thought in Buddhism. Palipana, unlike Anil, understands that Buddhism itself never stood outside the statist corridors of power and that such affiliations could ultimately turn out to be violent and repressive, as in the case of his deceased brother, Narada, and his daughter, Lakma. What Palipana tries to assert, through his critique of the secularist thesis, is that Buddhism and religion could be reinstated in a positive and progressive manner *vis-à-vis* the public domain to reconstitute the democracy of the future. The sacred grove of ascetics is not a traditional religious space per se; it suggests a differential order of religiosity that could be messianic as well as integral as the "other" to the positivist community of interpretation.

Jacques Derrida in his essay, "Faith and Knowledge", talks about religion as a messianicity without messianism or as a gesture towards the absolute "other" without a priori anticipation:

> This would be the opening, to the future or to the coming of the other as the advent of justice, but without horizon of expectation and without prophetic prefiguration. The coming of the other can only emerge as a singular event when no anticipation sees it coming. . . . The messianic exposes itself to absolute surprise and, even if it always takes the phenomenal form of peace or of justice, it ought, exposing Itself so abstractly, be prepared (waiting without awaiting itself) for the best as for the worst, the one never coming without opening the possibility of the other.
>
> (2002: 56)

Derrida differentiates between the paradigms of faith and knowledge and reinstates the kernel of messianicity in the realm of the former: "This abstract messianicity belongs from the very beginning to the experience of faith, of believing, of a credit that is irreducible to knowledge and of a trust that 'founds' all relation to the other in testimony" (Ibid.: 56). Faith or religiosity opens up the horizons to a radical and irreducible "otherness" that becomes the foundations of the democracy-to-come. The epistemic structure of knowledge reaches a saturating aporetic knot that could never transcend the ipseity of the sovereign Enlightenment "self" and thus could never gesture towards the otherness of the other of absolute justice in the democracy-to-come.

The final gesture of Ondaatje's novel enacts the religious ritual of the *netra-mangala* of Buddha by Ananda. Anil is coerced to flee the country with her findings on Sailor, which, by her own admission, have been inconsequential to the larger issues that plague the land: "So the war, to all purposes, is over. That's enough reality for the West. It's probably the history of the last two hundred years of Western political writing. Go home. Write a book. Hit the circuit" (Ondaatje 2011: 165). The final ethical reconciliation in Ondaatje's novel doesn't tread the path of positivist and Enlightenment categories of human emancipation through the scientific search for truth, being cut off from the doctrines of religion and faith. Anil couldn't prove that Sailor's predicament was only a recent phenomenon and that the splitting of the religious doctrine from the public realm of the ethico-juridical order of the state could guarantee a resurrection of future democracy in Sri Lanka. Ondaatje, on the contrary, posits the messianic realm of religion and faith as perhaps the only salvation available for democracy and ideal justice to resurrect itself. The *netra-mangala* ceremony undertaken by Ananda is not a private affair and thus transcends the secularist thesis that religion must be supplanted from the public realm in order to gesture towards the ethical in the public and statist domain of justice. The resurrection of the 120-foot Buddha statue, which had earlier been destroyed by insurgent forces, thus redeems the readers of the messianic hope immanent in the publicly visible domain of religion. The grounds around the fallen Buddha, which had once been "places of torture and burials," are to be reinstated through the ritual of the *netra-mangala* and re-invested with the messianic hope which lay at the heart of faith and religion. Although Ondaatje refutes the secularist thesis, he doesn't uncritically subscribe to the "sacred" realm of ancient Buddhist religious dogmas. Ananda's gesture of re-building the Buddha statue from earlier scraps is emblematic of the act of radically reinscribing the Buddha and its teachings away from the ipseity of its earlier "self." The statue that Ananda restores is no longer a homogenized and fetishized version of transcendental Buddhism that could be relegated to the politically sanitized and sacred spaces of the private realm; rather it is one that "would always look north" (Ondaatje 2011: 177), which was the most politically volatile part of the entire country. The radical secularism that Ondaatje gestures towards moves away from the calm and unifying serenity of the usual Buddha portrayals and reinscribes it with differential features and values that partake of the profane and the awry: "Up close the face looked quilted. They had planned to homogenize the stone, blend the face into a unit, but when he saw it this way Ananda decided to leave it as it was" (Ondaatje 2011: 174). The quilted and disintegrated stone and the northward-looking gaze of the Buddha, bereft of any calm and tranquility, gestures towards a coming-into-being of a political and social order that moves away from the constricting contours of secularism and laicism and reinstates the theological and the religious with radically messianic values and potentials.

Works cited

Derrida, Jacques. "Faith and Knowledge: Two Sources of 'Religion' at the Limits Alone." In *Acts of Religion*, edited by Gil Anidjar. New York: Routledge, 2002, 40–101.

Derrida, Jacques, and Elisabeth Roudinesco. *For What Tomorrow: A Dialogue.* Stanford: Stanford University Press, 2004.

Goldman, Marlene. "Representations of Buddhism in Ondaatje's *Anil's Ghost.*" *CLC Web: Comparative Literature and Culture* 6:3 (2004).

Guṇavardana, Raṇavīra. *Historiography in a Time of Ethnic Conflict: Construction of the Past in Contemporary Sri Lanka*. Colombo: Social Scientists' Association, 1995.

Habermas, Jürgen. "Faith and Knowledge." In *Frankfurt School on Religion*, edited by Eduardo Mendieta. New York: Routledge, 2005, 327–338.

———. "On the Relations Between the Secular Liberal State and Religion." In *Political Theologies: Public Religions in a Post-Secular World*, edited by Hent De Vries. New York: Fordham University Press, 2006a, 251–260.

———. "Religion in the Public Sphere." *European Journal of Philosophy* 14 (2006b): 1–25.

———. "Notes on Post-Secular Society."*New Perspectives Quarterly* 25:4 (2008): 17–29.

Kapferer, Bruce. *Legends of People, Myths of State: Violence, Intolerance, and Political Culture in Sri Lanka and Australia*. Washington, DC: Smithsonian Institution Press, 1988.

Ondaatje, Michael. *Anil's Ghost*. London: Bloomsbury, 2011.

Rawls, John. "The Idea of Public Reason Revisited." *The University of Chicago Law Review* 64:3 (1997): 765–807.

———. *Political Liberalism*. New York: Columbia University Press, 2005.

Scanlan, Margaret. "*Anil's Ghost* and Terrorism's Time." *Studies in the Novel* 36:3 (2004): 302–317.

Yates, Melissa. "Rawls and Habermas on Religion in the Public Sphere." *Philosophy & Social Criticism* 33:7 (2007): 880–891.

INDEX

For Product Safety Concerns and Information please contact our EU
representative GPSR@taylorandfrancis.com
Taylor & Francis Verlag GmbH, Kaufingerstraße 24, 80331 München, Germany